THESE
WICKED
DEVICES

Also by Matthew Plampin

The Street Philosopher
The Devil's Acre
Illumination
Will & Tom
Mrs Whistler

MATTHEW PLAMPIN

THESE WICKED DEVICES

b
THE BOROUGH PRESS

The Borough Press
An imprint of HarperCollins*Publishers* Ltd
1 London Bridge Street
London SE1 9GF

www.harpercollins.co.uk

HarperCollins*Publishers*
Macken House, 39/40 Mayor Street Upper
Dublin 1, D01 C9W8, Ireland

First published by HarperCollins*Publishers* 2025

1

Copyright © Matthew Plampin 2025

Matthew Plampin asserts the moral right to
be identified as the author of this work

A catalogue record for this book is available from the British Library

HB ISBN: 978-0-00-816366-2
TPB ISBN: 978-0-00-853879-8

This novel is entirely a work of fiction.
The names, characters and incidents portrayed in it are
the work of the author's imagination. Any resemblance to
actual persons, living or dead, events or localities is
entirely coincidental.

Set in Perpetua by HarperCollins*Publishers* India

Printed and bound in the UK by CPI Group (UK) Ltd, Croydon CR0 4YY

All rights reserved. No part of this publication may be
reproduced, stored in a retrieval system, or transmitted,
in any form or by any means, electronic, mechanical,
photocopying, recording or otherwise, without the prior
written permission of the publishers.

Without limiting the author's and publisher's exclusive rights,
any unauthorised use of this publication to train generative
artificial intelligence (AI) technologies is expressly prohibited.
HarperCollins also exercise their rights under Article 4(3) of the
Digital Single Market Directive 2019/790 and expressly reserve this
publication from the text and data mining exception.

This book contains FSC™ certified paper and other controlled
sources to ensure responsible forest management.

For more information visit: www.harpercollins.co.uk/green

For S and K

Historical Note

These Wicked Devices is set at a time when Italy was divided into a collection of city states, each with its own ruler and system of government. The Kingdom of Naples, which covered roughly a third of the Italian peninsula, had been controlled by Spain since 1504, when it was captured from the French. Governed by a viceroy, this territory was an important source of Spanish military and economic power.

And it was much envied.

Dramatis Personae

ROME
Donna Olimpia Maidalchini, princess of San Martino, first lady of Rome, sister-in-law to Pope Innocent X
Niccolò Ludovisi, prince of Piombino, confidant of Donna Olimpia, husband of her daughter Costanza
Olimpia Giustiniani, known as Olimpiuccia, daughter of Maria and Andrea Giustiniani, Donna Olimpia's granddaughter
Luigi Mattei, baron of Belmonte, professional soldier under the patronage of Donna Olimpia
Cavaliere Gian Lorenzo Bernini, master sculptor and architect, knight of the Cross of Christ
Alessandro Algardi, master sculptor
Flaminia Triunfi, painter and model
Lontra, creature of the streets

HOLY SEE
Giovanni Battista Pamphili, Pope Innocent X, brother-in-law to Donna Olimpia
Cardinal Federico Maidalchini, Cardinal Nephew to Pope Innocent X, son of Donna Olimpia's half-brother Andrea

Cardinal Giacomo Panciroli, Secretary of State to the Papal Curia, advisor and friend to Pope Innocent X
Cardinal Francesco Barberini, nephew of the late Pope Urban VIII, head of the Holy Inquisition, representative of the Barberini family in Rome
Bishop Fabio Chigi, Papal Nuncio in Cologne
Monsignor Francesco Mascambruno, priest and datary of the Vatican
Camillo Astalli, Vatican lawyer and personal secretary to Cardinal Panciroli, brother-in-law to Donna Olimpia's niece Catarina Astalli

CASTRO
Sister Orsola, servant nun of the Benedictine Order
Sister Serafina, choir nun of the Benedictine Order
Tullio Botta, soldier of Castro

MADRID
Rodrigo Díaz de Vivar Gomez de Sandoval y Mendoza, Duke of Infantado and Spanish Ambassador to Rome
Diego Rodríguez Silva y Velázquez, painter to King Felipe IV and Keeper of the Royal Pictures
Juan de Pareja, slave to Diego Velázquez

Rome

1650

PART ONE

Every Wolf and Every Lamb

Sorores

The hatch slides back to reveal a fine metal grille. Behind it, Orsola can see part of a laywoman's veiled head, silhouetted by candlelight. She gathers her breath; then she lets her shoulders fall, clasping her hands in abject gratitude.

'Virgin be praised,' she says, working the slightest crack into her voice. 'Bless you, Sister. *Bless you.* This is God's will, I am sure of it.'

'What do you want?'

'I have one of your own with me. A choir nun, she is – lost and quite alone. In urgent need of sanctuary.'

Orsola turns, inviting the laywoman to peer past her into the small, moonlit piazza. Serafina can be seen kneeling at the base of the fountain in its centre, her long limbs folded awkwardly on the step, praying the rosary with her usual ardour. Her habit is concealed beneath a worn, colourless cloak, but she still looks the part. She could hardly be anything else.

The laywoman is sceptical, however. 'Where did you find her? Surely she wasn't wandering the streets of Campitelli in the middle of the night?'

Orsola recites the story she has rehearsed. A week previously, the sister over by the fountain appeared in the yard of her family's farm, some thirty miles north of the city wall. She was ragged and half-starved, in a state of wild distress. They did what they could for her, and soon learned that she had been reduced to vagrancy after her convent was razed, the surviving nuns fleeing into the surrounding countryside.

'We knew it was our Christian duty to return her to her order,' Orsola says. 'My father could not leave our farm, so he charged me with bringing her here. Back to her rightful place.'

The hope was that this tale would be met with horror, and then a great rush of compassion, the lay sisters hurrying forth to bring Serafina inside; and that Orsola herself would be thanked, and blessed for her bravery, and perhaps even given some form of reward. But instead it prompts another, rather more difficult question.

'Is she from Castro?'

Orsola hesitates; she shakes her head. 'The poor sister's mind is . . . scattered. Her memories do not seem reliable. She talks only of being chased out by soldiers, and left to roam—'

'She is from Castro,' the laywoman declares with grim certainty. 'A razed convent cannot be anywhere else. Not since the peace.'

There is a mutter of agreement. Orsola realises that several others have assembled in the hallway beyond the door. Her heart sinks in her chest, for the tone of their voices tells her plainly how this will go.

'Its wretched citizens have been appearing all over Rome,' one of them says. 'I fear the coming of Spring will only increase their numbers.'

Orsola doesn't try to deny it. 'This sister is blameless,' she says more forcefully, moving closer to the grille. 'Please, you must listen to me. Whatever you think of Castro and its rulers, or the fate the town met, this sister is honest and true. She is committed to her vows. And she has a gift – if you would only listen to—'

'She is a heretic,' proclaims the laywoman. 'Castro was lost to heresy, to the very gravest sin. The Holy Father himself decreed this, and your lies are demonstrating it anew. There is no quarter to be had at the Tor de'Specchi. Leave here at once, both of you.'

With that the hatch snaps shut, dropping Orsola into darkness. She takes up the door knocker, rapping it loudly against the wood as she repeats her pleas. It is no use. The house stands silent and unyielding, like a back firmly turned. Orsola flattens her palms upon the door, closes her eyes, and grinds her teeth until her jaw aches. Then she swallows hard and steps away.

The Tor de'Specchi was supposed to be the place. In those final dreadful hours, the Mother Abbess took Orsola aside and made her memorise a long list of directions – along with much guidance about how to hide from their persecutors, the wilds, and then find their way through the vast city without mishap.

'Sister Serafina must be brought to safety,' the old nun said, raising her voice over the cannon fire. 'You are sharp, Sister Orsola, for all your wilfulness. And you have shown that you are capable. If you succeed in this – if you can deliver your sister to the Tor de'Specchi – you will have done a good deal to redeem yourself in the Lord's eyes.'

Orsola bowed her head and joined the Mother Abbess in prayer. By God's grace, here among the disaster lay a clear chance for atonement. Several years earlier, barely out of her own childhood, she had lain unthinkingly with Jacopo Bruni, the constable's second son. When her belly began to swell, she concealed it beneath shawls and tightly laced stays; and then, in her fearful confusion, gave birth in the stillness of the night-time washhouse, her tiny daughter perishing in minutes amid the tubs and paddles.

When this was discovered, Orsola was rushed in disgrace to Castro's Benedictine convent, the Blessed Visitation – where the other nuns never tired of reminding her that by allowing her child to die unbaptised, she had consigned the girl to the Limbo of the Infants. To the slopes of a grey, barren hill, far from the Holy Virgin's love.

In the months since they fled from Castro, Orsola has become convinced that returning Sister Serafina to the Benedictine Order will bring about the release of her daughter's soul into Paradise. Her imaginings of this have grown so potent, in fact, so filled with light and feeling, she has decided that they are divinely supplied; that the Madonna is showing her what she must do.

At the same time, however, Orsola has been plotting a more earthly form of salvation for herself. Before the Mother Abbess had even finished speaking, she'd realised that once Sister Serafina was back with the Order, she could simply slip away. It might have been assumed that she would rejoin as well, but it was never explicitly instructed. This is enough for Orsola. Shedding her servant nun's habit would cause her not a single instant's pain; indeed, the prospect is so joyous it makes her a little breathless to consider it. No more drudgery in convent kitchens and laundries. No more hours spent shivering in dark, draughty chapels, dragged from your pallet by the dictates of the Horarium. And no more *confinement* – the same pinched faces and sour expressions, day after miserable day; the constant complaints, reprimands and punishments; the hands whipped raw, the shoulders black with bruises, the ever-grumbling stomach.

It was no kind of life at all. That last afternoon, as she led Serafina through the conflagration, Orsola resolved that she would submit to it no longer. *Anything* would be better. And what, now, was there to stop her? The town of Castro, the only home she had known, had been wiped from existence. The Convent of the Blessed Visitation and its inmates would not be seen again. Her father and brother, so very ashamed of her, were most probably dead, or thinking that she had died herself.

And in a sense, this will be correct. Orsola will have atoned. A new birth will follow, a new beginning, with the sanction of Almighty God – for is this not what atonement truly means?

Sister Serafina is still crouched beside the fountain, rocking slightly as she prays, unaware of what has just occurred. Orsola starts towards her, recovering her determination. This is no disaster; it is merely another delay. The Mother Abbess had also provided the names of three other houses across the city, in case alternatives were necessary. She was less sure of these, and her directions are less precise, but it is something. The story should perhaps be altered, Orsola thinks, to remove even indirect reference to Castro. She only needs them to accept Serafina. What they might discover later on would not be her concern.

'We have to find shelter, Sister,' she says. 'We cannot stay out here.'

Serafina pauses in her prayer, her face hidden in the shadow of her hood. 'I must be inside for Compline,' she states.

Orsola crosses her arms against the cold. 'They had no room for us. We will go somewhere else in the morning.'

'I must be inside for Compline,' Serafina repeats. 'You told me that I would be. That this was certain.'

Over the past few months, Orsola has learned to anticipate the shifts in Serafina's mood – the way she can slide, often quite abruptly, to the outermost extremities of feeling. It is beginning now. The best course, always, is to keep calm, and hide your own impatience or irritation; to offer what comfort you can; to move her on quickly to other things.

'We will say it together, Sister,' Orsola tells her. 'As we did in the woods, at the altar we made. And by Compline tomorrow you will be inside once more. I swear it.'

She looks across the piazza, to where a number of pilgrims have bedded down beneath a low arcade. There are families among them, with women and children clustered around a couple of campfires. It is as good as they are likely to get.

'Come,' she says, holding out her hand. 'Over there. We can sleep for a few hours. Begin again at sunrise.'

Serafina appears to consider this. Then she puts away her rosary, grips onto Orsola's wrist and hauls herself to her feet. The choir nun is a head taller, and not agile; this single, ungainly movement almost overbalances them both.

Once they are steady, Orsola leads them across the piazza towards the arcade. The pilgrims watch their approach. They are foreigners, murmuring to each other in a northern language Orsola does not recognise. Rome is fast filling with such people, arriving for the festivals and solemnities of the Holy Jubilee. Many are sleeping wherever they can, having arrived too late to secure a place in a lodging house, or being too poor to afford one. On their way in from the wall, Orsola saw them laid out in alleys and stables, and camped upon stretches of waste ground, among the ancient ruins. It is only halfway through Lent, yet her impression was of a city already overloaded, barely able to contain the many thousands who sought to cram themselves into it.

Orsola hails the pilgrims. Their response is wary, but they do not try to stop her taking Serafina to a shallow alcove at the arcade's rear.

'We'll be safe enough here,' she murmurs, glancing along the arcade; at least a dozen faces are staring over at them. 'No one will . . . I don't believe they would . . .'

Serafina is shaking her head. Her hold on Orsola's wrist is growing uncomfortably tight, as if she wishes to cause pain. She has not been reassured, Orsola realises; indeed, her fears are now starting to run beyond her control.

'We are in hell,' the choir nun says, her voice hoarse and loud. 'You claim to be my sister but you have brought me into *hell*.'

Orsola hesitates, both hoping that this pronouncement will be all, and knowing for certain that it won't. 'Sister,' she says gently, 'if you would just—'

Serafina yanks her closer. The scarring on her brow and cheek looks darker in the campfires' light, like splashes of crimson wax. For an instant, her long face contorts with rage; then a sob bursts violently from her lips.

'Holy Virgin save me!' she gasps, covering her mouth with her black sleeve. 'This is a place of evil, of the most terrible evil! The demons here . . . I know them of old, Sister. They will surge forth from their pit and hunt down their victims without mercy or restraint. Spear their flesh. Tear out their hair. Drag them away for the most brutal torments and violations. Oh Lord, oh blessed saints! We are out in the open and they will come for us, they will surely come for us!'

The pilgrims are shifting about behind them, made uneasy by these frantic lamentations. Orsola lets Serafina rave on for a minute longer, selecting her moment; then she leans forward and looks directly into the choir nun's anguished, deep-set eyes.

'Sister,' she says. 'Tell me of Santa Catarina. She stood against the darkness, did she not – against the wicked tricks of the devil? Tell me of that.'

Serafina grabs at this with desperate eagerness. Holy stories are her solace, her refuge from the world – and Santa Catarina of Alexandria has a particularly exalted place in her heart. The

Blessed Visitation in Castro housed one of the saint's most precious relics, in a vault beneath the altar of its church. Her statue stood in the middle of the cloister, gazing heavenward with the martyr's palm in its hand; this was one of the first things to be destroyed, the white marble split from neck to hip by a shell fragment. But Serafina's devotion to Catarina remains absolute. When the mood is upon her, and it often is, she will talk of the saint's life for several hours without pause. She gulps in a few tearful breaths, pulling at her cloak and the black habit beneath; and then she begins to speak of a princess scholar, wise beyond compare, who defied a pagan emperor to give herself entirely to the glory of God.

With each word her panic recedes further. She forgets their plight, and the fears that pressed upon her so heavily. Her eyes flutter shut; she kneels down slowly upon the flagstones.

'Catarina was brought to the temple,' she says. 'It was filled with golden statues ten yards high, of men with the heads of birds and beasts. The priests there encircled the princess and demanded that she pay tribute to their idols.'

Orsola lowers herself to Serafina's side. She notices that the pilgrims are listening closely. She can't tell how much they understand, but their suspicions seem to have fallen away.

'Holy Catarina refused. She told these pagan priests that the idols they so revered would soon be dust, blown before the face of the wind. She bade them marvel instead at the heavens and the earth. At the land and the sea and all that was in them. To learn who made it – every pebble, every leaf, every wolf and every lamb. And to praise His heavenly name.'

The Mother Abbess believed it to be a gift. That one who found life so overwhelming, who was prone to neglect even the most basic needs of her body, could talk in this way, with such vividness and passion – it could only be the work of Almighty God, sending His angels to whisper holy truths in Sister Serafina's ear. On occasion, learned visitors would come to Castro, seeking an audience; and they would depart as moved and unsettled as the pilgrims who are before her now.

For Orsola, Serafina's words have long since lost their mystery. She has heard it all since they escaped Castro together, every last episode and incident, many dozens of times. The stories became wearying, after a while; then they were vexing, bringing an exasperation she struggled to contain; and now they simply wash over her, finding almost no purchase upon her mind.

But they have shown their worth in that arcade. Serafina has been calmed. She is caught up entirely in her tale, describing the bold words of the saint and the confusion they cause her hapless, grey-bearded adversaries. The pilgrims, also, are transfixed. Orsola decides that she will ask for a share of the food they are cooking over their fires. She and Serafina have eaten nothing that day but a handful of boiled chestnuts, and the smell from the blackened pots – a stew of some kind, she thinks, with pork and thyme – is difficult to bear. They have no more supplies and no money, just Serafina's silver rosary and the clothes upon their backs. She leans against the edge of the alcove and waits for an opportunity to make her request.

None comes. Serafina's envisioning seems more fluent than ever. Instead of growing impatient, however, Orsola is oddly soothed by the choir nun's recitation. Resting her head against the stonework, she watches the pale smoke from the fires as it curls up into the bare, vaulted ceiling; and she realises that in amongst her exhaustion and worry and constant, gnawing fright is a tiny flicker of relief.

Over these past months, despite the difficulties Serafina has caused, Orsola has begun to regret their separation. It is natural, she supposes – the bond God forms between ward and guardian. They must part. She knows this. Serafina must return to holy orders, whereas she most definitely must not. But that day, against long expectation, the moment has not arrived. For one more night, the sisters are together still. And Orsola is glad of it.

*

By daylight, Rome is staggering.

The previous evening, after coming in through one of the northern gates, Orsola cleaved closely to the route given to her by the Mother Abbess. This was direct, taking them down just two avenues, then around a hilltop palazzo to the Tor de' Specchi. The main thoroughfares were packed with pilgrims, advancing into the dark city. The nuns stayed among them as much as they could, walking quickly with their heads down to avoid drawing notice. Orsola glimpsed unruly tavernas, men spilling from their doorways; street plays, acrobats and several savage brawls; the mouths of numberless black alleys, unknown forms shifting in their depths. In her fear and haste, she gained little sense of where they were – but now, as they leave the arcade and start towards the piazza's edge, the sheer scale of this place leaves her stunned.

Orsola is a child of Castro: five avenues, three churches, and the plain barn of the Duomo, with a few larger houses on the main square. The city before her is like a hundred Castros stitched together. Off to the south, between two tenement blocks, she can see a vast spread of streets and rooftops sloping down gently into the valley beyond. Magnificent buildings loom in their dozens against the smooth morning sky, crowding it with towers, spires and domes. She blinks rapidly, whispering a word that would have got her birched in the Visitation.

'The next house is by the river,' she says, attempting to collect her wits. 'Close to the northern bank.'

Serafina is trailing behind, a fold of Orsola's cloak pinched between her thumb and forefinger. She is murmuring away as usual, snatches of Latin prayer mingling with litanies of her own invention. She doesn't appear to be listening.

As Orsola squints out at Rome, she realises that the directions she has are vague to the point of uselessness. She has barely slept, despite her fatigue. It was simply too terrifying, even with the pilgrim party there to serve as a barrier. Her limbs are stiff from a night spent huddled on bare stone, her head light and aching; she is cold also, and hungry, the meagre meal they begged from their protectors all but forgotten. The day ahead looks trying indeed.

'The Mother Abbess told me to make for San Pietro, the Holy Father's own church,' she says, unable to keep the frustration from her voice. 'She claimed that there is a dome on it you can see throughout the city. But there are a . . . more domes here than I can count Sister. How in God's name am I supposed to—'

Serafina cuts past her, moving with apparent purpose, heading out of the piazza and onto the winding lane beyond. Orsola swears again as she gives chase, scooping up the hem of her grey habit. Sister Serafina ran off many times out in the woods, after becoming convinced of something or other. It was both startling and increasingly tiresome.

The lane leads downhill, its cobbles interspersed with shallow steps. Orsola hurries along it with all the strength she has left, ignoring the pain that soon bites at her muscles. She would have no chance if this pursuit was to be decided by speed alone, but Serafina's gait has a careening quality; after twenty yards or so she collides with a stack of wicker baskets, knocking them all around and stumbling against a wall. Just as Orsola is about to reach her she starts off once more, weaving away between baskets and clods of refuse towards a bend at the end of the lane.

This brings the nuns abruptly into a new piazza, three or four times the size of the one beside the Tor de'Specchi. People are everywhere; Orsola hears shouts, laughter, and the dense murmur of innumerable overlapping conversations. On the far side, a stage is being prepared for a performance. Craftsmen are hanging gigantic painted screens upon a wooden frame, to be moved about by a system of pulleys. Orsola sees a scene of rocky wilderness; an expanse of the night sky, strewn with stars; an angelic host, brilliantly colourful, bearing harps, trumpets and drums. She realises that it is for the Holy Jubilee. Held every quarter century, this grand occasion is a time for the remission of sin – for forgiveness and pardon, and indulgences of all kinds. There is to be an entire year of parades, special services and sacred plays like this one; and a massive penitential procession, running in an endless circuit between the most ancient churches of the city. Orsola listened to much talk of this Jubilee among the choir nuns, before Castro met its doom – bittersweet fantasies of a glorious Christian spectacle that the confined women would never see. She shut it out as best she could, refusing to dispirit herself with unreachable wonders; yet now, by the Lord's will, it is she who has been brought among them. Orsola has no doubt what this means. Almighty God approves of her wish to atone, to free her daughter from the grey hill of Limbo and repair the damage she has done.

Sister Serafina has stopped by a water trough. She is quailing, trembling hard, taken aback by the noise, the colours and smells, the enormous quantities of people. Her cloak has come loose, revealing a long slice of her black habit.

Orsola rushes over to refasten it. 'Sister,' she pants, 'where are you *going*?'

In reply, Serafina looks to the side, away from the stage. Orsola follows her gaze – and between the marble façade of a church and a tenement's terracotta flank she sees a colossal silvery dome, ribbed with white stone and topped with a golden cross, perhaps a mile from where they are standing. It can only belong to San Pietro.

Orsola exhales, setting her hands on her hips. The meaning here is plain: Sister Serafina knows Rome. The dismay and horror it has prompted in her arise not from awe, but familiarity. She must have lived here before she took holy orders. This was the case with many of Castro's choir nuns, the convent being both of sound reputation and a long way from Rome, should a daughter need to be confined somewhere she could more easily be forgotten. Serafina hasn't mentioned this at any point, it is true. But then she never speaks of such things.

'Stay close to me,' Orsola says. 'We will find this house, Sister.'

She threads her arm through Serafina's and starts them off towards the giant dome. They leave the piazza and its stage behind, entering a crowded, shadowy avenue, where the huge buildings are still blocking out the rising sun. Many of the people there are pilgrims, from numerous distant lands; even with all the Lenten black, the clothes are unlike anything Orsola has seen. Rome itself is also beyond imagining. The nuns pass palazzos of astonishing grandeur; tiered marble fountains encrusted with statues, from which water leaps in glittering crescents; churches of a majesty and a richness that Orsola can scarcely comprehend. Jubilee banners hang all around, adorned with holy pictures. She gazes up at the Blessed Annunciation, with the Archangel Rafaello kneeling before the Virgin. The Holy Family's flight into Egypt. Christ wandering in the wilderness, rejecting the temptations of the devil.

Serafina does not look at any of it. She clings onto Orsola, her head bowed, saying her words more fiercely and fixedly than ever. With some consternation, Orsola senses that their journey to San Pietro will take them through the very heart of the city. As the sun's rays reach in over the rooftops, the multitudes grow even noisier and more difficult to navigate. The stench of unwashed bodies, dung and tobacco smoke grows eye-wateringly strong. Stalls come into view, hawking all manner of baubles and trinkets; musicians begin to play, several different songs competing with each other at any given moment.

And then the saints start to appear. They roam about wearing wide, beatific smiles, addressing the crowds from steps and stoops, or the pavilions of churches. Along the length of a single street, the nuns walk by a Lorenzo, half-charred, the griddle in his left hand and the martyr's palm in his right; a shivering Sebastiano clad only in a loincloth, his naked torso riddled with silver-flighted arrows; a Margherita chased by a black dragon, its jaws snapping, with a dozen street children running along behind. It is religion as Orsola has never known it before, alive and wild; she finds herself grinning as Margherita's dragon turns about and roars, scattering its squealing pursuers.

Serafina tenses, her fingertips digging into Orsola's upper arm. 'Sister,' she hisses, her mouth now a hand's width from Orsola's ear. '*Sister.*'

'It is an act, that's all,' Orsola says to her. 'A play. To show love for the saints.'

Serafina stares at her as if she is an idiot. Then Santa Margherita passes by them and she pulls yet closer, squeezing her eyes shut and rattling out a psalm with breathless speed.

The nuns press onwards, but their progress has slowed; it feels as if they are becoming hemmed in by people, market stalls and buildings. The silvery dome of San Pietro can no longer be seen, and Orsola begins to worry that they are wandering off course. She prays for guidance, and for speed — and that the Holy Madonna will keep any of Rome's Santa Catarinas from their path, for this would certainly cause them significant difficulty. As they advance, she scans the streets for saints, or players of any sort, along with any possible ways of enacting a quick escape.

It is futile; disaster arrives so suddenly that there is no hope of avoiding it. A woman walks from an alleyway just two steps ahead of them, wearing a yellow gown spotted with blood, a blood-soaked blindfold bound across her face. She is holding a silver platter, upon which are a pair of eyeballs, one brown and one blue, their bloody cords stretching away grotesquely behind. It is Santa Lucia, Orsola realises, a woman of such piety she cut out her own eyes rather than be admired for their beauty. Before she can move or speak, Serafina utters a harsh, wordless shout and brings her fist up beneath the saint's tray, flipping it into the air. Santa Lucia recoils with a cry, while Orsola lunges forward, making a fumbling attempt to catch the platter. She fails — and as it crashes onto the stones below, Serafina bolts like a horse, disappearing into the same alley from which the blind saint has just emerged.

Orsola is so tired and hungry she could weep. With a low groan, she steps around Santa Lucia — who is crouching down to retrieve her platter, releasing a torrent of extremely unsaintly language — and starts after the choir nun once more.

The alley leads into a dingy yard, where barrels are being unloaded from an ox cart; Serafina is on its opposite side, heading through an archway. Orsola follows, calling her name loudly.

The labourers there are turning to look, smirking at each other. One of them stands in her path: he is half a yard taller than her at least, with a matted black beard and grubby shirt, and for a second he fills her view.

'What's this?' he says. 'A little piglet, running loose?'

Orsola ducks to the left, squirming by – and he is gathering her towards him, chuckling lewdly, trying to work a callused hand beneath her armpit. It has been some years since Orsola has endured such attentions, but she remembers how to meet them well enough. Taking hold of the labourer's thumb, she twists it sideways as far as she can. The man releases her with a curse, and an ill-aimed kick that connects with the cart's wheel rather than her rump; and then she is gone, brushing against the ox's velvety muzzle as she darts out of the yard.

A short dash brings Orsola to a queue of Romans and pilgrims, funnelling down a lane. She worms in between the shoulders and backs, shouting again for Serafina. Before long, she finds herself moving from shade to bright sunlight; the chatter and music around her increases twofold, echoing out across a large open space. With some effort, she breaks free from the current and climbs up onto an unattended barrow.

The sight amazes Orsola anew. She is in a vast rectangular piazza with five-storey buildings lining its sides, and it is filled with people. A number are passing through, but many more are simply standing there, talking with their companions as if awaiting some kind of show or ceremony. Above the hundreds of hoods and hats, Orsola can see balconies draped with banners; a statue of the Holy Madonna set within a glorious golden pavilion, surrounded by worshippers; another half-built stage, festooned with ropes and pullies. The morning air is warming fast and already heavy with dust. She can smell cooking, also – frying fat, various herbs, freshly baked bread – all of it acutely delicious. She forces herself to concentrate: to search for Serafina's moss-grey cloak amid the masses before her.

To her surprise, she locates it in seconds. The choir nun is crossing the piazza at a diagonal, elbowing her way past the Madonna's pavilion. Orsola murmurs thanks, hopping down from the barrow to resume her pursuit. After only two steps, however, someone seizes a handful of her own cloak, nearly wrenching it from her shoulders. She wheels around, trying to stay under it and prevent her grey habit from being exposed. Her immediate fear is that she will be confronted by the labourer from the yard, bent on revenge – but there behind her is Santa Lucia, still in her bloody blindfold.

'Your girl cracked my eye,' she says angrily. 'It's broken – useless!'

Orsola glares back at her; out there in the sunlight, she can see that the saint's blindfold is made of a light gauze, through which a pair of undamaged eyes can just be made out.

'You walked into *us*,' she retorts. 'Leave me be!'

Santa Lucia is starting to reply, lifting up her platter like she means to hit Orsola with it, when a great murmur rises across the piazza. The numbers around them surge, pushing Santa Lucia against Orsola and bending her platter a little between them. The crush gets worse; the thickening mass of bodies sways and moans. Orsola and the saint clutch at each other, fighting to stay upright.

'What's . . . what's happening?' Orsola gasps.

Santa Lucia is gripping her shoulder. She has tugged the blindfold down so that it hangs around her neck; blood or whatever it is covers her cheeks, but there is none at all around her eyes and nose. The effect is alarming. Without looking, she jabs a finger towards what must surely be the largest building on the piazza – a fine palazzo with a façade of spotless white stone. Orsola can just see a cohort of black-clad guards opening a set of gates, pushing people back as they attempt to forge a path through the crowds.

'Donna Olimpia,' Santa Lucia says.

Orsola frowns, throwing out an arm to keep her balance. 'Who is—'

A row of trumpets sound a piercing salute from the palazzo's main balcony, causing a hush to fall across the piazza. The people stop jostling, many craning their necks to peer about; and a few seconds later, over by the stage, the shouts begin.

'Donna Olimpia! Here, Donna Olimpia! Here, here!'

The next moment, everybody is yelling and waving their hands in the air. This uproar has an odd tone to it, unusually high; looking around her, Orsola notices that the crowd out there in the middle of the piazza is made up almost entirely of women.

Suddenly the black-clad guards are close by, forming two parallel lines. Several splendid blue carriages are rounding the Madonna's pavilion, pulled by teams of chestnut horses with tall black plumes in their bridles. Orsola has a clear view of one as it passes – the polished, curving panels; the golden hinges and handles; the black-clad footmen standing at the rear. On the door, beneath the tiara and crossed keys of the Holy Father, a gleaming white dove has been painted with an olive branch clasped in its beak. The windows of this carriage are flawlessly clean, reflecting the morning sky, the buildings of the piazza, and the rapt, sweaty faces of the crowd. As Orsola watches, a black-gloved hand is raised close to the glass; whether this is to acknowledge the many dozens packed around or simply to block the sun, she cannot tell.

The women in the piazza continue to shout at the very top of their voices, appealing for help with varying degrees of despair.

'I have no one, there are men after me, I beg you, Donna Olimpia, in God's name!'

'My husband has died, I am a widow like you, my house has been taken away . . .'

'Donna Olimpia, I have been abused, abused most foully – oh dear lady, you are my last hope!'

The carriages do not slow down. Very soon the palazzo gates are closing behind them, the guards retreating with visible relief. The pressure eases rapidly as the crowd begins to disperse. For all their lamentations and tales of misery, the women do not appear to be disappointed. They begin swapping tips and predictions. Holy Week is coming, they remind each other; she's sure to be out a good deal then.

Santa Lucia did not add her voice to the chorus, or even look at the carriages as they passed. She straightens out her platter with her thumbs, glowering like she means to resume their fight at once.

Orsola steps back. 'Who . . . who was that?' she asks. 'Who is Donna Olimpia?'

The saint's eyes – her real eyes – are so dark they seem almost black. She fixes Orsola with a brief, quizzical stare, then grabs her cloak again and pulls it open. She takes in the grey habit beneath, along with the rope belt and worn sandals, and snorts with scornful amusement.

'How d'you get out?'

Orsola dips her aching head. She can see no point in lying now; a part of her welcomes the chance simply to speak the truth. 'Our house was attacked,' she says. 'Along with the whole town. My sister and I, we . . . we fled into the woods. We were—'

Remembrance of the situation comes like a sharp pinch. Sister Serafina is gone. Orsola looks towards the Madonna's pavilion, then to the stage and a couple of the other elaborate temporary structures that stand along the length of the piazza. No trace of the choir nun can be seen. Panic tightens painfully in her chest; the air in the bustling piazza feels thick and horribly warm, difficult to inhale. She starts to move away, urging herself to stay calm — but Santa Lucia is still on her, grasping her habit. Orsola rolls her shoulders, trying to break free. The saint is larger than she is, however, and obviously has experience of restraining people. As they struggle, Santa Lucia takes something from beneath the strap of her bloody yellow gown and holds it close to Orsola's face. It is the brown eye from her platter, now bisected by a neat white crack.

'Venetian, this is,' she says. 'Murano glass. Cost me thirty scudi. And your girl — your *sister* — she broke it.'

Her meaning is plain enough. The last of Orsola's patience disappears. She used to be known for her temper; back in the convent it led to beatings, days locked in the cellars, and many long hours of the Mother Abbess's counsel. The months Orsola has spent with Sister Serafina have taught her to keep it in check — but here, faced with the bloody Santa Lucia and her cracked brown eyeball, she feels the old fury rising in her once more.

'We have nothing,' she spits. 'Now *begone!*'

She brings her knee up against the saint's thigh, then snatches away the cracked eyeball and throws it with all her might, off towards the grand white palazzo. Santa Lucia turns to watch it go, swearing in disbelief, her hold relaxing a fraction — and Orsola gives her a hard shove, sending her lurching into the people behind.

Orsola runs on fearfully towards the Madonna's pavilion. It has been several minutes now since she last saw Serafina. What hope can there be of finding her amid these thousands — amid these chaotic, endless streets? This is God's doing. Of course it is. He knows what Orsola is planning – that she intends to leave Serafina, abandon the life of the convent, and betray her vows – and He is punishing her. He is seeing to it that she fails in this last duty. That she misses this great chance for atonement. That the soul of her innocent girl remains alone, stranded forever on the grey hill. Orsola's dismay is like a blow to the stomach, stealing her breath. Her eyes sting with tears. She attempts to compose a prayer – to explain her intentions, perhaps, and ask for forgiveness – but doesn't know where to begin.

And then, suspended above the throng, she sees Santa Catarina. The princess-saint is depicted upon a bright devotional banner, one of several that are displayed along the walls of a wooden, fort-like structure that stands in the centre of the piazza, past the Madonna's pavilion. Catarina is hanging high on a corner turret. She is twice the size of life, holding a martyr's palm, with a fragment of the shattered wheel propped behind her. Dark hair flows out across her shoulders, while above her head, set against purple storm clouds, is a ring of silver stars.

It is a sign, plainly; Orsola heads for it without another thought, wiping her tears on her sleeve. The Benedictine black is easy to spot. Sister Serafina is kneeling on the stones at the base of the turret, her cloak discarded, deep in her devotions. Orsola breathes out heavily, almost laughing as she whispers the most ardent thanks. She was mistaken. Their separation was a warning only – a divine caution against complacency and carelessness. Her chance is not lost yet.

As Orsola approaches, she sees that seven or eight others are kneeling at Serafina's side. The choir nun is speaking of Santa Catarina's first encounter with the pagan Emperor Maxentius, when she confounded him with her learning and God-given eloquence.

More passers-by are slowing to listen, taking Serafina to be another sight of the Holy Jubilee — part of the spirit and spectacle of the city. Orsola stops at the edges. She looks at the faces of Serafina's growing congregation. Many are captivated; several are lowering themselves to kneel as well, bowing their heads in prayer.

Serafina herself is lost completely in her tale and notices none of this. Around her knees and sandals is what seems to be a scattering of copper fish-scales, glinting against the stone. Orsola realises that they are coins — surely the smallest, thinnest coins she has ever seen.

But there are already quite a lot of them.

Domina

The grand staircase is loaded with people. They crowd along the balustrades, packing the balcony: prelates and nobles, the fashionable and the influential, dressed in every variation of black the mind can conjure. Donna Olimpia surveys them all unsmilingly as she starts up the stairs. The climb is agony, but she shows none of it. Her visitors begin to offer their salutations. She does not respond.

The chair in the audience chamber is a heavy, golden thing. Donna Olimpia's pace quickens a little as she nears it, and she barely contains a moan of relief as she sits down. Sucking air through her teeth, she gives her kneecaps a firm rub; the pain loses its awful, lacerating sharpness, subsiding to a nasty ache. After a minute or so, she straightens her back, arranges her satin weeds, and signals to her major-domo. This morning's business needs to be dispensed with as swiftly as possible.

The callers begin to file in. Their requests are standard: a petition to be set before the pope, a post in the Curia to be purchased, a papal indulgence to be secured. If Donna Olimpia can help, and usually she can, she directs her visitor towards an adjoining chamber. There sits Monsignor Mascambruno, over from his office in Trevi, ready with his ledger to inform them of the sums involved.

Just one item threatens to disturb this process. The Trinity Institute of Pilgrims – of which Donna Olimpia was made president, in an eye-catching display of her sense of civic duty – has sent a delegation of its ladies, apparently set on some form of challenge. It is the Trinity Institute's task to house the multitudes that have been pouring into Rome for several weeks now, to attend the Holy Jubilee. At Donna Olimpia's suggestion, an immense hostel was built in Regola, beside the river, by converting a block of warehouses. This was hailed as a mighty achievement, an unrivalled exercise of Christian virtue; but the Trinity council members before her are claiming that it has already proved inadequate.

'We fear that more charitable donations are needed,' one of them ventures. 'Perhaps the Institute should lead by example, with some gifts of our own. Might it be that you, Donna Olimpia, as our president, would like to—'

'There are several noble families who have not yet contributed,' Donna Olimpia cuts in. 'The Rinalducci. The Albani. I believe that they are our best chance here. Use my name, and make it plain what is at stake for them.'

This meets with uncertainty. The council members shift and pout; a couple adjust their skirts.

'Take heart, ladies,' Donna Olimpia says. 'You are doing God's work. The Holy Father speaks of it often.' She leans back to call a question across the huge room. 'Is that not so, Cardinal Maidalchini?'

Federico looks around. The boy wears the one red cloak among the black, but there is only vacancy on his donkey-like face, and all that is demonstrated by his stammering reply is that he has not been listening. Donna Olimpia grips her armrests, sinking her fingernails deep into the velvet. She has done all she can to correct her brother's wretched attempt at upbringing and school his son for holy office, for the office she worked so hard to win for him: that of Cardinal Nephew, the young prelate placed at the right hand of the pope. Yet at the end of it, Federico Maidalchini is even more incapable than when she began. It makes her want to throw something at him.

'Yes indeed,' she says loudly, as if the dullard has given her an assured and insightful answer. 'The Institute's mission concerns Pope Innocent greatly. It brings him much reassurance to know that you fine, pious women are overseeing it. You are in his prayers, every one of you.'

This does the trick. The prayers of a pope, even entirely imaginary ones, are enough for the Trinity delegation. They drop curtseys and retreat.

Donna Olimpia is tired now; she is riled, furthermore, by Federico's incapacity and is impatient to attend to other matters. Rising with a wince, she leaves the audience chamber through a different doorway, ignoring the bows of her visitors. Federico begins to follow, as might befit an intimate, but a single glance stops him dead.

The door leads into the antechamber where Monsignor Mascambruno makes his nest. Seeing Donna Olimpia passing through, the datary closes his ledger, slides from behind his desk and falls in at her heel, the usual touch of self-satisfaction on his pallid, dainty features. Together, they walk along a corridor, then up the half-flight of steps that leads into the gilded gloom of the chapel. On the altar wall hangs the Madonna in Glory, rising upon silver clouds and fringed with rosy-cheeked putti – a much-coveted piece by Maestro Sacchi, worth three hundred scudi at least, yet presented to Donna Olimpia on the feast day of San Martino for nothing at all.

Prince Niccolò Ludovisi, husband of Donna Olimpia's youngest daughter Costanza, is waiting before the reliquary, squinting through the glass-panelled doors at one of the holy relics displayed within. Noticing her approach, the fat prince plucks the pipe from between his lips and knocks it out; his efforts to conceal the thing inside the black velvet doublet he has stretched over his ample torso are so unhurried as to appear slightly contemptuous.

'Good morning to you, dear Mama,' he declares, waving away a wisp of smoke with his hand. 'May I say that you look especially fine this morning, in your way — wouldn't you agree, Monsignor Mascambruno? *Poised*, that is the word. Like a prosecutor, perhaps, at some grand trial, or a general about to announce a cunning manoeuvre.'

He laughs that coarse, loud guffaw of his. Donna Olimpia does not react. She has made her peace with the match — it was her doing, after all — but nearly six years on, Ludovisi still has the ability to aggravate her beyond measure. At times, she is sorely tempted to twist the ears clean off his skull. Peering around the chapel, she spies her granddaughter Olimpiuccia away in a corner, half concealed behind a marble column. The girl is kneeling on a cushion in an attitude of deepest prayer; her Lenten garb is needlessly austere, made from plain wool only, and her rich auburn curls are bound tightly beneath a black headscarf.

The sight brings Donna Olimpia a new twinge of annoyance. She has spoken repeatedly with the governess, the tutors and various relatives about this excessive piety her granddaughter has developed, that sees her praying incessantly, hiding out here in the chapel, and squandering the greater part of every day. All they can tell her is that it is common enough among the daughters of the nobility, when they are on the cusp of womanhood and coming to understand the matrimonial duties that lie before them; that it will burn brightly for a while, and then disappear.

'Olimpiuccia,' she says sharply. 'What are you doing here? Do you not have lessons?'

The girl attempts to make some excuse, but Donna Olimpia will not hear it. She orders her out, telling her to find Signor Rosselli, her Latin tutor, and ask him for additional exercises. Olimpiuccia considers resistance, pursing her lips; but after looking at her grandmother again she thinks better of it. She crosses herself and hurries away, keeping her head down.

'Good Lord,' Ludovisi murmurs. 'I had not the faintest idea she was in here.'

Donna Olimpia regards him with distaste — the collar of blubber beneath his chin, coated by a sparse, greying beard; the glassy, wide-set eyes; the slight falseness in his smile. 'You are her uncle,' she says. 'Do you feel no responsibility towards her at all? Must I see to everything myself?'

Ludovisi shrugs, nodding towards the reliquary. 'I fear that I was too absorbed in studying your latest acquisition.' He lets out a low whistle, as if awestruck. 'The issue of Santa Catarina, collected directly from her severed neck! How in heaven's name did you come by it?'

Donna Olimpia walks forward and they gaze into the cabinet together. There, between the shoulder bone of Santa Francesca and the tongs used to tear out the tongue of San Livino, rests a small phial, stoppered with a plug of molten lead. The glass is mottled and discoloured, but a quantity of dark sludge can be seen inside.

'Baron Mattei acquired it for me,' says Donna Olimpia, the pride of the collector stirring very slightly within her. 'During a recent campaign in the north. It has been verified by the offices of the Inquisition.'

'Praise God for the spoils of war,' says Ludovisi dryly. 'And the coming months will surely bring other opportunities as well. A great specimen box of humanity is being emptied onto Rome, and it is carrying all sorts of rare treasure in with it.' He points at the pride of Donna Olimpia's collection, placed on the reliquary's top shelf: a diamond-studded crucifix with a blackened fragment of the True Cross set in its centre. 'Why, you could complete your cross, Mama! Have the whole thing standing right there beside the altar, as if our Saviour had only just been prised off it!'

Donna Olimpia has heard a lot of such talk. It does not impress her. 'If all the pieces being sold out in the city were gathered together,' she says, going over to an upholstered chair, 'we could build a cross as tall as San Pietro.'

As Ludovisi chortles obediently, Donna Olimpia sits down and turns towards Mascambruno. The datary is standing just inside the chapel door, his ledger beneath his arm, eyeing Ludovisi with sly animosity. He has come to regard the fat prince as a rival — as a potential obstacle before his ambitions. Donna Olimpia has done nothing to discourage this; she finds it rather amusing, in fact, given Ludovisi's absolute obliviousness to the supposed contest. There is no question which of them she would dispense with, should it ever come to that. Ludovisi is family — and he maintains a dense web of spies and informants that spreads throughout Rome, which serves to outweigh his more irksome qualities. Nonetheless, there is much about Mascambruno that Donna Olimpia enjoys. He shares her love of coin and is pleasantly unburdened by scruple, despite his priestly vows. She has discovered a dose of real venom in him, also — a taste for the darker side of things that makes the gossip he shares with her quite unmatched in its viciousness.

'How did we fare today, Monsignor?' Donna Olimpia asks.

'Moderately well, Excellency. A shade past five hundred scudi, along with several pledges of plate and jewels.'

This is a lie, of course; the total was certainly higher than that. It is important that Mascambruno steals, however, and that his sub-dataries steal, and their clerks and footmen as well. Theft is the twine that binds all of this together.

'May I say,' the datary continues, 'that there is much gold to be made from the Jubilee indulgence. People would pay handsomely to obtain it without the need for the penitential procession.'

'Christ's blood, Masco,' murmurs Ludovisi, absently patting his belly, 'I swear I would fill your lap with rubies if you could get me out of that. The circuit must be twelve miles at least. And we Romans must do it *thirty times*. That is . . .' He pauses, making a vain attempt at calculation. 'That is a damned long way.'

'I have already talked of this with the pope,' says Donna Olimpia. 'He will not hear of it. He is set upon absolute propriety.'

'You will work on him, though, Mama,' Ludovisi says. 'You will win him around. You always do.'

Donna Olimpia shakes her head. 'I will not,' she says, with faint irritation. 'The Holy Father views the Jubilee celebrations as a chance to salvage his dignity, after the various humiliations he has endured of late – the shameful terms of the northern peace, and so forth. I see no advantage in trying to change his mind here. Great opportunities await us in this Jubilee year, but this is not one of them.'

It is time to move on to more confidential subjects. Donna Olimpia glances over at Mascambruno, who is no longer required; the datary seems about to protest, so she dismisses him with a flick of her hand, instructing him to draft the necessary papers ahead of her departure for the pope's residence at the Palazzo del Quirinale. He bows and leaves, radiating discontent.

'Come then, Ludo,' she says, when the chapel doors have closed. 'What have you heard?'

The fat prince's manner shifts, allowing a glimpse of the wily mind that he conceals beneath his jocular, dissipated exterior. He cocks an eyebrow, gesturing back towards the reliquary and the holy horrors housed within.

'It would seem that Rome's relic sellers are not the only ones taking advantage of the upheavals of the Jubilee. My people in Campo Marzio are in little doubt that Spain has spotted a chance to reassert herself, and increase her influence upon the pope. And she is moving fast. King Felipe's new ambassador is due to arrive during Holy Week, less than ten days from now.'

'What do we know of this ambassador?'

'He is the Duke of Infantado,' Ludovisi says. 'A big beast indeed, and among the most renowned and well-favoured of Felipe's generals. It is reported that he brings a complete staff with him, along with a company of fighting men.'

Donna Olimpia's mood sours yet further. The Spanish embassy in Rome has been without a master for some years now, a situation that suited her current schemes very well. The approach of this warrior duke is both disquieting and profoundly inconvenient.

'Our position is most precarious, Ludo,' she says. 'Keep that always in mind. Everything we have depends upon one old and fast-fading man. It could end with Pope Innocent. If my stratagem fails, all could be lost.'

It has long been Donna Olimpia's habit to plan meticulously for the future. Some time ago, she learned that King Louis of France had decided to seize the Kingdom of Naples from Spain. Louis intended to award the territory to his closest Italian allies: the Barberini family, relatives of the late Pope Urban. Exiled from Italy due to their rampant corruption, the heads of this once-mighty clan have been residing at Versailles since Urban's death six years previously. Now, though, the Barberini were plotting their return – and Naples was to serve as their new foundation.

Immediately, Donna Olimpia sensed an opportunity. Through secret channels, she offered to provide the French invasion force with funds and mercenaries – and, most importantly, with papal consent for the action, and a firm promise that the Vatican would recognise and support the kingdom's new rulers. Spain would be gravely diminished, France reinforced, and the Barberini family restored to power and prominence in Italy – and they would owe Donna Olimpia a very significant favour. There would most probably be another Barberini pope, once Innocent had been gathered to glory. Her place in Rome would be secure, along with the fortune she has accrued, and her family would all be safe – provided they played the parts required of them.

Ludovisi clears his throat. 'There is more, I'm afraid. Many Spaniards have come within our walls of late, to join in the Jubilee and attend to the renovation of the embassy, before the good duke's arrival. But there are a few whose exact business here my people have been . . . unable to ascertain.'

Donna Olimpia brushes impatiently at her black gown. 'Such as whom?'

'They speak of one fellow in particular – a courtier, a groom of the King's bedchamber no less, and the keeper of his pictures. It is known that he recently passed some months in the Kingdom of Naples, in the court of the Spanish viceroy.'

'Naples,' Donna Olimpia repeats. 'That cannot be a coincidence. What is his name?'

'Don Diego Rodríguez Silva y Velázquez. He has been travelling in Italy for some time. I met him at the Cavaliere's last year, as a matter of fact. An odd sort. He claimed that he was purchasing antique statues for the decoration of the royal palaces in Madrid.'

'Where is this person staying? At the embassy as well — that broken-down palazzo on the Piazza Trinita?'

'It would appear so. I am told that since his return from Naples he has been meeting with many Roman gentlemen.' Ludovisi pauses; his left hand wanders to the place where he stowed his pipe, as if he would dearly like to draw it out again. 'Including Camillo Astalli.'

Donna Olimpia stiffens in her chair, an unpleasant heat closing around the back of her neck. 'The traitor.'

'He is a painter as well,' Ludovisi offers. 'Velázquez, I mean. They say he is the finest in all Spain, whatever that's worth. Although I have yet to meet an Italian who has seen any of his works. He appears to have brought none with him.'

'This Velázquez is a spy,' Donna Olimpia states. 'He is obviously acting as a conduit between the viceroy in Naples and Spain's allies in Rome — men such as Astalli and his masters. Our enemies have caught wind of the French invasion, and perhaps of my involvement in it also. The stratagem could be at risk.' She sighs hard, her nostrils flaring. 'Adversity mounts, Ludo. Adversity mounts yet again.'

Ludovisi is unalarmed. 'How much does Pope Innocent actually know of this stratagem of yours, Mama?' he asks, his eyes narrowing. 'He . . . *approves* of it, doesn't he?'

Donna Olimpia sniffs. 'The pope is a spiritual man,' she replies. 'Such earthly machinations are quite beyond his understanding. But he is implicated, I have made sure of that. When the French have taken Naples from Spain, and gifted the kingdom to the Barberini, the Holy See will provide its sanction.'

Ludovisi grins conspiratorially, showing off a set of small, tobacco-stained teeth. 'It is just as I said earlier,' he chuckles. 'The pope is your pet, Mama. A blind, neutered pug, led along on a golden chain.'

Donna Olimpia shoots him a cold look. 'Listen to me, oaf,' she says. 'A threat is emerging here. This new Spanish ambassador, the duke of wherever; this devious picture keeper and his meetings with Camillo Astalli. The pattern is clear, and we would be most unwise to disregard it.'

Ludovisi cannot disagree; he shrugs once more and is about to make some remark, but Donna Olimpia no longer has any wish to hear him.

'They will fail,' she declares. 'I have been opposed before, many times, and they *always* fail. Our family will survive; it will surely flourish. So keep up your watch. We need only a few more months, then we will be beyond all interference.'

With that, Donna Olimpia gathers her will and starts to rise from her chair. Hot, needling pains throb out from her kneecaps, creeping around her thighs and prickling up her spine. She bites her cheek and grips a handful of her skirts, squeezing tightly; she contains it.

'Almighty God will ask much of us this summer, Ludo,' she says. 'Be ready.'

*

The Piazza del Quirinale is filled with the common crowd. At first, peering from her carriage window, Donna Olimpia cannot tell what is going on; then she spies a seam of clerical whites and reds running through the general drabness, accompanied in places by the stripes and halberds of the Swiss Guard. Many hundreds are kneeling, and there is singing as well – a chapel choir from the palazzo, trilling its way through a motet. A single splendid banner has been raised above all this: the crossed keys and triple tiara, with the dove and olive branch set below. Pope Innocent is out among his flock.

Donna Olimpia groans loudly. 'Old fool,' she says, striking the cushion beside her with her fist. 'Wretched old *idiot*.'

Across the carriage sits her daughter Costanza, left behind by Ludovisi to accompany her, and Carmela di Morrone, the wife of an important ally in the governor's retinue. They are glancing at each other, trying to work out how best to react.

'Praise God,' says Carmela carefully, after a few moments. 'The Holy Father is following the example of Our Saviour, as ordained by—'

'That milk-eyed dotard out there is not guided by *scripture*,' Donna Olimpia interrupts. 'He does this . . . this *nonsense* simply to . . .'

She cranes her neck, seeking out the papal party — and there he is at the fountain's edge, standing by the pope's side, his face concealed beneath the broad red brim of his hat.

Cardinal Panciroli.

Donna Olimpia wants to shout out an oath, she wants it very badly; but dozens of attentive faces are already directed at her carriage, so instead she takes a long breath, sits back upon her seat, and forces herself to remain as impassive and unfeeling as a marble bust. Her procession bears right, advancing along the edge of the piazza towards the palazzo's southern corner. Noticing its approach, the guards at the main gate begin clearing people back. More heads turn and a great hum of conversation starts up, rumbling beneath the warbles of the castrati.

Over at the fountain, the pope rises from among the pilgrims, clad in a white and gold mitre and a scarlet cloak. He is smiling through the discomfort Donna Olimpia knows he must feel, in his back and guts and everywhere else, attempting to shroud himself in an air of pontifical beneficence. Her lip curls when she sees the twist of cloth in his hands, smudged with grime from freshly washed feet. A page waits at his elbow with a copper basin; as he turns to wring out his cloth, he realises that his congregation has become distracted, and looks over towards her procession. Even at forty yards' distance, she can see his face fall.

There it is, she thinks with grim satisfaction. *He knows what he has done.*

The carriages enter the Palazzo del Quirinale, passing swiftly through a short tunnel into the main courtyard. Donna Olimpia steps out onto the stones, her chin held high and her sheaf of petitions under her arm. The servants here, like those in the mouldering halls of the Vatican, believe themselves to be special, as if fetching and carrying for the pope is itself a holy calling. Many act as if women, and Donna Olimpia in particular, are offensive to their sight. For a while she had them culled, casting more than a hundred out onto the street before a year was done, but eventually she grew weary of this. What did it matter to her, really? She is the first woman of Rome; while they are mice, flies, specks of dirt. They are nothing.

Donna Olimpia looks to the gates and piazza beyond. The huge crowd is shifting about as Pope Innocent heads back inside to offer her his explanations and excuses. She will not talk to him here, of course, in view of the Swiss Guards and the palace grooms, nor will she join his train like some kind of supplicant. The situation is plain: she must reach the papal apartments before he does.

Donna Olimpia calls for a sedan chair, as is her custom in the Quirinale, the doorways and corridors being more than large enough to accommodate one. The servants bring it promptly, whatever they might think of her. She pulls back the tasselled curtain and climbs in, hearing the slightest grunt from the man behind as they take her weight. These bearers rush her across the courtyard and up the endless stairs, continuing at a brisk trot through the glories of the Sala Regia. The pace slows only when they arrive in the principal reception room, first in the line of vast chambers that the pope inhabits.

'On, on!' she says, before the men can put the chair down. 'Quickly!'

They continue through the library and the study, into the dressing room. A team of valets is at work in here, sorting the papal cassocks, copes and surplices. Seeing the sedan chair, they scatter like rabbits.

'The window,' instructs Donna Olimpia.

The men take her over, setting the chair on the patterned marble floor with a smart *clack*. She climbs out and orders them to leave. The complaints of her accursed knees have eased off somewhat, thank God, after an application of frankincense oil back at the Palazzo Pamphili. Still, there is an odd, tingling sensation down in the bones — not pain, not quite, but a clear indication of what awaits if she makes any significant demands of them. Through the tall window, she watches the tail end of the papal entourage disappear from the courtyard, into the staircase. The pope is hurrying. It pleases her to imagine him panting along, a hand to his aching back, just to reach her and learn precisely how much trouble he is in.

There is an obstacle, however, between Donna Olimpia and her prey. She senses him walking at the pope's side as the company enters the dressing room. When she turns, all the others retreat at once; but Cardinal Panciroli holds his ground.

Donna Olimpia considers them, these two old men in their

clerical finery, and by the Holy Blessed Virgin it is all she can do to keep a lid on her disdain. Pope Innocent is inescapably sheep-like, with a bulbous nose and large ears, his narrow shoulders hunched atop an increasingly crooked spine. Panciroli is better, she has to admit; ten years younger, somewhat smarter and more upright, but so very *small*. He is like an aged boy, with a placid, complacent little pigeon face poking out from his crimson mozzetta.

'I will speak with my brother-in-law alone,' she says.

Panciroli feigns confusion. This is the standard tactic of these ecclesiastics — to act as if Donna Olimpia's utterances, in their feminine crudity, are somehow baffling to the pious male mind. 'It must be an issue of enormous urgency,' he says, 'to warrant the interruption of the Holy Father while he was engaged in that most sacred of tasks: the emulation of Our Saviour Himself.'

The cardinal then begins a discourse on the gospel of San Giovanni, trying to draw the pope into a comfortable, potentially endless meditation on something as familiar to them both as the shape of their own bony hands.

But Pope Innocent is too agitated by her presence to engage with Panciroli's words. He looks away, those large ears turning the colour of his cloak. Donna Olimpia says nothing. She does not sigh or shift her posture. She simply stands.

'It would be best, dear Panciroli,' the pope interrupts gently, after a while, 'if you left us. We have so much to attend to, Donna Olimpia and I. Family matters, you understand. I will join you for Vespers, before your return to the Vatican.'

This is a game, and Panciroli is a seasoned player. He knew from the moment he entered the dressing room that things would go this way. He has not lost here. As he bows, the look on his pigeon face tells Donna Olimpia that he is pleased enough with his day's work.

'What are you doing, you old booby?' she snaps, once Panciroli is gone. 'You mangy old sheep? You sad, stooped, shrivelled excuse for a man?'

As always, he cowers and winces, the corners of his mouth twitching now and again with something strangely like pleasure. 'They look to me,' he mumbles, 'for their connection to Almighty God. I must . . . I must do my duty.'

'So important, he is,' Donna Olimpia scoffs. 'So *vital*.' She moves closer. 'Do not forget, *never* forget, that I know you, Giambattista Pamphili. I know what you are.' She looks around the room. 'I know what lies beneath these vestments. The feeble heart. The *weakness*.'

'What do you want from me, Olimpia?' he moans.

She allows her expression to soften by the faintest degree. 'I want you to be careful, that is all. We do not know who might be in these crowds. Thousands are flooding into our city each and every day. They may be carrying diseases of the most grievous and deadly kind – *contagion*, Giambo, for heaven's sake. And then there are the heretics. The heathens. In a mob of that size, there could have been a dozen knives. Your guards would have been powerless. You could easily have been killed.'

And we are not quite prepared for that, she thinks.

The delivery is perfect – the subtle slide from anger to distress; the waver, very slight, that she puts in her voice. The pope's peevishness is transformed to contrition. He hangs his head and apologises, promising to exercise more caution in future. Then, removing his mitre, he sits wearily at a dressing table, running a hand through the few wisps of pale grey hair that still adorn his crown.

Donna Olimpia offers no forgiveness. She heaps the day's petitions before him and points impatiently to the writing materials at the table's edge. Standing behind, she watches him scratch out his signature, the Fisherman's Ring glinting heavily on his gnarled finger, barely reading a word of what he sanctions in his hurry to obtain her approval.

'And where is Federico?' she demands. 'The boy is your Cardinal Nephew, Giambo. You are his mentor, and must have him with you in public as much as you can. This Jubilee year is a God-given chance for him to prove himself at last.'

'Panciroli cannot tolerate him,' Giambo mutters, cringing a little more. 'He says that Federico is a . . . a doltish puppet, utterly unqualified for his role, who was appointed solely for your benefit. He will not have him present.'

This is true, of course. In that moment, Donna Olimpia sees quite clearly that the situation is futile: Cardinal Federico Maidalchini will never be of any genuine use. Fortunately, there are others among her relatives who can be brought to bear instead. She resolves to begin her preparations.

'What the devil does Panciroli know?' she says. 'Why do you insist on listening to him instead of me – your sister-in-law, your own family?'

Giambo scatters sand, moves the sheet, then signs another. 'He is my secretary of state, Olimpia. I must heed his views.'

'Your precious secretary of state is quite happy to put you at mortal risk,' Donna Olimpia retorts. 'It is almost as if he would have you die, to clear the throne of San Pietro for another man – a man named Giacomo Panciroli, perhaps.'

The pope sighs. 'Olimpia . . .'

'He has his backers, Giambo. It is well known that he is close to the Spanish faction. King Felipe himself is believed to favour him, and would gladly see him take your place.' Donna Olimpia hesitates. 'I will not lie to you, brother: Spain has become our enemy, and her influence in Rome needs to be curtailed. This is the reason for our stratagem — you remember, for the Kingdom of Naples.'

Giambo lifts his quill from the page, angling his head in query. As yet, Donna Olimpia has told him very little about her plans — for the less he knows the safer they will be, at least until the French invasion has begun. He is aware of the stratagem's existence, and that it involves Naples and the future security of their family, but almost nothing else. Thus far, the distractedness of his aged brain has prevented him from pondering it any further, and Donna Olimpia presses onwards now before he can request any clarification.

'The arrival of their new ambassador, this soldier duke, may herald all sorts of problems for us. I hear that they are busily planting their spies throughout the city. There is one gentleman in particular, a courtier and intimate of Felipe, who is already thought to be circulating intelligences. Perhaps you have heard of him.'

This is bait, of a kind old Giambo cannot resist; half a lifetime ago he was Pope Urban's nuncio in Madrid and fancies that he is still an authority on the workings of the Spanish court. Sure enough, he promptly forgets Donna Olimpia's mention of Naples and asks the gentleman's name.

'Don Diego Velázquez,' she tells him. 'He is the king's decorator, it would seem, and his principal buyer of statues — and some kind of painter as well, they say.'

Giambo sets his quill aside. 'Diego Velázquez,' he repeats flatly. 'Here in Rome.'

'You know this person, then?'

'I have not thought of him for many years. He was a young man when we met, but . . . a painter he certainly is, Olimpia. These works of his . . . these portraits . . .'

Donna Olimpia moves closer to Giambo's shoulder and pushes the unsigned petitions before him. 'He is accomplished?'

The pope shakes his head. 'The word is insufficient. Upon the unveiling of a new picture, the entire royal household would rush through the palace of the Alcazar to see it. And the likenesses were astonishing. King Felipe, already, would be painted by no one else.' Giambo's forehead creases. 'But I found something disquieting about them. It is difficult to explain.'

'He made them look foolish, you mean?' Donna Olimpia asks, tapping the papers with her forefinger. 'What manner of painter would do that?'

Giambo picks up his quill and sits forward. 'No, not foolish. These sitters, these proud nobles, they were . . . well, they were exposed. Laid bare, somehow.' He starts to write again, proceeding haltingly through his papal signature; then he stops mid-word and stares off towards the windows. 'It was ungodly.'

Servus

Juan de Pareja walks onto the piazza with the canvas held in his arms. Before him stands the ancient church of the Rotonda – once a pagan temple, he has been told, before it was cleansed of sin and claimed for Christ. That morning, several dozen men are clustered within its arcade of tall, scarred columns, gathered around the canvases and panels that have been mounted on easels or propped against the back wall. The annual exhibition of the Confraternity of the Holy Pantheon is underway.

De Pareja stops four paces into the square, attempting to prepare himself for what lies ahead. It is the Feast Day of San Giuseppe, and this occasion is being marked with all the vigour of the Jubilee. Red is the saint's colour, and many are wearing red sashes and rosettes along with their Lenten black, while lengths of red ribbon trail from every sconce, railing and door handle. Handfuls of sawdust – a tribute to the holy carpenter – have been thrown all around the piazza. These golden curls cling to hair and clothing, gathering in gutters and the cracks between stones, covering the city's reek with the tang of fresh resin. A group of young men stand at the fountain in the middle of the piazza – assistants and apprentices from the look of them, brought in to set up this exhibition and then dismissed. They are drinking from wineskins, playing at dice and sharing the rumours of the day, with much joking and laughter.

De Pareja shifts his hold on the canvas. It is about half his height and covers his body completely. The painted side is turned inwards and is not yet dry in places, the final strokes having only been applied the evening before. Bearing it like this is awkward, but Don Diego's instructions were plain: the painting was not to be shown until the Rotonda itself was in sight. This gesture is shot through with theatre, and involves a level of personal visibility, of *display*, to which de Pareja is entirely unused. Despite this, he cannot fault his master's reasoning. Don Diego needs to announce himself to the painters of Rome: to give a clear demonstration of his abilities. And what de Pareja is about to do cannot fail to achieve that.

A few of the young men by the fountain are looking his way. De Pareja eyes them with vague apprehension. He knows that he must cut a peculiar figure: his countenance, taken by so many in Italy as belonging to the heathen lands of northern Africa, coupled with his humble European costume, and what is plainly a large artist's canvas in his hands. Collecting his wits, he murmurs a quick Ave Maria – and then he flips the painting around, fitting his fingers inside the supporting frame so that he can hold it in front of him like a placard.

Almost at once, there is a shout: loud, wordless, intended only to raise the alarm. Several more come a moment later. De Pareja remains calm, firming up his grip. The apprentices are leaving the fountain, striding towards him over the sawdust-strewn cobbles. At a certain distance, the leaders' expressions grow slack with wonder.

'You must show yourself, Juan,' Don Diego told him, as he prepared to set out. 'This is paramount. Keep your face in view, above the canvas.'

Very soon a dozen stand before him, a strange enthusiasm breaking over them. De Pareja recognises this reaction from Madrid, when any new work of Don Diego's was revealed. It is a staggered disbelief, like a form of intoxication — an amazement that, in some instances, edges close to fear. They chatter at each other, the Roman slang spoken so quickly it is impossible to follow; they call to others elsewhere in the piazza, and to their masters at the Rotonda; they lean in close, studying the workings of the brush, then take themselves back a yard or two to marvel at the illusion that has been wrought. To de Pareja himself, the living man above his likeness, they ask only one question, over and over.

'*Who?*'

'Do not speak,' Don Diego instructed, 'until you are before the clerk. Not one word.'

Briefly, de Pareja fears that he will be crushed amid this astonished mob, and the portrait torn apart and lost — but when he starts to move again they all clear from his path, holding back new arrivals to ensure that he reaches his destination. He feels both like a priest parading with a sacred relic, and a criminal being led to a place of public punishment.

After the bright piazza, the Rotonda's arcade is cool and dark, with the dusty smell of old stone. Easels and canvases stand all about. De Pareja sees an array of the usual scenes: saints undergoing martyrdom, the holy family at various stages of their story, incidents from pagan legend unfolding in lush, mountainous landscapes. He is brought before a clerk who can barely look away from the portrait for long enough to make an entry in his book. As soon as he has given his master's name it is being spoken everywhere, in tones ranging from reverence to rank suspicion. An easel is produced, and others moved aside so it can occupy pride of place. De Pareja is then invited to place Don Diego's canvas upon it.

The Roman painters come before this easel like an assembly of elders, making a great show of their dignity, yet sight of the portrait strips it from them immediately. A number catch their breath, their eyes popping wide. One lets out a short, spluttering laugh, then lunges forward until his nose is almost in the paint, while another unleashes a stream of curses so vehement it reduces him to a fit of coughing. All of them look from canvas to man, and from man to canvas. De Pareja remains impassive, crossing his hands before him, and directs his gaze just above their heads.

'Truth,' somebody pronounces. 'My friends, it is *truth*.'

There is a strong murmur of agreement, followed by a lively discussion of the portrait's artistic qualities: the variations in tone, the great delicacy of the shadow, the richness and warmth of the colour. De Pareja cannot help looking as well. Back at the embassy, during his first viewing, he saw only the likeness. He stared, and offered fulsome praise – and as always had his words waved away, admiration being nothing to Don Diego but a source of mild embarrassment. Here, though, surrounded by Rome's artists and their works, he can perceive the portrait's deeper insights. A queasy chill spreads through him.

'You are yourself a painter, Juan,' prompted Don Diego, as the correct pose was sought. 'A painter of rare ability. And soon enough you will be a free man – a Spaniard, a subject of King Felipe. This must be shown.'

Accordingly, de Pareja arranged himself as a señor: back straight, hat beneath his arm, cloak just so. He summoned his pride, his confidence, his best sense of what he was; of what he had done and was intending to do. And this is there on the canvas. Don Diego has not betrayed him; for all his master's perversity, for all his odd tempers and habits of mind, he would never do that.

Yet somehow, the portrait also contains an entirely different aspect. There is a nervousness to it, even a trace of fear. It can be seen in the sidelong look of the eyes, and the slight awkwardness in the arm; the worn cloth of the doublet, with its missing buttons over the stomach; the scuff on the elbow, rendered in a single loose stroke. This sitter is a slave, an owned man no longer young, pretending to be what he manifestly is not. Whose chance in life is almost gone, if it ever existed.

Don Diego does this without thought. De Pareja has noticed it before, in his master's portraits of the king and his court. It has made several, including Felipe himself, increasingly reluctant to be painted by him. He cannot flatter or distort; he is incapable of it, whatever he might say or even intend. His brush seeks out the soul, depicting every side and part. There is no pose or disguise. It is unsparing.

Among the general acclaim in the Rotonda, a few dissenters are now making themselves heard. 'This is mockery,' someone declares. '*Spanish* mockery. Whatever painterly qualities it may possess are immaterial. This Señor Velázquez seeks to sully our most sacred place with the portrait of a heathen slave.'

De Pareja recognises the speaker as Maestro da Cortona, a highly sought-after painter and architect. Although well dressed, he is sallow and stooped, his face moulded by irritability.

'Forgive me, Maestro,' says a younger man in a black biretta, 'but there are many pagan pictures on display here. You yourself submitted an Apollo and Daphne. I suspect that Our Saviour will endure.'

Da Cortona ignores him. 'It was sent as a deliberate insult,' he continues. 'The Spanish know how much work the men of this Confraternity have done for the Barberini, for the French faction in Rome, and now they seek to demean us. A Mussulman, on display in the church of Santa Maria! Signori, it is close to blasphemy.'

The refutation de Pareja has made innumerable times across Italy stands ready in his mind: his place of baptism, his devotion to the true faith, his love for the Holy Virgin. But of course he has no leave to speak.

'And where *is* Señor Velázquez, anyway?' says da Cortona next. 'Why has he not come here to show his picture himself, as we all have? Why does he send this godless creature in his stead? Is he so used to the company of kings that he scorns us less exalted beings?'

A dozen voices begin to speak at once, debating the truly unfathomable subject of Don Diego's intentions. De Pareja glances off between the columns, wondering if he might simply bow and depart; before he can move, however, a black-gloved hand settles upon his shoulder. Its owner has a bony, eagle-like face, with the nose, chin and brow all somehow prominent, creating an impression of both grandeur and guile. His beard is well trimmed, fading to grey, and he wears an extravagantly large black hat, even by the standards of these artistic gentlemen. He seems to have appeared from the back of the arcade, in the direction of the church doors.

'Don Diego Velázquez,' he says, 'scorns no one.'

The company promptly halts its disputation. Many of them hail this newcomer, plunging into low bows and sweeping off their hats, saying '*Il Cavaliere*' in tones of deep regard – although de Pareja notices that several of the more senior artists are markedly less effusive. He tries to bow himself but the hand remains firmly on his shoulder, holding him upright. The newcomer turns towards the portrait and narrows his bright, dark eyes to slits, murmuring something obscene.

'This is knowledge,' he proclaims. 'By Almighty Christ, this is *love*.'

His admirers concur, praising this Cavaliere's perception – and abruptly de Pareja realises that the owner of the hand clamped upon his shoulder is Gian Lorenzo Bernini, peerless sculptor and knight of the Cross of Christ, outside whose palazzo he has waited for many hours while his master was entertained within. Cavaliere Bernini is responsible for much of the overwhelming beauty de Pareja has seen in Rome, works that scarcely seem believable as the productions of a mortal man.

Da Cortona remains unconvinced, however. 'Cavaliere, are you suggesting that Señor Velázquez loves an enslaved heathen? As a . . . brother, perhaps?'

The Cavaliere's laugh is loud, and laced very slightly with contempt. 'God bless you, Maestro,' he says, but explains no further.

His grip shifts, and for an instant de Pareja thinks that he is about to be gathered into an embrace; but he is released instead, swaying slightly at the sudden freedom. Cavaliere Bernini goes before the portrait, throwing his black velvet cape over his shoulder. He surveys the whole; then he steps in swiftly to examine the face, the sheen of the skin, the crumpled, grubby collar, talking under his breath as he does so. The company waits in silence. Even the dissenters do not dare disturb him.

Eventually, the Cavaliere steps back. 'The Holy Jubilee is a time of miracles, signori,' he says. 'And Don Diego Velázquez has just given us the first.'

*

Three blocks from the Rotonda, de Pareja takes his felt hat from his satchel, gives it a shake, and fits it onto his head. It is still an hour before noon, so he decides to allow himself some time to sketch before he returns to the embassy on the Piazza Trinita. Don Diego, if he is not out elsewhere in the city, will neither notice nor care. Back in the Alcazar, de Pareja was already granted the leeway of a dependable studio assistant, rather than that of a slave; and the months he and his master have now spent together in Italy have made Don Diego even less exacting.

Ahead of him now is the Corso, the great artery of Rome, which is as full of people as any street can be. It forms part of the penitential procession, the primary reason so many of these pilgrims are here, joining the basilicas of San Pietro and Santa Maria Maggiore. The atmosphere is one of open jubilation — so very different from the festivals of Spain, with their flagellants and clanking irons. Many liberties are being taken with sacred characters and tales, things that would not be permitted in Madrid. Some of what de Pareja has seen since their return from Naples has made him uneasy, but he cannot deny its appeal — the unmistakable quickening in his thoughts, in his soul, that comes with inspiration. He has prayed on this at length, examining his motivations and asking for guidance. Everything urges him to continue. A painting is the goal: a piece in oils at least a yard high, more ambitious than anything he has yet attempted. This picture will stand as an incontestable case for manumission, and his release into the life of a free and independent artist. Don Diego has a much-rehearsed plan for their mutual advancement, but de Pareja will not simply wait. He will show what he can do. He will make it impossible for them to keep him as he is.

De Pareja looks up and down the street, amazed all over again by the procession's vast, ramshackle splendour; the songs and chants, in Latin and several other languages, that echo off the many hundreds of mismatched façades; the countless banners, flags, and lengths of red ribbon; the sawdust curls that lie so thickly in places they are like drifts of golden leaves. Before long, he spots a troupe of players standing atop a set of church steps. There are six of them, all elaborately costumed, enacting a comical Annunciation that hinges around San Guiseppe's extreme old age. With a woollen nightcap and straggly white beard, the saint sits snoring on a stool as an archangel lands directly at his side, its huge wings shivering, to the startled, awestruck cries of his young virgin wife. It is lively, for sure; de Pareja suspects it will not serve his larger purpose, but he finds a vantage point nonetheless, takes his drawing folder and a piece of graphite from his satchel, and begins to sketch.

He has the principal figures and something of the grand doorway behind when he hears a lone female voice, oddly resonant, speaking above the noises of the procession. Looking around, he notices a patch of stillness amid the constant movement. Just to the side of the thoroughfare, tucked in between two market stalls, roughly two dozen people appear to be kneeling in prayer.

De Pareja stops sketching, lowers his folder, and weaves through the crowds towards them. The voice belongs to an Italian gentlewoman. She is talking of San Guiseppe in a long, faultless flow, describing the old saint's vigilance as he transported his wife and the newborn Christ child into Egypt, after the evil dictates of King Herod. De Pareja skirts a party of Milanese, ducking beneath their gold-fringed banner – and at the head of the kneeling group he sees a choir nun in Benedictine black, somehow released from her confinement. She is on her knees as well, her face obscured by shadow, a silver rosary wound around her clasped hands. There is no playfulness or cheap sentimentality here. This nun speaks fervently, and with an uncanny eloquence – of nightfall, out in the wilderness; the distant campfires lit by Herod's men; the horrible howls and barks of the desert dogs.

'But San Guiseppe did not falter. Much like Christ Himself

would do, he relied on the Lord God to guide him through the wastelands, and deliver him from the clutches of the devil. He looked to his wife. He looked to the holy infant. And he led their donkey on down the path.'

The nun's listeners cross themselves, murmuring amens and words of praise. She straightens up, raising her face and her hands, shifting inadvertently into a shaft of late morning sunlight.

De Pareja nearly drops his drawing folder. Her slender, solemn face is deeply scarred on its left side, a mottled trail that pulls the skin tight across her cheekbone and at the side of her mouth. The marks are old, three or four years at least, and give her complexion the look of scoured marble; of something that has been deliberately spoiled. Shock rings through him with a humming sharpness. His eyes feel like they have been locked wide open.

Everything is right.

Her pose, so urgent and full of yearning. The light that falls from above, illuminating the cruel pattern of her scars and the black folds of her habit. De Pareja sees it clearly: a figure the size of life, painted in the Sevillian manner, set against deep darkness, with all of her ardour and her torment laid out upon the canvas. This will be the painting. This will be the one that sees him freed. The feeling is acute, almost painful; it is like relief and panic intertwined.

The pose is broken as swiftly as it appeared, the scarred nun moving back into shadow and resuming her oration. De Pareja blinks, licking his dry upper lip; then he lifts his folder, flips over the unfinished sketch of the Annunciation, and begins to draw with all the speed he can muster. A smile spreads across his face. He feels Almighty God guiding his hand, bringing forth the very best of his ability. In moments, the shoulders are there, and the brow; the fine, straight line of her nose; the ugly spatter of the scar, and the enmeshing of those long, bony fingers.

'What are you doing?'

The speaker is at his elbow, standing so close that de Pareja starts a little, the graphite slipping in his grasp. It is a young woman, younger even than the nun, less than half his own age, clad in a shawl and a simple blue gown. She has green eyes and a wide, frank face; her voice is low, unrefined, with an accent different to any he has heard during his months in Italy. There is a plain note of hostility in it. De Pareja assumes that this will be a challenge, provoked by the affront of his supposed heathenism, or made perhaps as the preamble to an attempt at robbery. Such things are hardly uncommon.

'I am a Christian,' he says quickly, 'in the service of His Catholic Majesty King Felipe of Spain. I worship Christ Jesus as my Lord and Saviour, and revere His Holy Mother the Blessed Virgin Maria.'

He crosses himself and gives a shallow bow. Unlike so many here, however, this woman obviously doesn't care what he believes. She repeats her question. De Pareja turns his folder around to show her the incomplete sketch. This doesn't seem to interest her either.

'Ten *baiocchi*,' she says.

It takes de Pareja a couple of seconds to understand that she is trying to extract a charge from him for drawing the nun. He shrugs and pats at his doublet, as if searching for something that isn't there.

'I have no money, signorina,' he says.

This is true enough. De Pareja only ever has what Don Diego gives him for supplies, errands and so forth; at present, his purse contains just a few *quattrini*, the smallest Roman coin, not even near to the sum she has named. He suspects that offering this will make the situation worse.

The green-eyed woman lets out a sceptical snort. Another one arrives, more visibly Roman; she has gold rings in her ear, and a thin-lipped, glowering mouth with several missing teeth. They lean in yet closer, standing shoulder to shoulder. Both are none too clean and alarmingly fierce. The Roman splays a hand against de Pareja's chest, pressing her fingers against the breastbone. There is a disconcerting intimacy to it.

'What in the flaming hells is this?' she demands. 'You think the good sister is there for you to gawk at – you and any other dusky prick who happens to be strolling along the Corso? Perhaps this is how it is done in your heathen lands, but here in Rome we show *respect*.'

'I am a Christian,' de Pareja repeats, a little wearily. 'I was baptised in the Church of the Carmen in Antequera, a province of . . .'

The Roman isn't listening. She pushes him back a step and gestures at the Benedictine, who is talking still. 'These are precious words,' she says. '*Holy* words. There is a value to them. Any godly person can see that.'

De Pareja puts his drawing folder beneath his arm, raises his hands in surrender and begins to edge away. The two women are eyeing him with poisonous disdain. The Roman, in particular, seems ready to attack, to rip the button off his collar or knock off his hat; but then something else catches her attention, out in the crowds. She cranes her neck, on the alert.

'Could be trouble,' she mutters to the green-eyed woman. 'This one has nothing, Orsola. Let's be off.'

Forgetting de Pareja completely, the Roman sets about dispersing the audience and gathering up the coins they have left, while the green-eyed woman – Orsola – goes to the Benedictine. She touches the nun's shoulder, bringing her sermon to an uncertain halt, and then bends in to talk to her. De Pareja hears how very altered her tone is, how tender and patient, as she speaks of them rejoining the Jubilee procession and continuing on to Santa Maria Maggiore. The nun rises almost immediately; Orsola throws a cloak over her black habit and leads her along the Corso.

De Pareja watches the three women disappear into the crowds. He needs more if he is to bring about the painting he has imagined, of that he is certain, but it is not possible for him to follow them now. The nun's guardians would surely not tolerate it – and besides, he is running out of time, with the usual list of duties awaiting him at the embassy. He tells himself to take heart and make the best use of what he has already, as his life has well trained him to do. Closing his eyes, he impresses that moment in his memory as deeply and firmly as he can, working in every part of it like a seal in wax. Then he puts the drawing folder back in his satchel and starts in the opposite direction, towards the Piazza Trinita.

*

The key turns easily, admitting de Pareja into the cellar of the Spanish Embassy. The long, vaulted room has a church-like coolness, a floor inlaid with red and black bricks, and a couple of high, barred windows. Looking around, he sees a mansion's-worth of fine furniture, stacked methodically and covered with dust sheets; several sedan chairs awaiting repainting; and there, over to the right, the sixteen expertly constructed crates that have just been delivered to the embassy from Don Diego's dealer in Naples.

It is Holy Thursday, and the Duke of Infantado, Spain's newly arrived ambassador, has just gone to the Palazzo del Quirinale for his first audience with the pope. This grand event has served as an effective distraction, for barely anyone in the embassy even noticed the delivery being made. With some anticipation, de Pareja takes up a pry-bar and works off the fronts of a few of the crates. Inside are statues of various sizes, pagan wonders many hundreds of years old, selected by his master for display in King Felipe's palaces. He looks briefly at a naked Venus cast in bronze, emerging from the sea, then turns away to study the dealer's list. A faint mark, made to look accidental, has been left beside one item: crate number six, containing Mars with Helmet and Sword.

It is the smallest statue yet, only a half-dozen hands tall – a bronze cast like the Venus, but more weathered, the metal a faded, greenish colour, and slightly warped in places. De Pareja removes one of the crate's side panels as well, to enable closer examination; and there, running down the spine of the miniature god, is a seam of dark putty. He draws the short-bladed knife from his belt and carefully slices it away. Even after eight days on the road, it is still slightly moist to the touch.

The papers are rolled up within the torso. Fishing them out with his little finger, de Pareja discovers that the sheets are almost transparent, like the skin of an onion. There are eight of them in total, each covered in ciphered text and dense diagrams: reports from agents of the Count of Onate, Spanish viceroy of the Kingdom of Naples. De Pareja knows that they detail a growing hostile presence in the state, a force comprised both of spies and military men, who are rumoured to be preparing the ground for an invasion by the armies of France.

Life and nature have made de Pareja circumspect in all things, and handling these papers brings him an itch of discomfort. He can see clearly that this mission to Italy, originally one of simple service to the crown, has now been turned into something quite different. Don Diego's reasons for agreeing to this are plain enough: as always, he is thinking of his plan for their advancement and how best to bring it about. But it cannot be denied that a boundary has been crossed.

De Pareja takes a breath and tucks the pages inside his doublet, resolving to pray on the matter. Then he replaces the putty, completes an inspection of the remaining statues – all of which are surpassingly fine and unharmed by their long journey – and heads back upstairs.

The embassy is alive from top to bottom. The Duke of Infantado has brought many people to Rome with him, officials and clerks and footmen, as well as a tercio of Spain's finest soldiers. His procession to the Vatican is being spoken of everywhere; it involved more than two hundred carriages, they are saying, as well as a company of hunchbacks riding white mules, and dwarves brought over especially from Madrid. Every noteworthy Spanish gentleman in the city took part – including, in a very prominent position, Don Diego Rodríguez Silva y Velázquez.

De Pareja shares the general sense of pride. The duke, their new ambassador, has been received personally by Pope Innocent on the day of his arrival, and is attending the Mass of the Last Supper in the papal chapel. This is a great honour, and a clarion-clear announcement: the Spanish in Rome have a leader at last, and he sits at the side of the Holy Father.

Don Diego's rooms are six floors up, at the top of the building's eastern corner. De Pareja arrives on the landing a little out of breath, and with an ache in his lower back, but he is filled with purpose. He must return the used dishes and plates to the kitchens, empty the pots and fetch fresh water, and attend to Don Diego's wardrobe; and then clean the brushes, mix a full spread of colours, and prepare the new canvas his master has requested. Any time that remains is his own, however, and he means to devote it to the scarred nun. He will complete the sketch he began on the Corso the previous week, setting down the image Almighty God has preserved so vividly in his mind.

The door has been left unlocked. This is not unusual, but as he enters de Pareja hears something further inside the apartment. He goes very still. A thief, he thinks; or worse, a spy in the service of Spain's enemies. He wonders if they have learned somehow about the secret contents of the Mars, and come up here to steal them – to lie in wait for him or his master, and use bloody violence to achieve their ends. He puts one hand on his doublet, where the papers are secured, while the other moves to the hilt of his knife.

De Pareja is not, by disposition, a fighter. Part of him is aware that he should leave at once to fetch the guard, but instead he finds himself creeping forwards across the reception room, moving from the polished floorboards to the patterned rug. His heart thuds hard, his ears straining for the smallest sound. A raucous song rises up from the piazza, along with a peal of laughter from a street performance – and a few yards ahead, a woman yawns out the word *Maria*. He stops, his brow creasing; he releases his hold on the knife.

This woman is in the large, airy room they have made into the studio, on the same corridor as Don Diego's bedchamber. From where de Pareja is standing, he can just see in through the doorway. A hand comes into view, picking a cake of umber from atop a dresser, then turning it over to look idly for a merchant's mark. The wrist is bare, and the forearm too. After a moment, the pigment is replaced and the woman turns away; and the edge of her naked hip catches the sunlight, appearing almost white against the deep shadow behind.

De Pareja reverses course, heading rapidly along a windowless passage to the small storeroom that holds his pallet. Once inside, he drops his satchel and leans against the wall, pressing his shoulder blades flat on the pitted plaster. He looks up at the ceiling and asks for patience.

Flaminia Triunfi is back.

De Pareja's hope was that she would have drifted away while they were in Naples, carried off on the ceaseless current of Rome. He sees now that this was naïve. In the court of King Felipe, Don Diego was a man of respectable habits, who was married to the daughter of his own master while still a youth. Out here though, at the age of fifty and very far from home, he has become entangled with a Roman woman more than two decades his junior. He never speaks of her, but de Pareja is no fool: Don Diego, in his way, is infatuated. Flaminia's reappearance was all but certain.

In truth, de Pareja has managed to discover very little about her. At first, he assumed she was a courtesan, who had ensnared this fine Spanish gentleman as he played cards in some grand house or other. But almost nothing about her bears this out. There has never been any sense of an arrangement between them. Her clothes are wrong, also: of some quality, but too simple, too modest, with occasional evidence of wear or mending. Neither has he seen her wear jewels, and she barely uses any powder or paint upon her face. He has no idea where she lives, or how she traverses the city; she seems to come and go as she pleases. Flaminia Triunfi is a mystery. And now it seems that she is to number among his problems once more.

De Pareja strides from the storeroom, across to the small parlour where Don Diego takes his meals. He begins to make much noise with drawers and doors, and the moving of crockery, intending that Flaminia will hear him and realise that the time has come to depart – to sneak down the back staircase as she used to do, and out onto the alley at the embassy's rear. For her to be there on the day of the ambassador's arrival, when the building is so very busy, is infuriatingly reckless. If she was spotted, tongues would surely begin to clack. Such talk can be corrosive, leaving a stain that might endure across oceans, and bar a gentleman's rise – and the rise of those who depend upon him.

After a couple of minutes, de Pareja hears the soft creak of a foot upon a floorboard. In the reflection of a wine glass, he sees her slip from the studio into Don Diego's chamber, her body wrapped in a blue-grey coverlet.

De Pareja attends to his duties. He cleans and carries, he visits the kitchens and the laundry, and then he heads to the studio to begin his labours there. Something has changed since the previous day. The light is different, tinted by new colours; and there, in the middle of the room, a canvas has been fastened to the heavier of the two easels he acquired upon their return from Naples. De Pareja prepared this canvas a few days ago, mounting and priming, then applying a light grey ground. It is large, three yards by two; he assumed it was for a grand, full-length portrait of Cardinal Panciroli or some other worthy dear to Spain, but it stands on its side and bears the beginnings of a very different composition. Three long, loose curves of colour fan outwards from a point about a third of the way up the left edge. The top one is crimson; the next a pearly pink; and the bottom one, which extends all the way to the opposite edge, is a dark, greyish blue.

De Pareja's eyes narrow. It must be said that Don Diego has an unusual attitude towards his art. Prior to de Pareja's portrait, he had not lifted his brush since their departure from the Alcazar almost a year earlier. He didn't appear to miss painting, and mentioned it only rarely. But all this is changing. As was intended, the portrait in the Rotonda has made Rome suddenly aware of the Spanish maestro in its midst; and in turn, he himself seems to have been reminded of what Almighty God has given him. Of what he can do.

No preparatory drawings are nearby, or any other indication of what the subject might be. Don Diego no longer sketches unless it is absolutely necessary; indeed, the only papers de Pareja can see are a handful of unfinished letters. His gaze passes over the bowls of paint, which have been left uncovered; the dirty palette, with its smears of red, pink and blue; the long-handled brushes standing clustered in a wooden cup, their bristles soaking in lye soap. He looks to the left, beyond the doorway. A narrow bed stands there, which Don Diego has taken to using as a settee. Behind it now is a length of cloth, nailed to the ceiling so that it hangs like a curtain. It is satin, of a purplish, ecclesiastical red.

The apartment's main door opens, the hinges complaining loudly. De Pareja goes to the studio door – and he sees Flaminia directly opposite, responding to the same sound. Standing just inside the bedchamber, she is now dressed in a deep green gown, her dark hair bound up in a loose coil. He had almost forgotten what it was like to look upon her. Flaminia has a singular beauty, unlike that of any picture or statue; there is a power to it, a kind of shock. De Pareja is as affected by it as anyone, which he finds vaguely annoying.

Boots scrape upon the floorboards. Three men have entered the apartment. Flaminia meets de Pareja's eye. Hers are very dark brown, with an intent look to them, and a certain wryness as well. She gives him a slight, conspiratorial smile; then she pulls back and closes the bedchamber door.

*

'It is a joke,' says the Duke of Infantado. 'Such an abominable woman, in a position of such extraordinary influence . . . it is a terrible, terrible joke. And it is a testament, frankly, to the dreadful weakness of the pope. In the two hours of our meeting, the path of the past six years was explained to me entirely. I understood how the throne of San Pietro has become so debased. So *enfeebled*. Why now, in this Jubilee year, it is an embarrassment before the world.'

The new ambassador swivels on his heel, his hands on his hips, taking in the high, beamed ceiling of Don Diego's apartment. De Pareja is standing in the shadows holding three glasses of wine on a pewter tray. Surreptitiously, he looks Infantado over. The duke is tall and well made, with a fencer's upright posture and a jewelled sword at his belt. His face is not handsome – the nose is thin and long, and the forehead a shade too high – but there can be no mistaking either his status or his determination. The black of his Lenten garb is broken only by the ornate cross of the Knights' Order of Calatrava, which is stitched onto the breast of his doublet in crimson thread. Although still young, Infantado is renowned at the Spanish court as an experienced and effective general, having fought with distinction against both the Portuguese and Catalans. That such a man has been sent to Rome shows that King Felipe is aware of the city's travails.

'And that Cardinal Nephew,' the duke continues. 'Federico Maidalchini. He barely seemed able to follow our conversation. Is he even twenty years of age? How in God's name was this permitted?'

Signor Camillo Astalli smiles with his usual smoothness. Like Infantado, he is no more than thirty-five, but his bearing is very much that of a lawyer rather than a soldier. A Roman from a prominent yet impecunious family, Astalli is the personal secretary and apparent favourite of Cardinal Panciroli, leader of Spain's Italian allies. He is better favoured than Infantado in terms of his looks, with strong cheekbones, fine black moustaches, and clever, watchful eyes; but de Pareja senses an air of entitlement about him, as if he believes he should be afforded whatever he might desire without any need for effort on his part.

'That was Donna Olimpia's doing, your grace,' Astalli says. 'She installed poor Federico at Innocent's side, believing that he would be an effective puppet. But the boy has proved himself an abject idiot, as useless to her cause as he would be to any other.'

'Your master is ready to act, though?' Infantado asks. 'He is ready to dislodge this monstrous widow?'

Astalli nods. 'Cardinal Panciroli feels that it is time. The Holy Jubilee is relieving the pope's melancholy somewhat. Innocent can imagine, at present, that change is possible – that he can alter the direction his foul sister-in-law has taken us upon, clean out the wretched creatures she has crammed into the offices of the Curia, and begin his papacy anew.'

Infantado considers this. 'The Holy Jubilee,' he repeats, less than enthusiastically. 'What an outlandish prospect it is. Why, on our journey back just now, I saw the Last Supper of Our Lord enacted in the street no fewer than four times. And each one seemed to end with Iscariot being chased off by his audience, pelted with stones and dung. It is a wonder that anybody takes the role.'

Astalli laughs politely. Don Diego attempts to as well, but emits only a strangled cough; he is still out of breath after the climb up from the courtyard, which has taxed him rather more than the younger men. Aside from this, he now looks almost as he does in Madrid. His beard has been trimmed and waxed to points, while the loose lace of an Italian collar has been set aside for a starched

Spanish golilla, which de Pareja laid out for him that morning, along with the smartest of his three black doublets.

Infantado glances around him again. 'These are strange quarters Señor Morata has assigned you, Don Diego,' he says. 'A state apartment stands empty two floors below. I will have you moved.'

Don Diego dips his head and opens his arms, aiming for the pose of a grateful courtier. 'Please, your grace, do not . . . do not trouble yourself,' he pants – thinking no doubt of Flaminia and the back staircase. 'The rooms serve me perfectly well. And my man and I have just made a studio here. To relocate now would surely cost us time.'

Infantado studies him for a moment. 'As you wish,' he says, signalling for de Pareja to approach and taking a glass of wine from the tray. 'This is him, I assume – the Morisco slave whose likeness has so astonished Rome?'

'It is, your grace,' Don Diego says. 'My assistant, Juan de Pareja.'

The duke gives de Pareja a single second of his attention; then he looks away, sipping his wine with a faint wince. 'Your portraits in this city are set to follow a most unlikely course. From the base, one might say, to the apex.'

De Pareja keeps his eyes fixed straight ahead, upon a stretch of whitewashed wall; he adjusts his hand beneath the tray to stop it from trembling.

From the base to the apex.

The meaning here is plain: Don Diego is to paint the pope. De Pareja saw this coming, of course. His master's confidences are erratic at best, but he has made a couple of oblique remarks since their return from Naples that have indicated what might lie in store for them. All of a sudden, it feels inevitable. The will of God.

Astalli and Don Diego take their glasses; de Pareja lowers the tray, bows and steps back.

'Did you see this slave's portrait, Signor Astalli?' Infantado asks.

'I did, your grace, during its time in the Rotonda. I found its reputation to be richly deserved.' Astalli gestures at de Pareja with his glass. 'I had not seen this fellow here for some months, while he and Don Diego were in the south – yet that painting made me feel as if he had been brought before me, body and soul, and was on verge of speech.' He pauses meaningfully. 'I must say, I thought it a well calculated move on Don Diego's part. That portrait declared him to Rome in a resounding fashion, as the foremost painter of Spain. It quite dispelled any doubts about his purpose here.'

An unspoken communication passes between Astalli and Don Diego, who turns to de Pareja and enquires softly about the day's shipment. Understanding his meaning at once, de Pareja removes the Neapolitan documents from his doublet and hands them over. His master then offers them to the duke with a bow.

Infantado looks at the packet of papers. He does not take them. 'So this is the reason you had me come here,' he says. 'All the way up into the damned roof.'

'These are reports from the kingdom of Naples, your grace,' Astalli tells him. 'They concern a French invasion, to be supported by Donna Olimpia and her allies, intended to end Spanish rule and hand the kingdom to the Barberini, the family of Pope Urban.'

'They were exiled to Versailles, were they not?' says Infantado. 'For thievery and the like?'

'Indeed so,' Astalli replies. 'The Barberini were judged guilty of all manner of corruption and degeneracy. But now, having bound themselves ever more closely to France, they are beginning to return – and they unquestionably have fresh designs upon the papacy.'

Infantado holds out his glass at arm's length for de Pareja to reclaim, then he plucks the documents from Don Diego's hand

and begins to leaf through them with distinct scepticism. 'Is the widow named?'

'Not as yet,' says Astalli. 'But already there are allusions to funding, to political connections in Rome, that can refer to no one else. Donna Olimpia wishes to aid the Barberini – to ingratiate herself with the French faction here, for the sake of her future security. And she is prepared to completely undermine the papacy's alliance with Spain to do it.' He becomes slightly defensive. 'The Count of Onate is having these documents dispatched to us from Naples, as he readies his armies. He is a fine man, your grace, and well versed in this work. His people will provide us with what we need.'

'I know Onate,' Infantado says, in a manner that suggests he does not concur with Astalli's assessment of the Neapolitan viceroy. 'I must be honest – this does not seem entirely credible. What is the date for this supposed invasion? It cannot be imminent, for the bulk of the French Navy is committed elsewhere.'

'Next spring, it is believed,' says Astalli. 'Under the command of Henry of Guise.'

Infantado gives him a dubious look. 'You amaze me, Astalli,' he says. 'We have the king's painter here with us – a man of miraculous abilities, a true gift from God. But while I am striving to put his talents to their proper use, to strengthen the bond between Felipe and the Holy Father, you have him playing at spycraft.'

Back in the shadows, de Pareja feels a slight stirring of hope. The Duke of Infantado might change things, he thinks; he might extract Don Diego and me from this scheme, to which we are so very unsuited. Reason may yet prevail.

'These intelligences could prove useful,' Infantado continues. 'I do understand that. But such things must be handled with the utmost delicacy. The consequences of this espionage may run beyond anything you have anticipated, or have the ability to control.'

'Cardinal Panciroli thinks it is necessary,' Astalli retorts. 'Essential, even. With all respect, your grace, you do not know this woman. We must equip ourselves with every weapon that is available to us. These papers will provide evidence of betrayal, of her collusion with France and the Barberini, that can be taken to Pope Innocent. That will *damn her*.'

Infantado passes the papers back to him, obviously unconvinced. 'The other path we are preparing is both safer and surer,' he says. 'Carry on with this if you must, Astalli, but take every care, and involve Don Diego as little as you can. He has other duties to attend to – as do I.'

With that he departs, ignoring Astalli and Don Diego's bows and leaving the apartment door open behind him. Astalli immediately hands the documents to Don Diego and returns his untouched wine glass to de Pareja's tray. It was his idea to have them fashion a covert connection with Naples, using the sculpture shipments to evade the many spies of their enemy, and he is smarting at Infantado's dismissiveness.

'We will continue,' he says tightly. 'Cardinal Panciroli considers this a most worthwhile course and will support us. He is the ultimate authority here, not your ambassador. And he holds the keys to the Belvedere. Do not forget that.'

Don Diego lowers his head in acknowledgement. De Pareja's hopes for their extraction dissipate; he looks down ruefully at the two full glasses upon the tray, the circles of wine appearing almost black against the pewter. The truth is that Camillo Astalli has them trapped. The Belvedere gardens house the sculpture gallery of the Vatican, which is said to be the finest in the world. If the collection Don Diego is assembling for King Felipe is to be of the first rank, he will need access to it, along with permission to take casts from its most renowned pieces. This makes him very reliant indeed upon the continued good will of Cardinal Panciroli. The Belvedere was the reason Don Diego agreed to Astalli's plan, and let the Neapolitan statues be used as a conduit – for it was made extremely plain that if Panciroli was to allow him inside, a service had to be performed in return.

Astalli leaves as well, stalking out onto the landing after a rather cursory bow. Don Diego waits until the lawyer's footsteps have retreated down the staircase; then he swallows his wine in one gulp and throws himself into the nearest chair with such force that the wood protests beneath him. Without a word, de Pareja goes to the parlour to fetch the pitcher. When he returns, his master has torn off his golilla and cast it onto the floor, and is pinching the bridge of his nose with his eyes squeezed shut. Hearing de Pareja's approach, he holds up his glass to have it refilled, before drinking half of it and leaning back with a hollow sigh.

Briefly, de Pareja considers him: the heavy, pensive features, touched by moroseness; the lines scored beneath the dark, hooded eyes; the once-firm jaw, now broken slightly by the encroachment of age. 'You are to paint the pope,' he says.

The eyes slide his way; the lip curls beneath the moustache. 'There is Juan,' Don Diego murmurs. 'That fine deductive mind.'

'I imagine that it is to be a grand portrait,' de Pareja goes on. 'To commemorate the Holy Jubilee and the restoration of Spain in Rome. That is why you took my likeness and announced yourself to the artists of the city.'

Don Diego sits forward, swilling the wine around the glass before taking another swig. 'You heard his grace the duke. It is my duty.'

De Pareja catches the resentment in his master's voice. 'A papal portrait will bring much honour,' he says. 'You will be lauded, Don Diego. Spoken of everywhere.'

This prompts a bitter smile. 'As the painter of the King of Spain. As a creature of craft and toil, of labour and remuneration, rather than a gentleman of the royal court. And it will distract me from my true business here. The king writes to me nearly every week, Juan. He grows impatient for my return, and he expects marvels.'

At Don Diego's mention of distraction, de Pareja thinks of the new work underway in the studio; of the naked woman wrapped in the coverlet, slipping across the corridor. He sets this aside. 'It is surely part of the same campaign. You must retain the favour of his grace the duke, who is clearly set upon using this portrait to strengthen Spain's position in Rome. And you need to serve his Eminence Cardinal Panciroli, and Signor Astalli as well, if the collection you are assembling is to fulfil King Felipe's hopes.'

Don Diego mulls this for a few seconds, then finishes off his second glass. 'I suppose so,' he says, rising from his chair. 'I am a mere courtier, after all – a man at the mercy of his betters, and bound to obey. And now I am caught in a most damnable double bind.' He lays a hand momentarily against de Pareja's upper arm. 'You are right, though. Of course you are. If we hold our nerve, we can still return to Madrid in triumph. With God's grace, the cross of Santiago will be my reward. And my first act as a knight of the order, my very first act, will be to secure your manumission. This I promise you.'

De Pareja bows, and does his best to appear grateful, but he has heard these same words many times over the course of their travels. This is the covenant between them: when the goal is achieved, they will advance together – one to nobility, the other to freedom. Although de Pareja does not doubt Don Diego's sincerity, his master has been awaiting admission to the Order of Santiago for many years now. There is no guarantee at all that a collection of Italian antique sculpture, even one of unmatched excellence, will bring about its bestowal. De Pareja feels his time running away; he feels it acutely, in every new morning, every meal, every Mass. He is more certain than ever that he must have another argument prepared to win his liberty. A demonstration of his worth – of his God-granted skill. A painting of the scarred nun.

Don Diego has crossed to a mirror and is examining his reflection in the diminishing daylight, fussing at the moustache. De Pareja is attempting more reassurance, talking of the glory that is ahead, and how news of it will surely reach Madrid – when he notices that Flaminia has opened the bedchamber door and is leaning against the frame, watching them both. It is unclear how long she has been within earshot, or what exactly she might have overheard, but now she is laughing quietly, a sleeve of her green gown raised to cover her mouth.

'Only you,' she says to Don Diego, 'could be so vexed by the chance to paint the pope. You do know that Cavaliere Bernini is the only other artist that Innocent has allowed a sitting, in all the six years of his reign? He must like you and your duke very much.'

Don Diego glances over at her, away from the mirror. He is pleased, plainly, that she is there; his gloom lifts and he becomes a little awkward. 'No, he does not,' he replies. 'He did seem to know of me, but as Infantado made his proposition, I swear the old man looked ready to hurl himself through the nearest window. There are other reasons.'

'What other reasons can there be? Innocent will come before you in all his finery. You will take his likeness.' She pauses, her dark eyes gently mocking. 'And Rome will rejoice.'

Don Diego's cheeks are beginning to colour. 'I fear you do not understand.'

Flaminia crosses her arms. 'Did you meet with the pope in the *Stanze?* The Rafaellos there are among the greatest achievements in all painting. They must have been of interest to you.'

'I have told you already, Flaminia,' Don Diego says, with a trace of tiredness, 'I do not admire them. Nothing of life is shown there. You Romans esteem your art too highly.'

De Pareja firms his hold on the handle of the pitcher. He cannot explain how Flaminia is so familiar with the frescoes of the Vatican, but it is clear enough what is going on. She is calling Don Diego to her. This goading, these sharp exchanges, are a strange form of courtship. Sure enough, she makes a tutting sound at his last remark, as if disappointed by his dullness; and then she withdraws, slipping back into the bedchamber.

'Prepare a canvas,' Don Diego instructs, looking after her. 'It will be a seated portrait, taken at half-length. That is the tradition.' He starts towards the open doorway. 'Attend to it at once, Juan. We will be done with this at the first opportunity.'

Sorores

The piazza before Santa Maria Maggiore is seething with demons. Orsola stops by the fountain to watch them caper about, with their bat-wings, lizard tails, and twisting billy-goat horns, their bare torsos painted every colour from bird's egg blue to bright, blazing orange. They screech and hoot and bark, sounding rattles and banging furiously at blackened pots and pans, creating a chaotic wave of noise that rolls around the square and crashes off down the avenues.

It is Easter Saturday, and all across Rome the city's players are enacting the Saviour's descent into the Limbo of the Patriarchs, one of the outer regions of hell. Before long, Orsola spots a Christ, clad in a white burial shroud stained with the bloody wounds of the Crucifixion, marching into a knot of demons. They scatter to reveal a chained prophet — one of the patriarchs of the Old Testament, who lived before Christ's time on Earth and thus could not be saved. Christ breaks this prisoner's bonds with a righteous bellow; and together, to the cheers of the crowd, they begin to battle the baying satanic horde and carve a path to Paradise.

Orsola has been watching such performances all morning, a queasy, urgent feeling building within her. Many times, she has told herself that the Limbo of the Infants, to which her daughter has been consigned, is in a different, more peaceful part of the afterlife. The Mother Abbess at the Visitation and several priestly confessors have assured her that there are no demons on the grey hill, of any variety; that her poor child's soul is free from torment and terror. But Orsola has never quite been able to believe it. A heavy, suffocating guilt can close around her without warning. It can dog her for days on end.

She suppresses a shiver, trying to keep these thoughts at bay. For there is still hope. Her plan for atonement will still work. She will be able to bring Sister Serafina back to the Benedictine Order and deliver her daughter to heaven. It is just that the course of this plan has undergone an unexpected change.

The morning is fiercely, stunningly hot, like high summer rather than late spring. Orsola has been in Rome for nearly three weeks now and has yet to see even a hint of rain. The pale stone of the statues and columns on the Maggiore's façade glares so intensely in the sunlight that it hurts her eyes. Down below, dust coats everything, carried on the faintest breeze, undoing the city's efforts to wash itself in moments. The bloated line of Jubilee pilgrims queuing to enter the basilica wilts and stumbles in the heat, while a crowd jostles around the fountain, splashing faces and filling flasks. Orsola leans over to dip her hand in the cloudy, tepid water, then lays it on her forehead. The relief this brings is slight, and soon forgotten.

Serafina is kneeling a couple of yards away, at the base of the fountain's steps. She begins quite suddenly, her voice issuing from beneath the hood of her cloak. This is the third time she has spoken that day, and Orsola soon sees that the subject here will be the same: a meditation on Santa Catarina's first dispute with the pagan emperor Maxentius.

'Unable to match blessed Catarina's eloquence,' Serafina says, 'Maxentius had her cast into the dankest, filthiest dungeon in

Alexandria. Twelve days of confinement she endured, in darkness as black as the deepest well. But Catarina embraced it. She drew it within her. She made herself a vessel — a vessel of purity, a vessel for the Lord's holy light.'

Orsola looks around. Her partner is watching them from the shadow of a free-standing column, set beside the fountain with an ancient statue mounted on its top. It is the street player Orsola fought with on that first day, her bloodied Santa Lucia costume exchanged for a simple, slate-coloured gown and a straw hat with what appears to be a bite taken from its brim. Everyone calls her Lontra, the otter — and the nickname fits, for she is round-faced and broad-nosed, with large, shrewd eyes and quick, busy hands. Orsola is certain that she carries a knife.

It hadn't taken long for Lontra to find the nuns again. Still being set upon restitution for her cracked glass eye, and seeing what happened when Serafina spoke before a crowd, she made Orsola a proposal. She would guide them through the city and provide a safe berth — and they could use the money they earned to pay back the thirty scudi she was owed, along with a reasonable amount of interest. Orsola saw God's hand in this. A means of survival had appeared when they were at their most desperate, reduced almost to nothing. She was determined not to be taken for an easy mark, though, and demanded to keep half the coins collected. Lontra acted as if outraged, then offered a third — and their strange partnership began.

Lontra and Orsola swiftly established a system. They escort Sister Serafina around the Jubilee procession route, allowing her to hold forth whenever the mood takes her. Meanwhile, the two of them watch over the crowd that gathers, ensuring that they remain respectful and their donations are collected. Serafina is fast becoming known. Word of her former convent's location has got out, probably via Lontra; Orsola hears pilgrims and locals alike whispering reverently about the nun of Castro, the scarred Benedictine gifted with divine speech and a powerful, unaccountable insight into all manner of sacred mysteries. Wherever Serafina kneels, others will soon kneel also, and drop their coins into the platter that once held Santa Lucia's eyes. These are *quattrini*, mostly, Rome's very smallest, with the occasional copper *baiocco* among them – but the total is building.

So far, at least from Orsola's point of view, it has been an astonishing success. Foremost are the clothes. Shortly after they'd settled on their terms, Lontra produced a blue gown and a light woollen shawl.

'One nun we can manage,' she stated. 'Two will draw notice.'

Removing the grey habit of a Benedictine servant nun was a firm step away from the order, and Orsola took it without hesitation. The gown Lontra gave her was patched and faded, and far from clean, but by God it felt *wondrous*. Orsola had forgotten what it was like to wear clothes that actually fitted, made from material that did not itch or chafe your skin. Serafina would not look at her for several hours afterwards, but she didn't care. It was right.

The food, also, is astounding. In the Visitation, Orsola had only thin soups and stale bread. Here, though – after stating early on the importance of proper nourishment – Lontra uses a portion of their coins to buy roast birds and pickled fishes; paper cones of salted vermicelli; spiced sausage, fried peppers and cups of coarse wine. Orsola looks forward keenly to every meal and can barely stop herself from gobbling it in moments.

The berths Lontra promised are in the attic of a derelict grain storehouse, just along the river from the ghetto. The long, low room is home to an ever-changing company of players, orators and acrobats, all of them committed to wringing every last coin they can from the Jubilee year. They have found a space for themselves deep in the eaves, among battered props and trunks of grubby costumes, bedding down with various other women and girls of Lontra's acquaintance. This improvised female dormitory sleeps in shifts, taking turns to keep watch and raising a vocal alarm if any man tries to approach.

At first, it was disturbing to be up in that dark, lively place, listening to the loft's residents play at noisy games, couple in shadowy corners, and swap hair-raising stories of their battles, conquests and escapes. But each day, Orsola shrinks from it all a little less. For a while, she thought that a new person might be emerging within her, adapted to fit these much-changed circumstances. Slowly, however, she has come to realise that it is in fact an older one: a half-formed self, smothered by her confinement, now being coaxed back into existence.

And then there is Lontra herself. Despite her hard, sardonic manner, she has willingly adopted the role of the nuns' protector. She and Orsola are together almost constantly, relying on each other as they move Serafina through the swarming streets. Already it feels like a connection of many months, rather than just a few weeks. Orsola had no friends in the Visitation, or before really; but she is beginning to wonder, very cautiously, if she might have one now.

Lontra is especially vigilant that morning, for the usual sense of threat that simmers in the air has been made yet worse by the additional numbers that have come into Rome for the Easter observances. Orsola has discovered that at the Holy Jubilee, the love and charity Christ asks of his followers is in short supply. There is much enmity among the teeming crowds, in fact, and they frequently erupt into shouting and shoving. In barely the time it takes to draw breath, punches are being thrown, stones prised from the earth and slung about, and blades drawn from their sheaths. Orsola has seen men killed, often at the church door.

She has seen brothers expire in each other's arms; fathers cut down before their children. All she can do is pray for their souls and ensure that her own guard is never lowered.

Serafina is noticed straight away, the passing pilgrims halting their processions and alerting their fellows. People start to kneel alongside her, gazing at her rapt, scarred face, the black habit beneath her cloak, and the silver rosary wound around her hands. They listen to her almost nervously, as if believing themselves in the presence of God's anointed. Utterly unaware of them, Serafina is settling into her discourse, carried far away from the din of the overcrowded, sun-baked piazza.

'Every pagan who encountered Santa Catarina during her imprisonment was converted to Christ. There were twenty-four in total, two for each day. First was Agrippa, her gaoler and torturer – a brutal man with a taste for the suffering of others. But when he came before Catarina, he began to weep most fretfully. He cast aside his vicious tools and swore to use them no more. Agrippa's cruelty was peeled from him like the rough skin of an onion, exposing the pure white soul beneath.'

It goes on. Orsola knows this account intimately – how each conversion will be detailed, working through the various guards and soldiers, finally arriving at Messalina, Maxentius' queen, when God compels her to visit Catarina's cell. She looks over at Lontra again. Her partner isn't happy to be out on the piazza like this; Lontra prefers to keep to the avenues, from which a clean escape can usually be made, but she has enough experience of Sister Serafina by now to know that they are stuck for a few minutes at least. She leaves the shadow of the column and walks to Orsola's side, her eyes flitting between the cavorting bands of players and the numerous streets and alleyways that run off the piazza.

'Princes would really come to Castro to listen to this?' she asks, shaking her head at some new detail in Serafina's account. 'And churchmen too?'

Orsola shrugs. 'There were carriages at the convent gates. Teams of horses. I was told that they travelled great distances to hear her.'

Lontra thinks for a moment. 'How did she end up like that, anyway? Was it damage – a beating or violation? Or a terrible loss, pushing her into madness? I've known a few women who've suffered thus. They weren't like your sister, though, not one bit.' She snorts, reaching up to scratch behind her ear. 'You could barely get a word out of the wretches.'

'I think Serafina has always been . . . how she is,' Orsola replies. 'Nobody in the convent ever said otherwise.'

'What about that scar? She was scalded, no?'

Lontra has asked all this several times before; framing the same questions over and over seems to be a strategy of hers, designed to test the truth of what she has heard.

'I told you, I was a servant nun,' Orsola replies, waving a fat fly away from her nose. 'I mostly stayed down in the kitchens. I hadn't even spoken to Serafina before we fled the convent.'

'But you said you were in the woods for months. Didn't you talk of your lives?'

'Serafina doesn't do that. Surely you must have realised this.' Orsola shifts uneasily and crosses her arms. 'I never heard any story for the scar either. Some of the nuns did think it a holy marking, bestowed by angels or the like. Separating Sister Serafina from the rest of us.'

Lontra gives her a sceptical, gap-toothed smile. 'I've seen my share of scars, sister. Your girl there was scalded.'

Before any more can be said, the performances in the piazza reach a new peak of excitement and unruliness. It seems that a prophet has been recaptured by the demons, prompting a pair of

Christs to join forces and launch a vigorous counterattack. A lone trumpet plays a parody of a military charge; the crowds closest to the commotion begin to shout and jeer.

'This is too much,' Orsola says. 'We should move on.'

Lontra nods, only too glad to get back into the shade of the avenues. While she sets about collecting up the coins, Orsola picks her way through the kneeling pilgrims to crouch at Serafina's side.

'Noon is approaching, sister,' she murmurs. 'If we are to finish our circuit, we must say our prayer in the Maggiore and start for the Laterano.'

The Jubilee procession is central to Orsola's revised plan. Since the night of their arrival, to her surprise, she has heard much talk of Castro out on the streets of Rome. Along the procession route, and up in the grain loft, there is considerable sympathy for the ordinary people of the town and the awful fate that befell them. However, all servants of the Church seem to share the judgement of the laywomen in the Tor de'Specchi, believing that Castro was a place of heresy, deserving its destruction. Orsola became afraid that presenting Serafina at another convent in Rome could lead to their arrest and imprisonment, or worse. Their home had been destroyed for reasons she barely understood. Who could say what charges Castro's enemies might now press upon them?

And so she decided upon a new course. She told Serafina that God had barred their path, denying them re-admittance to the Benedictine Order; that penance was required for the time they had spent outside convent walls. They had to walk the route of the Jubilee procession, between four mighty, far-flung basilicas, as often as they must to gain the Holy Father's indulgence. Although upset by this explanation, Serafina seemed to accept it. The notion of penance is certainly one she can understand, and the routine keeps her steady amidst the constant clamour of the Jubilee.

Orsola's intention is to repay their debt to Lontra while gathering some funds of their own, and then leave Rome to find a holy house in a more remote and peaceable place; in the south perhaps, where the name of Castro is not known. There, things will proceed as before. Serafina will be returned to her confinement, and the soul of Orsola's daughter will be released to Paradise. As for herself, she cannot think with any clarity of what might come after that – but she is more sure than ever that she will not rejoin the Benedictine Order.

Here in the piazza of Santa Maria Maggiore, Orsola's gentle urging has no effect. Serafina remains oblivious, talking on about divine visions, stirring speeches and startling conversions, transported yet immoveable. Orsola can feel Lontra behind her, straining with impatience. She redoubles her efforts, raising her voice, earning disapproving glances from the nearest members of Serafina's congregation. Still it is futile.

Orsola glances back at Lontra and sees that she is looking intently to the north. A group of priests and soldiers has appeared around the corner of the Maggiore's grand façade and is moving into the piazza. Word spreads rapidly among the players. Demons, Christs and prophets all take to their heels, streaming away from the basilica in any direction they can.

'Inquisition,' says Lontra. 'No choice now, sister. We've got to go.'

The word alone is frightening. Inquisitors are dreaded by the inhabitants of the grain loft. Sacred plays and the impersonation of saints are generally tolerated by the Church, as acts of piety and veneration – but soliciting coin for these acts is imposture, and fraud, and blasphemy to boot. If witnesses spoke out against you, or if you could be made to confess, you would be subjected to a harsh penance and then locked up in the Tor di Nona, Rome's principal gaol. This last punishment is feared more than anything.

'The Tor di Nona,' Lontra has said, 'means death.'

Orsola takes hold of Serafina's shoulders and tries to look into her eyes. 'Come, sister,' she says. 'We must be gone.'

The choir nun continues as if she isn't there. 'And then Queen Messalina came forth. Sight of Catarina in her heavy chains roused a passion in the queen – a burning passion that no—'

Orsola tightens her grip; she is briefly aware of the knobbly ends of Serafina's shoulder bones, and the way her long neck bends beneath her veil. 'Sister,' she hisses. 'Hear me. *Please*.'

She looks towards the Inquisitors. They have cornered a stocky, red-faced Christ and are addressing him angrily, as the soldiers move in to make the arrest.

'The queen fell to her knees, her heart burning fiercely in her chest. She tore at her fine garments and begged forgiveness, pledging her soul to Christ Jesus. And Catarina—'

Serafina's listeners are beginning to leave as well, as if realising that one way or another her oration will soon be brought to an end. Losing patience, Orsola begins to ease the choir nun up from the stones. This is difficult; Serafina makes herself a dead weight, sagging in Orsola's grasp.

'And Catarina saw God's light upon the queen, and . . . and she did declare to her that . . .'

Lontra appears beside them, Santa Lucia's platter tucked under her arm; she has collected what coins she could and is stowing them in her bodice. 'Orsola,' she says sharply.

A couple of the black-clad Inquisitors are staring in their direction. They exchange a few words and start to stride over with grim, purposeful speed.

The women are out of time. Lontra drops the platter, hooks a hand beneath Serafina's armpit and nods towards the nearest street – which leads south-west, back to the centre of the city.

Together, she and Orsola hoist the choir nun up, cover a few yards of open ground, and shoulder their way into a dense bank of people.

*

They have just cleared the piazza when Sister Serafina starts to struggle.

'I have not *prayed*,' she insists, writhing between them. 'Let me *go*, sister! I have not prayed before the altar of the Maggiore – it will not count!'

'Please, sister,' Orsola gasps. '*Please*.'

She looks back, but the crowd is too thick, too mobile; she can't tell if they are being pursued. They head along the street as fast as they can, and are soon caught up in the swirl and churn of the Jubilee's perpetual fair.

'I *knew* it,' says Lontra, gathering in Serafina's flailing left arm; the choir nun is weak, fortunately, due to seldom eating or sleeping, and can just about be restrained. 'I knew there would be trouble today. Damn them, damn them to *hell!*'

The street is growing noisier. Music starts up somewhere nearby, competing with the cries of the stallholders. A group of devils from the piazza shoves past, one with a webbed orange fin on his head shouting at the others to hurry. Orsola's fear is mounting. If they are caught by the Inquisition, and the truth of the situation discovered, she will be judged without mercy. These agents of the Lord will surely see to it that she is tortured most horribly, and scourged, and then left to perish in the black bowels of the Tor di Nona.

Serafina goes limp, channelling all of her strength into a full-blown wail. A space promptly opens up around the three women.

People peer in with expressions of alarm, amusement or concern, unable to tell if this is yet another performance – an episode from the life of an obscure, cloistered saint, perhaps – or some kind of bold daylight abduction.

Lontra guides them away, elbowing and shouldering with urgent force, while locking an arm tightly around Serafina's head. They stagger off downhill, onto the long slope of a cobbled side street. Most of the crowd is left behind. The buildings become more spread out and are less festooned with Jubilee banners. Between them, away to the south, Orsola glimpses some of Rome's pagan ruins; the huge, crumbling arches and broken columns are surrounded entirely by pilgrim encampments, trailing smoke into the clear blue sky.

'Are they still . . .' she pants. 'Did they . . .'

'Halt!' someone cries, maybe thirty yards back. 'Halt there!'

Lontra seems to know where they are going. She leads them along a red-brick wall, then around a corner to a small, rusted gate. Releasing Serafina, she takes a quick breath and throws herself against it. After three tries it inches inwards, scraping over the stone. Lontra and Orsola squeeze Serafina through the gap, before following her and heaving the gate back into place.

They have been brought into a gloomy, overgrown orchard, the day's light obscured by branches heavy with unripe pears. Waist-high grass grows all around the gnarled, unkempt trunks. Serafina has gone very quiet, straightening her veil and gazing around uncertainly. Orsola can tell that she is thinking of the woods during the winter, and the times they had to hide; of the silence so often imposed upon her by the pursuit of men.

Lontra crosses the orchard, making for the small house that stands at its far end. The nuns go after her, brambles catching on their clothes, until they reach a narrow loggia half buried in the undergrowth. Behind them, Orsola notices a shadow move across the grass just inside the gate. Two men have stopped in the lane beyond it; one of them is wearing the black cap and cassock of an Inquisitor.

'Where did they go?' he asks. 'Did you see?'

'I did not, Monsignor,' replies the other, a soldier in a breastplate, helm and brightly striped breeches; then he turns on his heel and calls out something in a foreign language, like he is giving an order.

Lontra is standing by a door at the loggia's rear. 'This place is empty,' she whispers. 'We can get through.'

Orsola recalls the Inquisitors' faces when they spotted Serafina across the piazza. 'Were they looking for us?'

Lontra shakes her head. 'They're just out to put the fear of God into everyone. To show us all what they can do.'

The soldier moves off, shouting another order. The Inquisitor lingers, however, looking around him, as if sensing that they are still nearby. Suddenly, his attention fixes on a spot near his feet. Fear clenches coldly in Orsola's stomach. He has noticed the scraped stone. He can see where they forced the gate.

Lontra turns the door's handle, but it does not move. '*No*,' she hisses. 'Holy *saints*.'

'Lontra,' Orsola whispers.

'This wasn't locked before,' Lontra insists, turning the handle again, and a third time. 'I swear it, sister. Someone must've moved in, or . . . I don't know . . .'

They are trapped. The Inquisitor is leaning against the gate now, taking hold of one of the bars, flexing his fingers around the iron as he prepares to give it a push.

'We'll climb,' says Lontra decisively, stepping back from the door and glancing up at the pear orchard's low, tangled canopy. 'Come on. Won't be hard.'

Orsola feels a rush of hope – and then the steep, sudden dip of dismay. Serafina will be unable to do this. There is simply not enough strength or nimbleness left in her wasted limbs. Orsola turns towards her. Seemingly unaware of their plight, the choir nun is counting off her rosary beads, lost in a rapid, near-silent prayer.

Lontra sees where she is looking. 'Leave her. You *must*.'

Orsola says nothing.

'*Leave her*,' Lontra repeats. 'She's a nun. And she's plainly missing a wheel. They'll take care of her.'

Two contrasting visions pass fleetingly through Orsola's mind. One is of earthly freedom, of her life in Rome with Lontra, with all other considerations shorn away; while the other is of the grey hill, and that blameless soul left on its slopes for all eternity, her last chance for deliverance forever squandered.

'I can't,' she says.

Lontra takes another step back. 'You meant to leave her anyway, didn't you, once you'd found a convent? What difference does it make?'

There is much that Orsola has not yet told Lontra, and much she has failed to understand. Orsola knows that if Serafina is left to be captured, and she is identified by these Inquisitors as the so-called nun of Castro, a dire fate may well await her. She thinks of the months they have been together, facing the dark, dripping woods, and then the fearsome streets of Rome; of the feel of Serafina's fingertips absently pinching her sleeve, as they are now.

'No,' she says. 'Not like this.'

Lontra hesitates, a mixture of disbelief and scorn upon her face. She is about to speak, no doubt to issue a stinging verdict on Orsola's sentimentality, when there is a sharp, grinding noise from the gate. The Inquisitor is pushing against it, slowly working it open.

Lontra departs without another word. She selects a tree by the orchard wall, scales it with impressive speed, and is gone. Orsola watches her go, both frightened and profoundly annoyed. *Some friend,* she thinks.

Cries come from outside as Lontra is spotted, followed by the sounds of pursuit. Orsola draws Serafina into the depths of the loggia, behind a knotted screen of brambles. Their one remaining hope is that they will escape notice – that the Inquisitor will make a brief search, assume that Lontra was the only person hiding here, and move on. This seems less likely with each passing second. He has forced the gate about a third of the way open, and is about to come through.

Before he can do this, however, there is a flurry of movement, followed by the thud of impact and an exclamation of surprise. A short, thickset demon, stripped to the waist and painted bright green, has barrelled into the Inquisitor, and now snatches his biretta and runs off with it. The churchman reels, then shouts indignantly and gives chase. Orsola nearly laughs in astonishment; after waiting a few moments to make sure he is gone, she takes Serafina's hand and starts towards the gate. The lane beyond is bright with sunshine. There is no sign of Lontra or anyone else.

'Praise God,' Orsola gasps. 'He watches over us, sister. He . . . he is guarding us against . . .'

'The Maggiore,' Serafina says firmly. 'We must return there. We must pray at the altar.'

This is presented as a self-evident fact, beyond any dispute – as if the past half-hour, with its desperate panic and looming disaster and narrowest, slenderest, most God-granted of escapes, had not occurred.

Orsola feels something close to despair. 'But sister,' she begins, 'didn't you see what just . . . that we were so very nearly . . .'

She gives up. It is a waste of breath. The urge to grab Serafina, to shake her hard, rises powerfully – and is contained, as it has been a hundred times before. She puts a hand to her brow and closes her eyes, trying to convince herself that the Maggiore might actually be their best course. It is the last place a person of any sense would go, and thus the last place a pursuer would think to look. If Serafina is covered, if she can be persuaded to keep her head lowered and her mouth shut, all might be well.

The nuns head back by a different route and find the piazza looking much as it did prior to the Inquisitors' arrival. Pilgrims are queuing in ever greater numbers, while costumed players have returned to perform the same scenes of Christly heroism. Orsola and Serafina join the dusty line that winds in through the arches of the basilica's façade. Singing can be heard from a choir somewhere within. Serafina is plainly moved and would stop to speak – but Orsola pulls her onwards impatiently, reminding her of their penitential circuit and how little time is now left.

They enter the cool magnificence of the church. Orsola takes in the row of pale columns on either side of the aisle, the golden grid of the ceiling, and the shuffling hundreds all around. There is a priest by the altar rail, instructing the vast crowds to venerate the crucified Christ and the salvation that He brought. But not one holy thought registers in Orsola's mind. As the shock of their escape subsides, she can think only of the grain loft and what she will say to Lontra when she returns there. The truths she will tell. How their agreement will change. She wants to go now, this instant, and see the matter dealt with. The penitential circuit, or however much of it they can cover before the evening Angelus, seems to stretch out endlessly before her. Serafina is speaking as they leave the basilica, trying to relate some new vision or insight, but she doesn't want to hear it – she *can't* hear it. She walks quickly, deliberately keeping Serafina two steps behind her as she leads them from the piazza.

The shout comes at the head of the Via Merulano.

'There!' cries a man, quite close by. 'The scarred sister!'

Orsola flinches and prepares to run; but then she sees that this man is not an Inquisitor, or a soldier or guardsman of any kind, but a player — a demon in a fish-head mask, his arms gleaming with painted scales. A small troupe stands a short distance away, up on a raised section of pavement. There are three or four more demons, a couple of prophets, and a slightly haggard Christ, all pausing their performance to look over at the nuns. Orsola halts. Despite everything, she finds herself hoping that they are from the grain loft — that they have been sent by Lontra to ensure that she and Serafina escaped, and make amends somehow.

One of the prophets leaves the group, stepping out into the street. 'I don't believe it,' he says. 'It cannot be.'

'It is her, yes?' asks the fish-headed demon. 'The nun of Castro?'

The prophet ignores him. He walks nearer, weaving through a party of tall-hatted Dutch pilgrims, until he is only a few yards away. Orsola realises that he is not looking at Serafina but at *her*. His eyes are distinctly familiar: close set, yellowish brown, their effect oddly flat. He spies this recognition immediately. Breaking into a grin, he pulls off his woollen beard and drops it to the ground.

There can be no doubt: that lean, pockmarked face belongs to Tullio Botta, son of Castro's blacksmith, to whom Orsola once spoke daily but has not seen for more than four years. She blinks in amazement, opening her mouth, but cannot think of a single thing to say.

Tullio's grin grows wider. 'Gina Cassoni,' he murmurs. 'It is you.'

*

First of all, they tell Orsola of the dead. Taking turns, speaking with a peculiar, muted energy, the ragged troupe reels off a list of those who were shot, stabbed, or trampled by cavalry; drowned in the river during their desperate flight from the battlefield; or captured by the enemy in the days afterwards, and hanged from trees like bandits. As they talk, Orsola finds that she recognises at least three more of them. They were once the ordinary men of Castro, labourers, footmen and apprentices, who were marched from the city under the flag of the Farnese and routed in less than an hour. She begins to notice ugly scars beneath the false beards and body paint. One demon has missing fingers, yet to heal properly; another needs a stick to walk. Tullio himself has lost a part of his left ear, and has an angry purple line running along the side of his neck.

Their recitation goes on for some minutes. Tullio mostly keeps quiet; but towards the end he reveals the fate of Jacopo Bruni, who was struck in the throat by a German musket ball and expired in a ditch. 'Running away, he was. Not a good death.'

This is Tullio Botta, Orsola remembers: honest to a fault. Staying very still, she lets his news settle within her and is surprised by how little sorrow it brings. But why should she grieve for Jacopo Bruni, exactly? She never felt any love for him; she just gave in to an impulse, mainly through boredom, and regretted it at once. He pledged to marry her when she learned she was with child, but then he was gone – returning to Castro only after she had been committed to the Visitation, and their daughter had already been in the ground for half a year. At confession, Orsola told of her hatred for Jacopo again and again. The priest's response was always the same: all three of them, father, mother and departed child, were in the lap of Almighty God. Orsola's only concern now was to make herself worthy of His holy grace. She tried to obey – to let Jacopo drift away and lose all importance, if only to find a little peace. As she stands there so coolly among the crowds on the Via Merulano, she realises that she must have succeeded.

Sister Serafina has pulled out in front, walking beside the main flow of pilgrims in her slightly stiff-limbed manner, her head down. She was a stranger to Castro when she entered the Visitation, and knew none of these men; and even were they not dressed as they are, she most certainly does not care to know them now. The players do not laugh at this, or roll their eyes and mutter about madness, as so many others have done. Orsola realises that these men have heard of Serafina; that they will have seen the grand visitors she received in Castro, on account of her holy gift. She notices a couple of them looking over at the choir nun with wary reverence.

Eventually, almost grudgingly, Orsola asks after her father and brother. None of the players knows anything, not even whether they went out to fight. Neither man was seen in Castro's formations, though, or at any of the drills beforehand.

'They may have escaped into the valley,' Tullio says. 'I hear that many did, and then made their way through to Valentano or Orvieto.' He pauses. 'Did you not see any of this, Gina? Did you not find anybody after you got away?'

Orsola checks the street for Inquisitors. There are only pilgrims, hundreds upon hundreds of them, marching doggedly on. She thinks of the day Castro fell. The crush at the Porta Santa Catarina, and the panicked cries as the first cannonballs raked over the surrounding roofs. The great rush downhill, around the side of the immense rock upon which the town was built, into the bed of the valley. The soldiers waiting there, firelocks ready on their stands — and then the volley of shots, the bodies falling, the survivors screaming wildly as they fled in every direction.

'I found no one,' she says.

Tullio leans down, bringing his head close to hers. 'We know how it was,' he says. 'There is no shame in it, for any of us. We have all found each other now.'

These words strike an odd, jarring note. Orsola turns to meet Tullio's flat yellow eyes. She senses that he and his comrades have been looking for them — or for Serafina, at least. That they have a design of some kind, for which the nuns are being claimed.

'My name is Orsola,' she says.

Not once, in all of the time she spent longing to be free from the Visitation, did she consider going back to the way things were. How could she live in her father's house, and do his bidding? How could she bear his name, after how he treated her? No — whatever else might happen, wherever her path might now lead, Ginevra Cassoni is gone.

Tullio smirks, scratching the scar on his neck. 'Of course,' he says. 'Forgive me, sister. You were married to Christ, back in that convent. Made *pure* again. But what I don't understand is why you've come all the way to Rome.' He nods at Serafina. 'How did you end up with this one? And why in God's holy name are the two of you living like this?'

The flow of people slows as they reach the end of the queue to enter the Laterano. It must be a mile long, the longest Orsola has yet seen. As they come to a halt, she tells Tullio's troupe of the special duty she was assigned by the Mother Abbess, and their reception at the Tor de' Specchi — omitting her own intention to step away once Serafina was safely inside.

'The laywomen there told us that Castro was a place of sin,' she concludes. 'Lost to heresy.'

This prompts immediate, vehement anger; the players spit and curse, declaring it yet another insult that would have to be answered. Tullio swiftly restores order, beckoning his fellows to him so they might exchange a few words. Then he faces Orsola again.

'What do you know about our town's end, sister?' he asks. 'Why did they tell you Castro was razed?'

Orsola has not thought of this for some months. She attempts to recall the Mother Abbess's explanation, along with the snatches of talk she overheard as she went about her work. 'Our duke refused to honour a debt to the Church,' she says. 'The Holy Father showed patience, but in the end had no choice but to—'

'That is a lie,' Tullio interrupts. 'They were lying to you, to keep you loyal to this rotten old pope. There was a debt, yes, but it belonged to our duke's father, Odoardo. Why should Ranuccio inherit it? Why should he bear such an unjust burden?'

Orsola looks around her. 'I don't—'

'There was hunger in Rome, hunger close to famine,' Tullio continues, his voice quick with fury. 'And the pope's family, the damnable Pamphilis, they were profiting from it. Hoarding grain. Pushing up prices. They needed an enemy outside their walls, to draw the people's anger. A righteous cause. A *distraction*. They told you about Bishop Giarda, I suppose?'

Orsola nods. This could not be hidden, even from the sisters of a closed order. A new bishop for Castro, said to be wise and learned, had been hand-picked by the Holy Father and dispatched from Rome, but was killed by bandits on the road near Monterosi. There was much grief in the Visitation when this news arrived. Orsola lost count of the Masses that were said for the dead bishop's soul.

Tullio leans in again. His smell is strong and sour, like something curdled; the stitching on his prophet's robe is starting to come apart. He lowers his voice, disguising it beneath the sounds of the procession.

'On the streets of this city they blamed *us* for the murder. Giarda was a Pamphili spy, tasked with bringing Castro under control and laying us open for their thievery. So the pope's people put it about that it was Castro who killed him — a man of the Church cut down in cold blood, on the orders of Duke Ranuccio. This is why those wretched laywomen called you a heretic.'

Serafina has drifted back to Orsola's side. She was quietly praying the rosary; but now, as if spurred somehow by Tullio's revelations, she falls to her knees and begins to speak. This time, her subject is not Santa Catarina, but Christ's descent into the Limbo of the Patriarchs. There is an unusual fierceness to her recitation, as if she is rebuking the Jubilee players for their frivolity.

'Just as Jonah was swallowed by a leviathan,' she pronounces, 'and spent three days in the darkness of its belly, so Christ went beneath the Earth, away from the Lord's light. But He was not alone down there. Evil stirred in those black shadows — the most vicious and abandoned evil ever to exist.'

Orsola is numb with horror. 'It . . . it isn't true, then?'

Tullio snorts. 'How can you ask me that? We are God-fearing people, sister. We don't kill *priests*.' He glances at his comrades. 'And we have friends in Monterosi. Men were seen in the woods, armed men, on the day of the Bishop's death. A hunter overheard their talk. They were mercenaries from the north, belonging to a company in the pay of Baron Luigi Mattei.'

'Who is that?' Orsola asks.

'The hero of Castro,' says Tullio bitterly. 'The general sent from

Rome, who defeated us and destroyed our town, and then came back here to be heaped with gold and honours by the Pamphili.'

Orsola eyes the queue of pilgrims. Serafina has been recognised; the nearest are listening closely, edging towards them. 'So you're saying that they had their own man killed, that they had a *bishop* killed, to give them an excuse to break apart our town and carry off whatever was left?'

'Not *they*,' says Tullio. 'You must have heard what the Romans say about it. Pope Innocent is old and frail. His grip was failing on the day he took charge and has only grown weaker since. No – it is Pimpaccia.' He bites out the word savagely, showing stained and crooked teeth. 'She is the one who ordered Bishop Giarda cut down and had Castro looted to the last candlestick. They took everything, sister. Her men even carted off the damned bells from the campanile.'

Orsola recalls her first morning in Rome, when she ended up among the imploring crowds on the long, grand square she has learned to call the Piazza Navona. 'Donna Olimpia,' she says. 'You are talking about Donna Olimpia.'

This woman is a sight of the Holy Jubilee, as much as the banners, acrobats or sacred plays. Multitudes gather to watch her magnificent carriages pass by, hoping to catch a glimpse of her – a widow with only the faintest claim to nobility, who is now more powerful and wealthy than any queen. And she seems to inspire as much loathing as admiration. This name they call her in the streets, *Pimpaccia*, is fit only for the most greedy and horrible of women. Many consider her a wicked influence upon the pope, guilty of all kinds of thievery and corruption. A good deal of this is deserved, according to Lontra – but none of the stories Orsola has heard come close to what she is being told now. She bites her lip, trying to think.

Tullio is raging on, meanwhile, listing further crimes and the forms justice should take. It is plain enough that he and his companions are planning revenge, making preparations for the spilling of the widow's blood, to gain forgiveness for their disgrace upon the battlefield. Orsola wants no part of that: Castro was not kind to her, not in the least, and she won't risk herself or Serafina for its honour. But once again, she can detect the Lord's hand at work here. As Lontra's limits are revealed, another path is surely being opened before them.

A group of seven or eight pilgrims has kneeled around Serafina in a close semicircle, gazing at her in wonderment as she talks of radiant virtue meeting dark, smothering evil; of demons burned and slashed apart; of the sword of divine might slicing through the bonds of the righteous, releasing them for the march to Paradise. The coins have already started to come, a smattering of shiny *quattrini*. With sudden clarity, Orsola understands that these tiny sums will never be enough, even after a hundred circuits. If she and Serafina are to have any chance at all, they will need more. Much more.

'It cannot be left unmet, sister,' says Tullio. 'We are the people of Castro, and Pimpaccia ordered our doom. She must pay for that.'

The line around them advances a few steps. Three or four more pilgrims are snagged by Serafina's account, sinking to their knees. The sound of singing drifts along the avenue from the piazza ahead.

'You are right, Tullio,' Orsola says. 'She must pay.'

Domina

Donna Olimpia plucks her third zeppole from the plate and places it in her mouth. She chews slowly, savouring the slight crunch of the caramelised shell and the soft, honeyed warmth within. Her eyelids flicker shut, and for a single luxurious moment her knees do not hurt, her back does not ache, and her mind does not strain beneath the weight of the plans and stratagems that she must constantly be devising. Then she swallows, and it is gone; and she is licking her fingers, eyeing the plate, considering a fourth.

'They are delicious, Excellency,' says Mascambruno from his armchair. The datary is still on his first, taking ridiculous nibbling bites, extending his lips as he does so like a cautious horse. 'Truly delicious. Signor Gallo is the finest *pasticcere* in Rome — which is to say, the world.'

Donna Olimpia cannot help smiling faintly at his obsequiousness. She has called the datary up here to her private apartments to discuss the usual matters of finance: gifts received by certain prominent Jubilee pilgrims, saleable Vatican offices that might soon become vacant, and so on. Now, though, lifted by the zeppole and the rich Corsican wine she had brought in to accompany them, she decides to tell him of her triumph over Princess Maria Apollonia of Savoy.

A woman of famous piety, who set aside her crown to wear the mantle of a lay Capuchin nun, Princess Maria snubbed Donna Olimpia most impolitely upon her arrival in Rome three days previously, proceeding directly from a private audience with Pope Innocent to her convent lodgings. So Donna Olimpia sent her a message, inviting her to the Palazzo Pamphili for a viewing of the reliquary, and mentioning a couple of the astonishing objects it contained. The devout Maria promptly forgot her objections to her hostess and arrived at the appointed time, her pinched little face flushed with excitement – only to discover that a large part of Roman society had been assembled there for a reception in her honour.

'Imagine it, Masco,' Donna Olimpia says. 'A woman of such modesty, so severe in her religion, so dismissive of worldly glories, made to endure a shower of compliments of the most effusive sort. Her coachman barely had time to water the horses before she asked – nay, *demanded* – to be returned to her convent.'

Mascambruno's small black eyes are glinting with mirth. 'And the reliquary?'

Donna Olimpia reaches for the fourth zeppole. 'Poor Maria did not come within fifty yards of it.'

This elicits a genuine laugh, a high, nasal honk, free from sycophancy. 'Vengeance, Excellency,' the datary declares. 'Sweet vengeance.'

Mascambruno is a good audience – and as a devotee of the Florentine vice, with boys stowed all over the city, he understands discretion better than most. When alone with him, Donna Olimpia feels that she can talk without inhibition; they each know enough to destroy the other several times over, so there is an odd safety to it. She looks around with some irritation, therefore, when her major-domo enters to inform her that an important guest is waiting to speak with her in the sala. Mascambruno rises immediately, offering his arm. She finishes the zeppole and heaves herself up, muttering a prayer at the protestations of her knees before starting gingerly towards the doorway.

The Palazzo Pamphili is filling with her people. On the main balcony alone there are ambassadors and bishops; three or four cardinals, all from the French faction, of course; artists and architects, hopeful of patronage; and numerous nobles of the first rank, many from her own family. When they see her on the stairs above them they burst into rapturous applause. Mascambruno remains at her side, supporting her descent. As they approach the doors to the sala, she glances at him and he steps away with a bow; this lesson, at least, appears to have been learned.

A pair of footmen ease the huge gilded doors open just enough for Donna Olimpia to pass through, and then close them promptly behind her, to prevent the crowd on the landing from seeing too much. The sala is the palazzo's largest room, most commonly used for balls, banquets or grand gaming evenings. That day, however, it is being turned into a theatre. Cavaliere Bernini's people have built a stage at the western end, upon which an elaborate set is still being painted and nailed together. These performances in the Palazzo Pamphili are a tradition of Carnivale: collections of comic scenes from modern Roman life, conducted always under the Cavaliere's tirelessly inventive direction. The pope had ordered that Carnivale be left uncelebrated during the Holy Jubilee, Rome already having quite enough unrestrained gaiety to contend with, and Donna Olimpia had intended to include her play in this general prohibition. But the Cavaliere had begged. *Such subject matter this year,* he cried; *such glorious, unmissable targets!* Donna Olimpia had conceded, setting a date after Easter and opening up her coffers once again. The play was worth it for the attention it drew, she reasoned, and the aggravation it never failed to cause her enemies.

The Cavaliere is across the enormous room, delivering instructions to a small group of workmen, his wiry frame taut with stress. Seeing her, he bows low – and then strides towards the stage with a shout, gesticulating wildly at some error in the rigging.

The shutters are still open, flooding the sala with soft evening light. Donna Olimpia soon locates Cardinal Francesco Barberini, sitting alone in the rear row of chairs, his pale, spotless hands crossed in his lap. She approaches unhurriedly. Francesco's face is sharp and scholarly, with a large, bony nose; he is reputed to be the more serious of the surviving Barberini brothers, the true churchman of the pair. This is why he has been allowed to return from exile and resume his duties in Rome – commanding the Holy Inquisition, among other things – while Antonio is required to languish in Paris a while longer. Donna Olimpia has never found this distinction to be particularly true. Francesco might hide it better, but to her he seems just as avaricious and power hungry as the rest of his family.

They exchange greetings and she sits with a groan, two chairs to his right. She soon sees that for all his composure, Cardinal Barberini is gravely worried.

'I am hearing much about the Spanish, Donna Olimpia,' he says. 'About their new ambassador, this Infantado. About great spectacles and parades staged around the city. About a painter, furthermore, an unparalleled genius in art, who will cement their favour with a portrait of the pope.' He pouts in disdain. 'A Spanish painter! Whoever heard of such an absurdity?'

Donna Olimpia looks at the Cavaliere's stage set, where a final, central piece is being fixed in place under his personal direction. It represents Rome itself. She can see pasteboard depictions of the dome of San Pietro, the battlements of Sant'Angelo, and fragments of pagan ruin. Everything is draped in lurid Jubilee decorations, the banners featuring holy figures in unlikely poses and misspelled words of prayer.

'Do not concern yourself, Eminence,' she says. 'It is nothing.'

The cardinal is not convinced. He leans over the empty chair between them, the satin of his mozetta gathering against its upholstered arm. 'I am also hearing that they are aware of our preparations in the south, for the movement upon Naples. Our ship numbers and supplies. Our supporters among the local population, and the actions they will take. I am told that they are making plans to resist us.'

Donna Olimpia regards him with a trace of impatience. 'It is *nothing*, Eminence. All will proceed as planned. Your brother will leave his exile. Your family will receive its rightful due. The Barberini will not lose their footing in Italy again.'

The cardinal sits back, twisting the point of his neat little beard. 'And what is the Holy Father's opinion? How does he regard this . . . increased confidence among Felipe's subjects? Or this imminent restitution of my family, for that matter? It was not so long ago that he was our most determined enemy.'

Donna Olimpia is now barely managing to mask her annoyance. 'We are thinking of the future, Eminence, are we not?' she says crisply. 'Pope Innocent's objection to your family, and to his predecessor, belongs to the past. My brother-in-law is reconciled to the return of the Barberini, along with whatever that may entail. I will ensure that he numbers among your keenest allies.'

At the far end of the sala, the stage curtain is being winched into place – a single, giant sheet of sumptuous blue velvet, designed merely to drop from the ceiling at the start of the performance. As Donna Olimpia and the cardinal watch its climb, she attempts to nudge their discussion in a slightly different direction.

'The pope has sanctioned me to speak of another matter, in

fact,' she says. 'A rather happier means of binding the Barberini to Rome.' This is a lie, of course; Innocent has no idea whatsoever of her ambitions in this quarter — not that he would dare to interfere with them.

Cardinal Barberini sees her meaning at once. 'You are referring to your granddaughter, Olimpiuccia, and the possibility of a union with my nephew Maffeo.' He looks off towards the windows with an expression of mild distaste. 'She is still a child, surely.'

'Olimpiuccia is ready,' Donna Olimpia replies firmly. 'I see the Lord's will in this, Eminence — that these two young people are of age at this precise time, just when you need to establish your return.'

'With you, Donna Olimpia, there is always a marriage,' the cardinal says; then he sighs, raising his thin eyebrows. 'It might be possible at some point, I suppose. My brother will have to be consulted. But I can tell you now that Naples will remain his primary concern. Antonio is a straightforward soul, you understand, and quite wedded to the view that territory is the only sure foundation for power. If the Spanish and their friends in Rome are allowed to threaten this, he will—'

Donna Olimpia wags a forefinger. 'There is no threat,' she interrupts. 'We are watching them very closely, I promise you that. Any move they consider will be known well in advance and brought to a decisive halt.' She sits up; the knees emit a deep, aching throb. 'Rome is our city, Eminence. They cannot hope to best us here. By this time next year, your Maffeo will be the duke of Naples, with a French fleet moored in the harbour to ward off any attempt by the Spanish to reclaim her.'

The cardinal cannot help but be impressed by her certainty, although whether he is actually comforted is harder to discern. He still has much to say about his brother's lofty standing in Paris, and his frequent conversations with Cardinal Mazarin – who is apparently taking a close interest in this affair and keeping King Louis himself apprised of its progress. Donna Olimpia folds her hands together, feigning interest. She decides that further discussion of marital matters can wait.

After only a minute or so, to Donna Olimpia's relief, Cavaliere Bernini orders his people to start closing the shutters and lighting the sconces. As the panels creak over the windows, steeping the sala in a theatre-like gloom, the black-clad Cavaliere stalks down the side of the room towards them. Donna Olimpia perceives that he is reluctant to approach the cardinal. The Barberini were known to have been affronted by the speed with which the renowned sculptor embraced their enemies after their exile, having been almost entirely dependent on their patronage for so many years. He overcomes it, however, and he and the cardinal choose to ignore each other completely.

'Excellency,' says the Cavaliere, clasping his hands behind his back. 'If you would be so kind as to move yourself to the front row, I do believe that with God's almighty grace we are ready to begin.'

*

Donna Olimpia has her family sit around her – apart from the pope, of course, who is over in the Palazzo del Quirinale, and those she has seen exiled from Rome. At the row's end is Federico, her hapless Cardinal Nephew, looking like he himself is an actor in costume, and badly miscast. Along from him is Costanza and her husband Prince Ludovisi, who appears very tired; the demands of the Jubilee calendar, with all the wine and grappa he must drink, are clearly extracting their price.

At Donna Olimpia's side, in the most privileged position, sits Olimpiuccia. Amid the general murmur of anticipation, the girl is unwillingness personified. Her plain, clever face — so like her grandmother's own, many have said — is dark with displeasure. In an attempt to cheer her, Donna Olimpia starts to talk of the many plays she has staged in the past and the enormous fun they have been. Before she can say very much, however, there is a crash of cymbals and the blue curtain drops heavily to the floor, billowing warm air over the front row.

The stage is lit by a great many candles, their light reflected upon sheets of polished metal, which have been positioned in the wings. After a brief, expectant silence, Cavaliere Bernini walks onstage. He is clad now in the colourful costume of a Swiss Guard, a pasteboard halberd on his shoulder. With a flourish that causes his helm to slip a little to the side, he announces the title: *Jubilee of Dust, or Rome turned Upside Down*. A drum rolls, trumpets sound — and a cavalcade of crudity begins, as irreverent and obscene as anything ever staged during Carnivale.

In the first scene, a stooped figure in papal robes and mitre hobbles onstage to wash the feet of the poor. So short-sighted is this pontiff, though, so infirm and weak-minded, that he tries to wash his Swiss Guards instead — and then parts of the assembled crowd's anatomy that are certainly not mentioned in scripture. Next, a painter struts into view, brush and palette in hand, sporting pointed Spanish moustaches and one of those high collars favoured by King Felipe and his court. In a ridiculous accent, he declares that he will dazzle Rome with a portrait of his Moor. Enter Bernini, his face now oiled to a light shade of ochre, carrying a golden frame and presenting himself, a living man, as if he was a painting. The illusion is successful, causing a group of artists and connoisseurs to fall about in admiration — until the portrait breaks wind loudly and both the painter and his subject must make themselves scarce.

This causes much hilarity among the audience, who let out cheers, hoots and heckles, to which the actors gleefully respond. Donna Olimpia manages to smile, but in truth she is finding it all rather tiresome. She begins to think of the various estates in her possession, in Rome and beyond; in particular the walled town of San Martino, close to Viterbo, which she is presently renovating in the finest style so that it might serve her as a retreat. Her eye wanders to her granddaughter. Like her, Olimpiuccia is sitting almost motionless among the mirth. Donna Olimpia feels a momentary kinship – but then she notices that the girl has a rosary hidden up her sleeve and is working her way through a surreptitious prayer. She leans over and slaps Olimpiuccia on the arm.

'*Watch*,' she hisses.

The girl jumps, startled by her grandmother's rebuke, looking up obediently at the stage; and her lower lip falls in amazement. Donna Olimpia turns back. Off to the side, she sees the black habit of a Benedictine nun, worn by an actress with a long, jagged scar painted across her face. Emerging from beneath a replica of the Arch of Constantine, this character hurries to the centre of the stage, where she begins to babble in an unbroken, barely comprehensible stream about saints and angels and grisly acts of martyrdom. Donna Olimpia is struck through by a peculiar sensation, as if a long-buried memory has been dragged back suddenly to the surface. It is a powerful feeling indeed; but also frustratingly, disconcertingly vague.

Around her, the audience is laughing with recognition. 'The scarred sister!' they cry. 'I have seen her, I have seen her!'

Up on the stage, worshippers have gathered around the nun, kneeling and praying, but it soon becomes clear that this is not simply a sacred exercise. A toll-taker appears – the Cavaliere again, the oil wiped off his face, wearing a long black wig – who unfurls a list of available services and the prices involved, and pins it to the wall of the pasteboard Rotonda.

Donna Olimpia's eyes widen. Across the top of this list is written *The Nun of Castro*.

The scene continues, to the great delight of the audience. Fat sacks of gold are collected from the gullible crowd – but then a number of Inquisitors appear, rapping skulls with their large wooden crucifixes and threatening all with the Tor di Nona. Donna Olimpia watches as they corner the nun and attempt to interrogate her. She seems deranged in some way, however, unable to dam her holy discourse, and can only respond with odd details from the life of Santa Catarina. Snarling at her blasphemy, the Inquisitors close in, preparing to clap her in irons.

Donna Olimpia's patience expires. She stands, bringing on a jolt of pain – just as this nun of Castro somehow rises three yards directly into the air, a pair of gleaming white wings unfolding from her back. The audience is caught: poised to applaud the Cavaliere's ingenious mechanisms, to applaud them vigorously, but also very aware that their beneficent hostess is now upright before them, partially lit by the stage lights and wearing a noxious frown. The silence grows longer and more awkward. The flying nun hangs above, her beatific grin fading as she rotates a little on creaking ropes. Donna Olimpia glances up at her, breathing in hard through her nose; then she marshals her agony and marches from the room.

The servants out on the balcony come to attention, opening doors smartly at her approach. She heads through the library into a small adjoining chamber, often used for confidential exchanges. The shutters of the single window are still open, admitting a dull, blueish light. Donna Olimpia goes to the sill and glowers out at the darkening rooftops of Parione.

Ludovisi enters a minute later, padding across the room to place a candle on a dresser. For all his apparent insouciance – and his current rather depleted condition – her son-in-law has a knack for knowing when his counsel will be required.

'Castro in Rome,' Donna Olimpia says. 'How can this be?'

'It is to be expected, Mama,' Ludovisi replies. 'Honestly, I'm surprised we've heard nothing sooner.'

Donna Olimpia scowls at him: the dishevelled costume, the red-rimmed eyes, the clammy, greyish skin. 'And yet you speak of it only now. I swear, Ludo, sometimes I wonder if these fabled brains of yours actually exist.'

The fat prince lets out a low, hoarse laugh. 'I do admit that my brains are not serving me particularly well today,' he says, rubbing his brow. 'There was a reception, you understand, at the Mantuan embassy – and a most intriguing company, among whom I found a young—'

'I will speak with Bernini,' Donna Olimpia interrupts. 'This instant.'

Ludovisi props himself wearily against the wall and nods. 'I told him as much on my way from the sala. He will be here shortly.'

Gripping the sill, Donna Olimpia attempts to concentrate – to unearth more of the memory that came upon her so forcibly at first sight of the nun. It was trouble, she recalls. A beleaguered family, and a dreadful act of rupture; then banishment, disgrace, oblivion.

Cavaliere Bernini arrives still wearing his wig. He fills the small chamber with a strong citrus scent, mingled faintly with the smell of fresh sweat. His demeanour suggests concern, a degree of contrition, and a slight defiance.

'Holy saints, Donna Olimpia, whatever is the matter? Are you unwell, dear lady? Are you overcome, perhaps, by the vivacity of the performance — by the energy and the deftness with which we are—'

'The nun,' says Donna Olimpia. She points back towards the sala. 'Where did all that nonsense come from?'

The Cavaliere bridles at this description of his work, but manages to keep his response in check. 'Have you not seen her then, Excellency, as you travel about the city?' he asks with a tight smile. 'The scarred sister is a sight of the Jubilee, plying her tales along the route of the procession — in the piazzas, on the steps of churches . . .'

'And Castro? What do you know about that?'

Bernini shrugs. 'Just a rumour I heard. They say the poor creature fled that wicked city like one of Lot's daughters — and then, after months of wandering, washed up at the gates of Rome. I am told that there is a little community of Castro's former citizens here, in fact, living in vagrancy, squeezing what coins they can from the pilgrims.' The Cavaliere hesitates, turning on his heel to glance questioningly at Ludovisi. 'If my play has *displeased* you in some way, Excellency, I would be happy to rewrite a part of it. I mean, it would run against the spirit of Carnivale, and everything I have staged for you in the past, but I suppose it can be done.'

Dear God, this man is tedious. Were it not for his genius, Donna Olimpia would have nothing whatsoever to do with him. She takes a long breath, then moves away from the window to sit in a high-backed chair. 'The Spaniard,' she says. 'This portrait painter. Tell me of him.'

Another shrug. 'What is there to tell? Don Diego keeps his distance, shall we say, from the painters and sculptors of Rome. I do have friends who have attained a certain intimacy — yet they too claim that the man gives very little of himself away.' The Cavaliere joins his hands, pressing the palms together, and looks off briefly to the side; Donna Olimpia spots a dark drip of oil running down his neck. 'I would be happy to discuss this with you later, Excellency, but a performance has been left in suspension — quite literally, in the case of my poor Luisa, who is still dangling up in the air. With your permission, we should—'

Donna Olimpia waves her hand. 'Continue,' she says. 'I shall not be returning.'

Bernini makes a halfway convincing display of disappointment; then he bows low and departs, no doubt cursing her passionately as he strides back to the stage.

'Watch him, Ludo,' Donna Olimpia says. 'Have your people find out what he knows. *Who* he knows.'

'And the nun?' asks Ludovisi. 'This . . . community he spoke of?'

Donna Olimpia stares at the candle's flame. She pictures these survivors of Castro gathered around a fire out in the ruins somewhere, sharing tales of woe and outlandish theories. Preparing blades, firearms and who knew what else. Plotting her demise.

'Pope Innocent may be at risk,' she says. 'We will do what we must.'

*

'I hear that a fine play was staged at the Palazzo Pamphili last night, Donna Olimpia,' observes Cardinal Panciroli. 'The Holy Father himself was featured, they say. With the part taken by an apprentice from the workshop of Cavaliere Bernini.'

Donna Olimpia smiles, wishing a blade driven directly into that placid, evaluating eye. 'You know how these things are, Eminence.

The Cavaliere writes in the tradition of the *Commedia* – gentle mockery is employed to express the most profound respect. And besides, the play's subjects were many. Sacred frauds, for example. Corrupted priests.' She pauses. 'The antics of a certain Spanish painter.'

Panciroli nods his little head slowly. 'That I can understand,' he says. 'Don Diego Velázquez is certainly one of the remarkable blessings of this holy year. All are agreed that his portrait of the Holy Father will stand as a glorious memorial. Did you know that a date has been arranged for the sitting? It will occur between Corpus Christi and the Chinea – why, only two weeks from now.'

Donna Olimpia sees that she is being goaded, but cannot help growing angry nonetheless. 'Why wasn't I consulted?' she demands, tugging at the neck of her black cape. 'This is an exceptionally busy season, Eminence. Every hour, every *minute*, is accounted for. The pope cannot spare—'

'A single morning is all Don Diego requires,' Panciroli breaks in. 'He is quite famous for it in Madrid. And then, by God's grace, an image will have been made, a captured moment of holy creation that will endure until—'

'Please,' says Giambo, quite loudly. 'Be quiet. Both of you.'

They are before the Palazzo del Quirinale, atop the steps outside the main gate. The piazza is full, yet more people are arriving constantly, pressing in from the surrounding avenues in massive numbers. Dust hangs heavy in the air. It is late morning, and the heat is punishing; the pope and his attendants stand beneath a crimson awning, their faces coloured deep pink by the sunlight that blazes through the fabric. Following Donna Olimpia's concerns about the foot washing ceremony, a full detachment of Swiss Guard has been deployed, forming a tight, steel-edged cordon around the steps. It is still distinctly frightening, however; Donna

Olimpia keeps eyeing the shifting, murmuring crowds, fearing the worst.

Giambo is dressed again in full golden garb, his ferula in his hand. He is to bless this enormous gathering – and then is determined to grant the Jubilee indulgence on a *personal basis*, to all the pilgrims who claim to have completed their penance within the past week, appraising the honesty of each and every one. Donna Olimpia declared this to be madness, and a practical impossibility – but the wretched Panciroli encouraged it, implying that a woman had no chance of understanding a truly divine impulse, and trotting out endless passages from the gospels about the guidance of multitudes. This closed the matter. Giambo would disregard her and proceed.

Donna Olimpia takes in the prelates assembled beneath the awning, assessing as always the balance between allies and enemies. With slight concern, she notices that her lumbering idiot of a nephew is not in attendance. This is the second occasion Federico has missed of late, having been omitted from the papal entourage during the Ascension Day services the previous week. She hadn't given this much thought at the time; the dolt had hardly distinguished himself during Holy Week, at one point dropping a censer down a flight of steps. For the Cardinal Nephew to be excluded again, though, and so soon – that could mean something.

It is then that Donna Olimpia sees Camillo Astalli, Panciroli's private secretary, standing next to the musicians: the traitor, whose brother she'd helped into an extremely advantageous marriage to one of her own nieces, yet who had since chosen to join with her most relentless foe. Rather to her surprise, this arrogant, over-groomed weasel is wearing the black cassock of a priest. All Vatican lawyers are ordained, of course, but she has never seen Astalli wear one before; she has heard that his life is hardly lived in the appropriate manner. His poise irritates her, being so unaffected by the heat — which she is beginning to think might overwhelm her completely.

Seeming to sense her glare, Astalli looks back at her, holding her eye impudently for a few seconds before lowering his head. Donna Olimpia's nostrils flare. This cannot stand. Camillo Astalli is several ranks beneath the next most lowly man, several ranks *at least*. He should not be there; he has *no reason* to be there. She tugs on Giambo's robe, making the gemstones rattle.

The pope turns, and he looks so frail and harried Donna Olimpia nearly forgets the cause of her complaint. What must all these pilgrims think, she wonders, when they see that their Holy Father, the man closest to Almighty God, is so very diminished? It is worry that weighs him down, worry about everything — from the pilgrims' copious pipe-smoking in the basilicas, to the machinations of kings and princes in faraway lands. And there is grief too, more than a month old now but still making itself felt in every conversation they have. Prudenzia it was, his second sister — a nun of stern disposition, implacably opposed to Donna Olimpia, and adamant in her cessation of all contact while she remained at her brother's side. As a result, Giambo had not spoken to Prudenzia for several years, yet this does not reduce his sorrow in the least. Donna Olimpia knows that he needs sympathy, and she tries to provide it; but Holy Virgin, it is difficult.

Just as she begins to speak the trumpets sound, announcing the blessing. Giambo gives her a miserable smile before inching forward across the crimson carpet. He raises his ferula and commences his address — and there is a colossal, inexorable movement as every soul in the piazza pushes towards him in unison. The captain of the Swiss Guards yells an order and the soldiers close ranks, interlocking their striped arms. At first, the prelates gathered beneath the awning are gratified, praising the Almighty for this display of pious enthusiasm; but within moments it becomes plain that something is going very badly wrong. The Guards strain and shout as their line starts to buckle; Donna Olimpia sees a helm knocked off, the sound of it striking the stones all but muted by the uproar. The crowds are pressing against the soldiers with an elemental force, those at the front now no longer able to stop or pull back. Individual forms are lost, the thousands of people merging together into a gigantic, tangled compression of limbs and hats and anxious, sweaty faces. Their smell rolls among the perfumed churchmen; it makes Donna Olimpia think of livestock. Of dirt and degradation.

She moves herself closer to the gates. Tragedy is surely approaching, at a speed that outstrips comprehension. The noise alone is staggering. Among the mounting appeals to the Holy Father, to the Madonna, to God Himself, she can hear women calling out for *her* — for her intercession in their plight, as they do in the Piazza Navona. For some reason, she finds this acutely annoying. She turns to Panciroli, whose pigeon face is alive with alarm.

'I told you!' she bellows. '*I told you!*'

He blinks and swallows, but does not reply; he seems incapable of any speech or action.

Soon there are screams, panic spreading through the crowds like fire in straw. Another surge gathers, breaking the Guards' line. The foremost pilgrims spill onto the steps, stumbling forward to prostrate themselves at Giambo's feet and bawl out their prayers. The old sheep looks around him in distress and helpless confusion, the ferula limp in his grasp; Donna Olimpia swears that his lips are forming her name. Guards encircle him in seconds, shoving and kicking people back. Their captain gives a signal and the gates are opened a short way. Giambo is bundled inside, with Donna Olimpia and the rest of his entourage a half-dozen footsteps behind.

The screams are growing louder and more desperate. As she enters the Palazzo del Quirinale, Donna Olimpia sees bodies being lifted above the swaying, keening crowd – children and the elderly, their skin a deathly white – only to be dropped as a third mighty push causes many hundreds to fall as one.

The gates are closed and barred. There is a great flap of genuflection as the shocked prelates struggle to understand what has happened – what is happening still.

'Oh, Lord aid me!' Giambo moans, banging the end of his ferula on the floor. 'It is going wrong, so very, very wrong! Holy Christ, save your subjects, I beg of you!'

Panciroli, now recovered, suggests going upstairs to the balcony, so they can witness the scale of this awful accident and help in whatever way they can.

'A most stupid idea,' pronounces Donna Olimpia. 'What good can you possibly hope to do, Panciroli? You only risk exciting the people further, and causing the pope yet more anguish.'

The prelates seem to draw together, staring over at her with a scorn so cold and absolute it can almost be felt upon the skin.

'We will offer our prayers,' Panciroli informs her. 'The Holy Father will appeal for calm – and with God's assistance, the people will hear him.'

The churchmen head for the stairs, sweeping the dazed, docile Giambo along with them. Donna Olimpia stands for a moment, listening to the dreadful cries outside. She knows that she must follow. Panciroli cannot be allowed this victory. There are no servants to be seen, who she might order to bring her sedan chair; she suspects that Panciroli's people have dismissed them for this precise reason. But this will not stop her. She summons her strength and her resilience and sets off.

By the time Donna Olimpia reaches the corridor above, the tears are dripping from her chin. She would give much – plate, coin, even one of her holy relics – simply to sit upon the top step and rub her kneecaps. However, through a double doorway ahead, she can see that the prelates are about to venture onto the balcony of the palazzo. She can make out Giambo's mitre silhouetted against a window, dipping in despair. And there is Panciroli, trying to rally them with the words of San Paulo, proclaiming that they must glory in their sufferings and use them as a path to valour.

This is all the encouragement Donna Olimpia needs. Ignoring the gnawing torments of her knees, she wipes her cheeks on the edge of her widow's hood, sets her features into a resolute grimace, and continues.

Just as she nears the threshold, a black-robed figure appears before her. It is Camillo Astalli, his urbane manner exchanged for one of vicious satisfaction.

'Step aside,' she orders.

Astalli smiles icily and opens his arms. For an instant, Donna Olimpia wonders if he is making a misguided, condescending attempt at benediction. Then she sees that he has taken hold of the double doors, one in each hand, and is preparing to shut them in her face.

She pushes herself onwards, thinking to pass into the room before he can act. Searing wires seem to whip around her shins, winding tightly enough to splinter the bones. An involuntary squawk breaks from her lips – which is obscured by the slamming of the doors, the bang resounding along the marble-clad corridor.

Donna Olimpia's pace is such that she almost collides with the dark, polished panels. She sets her hands against them and leans in close, her heaving breaths misting upon the varnish. A metallic jangle comes from inside the room – the sound of keys being readied. She hesitates in sheer disbelief, before grabbing at the handles and shaking them hard. But it is too late. The lock is already being turned, the parts slotting into place.

'Open these doors, Astalli!' Donna Olimpia commands, just managing to keep her voice steady. 'You have no right to keep me from my brother-in-law, no right at all! Do you hear me, villain? Open these doors immediately!'

Nothing happens. Beyond the palazzo, the bells of several nearby churches begin to peal in a frantic, tumbling cacophony, announcing the emergency in the piazza to the surrounding city; and suddenly, there in the corridor, Donna Olimpia receives a clear intimation of danger. The exclusion of her nephew Federico, no doubt to satisfy the insufferable Panciroli. The presence of the traitor Astalli, in all his insolent overconfidence. And now this concerted effort to shut her out, to bar her from Giambo's side. A scheme is underway.

Donna Olimpia steps back across the patterned floor, onto a rectangle of Verde Alpi. She is infuriated, of course, and aghast, yet also oddly relieved. It has arrived. Those damnable clerics have found their spines at last. After so many years of muttered gripes and sly intimidation, the battle lines are finally being drawn.

Camillo Astalli's eye appears in the thin crack between the door panels. 'Whore,' he says. 'Your time is at an end.'

PART TWO

The Fisherman's Ring

Servus

Don Diego rides to the Palazzo del Quirinale in the ambassador's own carriage. This honour is due to the extraordinary task he is to perform, but de Pareja senses that there is more to it than that. His master will be receiving a few final instructions about how the portrait is to be approached, and Spain's expectations of the result. He himself is up on the roof, with a couple of Infantado's tercio; the soldiers sit in silence, ignoring him completely.

The morning sky is a blue so deep you would need to mix in a pinch of black to paint it. Rome is quiet, a lull of sorts having descended after the celebrations of Corpus Christi two days before. Crumbling flower wreaths still hang everywhere, while the gutters are heaped with carnations, lilies and roses, all withered by the heat and starting to decay. Not for the first time, de Pareja finds himself worrying about contagion. It is commonly claimed that God will protect Rome during this holy year, its countless pious acts surely forming a shield against disease. But if this is not so, he can easily imagine the city being consumed in a matter of days, and his journey with Don Diego coming to a premature and terrible close. Death is everywhere at the Jubilee; already, during this brief ride, he has glimpsed two men laid out in a soot-stained arcade, their blood forming a blackening lattice across the cobblestones. It can take you without warning, in any number of ways. De Pareja prays with all his soul that plague will not be added to the list.

Their short procession circles the walls of the Quirinale, then rattles in through the gates. A company is waiting to receive them in the courtyard. At its head is an old, neat, mild-looking cardinal who can only be Panciroli. Beside him is Camillo Astalli – now clad in cardinal's robes as well, with a magnificent silver cross around his neck. De Pareja is expecting this sight, but he is still impressed by the boldness of what these men have done. Astalli has been raised to the Sacred College, and then promptly appointed Pope Innocent's Cardinal Nephew, dislodging Federico Maidalchini without ceremony. Panciroli reportedly convinced the pope of the wisdom of his plan in the course of a single conversation, on the evening before Corpus Christi; it is to be announced to the people of Rome the following day.

'Were the widow not so despised,' observed Don Diego, as he told de Pareja the news, 'there might well have been some objection from the Curia at the remarkable speed of it – not to mention the fragility of Astalli's connection to the papal family. But they are all thinking of who will be the next pope, and very probably the one after that. They are trying to drive her out for good.'

The Spanish party disembarks. The Duke of Infantado is half a head taller than everyone else and dressed in the sober magnificence of the Order of Calatrava. He bows to the cardinals; and then, after Don Diego has done the same, he draws them all to him for a short conversation. The duke's decision to accompany them to the sitting is unconventional, yet easily explained: Infantado clearly means to lay absolute claim to Don Diego Velázquez and his works, on behalf of the Spanish Crown. From atop the carriage, de Pareja can hear a little of what is being said. The duke and the churchmen are speaking of their anticipation, and the anticipation of all Rome – of the great statement of friendship that this memorial portrait will represent.

'I would be most happy, Don Diego,' Infantado says, 'if the likeness were ready for presentation on the day of the Chinea. Can this be done?'

Don Diego bows. 'Of course, your grace. It will be my honour.'

The swift certainty of Don Diego's reply wins him a few approving words as the company moves off towards the grand staircase. De Pareja climbs down from the carriage, retrieving a wooden colour box, a mid-sized easel, two half-length canvases and a folder of buff paper from the rack at the cabin's rear. Along with his satchel, this is a full load indeed; it takes him a minute to arrange it all and follow after them.

The Palazzo del Quirinale is glorious but de Pareja hardly sees it, so intent is he on balancing his load and attempting to catch up with the party ahead. At the top of the stairs is a broad corridor, with two Swiss Guards standing by a set of double doors at its end. They exchange a glance as de Pareja approaches, then one of them raises his hand, instructing him to stop. Through the doors, de Pareja can hear Infantado paying obeisance to Pope Innocent and making sweeping predictions of the portrait's greatness. It goes on for some minutes. De Pareja puts down the easel, scratching apprehensively at a flea bite on his wrist. He waits.

Then the doors are opened and Infantado, the cardinals and a couple of others come into view, bowing as they take their leave. De Pareja quickly picks up the easel and moves aside; they are heading left though, fitting hats on their heads and starting down another passage, conversing in low tones. As the doors are closed again, one of the guards whistles softly through his teeth and jerks his head at the narrowing gap, indicating that de Pareja should enter.

The audience chamber beyond is as huge and majestic as the rest of the palazzo. Tapestries line the lower parts of the walls, while masterful frescoes cover the plaster above, all of it crowned by a gilded ceiling of luminous intricacy. Pope Innocent stands in the centre of the chamber, clad in a white robe with a red mozetta over his shoulders, his large ears pushed out slightly by his bell-shaped crimson hat. De Pareja feels an unexpected disappointment. He isn't entirely sure what he thought he would see – an inner radiance perhaps, a sense of beatitude, an aura of great and otherworldly wisdom – but it is not there. The Holy Father is very much a mortal man. Nevertheless, he sets down his load, removes his hat and drops to his knees; in his haste, he bends over rather further than necessary and nearly cracks his forehead against the marble floor.

'Who is this person?' The pope's voice is thin, refined, and faintly strained; to de Pareja's surprise, he is talking in Spanish.

Don Diego is strolling nearby, a hand on his hip, appraising the light. The trace of nerves de Pareja noticed back in his rooms has been banished; he has assumed the calm, assured manner of the courtier. 'My assistant, your Holiness,' he replies.

'I remember these people from the Alcazar,' the pope says. 'Your Morisco slaves, so quiet and busy. He is Catholic, I presume?'

'Naturally, your Holiness. And as good a Christian as I have known.'

The pope nods, seeming to accept this. 'Please send him out when you are ready to begin.'

This is not an unusual request, especially among Don Diego's less willing sitters – and this particular man, the vicar of Christ, Almighty God's voice upon the Earth, can be placed among the most reluctant. He appears agitated, as if awaiting interrogation or a painful medical procedure.

Don Diego is now studying the impressive golden throne that is situated at one end of the room — surely the place from which the pope receives his many visitors and supplicants. He suggests that the Holy Father sit himself upon it, as this is the form. Innocent assents and begins to shuffle over. Meanwhile, Don Diego instructs de Pareja to set up the easel, indicating the position of its legs with his forefinger.

When this is done, and a piece of primed canvas attached, de Pareja opens the colour box and begins to prepare his master's palette. He does this as rapidly as he can, but with careful reverence as well, almost as if he is observing a ritual. The colours themselves were ground up and mixed early that morning, and stored in small covered bowls. De Pareja now spoons out the glistening gobbets of pigment, setting them across the board in Don Diego's preferred order, fanned immaculately around the thumb hole. All must be exactly right; it has not been revealed how long Don Diego would have with Innocent, or if this opportunity would ever be repeated.

'I will take what I can, Juan,' Don Diego said. 'Let us pray that it is enough.'

De Pareja hands his master the palette, along with five sable brushes of various degrees of fineness and a yard-long mahlstick. Then he looks back into the box and conducts a quick inventory. Still within are a twist of clean rags; flasks of water, linseed oil, and white vinegar; half a dozen palette knives; charcoal, several pens, and a bottle of brown ink. Everything that Don Diego might need.

He nods to his master, bows low and retreats. At the doors, he risks a final glance back at the pope. Innocent is sitting squarely upon the throne, shoulders sagging slightly and elbows hanging out over the arms. His heavy old face, framed by shining crimson satin, crisp linen, and gleaming gold, is watching Don Diego with distinct suspicion.

The corridor outside is empty save for the Swiss Guards at the door, who pay de Pareja no further attention. He walks a short distance, selecting a spot beneath a tall window. There he sits cross-legged, taking his sketching folder from his satchel and opening the cover – and the scarred sister is before him, her habit falling in black folds, her disfigured cheek angled imploringly towards the heavens.

Each time he sees these drawings, de Pareja experiences the same sequence of emotions. Having convinced himself that they are bad, he is struck by how they are not *entirely* bad; how actually, in some respects, they could even be said to have a certain promise. But then, as his eye grows accustomed to them once more, and he remembers the struggles he had, and the many challenges and problems still unresolved, he realises that they are in fact without any merit whatsoever. The absolute opposite of what he wishes to achieve. Worthy only of the fire.

Several dismal minutes pass. Gradually, de Pareja recovers something of his spirits. He knows very well that this is what it is to be an artist. Success is built upon the backs of many failures. You must turn the page; you must try again. He readies a stub of graphite, locates a blank patch among the sheets of sketches, and attempts to summon her once more, kneeling upon the Corso in that shaft of strong sunlight.

After a while a Swiss sergeant stalks by, eyeing him with close, unkind curiosity before extracting an explanation from one of the guards on the door, in what de Pareja assumes is a form of German. Ignoring them, he abandons his drawing and begins anew, delineating the sister's back with a long, decisive stroke, then hatching in some shadow to establish the position of her clasped hands. When this is done he stops, holding up the sheet to consider the effect. His eyes widen in amazement, for these few lines have the clear ring of truth. *Holy saints,* he thinks, *could this be it? Could I have—*

A carriage arrives at speed in the courtyard below, drawing to a noisy, clattering halt. Its door is thrown open with great force and a woman begins to shout.

'Chair! Chair, damn you, this instant! *Chair!*'

The Swiss sergeant goes to the next window, muttering something that can only be a curse. De Pareja sets aside his page and rises to his feet. The carriage is a deep, lacquered blue and as fine as they come, with several smart footmen riding atop it. He cannot see its occupant – who continues to shout that same word over and over – but on the door beneath his window, above the papal tiara and keys of San Pietro, is a dove with an olive branch in its beak.

A sedan chair appears from under the arcade, carried by a pair of palace servants, hurrying to the other side of the carriage. The same female voice can be heard, talking more quietly now but with no less anger, as the chair sets off and disappears between the arches. The sergeant curses again and heads into another region of the building, plainly seeking to get himself well out of the way.

There is a brief, ominous quiet – and then the sedan chair appears at the end of the corridor, the lead servant red-faced and puffing. In anticipation, the Swiss Guards step forward smartly to open the doors of the audience chamber. The chair charges by de Pareja, barely a yard from where he is standing, and for a single second she is beside him: Donna Olimpia Maidalchini, clad in widow's black, seeming to fill the little box completely. He can discern next to nothing of the features behind her veil, yet she still radiates an alarming fury.

The chair races into the audience chamber and the shouting

resumes. 'What *is this*, Giambattista Pamphili? You would betray your own family – betray your *blood*? What in heaven's name is the matter with you?'

'Olimpia,' says Innocent, sounding pained and tremendously weary, 'if you would just—'

'You did not even have the courage to tell me yourself. I must discover it from Ludovisi – from *Ludovisi*, Giambattista! How did I deserve such a harsh humiliation? All I have done since my marriage is champion your cause. You sit there because of *me*. I neglected my husband for you – your own dear brother! I paid bribes, I courted favour, I gave presents and hosted banquets and made donations. All for you!'

De Pareja moves closer, looking into the grand room, hoping to catch sight of his master and get a sense of what he might do. The sedan chair and its bearers have vanished; they must have left the chamber by a servants' door. Donna Olimpia is standing bolt upright before the throne, her chin raised high, pointing at the pope in a gesture of violent accusation. Rather to de Pareja's astonishment, Don Diego is still working – dabbing at his palette, then darting the brush over the canvas with the haste of one who knows that he has only seconds left.

The pope attempts defiance. 'I will do what is best for the Holy See,' he says, gripping the arms of his throne, a dull purple colour gathering in his cheeks. 'If you cannot understand that Federico was ill-equipped for his position, Olimpia, then I—'

'Oh, quiet! Speak no more, I implore you! You who are so *busy*, so very *important*, that you can spend an entire morning sitting before this . . . this mountebank, this Spanish trickster! You are in here *alone* with him, Giambo! Holy Madonna, what if he is diseased? What if he is in truck with our enemies, or has taken gold to stick a knife between your ribs?'

'Our enemies? Olimpia, I do not think that—'

'Federico is *ours*, Giambattista. He is growing still, yes, that I grant you – but there is a great and worthy man in him. He simply needs schooling and patient guidance. What he does *not* need is for his dear uncle, his papa, to betray him, to cast him out so cruelly, to strip him of all he has attained in such a . . . a base and perfunctory manner. To side with his detractors, his abusers, and . . .'

The widow runs on, becoming yet more impassioned and outraged. Innocent merely sits and listens, his head bowing down, like a man enduring punishment for an acknowledged sin. Footsteps sound nearby, walking with urgent speed. De Pareja turns to see a large detachment of churchmen, headed by Panciroli and Astalli, rushing to the pope's relief.

As soon as this party enters the chamber, Donna Olimpia's ire switches to them – and to Cardinal Panciroli in particular. Pope Innocent has disappointed her, disappointed her most grievously, but this man she truly hates.

'*You* have done this,' she spits. 'You, and you alone! I knew it on the day of that calamitous blessing, when the piazza outside these very walls was piled with the bodies of the faithful! You have been toiling to dispose of me, bringing all of your dark mischief to bear. You cannot tolerate my influence, can you, Panciroli? You cannot abide the love that exists between the Holy Father and I – an honest and loyal bond that you cannot break. It maddens you, admit it!'

The Swiss Guards have gone inside, in case the pope needs an actual rescue. De Pareja walks to the doorway. All he can see now are black and crimson-clad backs; and Innocent's face in among them, just for an instant, wearing an expression of abject terror.

'This is the correct decision, Donna Olimpia,' says Panciroli, attempting loud, measured reason. 'It has nothing to do with influence, as you claim. Federico Maidalchini is unworthy – you know this better than anyone. He could not remain as Cardinal Nephew. This step is for the good of the Church. It is the will of Almighty God.'

Donna Olimpia snorts. 'The person you have chosen to replace him is inappropriate,' she announces. 'He is deeply, *offensively* inappropriate. He is neither Maidalchini nor Pamphili. How can that . . . that *greased knave* standing there hope to serve as Cardinal Nephew to my brother-in-law?'

'Cardinal Astalli's relation to the pope is quite clear, Donna Olimpia,' Panciroli counters coolly. 'I am sure that you recall bringing about the marriage of your niece Catarina to the cardinal's brother, Tiberio. He is entirely eligible for the position the Holy Father has granted him.'

There is some laughter at this rebuttal, but the widow will not back down or retreat by the slightest amount, launching into a new round of enraged shouts. De Pareja has never witnessed anything like it. The whole spectacle is utterly beyond the protocols of the Alcazar – a woman confronting so many churchmen, and with such savage contempt. He finds it unsettling.

Just as he is debating whether to enter the tumultuous chamber in search of his master, Don Diego appears before him, edging out between two archbishops. He holds the colour box in one hand and the canvases in the other, with the easel gripped under his arm; unused to carrying his own materials, his progress is awkward, to say the least. De Pareja slips his sketching folder back into his satchel and goes to help. He sees that the surfaces of both canvases are gleaming with fresh paint.

'It is done,' says Don Diego, as the dispute behind them reaches a furious crescendo. 'Let us leave this godforsaken place.'

*

Directly upon their return to the Spanish Embassy, Señor Morata, the assistant consul, is sought out to explain the Chinea. He informs Don Diego that it is an annual ceremony staged in the Vatican on the feast day of San Pietro and San Paulo, during which Spain pays her rent for the Kingdom of Naples.

'You mean it isn't ours?' asks Don Diego. 'My understanding was that King Felipe's great-grandfather captured it from the French.'

'That is so, Don Diego,' Morata replies, 'yet the kingdom remains a papal territory. A symbolic remuneration is made in the form of a fine white horse, to be led across the piazza by our king's representative. This year, of course, that honour will fall to his grace the Duke of Infantado. He will take it inside the basilica, as far as the transept, where it will kneel before his holiness the pope.'

'The horse will kneel,' repeats Don Diego doubtfully.

Morata nods, as if this is obvious. 'To serve as a demonstration of Spain's unswerving loyalty. Its reins are then passed to the Cardinal Nephew, and it is added to the Vatican stables.'

De Pareja understands at once. This Chinea ceremony will serve Panciroli and Infantado in multiple ways. It will make a public declaration of Spanish dominion over Naples, of King Felipe's absolute obedience to Rome, and of Astalli's appointment as Cardinal Nephew. And it will also provide the ideal moment for the presentation of a papal portrait from the hand of Felipe's own court painter.

Work begins that same day. Don Diego appears to have overcome his initial objections, or is perhaps determined to dispense with this unwanted duty as swiftly and completely as he can. The oil sketches he made in the Quirinale, the labour of rather less than an hour, are remarkable. One shows the figure upon its throne, taken from three different angles, while the other concentrates on the face. De Pareja grins when he stands before them, for Pope Innocent is *there*. The old man has been captured in a number of strokes that can almost be counted, they have been left so visible. Don Diego has perfectly rendered the drooping nose; the wide, moist mouth, and the wisp of a beard; and those eyes, so small and suspicious, peering out from beneath a knitted brow. De Pareja offers the usual words of praise, which are as insufficient as ever.

Don Diego does not hear him anyway. 'My first impression was correct,' he says. 'The Holy Father told me that he remembered my works from when he served Pope Urban in Madrid. He attempted politeness, but it was plain enough that he did not care for them.'

'Could he not have refused to sit?' de Pareja asks.

Don Diego shakes his head. 'He does not have the nerve, Juan. You saw it just then. He is caught between Panciroli and the widow, like a rag pulled by two dogs. And at present, Panciroli seems to be the stronger.'

De Pareja is instructed to clear the studio of all unnecessary items. He decides to move the other large canvas, the one with the three mysterious curves, into his own chamber. As he walks towards the shadowy corner where it has been propped, however, he sees that the curves are mysterious no longer. Darker tones have been added to both the crimson and blue stripes, forming creases that transform them into fabric – into a curtain and a coverlet. The pearly pink, meanwhile, has undergone a still more profound change. Soft greys have begun to shape a smooth, naked hip, the line of a backbone and a buttock, while a loose, creamy highlight traces the edge of a shoulder blade. Between this partially defined body and the deep red curtain are patches of white, green and black that he realises are discarded clothes: a dress, a shawl, petticoats.

Without another thought, de Pareja grabs the canvas up, carries it to his chamber with all possible speed, and stows it away behind their travelling cases. He stands for moment; then he gathers in two handfuls of his hair and pulls it hard, snarling through gritted teeth.

This is madness.

To find a woman is one thing; it is expected, even, for a man of Don Diego's station, away from home for so many months. To bring her here, though, to admit her into his chambers in this heedless manner, and to paint from her in this way – it almost suggests a desire for self-obliteration. Among the Italians now for nearly a year, Don Diego must imagine himself to be one of them. He has forgotten that he does not share their liberties; that his life in the Alcazar, in the service of King Felipe, must be held to a quite different standard.

De Pareja releases his hair and sits heavily upon his pallet. His scalp smarts painfully; he is out of breath, also, as if from some great physical exertion. He allows a minute or so to pass, listening to some cats yowl and hiss on the rooftops. Then he wipes his face on his sleeve and tells himself firmly that there is nothing to fear. The canvas half-hidden beside him will be abandoned and painted over, or gifted quietly to some Roman gentleman. Don Diego is certainly strange, a master like no other, but he remains a singular blessing, a bridge to a better land, granted by the wisdom of Almighty God. This cannot ever be forgotten or understated.

To restore his equanimity, de Pareja runs through the stages of their plan – how they will perform their duties, both official and clandestine, and return to Spain for their reward; how Don Diego will be admitted to the Order of Santiago and give de Pareja his liberty. And then his life will finally be underway. His youth may be gone – his body beginning to slow and ache, and his hair starting to lose its colour – but he will be a slave no more. He will be able to seek out commissions, and earn, and open a workshop of his own. He will go to Señora Inés at her stall on the Plazula de Santiago, where he has bought cinnabar, lapis and much else for several years now, and say to her: I am free. We would joke about it, do you recall – of how we were both alone and could marry; of how, if I were my own man, we might have a house on this very square, and a clutch of happy children? Well, it is a joke no longer. I am free, Señora Inés. I may do as I please.

De Pareja stands with a grunt, straightens his doublet and smooths down his hair. He just has to keep this end in sight, ensure his wits are about him always, and all will still be well.

*

The portrait proceeds quickly.

A papal mozzetta, rochet and camauro arrive from the Palazzo del Quirinale, sent over by Innocent's major-domo. De Pareja worries that he might be made to wear them, and sit before Don Diego for a second time, despite the differences between his build and that of Pope Innocent; or perhaps to venture out into the city to locate a sufficiently stooped, fragile old man. But Don Diego barely notices the major-domo's parcel. He already has everything he needs.

Word goes around the embassy that the gentleman in the uppermost guest apartment, previously of little interest, is painting the Holy Father. De Pareja finds himself questioned in the kitchens and corridors, or asked to verify the stories that have started to circulate. Is his master having to paint entirely from memory, the pope having refused to let him work in the Quirinale – being too afraid that his paints might be poisoned somehow and taint the air? Did Donna Olimpia really stand behind him throughout his audience, dagger in hand, lest he prove an assassin? De Pareja offers neither confirmation nor denial.

The city outside is changing at a similar pace. Amid much clerical pomp, Cardinal Astalli is formally installed at the pope's side. Her complaints disregarded, Donna Olimpia has locked herself away in her grand palazzo on the Piazza Navona, seeking to torture her brother-in-law's conscience with a display of distress. It seems unlikely to succeed; de Pareja hears that even this palazzo is in actuality hers no longer. Pope Innocent — advised by the Curia, and his secretary of state Cardinal Panciroli in particular — has gifted it to the new Cardinal Nephew, to serve as his Roman seat. All that remains is for him to take possession.

Early one morning, a second shipment arrives from Naples — far smaller, brought in by a courier rather than a line of oxcarts. De Pareja goes down to the cellar to discover three slender boxes, each containing an ancient figurine cast in bronze: a nymph, a wrestler, and a minor goddess he can't identify. The last of these has a hollow base, within which are several ciphered sheets, folded into small squares. De Pareja takes them over to the Mars with Helmet and Sword, to which he returned the other documents, it having seemed altogether too dangerous to keep them upstairs. In barely a minute he has removed the putty, added the new papers, and sealed the little statue up again.

He heads straight back up towards the apartment. Since Pope Innocent's turbulent sitting, he has begun a new sketch of the scarred sister, this time painted in oils upon a scrap of leftover canvas, and is keen to return to it. He is so immersed in thoughts of this sketch that he doesn't notice Flaminia Triunfi until she is a half dozen steps in front of him. She is on her way out of the building. In one hand she holds her shoes, which are quite plain and hard wearing, along with a gauzy black shawl and a simple black hat; while the other pinches up the hem of her bottle-green gown, revealing stockinged feet bruised with dirt. Her hair is tied back, and her fine dark eyes are looking directly ahead. She is unsurprised to meet him, and smiles with apparent friendliness. De Pareja hasn't seen her for a week or more and assumed that Don Diego must have ordered her away, so that he could concentrate upon the portrait. But evidently not.

Rather to his consternation, she comes to a halt and inquires about the statues — exemplary pieces, Don Diego has told her, pagan glories from the greatest days of Rome.

'I am sure he will show them to you if you ask,' de Pareja says.

Flaminia sits to slip on her shoes. They are on the rear staircase, which is dim and narrow; he cannot get past without specifically requesting her to move aside, something he is not wholly sure he has leave to do. A silence grows between them. Spanish voices can be heard below — clerks arriving for the day's labour. Part of de Pareja hopes that they will be spotted, interrupted, despite the trouble this might bring.

'Do you not hate them?' she says.

De Pareja hesitates. 'Signorina?'

Flaminia gestures at the embassy. 'These people. Your masters. These *knights*. That pig of an ambassador. Diego tells me how things are in Spain — what was done to the Moriscos. How they made your people choose between expulsion or enslavement.'

A slight crease appears in de Pareja's brow, for this question seems to throw a new light upon Flaminia Triunfi. She is someone who would contest the authority of princes and knock the hats off priests — who chooses to live outside the bounds of convention, and imagines that he must as well, in his thoughts at least. He notes that 'Diego' also, and the sympathies she implies. When telling this woman of his life in Madrid, his master — as a courtier and aspirant nobleman, and close friend of the Spanish king — has plainly made some careful omissions.

'I was hardly born then, signorina,' he replies. 'I serve Don Diego, that is all.'

She nods, as if acknowledging his refusal to answer, and looks down at her hat. 'He says that you paint also. That you are an excellent painter. That he means to free you as soon as he is able, so you might take on your own work. Start a shop, even.'

Here, de Pareja catches something quite different in her voice: a trace of envy. 'I have always painted,' he says, a shade more softly. 'It is my profession.'

Flaminia looks at him again and de Pareja could swear that there is fellow feeling in her eyes. She rises from the steps, angling herself so that her back is against the wall, the whitewash reflecting a little of the green in her gown.

'Show me your works,' she says. 'Your latest pieces. I would very much like to see them.'

De Pareja blinks, beset by contradictory feelings. He is irritated, profoundly so: Flamina should leave the Piazza Trinita straight away, where one glimpse of her could do so much damage. But he finds that he is also oddly eager to grant her request. Perhaps her reaction will confirm his growing sense that this oil sketch represents a new standard in his art, worthy of an independent painter. Of a free man.

He clears his throat. 'Don Diego requires that I—'

Flaminia is shaking her head. '*Don Diego* is already occupied completely with his pope. I mean no offence, señor, but he would not notice if you spent the day down in the lanes, playing at *pallacorda*.'

This is undeniable; his sense of art now fully reawakened, Don

Diego has taken to rising before dawn and working until the sun has all but set. De Pareja reasons that showing Flaminia the sketch will actually be the quickest way to get her off the staircase and out of sight. He can detect nothing false in her even, intelligent features, no mockery or anything like it; and God help him if he does not feel his soul unfurl a little before her interest. He nods.

They go back up to the apartment. De Pareja thinks that she will wait for him in the reception room while he fetches the sketch, but she follows him along the corridor to his chamber, stopping in the doorway to survey the cramped, dingy interior. If she spots the long canvas tucked behind the travelling cases, and the stretch of her own naked thigh that is clearly visible upon it, she gives no indication.

By now, de Pareja is too concerned with the oil sketch to be alarmed by any of this. He has pinned it to a board and propped it atop a crate just across from his pallet, so that he is forced to consider it numerous times a day and become thoroughly acquainted with its shortcomings. When he looks at it now, though – viewing it, he supposes, as Flaminia might – he is genuinely struck by its quality. The image has a shock to it, a vividness, a true holy presence. It shows him at his best.

De Pareja turns to indicate the sketch to Flaminia, but she has seen it already. Her air of honest, amiable attention has disappeared. She is locked in place, the colour draining from her cheeks, staring at the little painting with horrified amazement. It is not the response de Pareja was hoping for.

'Signorina,' he says uncertainly, 'are you—'

'Where did you see her?'

'I beg your pardon?'

Flamina makes a sharp *tsking* sound, then steps forward into the room and points to the Benedictine's face. 'This nun here. Where did you see her? Was it in Rome?'

De Pareja realises that something else is afoot: a matter that involves his subject, rather than his rendition of her. Flaminia is angry, deeply perplexed, very close to tears, and trying hard to contain it all.

'Upon the Corso,' he says. 'A few weeks ago.'

'And have you seen her since? Have you had her pose for you?'

De Pareja has thought of this, of course: a formal offer, with scudi loaned somehow from Don Diego, and sittings wherever the nun is housed. He has watched out for her avidly, every time he has left the embassy, and especially while close to the procession route. But although he has heard others talk of her on many occasions – the scarred sister, with her holy sight and endless litany of sacred truths – he has seen nothing.

'I have not,' he says. 'I came upon her by chance, and only for a minute. Yet I . . . I felt the Lord's hand, signorina. I do not know if—'

De Pareja stops, for Flaminia has gone. She has left the storeroom and is walking rapidly along the corridor. A moment later, the apartment's door slams behind her.

*

On the morning of the Chinea, de Pareja is dispatched to the Vatican with the completed papal portrait, to set it in place ahead of the formal presentation. He arrives early in a small cart with two of Infantado's soldiers; one of them helps him carry the canvas, which has been magnificently framed and wrapped in a length of heavy purple velvet, while the other hefts the larger easel onto his shoulder as if it were the stand for a swivel gun. A steward leads them through a series of musty halls and up a wide, vaulted stairway. De Pareja has never been inside the Vatican before, and he looks around with interest. It is said that this ancient palace of the popes hums with disease in the summer months, due to its low elevation. Innocent has long since abandoned it for the clean air of the Quirinal hill, returning only to perform his ceremonial duties. There is an air of absence, of emptiness; of great grandeur slowly gathering dust and mould.

The presentation is to occur in an octagonal atrium clad in red marble. The steward points out a place; they erect the easel and set the covered portrait upon it. De Pareja then loosens the velvet shroud and lifts it for a final check. The varnish is intact, thankfully, the smooth, liquid surface undisturbed; he applied the second coat after the Vesper bell, and then walked up and down with the canvas for over an hour, to hasten its drying. It is faintly unnerving to be this close to the painting, his face only inches from its surface, the eye of the wary old man on the throne seeming almost to seek his own.

De Pareja hears the drumming and fanfares of a large procession. The Chinea is about to begin. He lowers the sheet again and follows the soldiers to a nearby corridor, where a narrow balcony provides a view of the square before the basilica. Carriages are pulling up in orderly lines, a dazzling panoply of Habsburg flags flying from their roofs. A contingent of Spanish cavalry appears, its spears raised and breastplates glittering; an unseen officer shouts a command and the soldiers move to seal off the square, holding back the great crush of Rome. The carriages continue to arrive, dozens and dozens of them, forming a total that is surely in the hundreds. De Pareja has seen a good deal of royal spectacle at the Alcazar, but there is a splendour and scale to all this that his mind can scarcely encompass.

The Duke of Infantado walks out in front, the feather on his hat like a creamy curl of paint. A groom comes behind him, leading the tribute: a mare of absolute, unmixed white, shining against the tumult of colours around her. She tosses her head and steps from side to side, unsettled by the music, the numbers, and the many strange smells. Infantado goes over to calm her, taking hold of her bridle and patting her neck. The rest of the Spanish company begins to climb from their carriages; Don Diego is prominent among them, walking stiffly in his stitched-up golilla.

Cardinal Camillo Astalli and a retinue of deacons emerge from the cathedral doors and make some inaudible proclamation. Infantado bows low, crosses himself and offers a response; then he presents the white mare's reins to the new Cardinal Nephew, thus settling Spain's account for another year of rule over Naples. Astalli accepts the horse with noticeable uncertainty. After a short prayer, he begins to lead the assembled Spaniards inside San Pietro to meet with the pope, the tribute tottering a little beside him as she mounts the steps.

The two soldiers on the balcony are discussing the chances that the mare will pull off the kneeling trick that the Chinea ritual demands of her. 'Not a hope,' opines one. 'Look at her twitching there. She's more likely to shit on the Holy Father's slippers.'

A special Mass is to be said, once the kneeling has occurred; de Pareja estimates that the papal party will not arrive in the atrium for the better part of an hour. He heads back inside, finds a shallow alcove out of the soldiers' sight, and takes his drawing folder from his satchel. His intention is to make detailed sketches of certain parts of the composition – the nun's head, her clasped hands, the knot of her rope belt – but instead he loses many minutes simply staring at the drawings he has already made. Flaminia's reaction to the oil sketch has disturbed his sense of the scarred sister. Before that morning she was something removed, not quite real, almost holy in herself. Now, though, he cannot help thinking of her mortal circumstances. How did she come to leave her confinement? Does she wish to go back? What precisely was her relation to those two women – the ones who had demanded money from him? He has no answers.

Three dozen intermingled footfalls herald the approach of the papal party. As de Pareja hurries to put away his sketching folder, they enter the atrium and fan out around the easel, arranging themselves according to rank. An air of triumph prevails; the Chinea has proved a success, it seems, with the white mare defying the soldier's prediction and making the necessary display of equine reverence. Even Don Diego shows every sign of being pleased. De Pareja knows that his master does not savour these moments. He is satisfied with his work, however: he has done what was asked of him, he has done it surpassingly well, and advancement will surely follow.

The one inharmonious note in this scene is the Holy Father himself. Pope Innocent has the look of a man undertaking a painful obligation; he seems as reluctant to view the portrait as he was to sit for it in the first place. He appears distracted also, and extremely tired. De Pareja guesses that Donna Olimpia is the cause. It is rumoured that after a few days barricaded inside the Palazzo Pamphili, claiming life-threatening illness, she has now fled the city – behaviour no doubt engineered to cause Innocent the largest measure of suffering.

The Duke of Infantado quickly places himself at the centre of things, making an address along the expected lines, praising Don Diego's genius and stressing the unbreakable bond between Spain and Rome. Then he draws back the velvet sheet with a flourish, letting it cascade onto the floor.

First, there is a collective intake of breath, and a couple of seconds of stunned silence; then words of prayer, and a stifled laugh or two; and then a great torrent of superlatives, spoken with increasing volume and conviction, the viewers competing with one another to make the most resounding declarations of praise.

'The likeness is a marvel. A *marvel*. Holy saints, the presence of that stare!'

'Indeed yes, the pure power of it! Praise God, it is *wondrous*!'

'This is the Lord's work, brothers – the Lord's glorious work!'

De Pareja shifts slightly to the side, so that he too may consider the finished portrait. Here in the cool light of the atrium, it is the strength and subtlety of the colours that strike him with the most force. The scarlet and ripe vermillion of the walls behind; the greens, greys and yellows in the shadows of the white papal robe; the pinkish sheen of the satin mozzetta, light crackling across the fabric where it falls to the Holy Father's lap. These are pigments he himself prepared: minerals and oil, refined and distilled, mulled and sieved and mixed together. That his master can employ them to fashion an image so like life itself, held there on a rectangle of cloth, removed forever from the flow of time, never fails to stir something in de Pareja's soul. It is like holiness, as all these excited prelates are saying.

Once the initial effect has been absorbed, the party turns to the painting's subject, wishing to gauge his reaction. The pope's discomfort has only increased; it is so obvious and acute that de Pareja feels a pang of pity. Innocent's small eyes blink uneasily beneath his jewelled mitre; his protuberant ears throb beetroot red. The silence around him lengthens, growing almost palpable in its heaviness.

'Too true, señor,' he says at last. 'Too true.'

The company lets out a low, obsequious laugh, before resuming its admiration of the portrait. Innocent's subdued response has brought about a change, however, very slight but irreversible. The private misgivings that these men harbour about Giambattista Pamphili — the weakness of his nature, the extraordinary corruption he has allowed, the influence granted to his demonic sister-in-law — are there with them now, collecting above their heads like a light mist.

De Pareja finds himself looking at the portrait anew, and he detects what he saw in his own likeness, back among the columns of the Rotonda: a face that asserts one thing, one set of qualities, and yet also suggests its opposite. Pope Innocent is enthroned, with the Fisherman's Ring upon his finger, a man of stern, watchful power, taking the measure of whoever stands before him; and at the same time he is aged, faltering, the hand that wears this ring hanging limply over the arm of his throne. There is distrust in his eyes — a trace of fear, even, that spreads through his large, unlovely features. This is a man who has come to doubt everything and everyone. Who feels that he is alone.

Cardinal Panciroli takes charge. Whether he senses this awkwardness or not, he pushes the proceedings onwards, proclaiming Don Diego's work a miracle of art, a gift from the Divine, for which he must be rewarded. The pope is still regarding the portrait with something akin to dread. He does not register the cardinal's prompt until a servant arrives beside him, bearing a velvet cushion. Brought back to the present, he summons Don Diego over and has him kneel, then takes a gold medallion and chain from the cushion and hangs it around his neck. It clinks softly, glinting in the light; Don Diego retreats with a deep bow.

Panciroli is not finished. 'Most noble and pious friends,' he says, 'there is more. A gesture is to be made — a recognition of what we have celebrated today, with our Chinea and now this . . . *astounding* display of God-given genius.'

He looks to the pope, so that he can make a rehearsed announcement — but Innocent is done, quite worn out and barely interested. He waves a hand, giving his secretary of state leave to continue. Panciroli is only too glad to oblige; this is a man enamoured by authority, thinks de Pareja, who pictures himself sitting upon that papal throne before too long.

'As the noble Duke of Infantado returns Spain to Rome in the truest sense,' the cardinal declares, 'as she is restored as the Holy See's best and most loyal servant, so Rome shall allocate her a permanent berth. It has been decided that the square of Santa Trinita shall be renamed for her. From this day forth, it shall be the Piazza di Spagna; and with God's will, it shall be hers forever.'

This is news, and evidently a surprise to all but the innermost circle. The company hesitates, unsure what to do; to offer congratulations, to cheer, to applaud? Infantado steps forward, going before the pope as if overwhelmed. He hesitates, then sweeps off his hat and drops to his knees. At once, every Spaniard follows suit, with the Italians joining them a second later; and together, led by the duke, they offer up a prayer of thanks.

Sorores

The signal comes in the middle of the morning, within an hour of the Terce bell. Orsola takes a breath, trying to ignore the flat, nauseous feeling that fills her insides. Marco Moretti, the nearest Castro had to a tailor, has appeared at the end of a street; today he is clad as San Paulo, with a bristling black beard, and is waving a pasteboard sword above his head.

The rumours are true. After several weeks holed up in her palazzo, Donna Olimpia is leaving Rome, using the feast of San Pietro and San Paulo as cover for her withdrawal. Orsola has heard that a group of scheming, jealous cardinals has turned Pope Innocent against her, disposing of her own Cardinal Nephew and setting up a pretender in his place. Out on the Piazza Navona, there was disagreement among the widow's admirers as to whether she was fleeing into exile, fearing imprisonment and death, or if she was departing in a state of lofty disdain, having refused to bend her knee to her enemies. One thing seemed certain, however: she would be heading for that town of hers, San Martino, in a procession of carriages loaded with all the portable treasures they could contain.

Orsola nods to Lontra; together, they curtail Serafina's sermon, disperse her audience and get her back to her feet, covering her habit with a cloak. That morning, influenced by the feast day, she has mostly been telling the sorry tale of Ananias, a follower of San Pietro, who pledged to give all his gold to the new church but secretly kept a portion back for himself. She accepts the interruption readily enough, believing that they are to continue with their penitential circuit. Serafina seems content to circle Rome endlessly; Orsola does not know how many laps they have completed by now, but it surely exceeds that asked of the very gravest of sinners.

They are at the midpoint of the Corso, in a corner of the Piazza Colonna. In preparation for the feast, the ancient pagan column that stands in the centre of the square has been generously draped with flower garlands, obscuring many of the dozens of tiny carved figures that wind around its surface. Tables are being dragged out beneath sagging, sun-bleached awnings as shops and tavernas open up, while musicians sit in small groups, cleaning and tuning their instruments. All around, the austere faces of San Pietro and San Paulo stare down from the walls, the first brandishing his keys, the second his holy book and the sword of his martyrdom. It is set to be another day of great colour and noise; of merriment and thanksgiving, and astonishing sights; of violence, fornication and death. A day of the Holy Jubilee.

Their plan is simple. Tullio Botta and his comrades have fanned out through the streets and alleys to the north-east of the Piazza Navona. They will track Donna Olimpia's carriages, discerning the route she is taking to the city wall, and will then alert Orsola so that she can place Sister Serafina in the widow's path. The coachmen of noble families are renowned for driving at almost anyone, not much caring who might be trampled beneath their horses' hooves. A nun, though – a choir nun in the black habit, with her face so scarred – that will urge them to stop. On this, Orsola, Tullio and the rest of them are agreed.

The three women move past the garlanded column and look into the street where Marco was just standing; he's now a couple of blocks away, pointing off to the left.

'It's working,' says Orsola, quickening their pace. 'Come on.'

'They mean to kill her,' says Lontra matter-of-factly. 'You realise that, sister, don't you?'

Orsola rolls her eyes; of course she does. On that first afternoon, after a cup or two of wine, Tullio stated plainly that his aim was to cut Pimpaccia down, followed by her entire accursed family. The daughters and their fat, worthless husbands. The son in exile – an oaf so debauched, so devoid of shame, that he had been obliged to hand back his cardinal's hat. The many pampered nephews and nieces, none of them good for anything whatsoever. Even the granddaughter, Olimpiuccia, who Pimpaccia loves so much that she removed the girl from her parents and had her raised in her own palazzo.

Orsola baulked at this last part. 'You would really kill a child?'

'How many of our children did she have killed, Gina?' Tullio replied. 'They all must die. *All* of them. It is the only way to make it right.'

He insisted upon bringing Orsola and Serafina to his camp, out among the pilgrims in the sprawling ruins of Celio. It was less comfortable than the grain loft, and a good deal less safe. The most wretched, debased people hid themselves among the rubble and bushes, scuttling between hiding places like crabs on a riverbed, while dogs roamed in ragged, starving packs, their eyes gleaming in the firelight. Tullio promised to watch over the nuns, but Orsola soon saw that he and his band were not to be relied upon in any way. They were reckless, always boasting and picking fights, acting as if they held a bitter grudge against anyone who crossed their path. It was clear enough, however, that their deepest hatred was for themselves. They spoke ceaselessly about retribution, about justice and bloodshed, but never about escape, or what might come afterwards. Orsola began to suspect that they longed for their own destruction, as only this would release them from the shame of their defeat. Lying in the dark nook she'd claimed for Serafina and herself, listening to them rant, curse and sob, she'd decided upon a scheme of her own.

The first step was to broker some form of peace with Lontra. It could not be denied that she'd failed them in that pear orchard, abandoning them to the Inquisition – to the Tor di Nona and whatever horrors lay within it – but who else in Rome could Orsola turn to? A few days after the end of Holy Week, she went at dawn to the stoop of the grain warehouse. After an hour or so, Lontra emerged dressed as a serpent, with a trailing, scaly tail and a forked tongue poking from between her lips. Predictably, she didn't think she had anything to apologise for.

'We each look out for ourselves,' she said. 'That's just how it is, sister.'

Orsola had readied herself for this. She said that she understood, and sought to place no blame; and then she spelled out her new circumstances, so strange and unanticipated, and what she was planning to make of them.

At first, Lontra was appalled. She declared that Orsola's scheme was madly dangerous, almost certain to fail, and absolutely not worth the dire risks involved. But it quickly became apparent that the streets of Rome were beginning to turn against her. The Inquisition had captured three of her friends during Easter, she revealed; another had died in a brawl, while a fifth had been found drowned on the riverbank, having been the victim of a brutal violation. So when Orsola talked of magnificent plunder, of jewels and chests filled with coin, of riches so plentiful that their lives could be started over again, she listened despite herself; and before very long she had reassessed her reservations and found them to be not so insurmountable as she had thought.

Briefly, Orsola worried that the pear orchard might have changed everything; that Serafina would reject Lontra as a false-hearted betrayer, or the like; that their damaged partnership simply couldn't work any more. Yet this was not the case. Serafina did not react to Lontra's reappearance at all; and once they were out again among the perils of the city, walking the procession route and gathering their coins, everything felt much the same. Orsola was encouraged. God knew her heart. He was surely indicating His consent for what lay ahead.

'Donna Olimpia is safe enough,' she says now, as the three of them follow after Marco. 'Tullio and the others might have seen death, but they aren't killers.' She lets out a hollow laugh. 'The widow's army didn't give them the chance.'

Lontra is unconvinced. 'This isn't soldiers on a battlefield, sister. It's an old woman – someone they hate, sitting there helplessly in front of them. It could happen so easily.'

Since their reconciliation, Lontra has encountered Tullio a few times about the city, and whatever kinship she feels for Orsola she most definitely does not feel for him. As a condition of her further involvement, she made Orsola promise never to bring him or his comrades anywhere near the grain loft, seeming to think that they would move in and take over, and that a rare haven would be lost.

'You just don't like them, that's all,' Orsola tells her.

'And you don't know them like you think you do, Sister Orsola. These are men. Their pride and lust will drive them to the darkest, wickedest places.'

'Holy Madonna,' Orsola murmurs. 'You sound like the Mother Abbess.'

The scene has been rehearsed in Orsola's mind a hundred times over, and in such detail that occasionally, upon waking, she thinks for an instant that it has already occurred. The lead carriage will stop, and Donna Olimpia herself will lean out of its door. Orsola hasn't ever seen her before; she pictures a round, jowly creature, rather like a mole, softened by fine living. She will sprint ahead of Tullio and the rest, as if eager for her own vengeance, and shove Donna Olimpia back inside. Working fast, she will remove the widow's rings and rosary, along with any necklaces, earrings or bracelets. Lontra will be there by then, rushing into the cabin – and together they will claim a good share of whatever riches Donna Olimpia is bearing away with her into exile.

It will all take a matter of seconds. The widow will make spluttering protests, appealing to the saints and the Holy Virgin – but they will be gone, out and off, vanishing into the alleyways. Tullio will be advancing on the carriage with his blade drawn, set on slaughter. By then, though, the alarm will have been raised. The Corsican Guard, charged with keeping order in the city, will be approaching at speed, along with any number of others. Chaos will follow, that much is certain; while they escape across Rome unnoticed, with enough wealth to go wherever they choose.

Orsola finds an unexpected excitement in all this deviousness. It is so very satisfying to use these men as they think they are using her; to recruit Lontra, and tell her how things will proceed; to dream of her atonement, and the dizzying sweetness of true freedom. Obviously, she is aware that it is wrong. There will be theft, and quite possibly bloodshed as well. The nuns go to morning Mass each day, in the church of Santa Maria in Monticelli, and they pray in every basilica of the penitential procession. Kneeling beside Serafina, Orsola has waited for God to order her to desist – to indicate His displeasure, or an alternative path. But He does not. He knows that her aim is to remove Serafina from Rome, to a place of holy sanctuary. To wash away the great sin of her life, and see her daughter guided from the grey hill. And He has surely brought about this change in her so that she will be able to achieve it.

They leave the Piazza Colonna, skirting a gaggle of street women who are spilling out of a back-alley brothel, left bruised and haggard by the night's business. Orsola avoids their gaze, knowing that offence can rapidly be taken, and that confrontation is common indeed; the women barely notice her, though, laughing at a salacious joke as they pass around a taper to light their pipes.

'This is not the way to the Maggiore,' says Serafina. 'We must get to the Maggiore, sister, with all haste.'

'We need to stop somewhere first,' Orsola replies. 'Only for a minute. Tell me of Ananias, as you were back on the Corso.'

Such crude distraction does not always work, but that morning Serafina begins to talk at once. She picks up her tale at the same point, when the shameful Ananias came before San Pietro in the marketplace and laid the incomplete sum at the holy apostle's feet.

'Pietro looked at him and said, "You have sold your clothes, and those of your wife. You have sold your fine house; your carpets and spoons and lamps. But Ananias, it is for naught. It is for naught."'

They follow Marco past a large palazzo, its sealed-up façade bright with flags, and along a short, broad street. He exchanges a series of whistles and gestures with a distant comrade, and directs them into an alley. A shadowy hush falls as they move away from the main thoroughfares. The rancid smell of Rome grows closer, more full-blown; flies descend in clouds, clustering around eyes and at the edges of lips; rats wriggle messily through the grates of clogged drains.

Lontra is becoming ever more tense, chewing her thumbnail;

she is escorting Serafina like she has her under arrest. 'You're sure there'll be riches?' she says. 'Jewels and coin?'

Orsola sucks her teeth in annoyance, for they have been over this at length. A reversal of sorts has occurred since the events of Easter Saturday: she now leads while Lontra hurries to keep up, filled with foolish questions and miscomprehension. It is good, she supposes, for addressing Lontra's fears does serve to keep her own in abeyance.

'The widow is leaving Rome,' she says. 'Leaving her palazzo. She'll be taking all of her most precious things, along with enough gold scudi to fill a cider press. You'll see.'

Tullio is waiting at the mouth of a quiet, crumbling lane. He is dressed as San Pietro in flowing robes of blue and yellow, his beard and hair greyed with chalk-dust and two rusty, mismatched keys in his hands. When he sees them, he tosses these keys into a gutter, draws out a dirty knife, and whistles to a handful of his fellows, who have just come around the lane's far end.

'We'll do it here,' he says to Orsola, nodding to a spot about ten yards from where they are standing. 'Get your sister ready. She'll be on us at any moment.' He tries to smile, but there is wild terror in his eyes. 'This is it, Gina. God willing, this is it.'

The scene is not how Orsola imagined it at all. The lane itself is far too narrow; furthermore, the men of Castro are hiding themselves uncomfortably close to where the lead carriage will stop. She'd pictured them running up behind, having to get past the other vehicles in the procession, allowing her and Lontra to reach Donna Olimpia first. But these men could be at the cabin almost immediately. Everything would be ruined.

Orsola's stomach suddenly hollows out, and an odd coldness creeps up her arms and back. She opens her mouth to say something to Tullio but he's already marching off down the lane, issuing last-minute instructions; then he pushes his way into a small butcher's shop and conceals himself behind a row of plucked, dangling chickens.

Lontra has seen the problem as well. 'We should go,' she mutters. 'It can't be done. Sister, we should go right now.'

'No,' Orsola says. 'God is with us. We just need to be quick.'

'Quick?' Lontra repeats. 'Orsola, it won't matter how damn quick we are when—'

'This is wrong,' states Sister Serafina loudly. 'We are not going to the Maggiore. We are not performing our penance.' She works her elbows, trying to throw them off. 'This . . . is *wrong*.'

'What of . . . what of Ananias?' Orsola asks, wrestling to contain her. 'What of him, Sister? Tell me what happened. Tell me . . . tell me God's truth.'

But Serafina will not have it this time. She begins to fight with real passion, flailing those long limbs. After a few seconds, Orsola is thumped hard on the lip, her head jerking back; she feels a flare of anger, her own fist clenching.

'Ananias,' she gasps, as she struggles to repress it. 'What happened when—'

'*You* are Ananias!' Serafina shouts in her face. 'Satan has . . . has filled your heart with his diabolical ichor! You have lied to the Holy Spirit, you have lied to Almighty God! And like Ananias, the Lord will strike you down where you stand!'

Teeth bared, she stamps on Orsola's big toe with the bone of her heel. There is a distinct snapping sensation and a blinding burst of pain. Orsola doubles over with a curse, while Serafina slips from beneath her cloak and lunges off down the lane. Lontra gives chase, reaching out to stop her – but just as she is about to grab at the black Benedictine habit, two fine chestnut horses round the corner at the lane's end. They are moving at a swift trot, with two more yoked behind; and then comes Donna Olimpia's dark blue carriage, the very same one Orsola saw on her first day in Rome.

The enormous vehicle only just fits onto the thoroughfare. It speeds up further, rushing relentlessly along the lane towards them, the horses' hooves pounding out an accelerating rhythm upon the stones. The sight makes Serafina stumble to the ground, directly in its path, where she gapes at the approaching carriage as if stupefied. *We were wrong,* thinks Orsola. *It will run straight over her, over all of us. Donna Olimpia will stop for nothing.*

But no – it seems that Sister Serafina had simply not yet been seen. Spying her, the coachman pulls sharply on the reins and calls to the horses; and over the space of a few awful yards, the beasts slow and snort, their bridles jangling, and the carriage draws to a dusty halt.

Orsola's split lip throbs, a hot bead of blood running down her chin. She stares at the carriage and the chestnut horses, and the choir nun kneeling such a very short distance before them. She cannot move or breathe. Everything is held in a strange suspension.

Lontra has returned to her side. 'There's only one,' she says.

'What?'

'Donna Olimpia always travels with three carriages, sister – three carriages *at least*. But there's only one. And no guards or footmen neither. Just that coachman.'

Orsola looks more closely. This man is wearing a leather jerkin, rather like a soldier's. He has short, disordered hair and a wide, thin-lipped mouth, and seems to be missing part of his nose. Setting the reins aside, he leans back in his seat and folds his thick arms. He is watching them carefully, but does not speak. He appears to be waiting for something.

'She's trying to leave in secret,' Orsola guesses. 'Without anyone noticing.'

'Then why the fine blue carriage?' Lontra asks. 'Everyone in Rome knows it. Why—'

The men of Castro emerge from their hiding places, dressed as apostles, angels and lepers. One takes hold of the lead horse's bridle; another points a blade at the coachman, who raises his hands with only the faintest semblance of alarm. Tullio exits the butcher's shop, his face set in a resolute frown. Forgetting her burning toe, Orsola charges forward along the lane, past Serafina and the team of chestnut horses, thinking only of getting to Donna Olimpia before he does. As she reaches him, he is already gripping the golden door handle and wrenching open the smart blue door; so she braces herself, barges him aside, and darts up the steps into the carriage.

The shutters are closed, creating a darkness so deep and still it takes Orsola a couple of breathless seconds to understand that the cabin is completely empty. She catches a whiff of stale perfume, mixed with something cloyingly sweet. Her mind seems to slacken; she blinks and swears, her voice a terrified croak.

'The . . . the widow isn't here!' yells Tullio, somewhere behind her. 'It's a *trap!*'

Horses are arriving outside, a good number of them, to cries of warning from the men of Castro. Orsola glances down at the green velvet upholstery, trimmed with gold so rich it glows softly in the low light – and she thinks momentarily of staying in there, of hiding out beneath the cushions and blocking up the doors.

There is a loud bang beside her, like a gate slamming in the wind. She starts hard, then sees that a crossbow bolt has punched through the back of the carriage, its diamond-shaped tip protruding only inches from her arm. A scream follows, and the scrabble of panicked footsteps; Tullio calls out names, trying to give orders; and abruptly Orsola is outside again, the lane seeming bright after the shuttered cabin, rushing back towards the front of the carriage. Towards Serafina.

A thunderclap sounds, so startling and close that she nearly trips over her own feet. She looks up. The coachman has taken a pair of pistols from beneath his seat and unloaded one into the side of Tullio's head at three yards' range; he is splayed out on the ground, his body juddering, blood spattered on the cobbles around him and soaking his chalk-powdered hair. His killer, meanwhile, is standing up to look around the carriage, calmly selecting his next target.

For a second, Orsola thinks that she's going to be sick; that she'll start screaming and be unable ever to stop. Instead, she covers her head with her arms, crouches low and forces herself onwards. Ahead, through a thickening veil of pale, gritty dust, she sees five or six horsemen armed with crossbows, blocking off the lane. A San Paulo – Marco Moretti, Castro's almost-tailor – lies face-down before them, arms neatly by his sides, two bolts jutting from his back.

Sister Serafina has not moved but is quivering with an uncontrollable tension, growling wrathfully under her breath. She pulls away from Orsola's touch, raising her hand, the silver rosary wound around her palm and fingers like a bramble. Orsola looks along the lane. Lontra has vanished as utterly as if she'd been lifted straight up to heaven. Despite everything, Orsola wants to laugh; Lontra is consistent, at least.

There are horsemen behind the carriage as well, sealing off the other end of the lane, trapping the men of Castro as they'd meant to trap Donna Olimpia. Several of them are dismounting, drawing swords and swinging them in tight loops, to limber themselves up. Tullio's comrades are caught between defiance and crazed panic. A few are rattling on tenement doors or hammering against shuttered windows, searching vainly for a way out. Two of them go for the coachman; he kicks one in the face and shoots the other through the eye, grinning as he does so.

Serafina clamps her hands over her ears. 'Demons will come,' she moans. 'Oh, demons will come as they came for the soul of Ananias. I see one with the head of a dragonfly. The horns of a bull. A trident . . . a rusted trident . . . a . . .'

Orsola leans in closer, her cheek brushing against Serafina's shoulder. 'Sister,' she says, 'we have to go. We have to leave this place. We have to . . .'

Her voice trails off. It is pointless; there can be no escape here. This trap they have sprung is far better made than their own. No last-minute reprieve is coming; no unforeseen disturbance that will allow them to slip away, as it had done in the pear orchard. The men of Castro are readying their weapons, attempting to rally. They cry out curses and promises of revenge, urging their enemies to attack.

What follows cannot properly be called a fight. For all their bravado, these last men of Castro are killed in moments, landing not a single blow between them. Their executioners are dressed like grooms or gardeners, but it is clear that they are well used to this work. Their movements are direct and efficient. They do not speak a word.

We are to die, Orsola thinks. *We are to die here and now.*

She wraps her arms around Serafina, hunching over her as if they were caught in a gale. This meets with no resistance; sensing the danger as well, the choir nun seems to shrink inside Orsola's embrace, her recitation becoming a breathless whisper.

'The next demon had the snout of a . . . a shrew, with teeth like poisoned needles, the wings of a beetle, and the hairy limbs of a . . .'

A final man of Castro is dragged from the butcher's shop in which Tullio hid himself: a ragged, one-winged angel, around Orsola's own age, who is cursing his foes viciously even as they push him to his knees. Before Orsola can look away, one of the horsemen angles his sword with a practised swivel of the wrist and pushes it deep into the base of the angel's neck, driving the blade through his collarbone and into his heart. He dies immediately, his eyes wiped blank; the sword is withdrawn and he topples forward, his insensible head cracking against the stone.

The coachman jumps down to join his fellows, and they all turn towards Orsola and Serafina. Fear roars in Orsola's ears, seeming to press upon her back with excruciating force. She thinks of her life and the vital task she has left undone. Her daughter's last hope for salvation has surely been wasted through her rashness and sore lack of judgement. For it is clear now that she was gravely mistaken. Almighty God has not been helping her, or approving of her course. Perceiving her sin, He has left her to become lost; to falter, and fail, and meet her end. And her blameless child will stay in the Limbo of the Infants until the end of time.

'There's the scarred nun,' says the coachman. 'The prince's information was sound.'

'Who's the other one?'

'Some whore. Here, give me your blade. I'll see to her.'

Orsola watches dazedly as a sword is passed over and whipped from side to side to shake off the angel's blood. Then the coachman comes up to them, drags her apart from Serafina and casts her into the gutter. One of the others attempts to take hold of the choir nun's arm. Jerking away from him, she falls onto all fours and emits a shriek that is piercing enough to startle the horses, even after the pistol shots and screams.

The coachman seizes a handful of Orsola's hair, twisting it

violently to pin her in place. He draws back his sword arm, squinting in concentration as he aims for her throat. Grasping at his wrist, she is about to beg for her life – when suddenly she realises the importance of what was just said.

'I . . . I am a nun,' she gasps. 'I am a nun also. Please, signor. I swear by our Holy Lady. I am a nun of the Benedictine order, like my sister there.' She begins to pray as loudly and quickly as she can, reciting the only Latin she has ever been able to commit to memory. '*Ave Maria, gratia plena, Dominus tecum. Benedicta tu in muli . . . in mulieribus, et Benedictus ventris tui . . .*'

This is enough to give the coachman pause. Keeping the sword raised, he turns to his comrades, who are forming a loose circle around Serafina. One rushes forward with his arms outstretched, as if to scoop her up – and gets punched squarely in the face, knocking him away again. Another comes at her from the opposite side, like he is approaching a rabid animal. Sliding a short blackjack from his sleeve, he delivers a single deft blow to the back of Serafina's head, dropping her into the dust.

'No,' Orsola groans. '*No.*'

'What is it?' someone asks the coachman.

'This one says she's a nun too,' he replies. 'Says that they're sisters.'

The horsemen confer for a minute, then one of them faces the end of the lane and makes some kind of signal. A rider trots up shortly afterwards. Orsola squirms about, trying to catch sight of him, which causes the coachman to tighten his grip yet further; she yelps as the hair starts to tear from her scalp. From her place in the gutter, she can just see that this rider is a gentleman in a hat and cape, older than the rest, with oiled black moustaches.

'We must be off,' he says, in a tone of impatient command. 'The Corsican Guard will be arriving soon. She wants this done quietly.'

'Apologies, *barone*,' says the coachman. 'We've caught ourselves a second nun. Or so she claims.'

The *barone* comes nearer, peering down at Orsola from his saddle, his piebald horse pacing beneath him. He is well made and somewhat weathered, his left eye clouded by a film of grubby white. Several agonising seconds pass. Orsola looks over at Serafina, her body barely discernible beneath the black heap of her habit; and then at the coachman's borrowed blade, still poised to deliver her to God. She is petrified, steeped in terror, but also immensely, achingly tired. She wonders vaguely if she should resume her prayer.

The *barone* sits up. 'Very well,' he says, flicking his reins. 'Bring them both.'

Domina

Donna Olimpia starts up towards the pope's apartments. It is two hours after Compline and the Palazzo del Quirinale is quite dark. Her aim, her last gambit, is to catch Giambo by surprise — and very probably in his bed, groggy and disarmed in the papal nightshirt. She will sit upon his coverlet, and remove her widow's hood and slippers; slide in beside him for a time, as she used to when he was a younger, less fretful man; and then talk to him frankly about what he is doing to her. About what he has already done.

There is uncertainty on the faces of the servants and Swiss Guards, but they dare not stop her. The sedan chair is left in the black cavern of the audience chamber, Donna Olimpia having decided that it would be better for her to arrive on foot. She took a draught before leaving the Palazzo Pamphili, given to her by her physician — an efficacious solution of opium, saffron and ambergris — to silence her knees for the duration of the evening. She resorts to this only very rarely: the poppy tends to dull the mind's edge and engender a sense of goodwill, effects she finds distinctly undesirable. But this might well be her final chance to retain her position. She cannot be gasping and whining in Giambo's presence, her brain fizzing with agonies — so she swallowed her medicine, and the knees' complaints were swiftly lowered to less all-consuming pitch.

Climbing from the sedan chair now, Donna Olimpia finds herself suffused with a pleasing inner warmth. She seems to drift across the smooth stone towards the library, unable to account for her individual footsteps. When she opens the doors, the light that falls out makes her screw up her eyes, so blindingly bright does it seem – and as her vision settles again, she sees that she is in for a very different encounter to the one she has imagined.

Giambo is still some way from his bed. He is dressed and appears to be attending to business, with the cardinals Panciroli and Astalli both close by. Donna Olimpia's comfortable glow promptly recedes. These two scoundrels have been glued to Giambo's side since the day of the portrait sitting, when they harangued her so disgracefully after she protested at their cruel defenestration of her nephew Federico. She'd assumed that the late hour of this expedition would enable her to sidestep them and secure a private conversation with the pope. But it would seem not.

The three men are standing in an inward-facing triangle, the red of their robes and caps humming like fresh blood on a bedsheet. Donna Olimpia cannot see exactly what they are doing – conferring closely, praying? A mixture of the two? – but they give no sign of having noticed her arrival. She is angry to discover the cardinals there, of course, but finds an unusual peace within her as well. The landscape is different, that is all. She merely needs to adjust her plan of attack.

Before she can speak, however, she catches an odd odour. The library of the Quirinale smells normally of beeswax, old leather and dry, dusty paper, but that night there is something else, cutting through these other smells: the acrid scent of linseed oil. Donna Olimpia looks around her, into the depths of the room.

Off in a corner, upon an artist's easel, is the Spanish portrait. The sight makes her catch her breath so sharply that she lets out an abrupt, hiccupping sound.

'Christ alive!' she exclaims.

At this, the three churchmen turn towards her. 'Why, Donna Olimpia,' says Cardinal Panciroli, without enthusiasm. 'I'm sure I heard that you had left the city.' He hesitates. 'What could possibly bring you to the Quirinale at this hour? I trust that all of the Holy Father's family are well?'

Donna Olimpia is still staring at the portrait. Somehow, in this one image, she can see the young scholar, in all his brilliance; the admired, ambitious cleric whose cause she took up, and whose campaign for advancement she directed with such unflagging devotion; and the depleted, crumbling pope, so reduced in mind, body and will, whose end now lies not so very far ahead. She can see the infuriating hesitancy, the desire always to do *both things*, rather than make the necessary choice between them. And most clearly of all, she can see the appalling waste of it: the monumental prize she won for their family, and how this weak fool is surely frittering it away. It is there on the Spaniard's canvas, laid out for all eternity. It may well be the only thing from this sorry papacy that will survive.

'Is it not remarkable?' says Panciroli, noticing the direction of her gaze. 'Does it not capture the Holy Father's presence – his authority, his great shrewdness? Already, several have mistaken the painting for the man himself. Even one so wise as his Eminence Cardinal Melzi, returning from Vienna, did drop his deepest bow before it, and begin to make his report on the court of Emperor Charles. There was much laughter when his mistake was revealed to him.'

'Indeed,' says Donna Olimpia.

'We Italians may lead the world in many things,' declares Cardinal Astalli, 'but in the field of portraiture, our Lord God has unquestionably handed the palm of genius to Spain.'

Donna Olimpia glares over at him, the detestable traitor who has bounded in a single season from obscurity to ubiquity. He looks vexingly handsome – and vexingly young. This is a foe who could stand against her family for thirty years or more, should he wish it; and to judge by the antagonism that simmers in his sly, calculating eyes, he most certainly does. With a slight lift of his brow, he now reels off a passage from the gospel of San Giovanni, something about how he who believes in the Lord cannot fail to do great works.

'Amen,' says Panciroli approvingly, glancing at the pope. 'Amen.'

A few seconds later Giambo nods, and mumbles the word as well. This has been the enemy's strategy – and it is so obvious, so very *simple*, it makes Donna Olimpia flinch to consider it. For these past weeks, they have hemmed Giambo in, blocking him off from her behind a barrier of cardinal's crimson, whispering all the while into those large, hairy ears. Together, Panciroli and Astalli have poked at his greatest fears; at his keenest, most troubling worries. They are now the two most senior members of his cabinet, the pillars supporting his throne, and are working hard to make her irrelevant. A nuisance to be swatted away.

Donna Olimpia studies her brother-in-law for a moment. He is so weary he can barely keep his head up; and he appears, furthermore, to have a strong aversion to the uncanny, much-lauded portrait. As the two self-satisfied cardinals praise and pontificate, he looks instead to the bookshelves, to the chandelier – anywhere but at the canvas. Or at her.

'All Rome is now rushing to the Spaniard,' Panciroli continues, 'asking him to capture them as well, but his grace the Duke of Infantado is policing them quite diligently. Only the most favoured are permitted to sit before Don Diego Velázquez.' He leaves one of his careful pauses. 'I believe that he has agreed to prepare a likeness of Cardinal Astalli.'

After an unconvincing show of modesty, Astalli starts to talk of his long association with the Spaniard, and how he is assisting him with the assembly of a sculpture collection for King Felipe. 'In several ways, Don Diego is a rather ordinary man,' the young cardinal observes, 'wholly devoid of the monstrous vanity demonstrated by so many of Italy's own artists. He is a vessel, one might say, for his remarkable eye.'

Donna Olimpia is pouting hard, as if tasting something horribly sour; the conversation is beginning to seem like a species of torture from which even the poppy can offer no respite. These cardinals are plainly attempting to drive her off with their interminable discussion, flaunting their success at drawing the papacy closer to Spain, at the expense of the French and their Barberini allies, and Donna Olimpia's own plans for the future. She will not have it.

'Holy mother of God!' she cries, with all the passion and energy she can muster. 'It is me, Giambattista, it is Olimpia! So much have we endured together. So very far we have come. Think of love, I implore you, and the bonds of family! Think of your dear departed brother, my beloved husband, who is watching us from above! What must he be thinking? What damage are we inflicting with this senseless rift?'

The cardinals launch immediately into murmured counter-arguments that Giambo is unable to resist. Think of the Church, they say, and its holy mission; of the place of Innocent X in history, and the legacy your papacy will leave; of all the things you could still accomplish. The pope, to Donna Olimpia's horror, is nodding again. Panciroli knows her well, and he knows Giambo too; she realises that he has prepared for this exact circumstance.

'Go, Olimpia,' Giambo mutters at last, still refusing to look at her. 'Leave this city. Leave the Palazzo Pamphili, as I ordered you to do almost a month ago now. Cardinal Astalli will be taking possession of it shortly, as is his right.'

'My people are ready,' Astalli confirms. 'With my furniture and so forth. It could happen in an afternoon. And I can only thank you, your Holiness, thank you with all my soul, and assure you of the service I will perform.'

At this, Donna Olimpia's conciliatory intentions are forgotten. The lightening gauze of the poppy is consumed in a trice by a fierce, leaping flame of indignation. She feels herself rise and grow on the library floor, becoming formidable once more.

'That palazzo is mine,' she states. 'I built it with my gold – every hearth and column and roof tile, every bolt of cloth, every precious decoration. It is *mine*, Giambattista!'

Strictly speaking, this is incorrect. The palazzo is the ancient seat of the Pamphili family, and ultimately it belongs to the pope. But Donna Olimpia has transformed it since her marriage to Giambo's older brother Pamphilo, supervising a programme of expansion and renovation that has turned it from a run-down embarrassment into one of the most glorious residences in Rome. She has far more right to live there than anyone else, especially this fraudulent Cardinal Nephew.

The Giambo of old would have cowered before such a declaration; he would have relented before a half dozen words had spilled from her lips. But Panciroli's hand is there upon his elbow now, and Astalli's is on the other. The two cardinals are quite literally propping the old booby up.

'I will not discuss this, Olimpia,' he says. 'I will not, do you hear? I can see that I have allowed you to steer me, to steer my papacy, in a poor direction indeed. In an ungodly direction. It cannot continue.'

'This is right, your Holiness,' says Panciroli reassuringly. 'A woman should not even be admitted within these halls, let alone given leave to confer with a pope. But Almighty God is guiding you now. He is guiding you back to the light.'

'And where am I supposed to go?' Donna Olimpia demands. 'What am I supposed to do? My place is here with you, brother, as it has always been. I have given my life to you, as you well know. I have nothing else – nothing!'

She continues in this vein for a while, her attention fixed on Giambo's miserable visage, inwardly weighing the first moves she might make. The wretched cardinals begin to shake their heads in exasperation and raise their eyes to heaven; then they lean together to shield the pope more completely, as if deeming her too vulgar and impious for any further engagement.

'I am afraid, Donna Olimpia,' says Panciroli, with grotesque mock-delicacy, 'that I must ask you to withdraw, lest the Holy Father become—'

'Is this honestly how it is to be between us, Giambattista?' Donna Olimpia snaps. 'They have sheared off your balls, have they, these red rogues here? They have entranced your tongue, to prevent you offering me any further explanation?'

The cardinals cross themselves now at this talk of *balls* and *tongue*; there is a short exchange in Latin about perhaps calling for the guard. And still Giambo does not dare to look at her. Instead, he angles himself towards the door to the papal study, and the dressing room and bedchamber beyond, seeming almost to hide behind Panciroli's boy-like shoulder.

Overcome by frustration, Donna Olimpia folds her arms and

turns away. In stark contrast to the living man, the pope's likeness meets her eye at once; it seems to seek her out from across the chamber, in fact, subjecting her to suspicious scrutiny, as if this eerie replication of Giambo is evaluating the case she has just made and finding it somewhat lacking. In that instant, she is claimed by a hatred so sun-bright and vitalising, she would snatch the damned Spanish portrait from the easel and consign it to the library fire. She would tie it behind her carriage and drag it through the streets of Rome until every scrap of pigment had been scoured off and nothing whatsoever remained. She would break apart that frame like so much golden kindling and tear the damned canvas in half with her teeth.

The knees stir, provoked perhaps by this vision of violent activity – a stippling of discomfort, not much in itself, but a sure and certain flavour of torments to come. Donna Olimpia swallows; she flattens her hands briefly against the front of her black gown, trying to keep steady. Reaching up to adjust her hood, she swivels around to face the doors to the darkened audience chamber, where her sedan chair is waiting.

'So be it,' she says coldly, as she starts to walk; and then she shouts, at the very top of her voice, '*so be it!*'

*

Monsignor Mascambruno enters the alleyway, swerving past a huddle of dozing, sackcloth-swaddled lepers, and glances behind him to check that he is not being followed. As he hurries up to the small grey carriage, Donna Olimpia sits back from the shutter, which she has opened by the slightest degree, and attempts to collect her thoughts. To pack away her rage, her sorrow, and her intense, blistering bitterness. To present only calm control.

'And how are things,' she asks, once he is settled on the seat opposite, 'in the office of the datary?'

Mascambruno is taking in the cabin, no doubt noting the faded paintwork and thin cushions of this temporary conveyance – this disguise Donna Olimpia has been forced to adopt. 'There is great dissatisfaction, Excellency,' he replies. 'Every soul in the building believes that the Holy Father has erred most gravely and is already beginning to realise it.'

Donna Olimpia eyes him dubiously. She knows from Ludovisi that Mascambruno has been playing a most delicate game during these past weeks: doing his work, and limiting his more blatant thefts and deceptions, while busily courting whatever favour he can. All Rome might think him her creature, but he has been signalling with velvet discretion that he could just as easily belong to another. At the same time, it cannot be denied that Mascambruno is exposing himself to significant risk simply by having this conversation. He is a senior official of the Church; stepping outside in the middle of the morning without his personal guard is precisely the sort of thing that draws notice. Also, to judge by the solid little coffer he is now taking from beneath his cape and setting on the floor between them, he has come ready to honour her.

She beats her palm against the back panel, ordering the coachman to move them off, then crosses her hands in her lap and inquires about the state of the Curia. Mascambruno proceeds to tell her of the papal court with his usual fluency, but the account he provides is subtly evasive. There is much detail on irrelevances, and only carefully selected morsels on the key matters of the day. Donna Olimpia is mildly affronted, both by the subterfuge itself and the fact that he must imagine she will not notice. Doesn't he know her at all, after so many conversations, so many shared plots and deceptions? She shows nothing, of course, even feigning interest as he runs through the ceremonies that have been staged to welcome visiting dignitaries, the robes and bejewelled hats that Giambo wore at each one, and the splendid effects of his retinue.

'And the new Cardinal Nephew?' she asks coolly, after a minute or two. 'How is he faring amongst all this wonderment?'

Mascambruno rubs his eye with a pale, slender finger. 'Well enough,' he says. 'Some are surprised by his lack of . . . initiative. By his willingness to let his master Cardinal Panciroli rule over the papal cabinet, and be the principal source of support and guidance for the Holy Father. But Cardinal Astalli's connections with the Spanish, with their noble ambassador and this portrait painter as well, seem to have placed him beyond any serious criticism.' The datary shoots her a cautious look. 'And I must say that he is widely preferred to the previous incumbent.'

The muscles in Donna Olimpia's buttocks clench tight, lifting her slightly in her seat. 'The pope is to blame for that,' she declares. 'He neglected poor, foolish Federico, neglected his most basic familial duties, and left my nephew half-formed and inept. He has allowed our blood relations to be sidelined and abandoned, and the Vatican to be brought entirely under the sway of Giacomo Panciroli. That scapegrace. That *louse*.'

Mascambruno pauses meaningfully. 'Forgive me for asking, Excellency,' he murmurs, with an irritating note of sympathy, 'but why have you chosen to remain in Rome? Surely the best course would be for you to leave for a season or two. I say this only as your most devoted friend and servant. Go to San Martino and apply yourself to overseeing the works underway there. All you do here is invite exhaustion and squander your reserves.' He leans forward. 'This Spanish faction will falter. I am sure of it. They are relying too much upon Cardinal Panciroli and his preening pupil, and the Holy Father's own resolve.'

Donna Olimpia almost laughs in his face. *That would suit you extremely well, wouldn't it?* she thinks. *Me safely off the stage. You left to pursue your little ploys.* 'I am the Holy Father's resolve, Masco,' she tells him. 'I am his backbone, and his guts, and his damned brain to boot!'

The datary moves back in alarm. 'That has never been in doubt, Excellency,' he says, nodding quickly. 'Pope Innocent needs you. Allow some time to pass and he will come to feel it most acutely. That is all I meant.'

Staying very still, Donna Olimpia wonders what use a man such as this can ever really be; then she looks down at the little coffer and taps it with her toe. 'How much is in there?'

'As much as I could chance without attracting attention. I fear that your enemies are expecting me to assist you.'

Donna Olimpia purses her lips, noting that he says 'your enemies' rather than 'our'. She reaches down for the coffer, her knees tingling hotly as she shifts her legs. Mascambruno is watching her, she realises, the oily smile slipping from his face. She glances up at him and he looks abruptly to the side, out through the narrow gaps in the shutter.

'Would you, ah, be so kind as to have your man drop me here, Excellency?' he asks, with slightly self-conscious ease. 'I see that we are about to pass Santa Maria in Via, and I have some business with a deacon there – a petition he wishes to draft. It is the reason I gave for my absence from my office, as a matter of fact.'

Donna Olimpia assents. The grey carriage halts, and after a further vow of fealty, and a kiss of her hand that lingers for several seconds too long, Mascambruno disappears among the dusty crowds of Trevi.

Alone again, Donna Olimpia studies the coffer with a little more circumspection. For all his deviousness, Mascambruno is easy to read; he was very keen to be gone before she opened up this gift of his. Could it be poisoned, its contents smeared with some invisible, deadly concoction, or the lid's hinge primed to release a cloud of noxious gas? She dismisses the idea. Masco simply doesn't have the courage to embark upon such a course of his own volition; and if one of the Spanish faction had bribed or blackmailed him into an attempt on her life, it would have been evident in his every word and movement.

With a groan, Donna Olimpia takes the coffer by its moulded iron handles and heaves it onto the seat beside her. Inside are a dozen coin stacks, each one tied neatly with scarlet ribbon. She makes a quick count: Mascambruno has brought three hundred and sixty gold scudi, a tiny fraction of what he has been holding for her, but enough for now.

As she goes to pick up one of these stacks, she notices something tucked between them – a single metal disc, slid all the way down to the coffer's base, as if to avoid immediate detection. She fishes it out. It is not a loose scudo or currency of any kind, but a medallion the size of an apple slice, cast in some bright, reddish alloy. She brings it close, angling it in the light, and sees that it is well made; rather better made, in truth, than the coins among which it was concealed. Upon it, depicted in light relief, is an old man with enormous ears seated on a stool. His hair is worn long and is arranged in elaborate, effeminate tresses. The pose of this grotesque figure is formal, but his accessories absurd: a distaff in one hand, and a spindle in the other, as if he is preparing to spin yarn. Donna Olimpia snorts with disbelieving laughter – for it is Giambo, quite unmistakably, a precise likeness the size of a thumbnail.

She turns the medallion over. On the reverse is a plain, rotund woman enthroned like a pagan goddess, her expression distant and imperious. With a twitch of the eyebrow, Donna Olimpia realises that it is her. The papal tiara is upon her head, and the keys of San Pietro in her hands. This medallion has obviously been made to taunt the pope: to claim that he is ludicrously weak, fit only for womanly pursuits, and has even allowed a woman to rule in his stead. And there it is, in fact, spelled out around the disc's edge in large, expertly rendered letters.

Olimpia I, Pontifex Maximus.

*

The grey carriage comes to a stop in the shade beneath a gigantic rose bush. Donna Olimpia climbs down carefully from the cabin, then stands for a moment to take in the garden at Ripagrande. Facing onto the filthy, shrunken river, it is laid out in the style of the previous century. It has an air of having been entirely forgotten – the shrubs overgrown, the statues coated in moss, the trees wild and ragged – making it an ideal meeting place. She tells the coachman to stay put and begins to wince her way across the weed-spotted gravel.

There is only one building on this plot, a dilapidated three-room villa that Donna Olimpia will soon have replaced with something far grander. It has a loggia, though, offering shelter from the punishing sun; Prince Ludovisi is sitting there on a stone bench, propped against the inside wall with his feathered hat hung upon his knee. It is not clear how or when he arrived, but he appears pink-cheeked and moist, as if freshly poached.

'Stay seated,' she says as she moves between the loggia's chipped columns; then she slips the medallion from her sleeve and flicks it into his lap.

The fat prince studies it unhurriedly, turning it this way and that. He seems to be fighting down a smile. 'Finely wrought, is it not?'

Donna Olimpia sits on the bench beside him, grimacing at the complaints of her knees. 'Have you seen it before?'

Ludovisi inclines his glistening head. 'They have started to appear across the city. I did hear that one was even being passed around the Quirinale.'

It is as Donna Olimpia suspected: the medallion is another part of the campaign against her. Giambo will surely have been shown it by a concerned confidant, stating that the pope needed to know precisely how he was regarded. And it will have struck him at his very core.

'It would seem that they were made abroad,' Ludovisi continues. 'I'm told that they have been circulating in several foreign courts.'

'Foreign courts,' repeats Donna Olimpia; she recalls Panciroli's tale of a nuncio bowing mistakenly before the Spanish portrait. 'Cardinal Melzi has recently returned from Vienna. Could he have brought them here?'

'That is almost certain,' says Ludovisi. 'May I ask how you came by this one?'

Donna Olimpia plucks up a fold of her black silk gown, shaking it free of the ever-tender kneecaps, and tells him of Mascambruno's coffer.

Ludovisi chuckles, patting at his meaty thigh. 'The snake put it in there to unnerve you, Mama,' he declares. 'To seed disquiet in your mind. I believe old Masco wishes to demonstrate to you just how bad this little coup is – how very deep the rot is supposed to run.'

Donna Olimpia gives him a sidelong look, displeased by the amusement in his voice. Despite the abrupt plunge in her fortunes –

and by extension, those of their entire family – his demeanour is unchanged. She is reminded of her enduring misgivings about Niccolò Ludovisi: that, born into great privilege, he cannot truly picture its decline; that although cunning, he is shallow, too disposed towards flippancy, and unequal to the severity of their plight; that as always, she can only really rely upon herself.

'Mascambruno advised me to leave Rome,' she says. 'To watch from a distance as this Spanish faction underwent an inevitable collapse.'

'Of course he did! He imagines that he can turn your absence to his advantage, while he waits to see which way everything will go.' Ludovisi shrugs, hooking a thumb inside his straining lace collar. 'I mean, we are beleaguered at present. There can be no denying that. My sources have also reported that the good Cardinal Melzi possesses a book of cartoons – drawings of a most licentious nature, showing yourself and the Holy Father in a range of . . . unseemly positions.' He hesitates, biting his lower lip to contain his mirth. 'It is nothing we haven't seen in Rome a hundred times before, but I understand that this particular volume was presented to Melzi by Emperor Charles himself. Apparently, his Imperial Majesty is concerned that such material might find its way to the Protestant kingdoms and make the Holy See look ridiculous in the eyes of the heretics.'

Donna Olimpia watches the brown Tiber, feeling a rising swell of foreboding. 'And Melzi has now relayed all of this to the pope – in the very darkest terms, no doubt. He has long been a determined enemy of mine.'

'A large number have declared against you, in truth,' says Ludovisi. 'Ambassadors. Ministers. Even members of our own family.'

Donna Olimpia stares at him. 'I take it that you are referring to my son.'

In less fractious times, any mention of this matter is forbidden. Camillo Pamphili, Donna Olimpia's only son, was once Cardinal Nephew himself, an appointment in which his mother had played no small part. But three years previously, in an act of unforgiveable ingratitude and near-sightedness, the fool cast aside this exalted role to marry Olivia Aldobrandini, Princess of Rossano, a woman as ambitious and stupid as she was deceitful. In her fury, Donna Olimpia had seen to it that the devious couple were sent into exile at Frascati. It was this first betrayal that had made her reliant upon the idiot Federico, who was so easily deposed by Panciroli and his band. How predictable that they would return the instant her power was diminished! She can clearly imagine their rush to Giambo, where they would dangle their infants before him, exploiting the old sheep's sentimentality to win back his favour. The notion is maddening.

'It was always going to be thus, Mama, once you stepped away,' says Ludovisi. 'A crowd has clamoured in, seeking to claim your spot.'

Donna Olimpia lifts her chin. 'I did not *step away*,' she says sharply. 'I was shoved from my rightful place, shoved out into the mud. But I will not be down there for long, Ludo. Of that you can be sure.'

Ludovisi is now regarding her with wry affection, which only stokes her annoyance. Before he can say anything, she asks about Castro in Rome and whether her orders have been carried out. This sobers him somewhat; he tells her that they have, with Baron Mattei's usual thoroughness, and that the person in whom she is interested awaits her pleasure.

Donna Olimpia nods. This is something, at least; one cause for worry struck from the list. 'And what of my granddaughter? Has Olimpiuccia been taken to her parents, as I instructed? She must not remain in the Palazzo Pamphili. This is paramount, do you hear?'

The loss of this palazzo is among the worst of the wounds they have inflicted. To think of the traitor Astalli walking her hallways, dining off her table, kneeling in her chapel and praying before Sacchi's Madonna . . . Well, Donna Olimpia cannot. She simply *cannot*. The cardinals ensured that she was obliged to leave many things behind, that treasured painting among them – but she will surely die before she allows her Olimpiuccia, upon whom so much could still rest, to be brought under Astalli's illegitimate dominion.

'It is done,' Ludovisi replies. 'I had someone take her to the Palazzo Giustiniani within an hour of your final expulsion, rather to the bemusement of both the girl and her parents. She's a strange fish, Mama, is Olimpiuccia. I swear, if you were to permit it, she would take her holy vows tomorrow. She sees herself as a junior Santa Teresa. As a holy scholar in waiting.'

Donna Olimpia is not about to discuss this matter with Ludovisi. She decides to advance to the next item on her list, a letter received the previous evening from Cardinal Francesco Barberini – an unpleasant missive from an increasingly unlikeable man, the page practically crackling with discontent.

'What news is there of Spain?' she asks. 'The Barberini are most alarmed by these recent developments, Ludo. They fear for my Neapolitan stratagem now that I am no longer at the pope's side. They are concerned that Panciroli will turn Innocent against them – against France, even. That the Holy See will condemn any invasion of the Kingdom of Naples in the strongest terms, and perhaps raise an army to aid Spain in its defence.'

Ludovisi idly plumps the feather of the hat upon his knee. 'I have heard no word of anything like that,' he says. 'At least, not yet. I continue to watch every notable Spaniard in Rome, and to move among them whenever I can. The Duke of Infantado rather likes me, I think. I am learning much – although nothing, I must admit, that pertains to your stratagem. Infantado seems to regard Naples as completely secure, and the French as no threat at all.'

'And the painter, this Velázquez?' asks Donna Olimpia. 'Are you watching him also – his movements, his visitors, his routines?'

Ludovisi sighs. 'What can I tell you, Mama? The scene is largely unchanged. Statues continue to arrive at the embassy, but my people can find no obvious sign of espionage. The fellow seems to be doing what was claimed – gathering in artworks for his king. He is a quiet man, very quiet indeed. *Distant*, I would say. He emerges from his studio only with great reluctance.'

Donna Olimpia feels a glimmer of satisfaction. These are the tidings she wanted: the latest action she has conceived depends upon this painter's habits remaining the same. She pulls herself upright and looks off into the gardens.

'Where is Algardi?' she asks. 'Did you bring him here with you?'

The fat prince gestures towards the river. A man in a cape and hat can be seen pacing along the proposed boundary of Donna Olimpia's new house, which has already been pegged out across the sun-browned lawns and long-dead flowerbeds. Clearing his throat, Ludovisi cups a hand around his mouth and calls the sculptor's name. He comes over at once, bowing low as he nears the loggia.

Maestro Alessandro Algardi has forced his blacksmith's frame into a half-decent green doublet and his leathery complexion shows the recent attentions of a barber. After the usual compliments, he makes a broad enquiry about the house – the architect, the decorative scheme and so forth – no doubt looking for some personal opportunity, or an insight into the activities of his competitors.

Donna Olimpia tells him nothing. 'You should attend to your work, Maestro,' she says. 'I can only spare you a half-hour.'

Algardi bows again, and takes a drawing folder from under his arm. The sculptor has brought a stool to sit upon; some unhappiness with the light causes him to seat himself in three different spots before he is content. When he is finally positioned, he unlaces the cover of his drawing folder, slides a length of graphite from its spine, and fixes a pair of spectacles to his nose. Algardi gazes at Donna Olimpia for a few moments before requesting that she turn slightly to the left, raise her nose, and adjust the fall of her hood. There is a pause; he seems to clear his mind, or perform some vital inner preparation. Then he makes a mark upon the paper.

'I must admit, Excellency, that I was surprised when your people sought me out,' he says, as he makes two more. 'I had supposed that your current travails would mean a significant delay to this commission.'

Algardi has a careful, kindly air, almost avuncular, even though he must be ten years younger than her. Donna Olimpia has no patience for it.

'These *travails* of mine are merely temporary,' she informs him. 'I will be back in the Palazzo Pamphili soon enough, and this bust of yours – assuming it is finished to your customary standard – will be given pride of place.' She can picture it very clearly, on a plinth at the base of the main stairs: Donna Olimpia Maidalchini in white Carrara marble, confronting all who come through the doors, immutable and unyielding. 'Besides, it is nearly complete, no? Only a few fine details left? This is what I was led to believe, Maestro.'

Algardi nods, squinting as he sketches. 'The end is close, certainly, but we are at a crucial stage. The face, Excellency, is an endlessly complex thing. A number of the very smallest touches combine to create the mood. In your case of nobility . . . of resolve . . .'

Donna Olimpia sets her brow, imagining posterity; the great and constant churning of history; the inspection of countless souls not yet born. She remembers the Spanish portrait also, and the more unfortunate aspects it contains – the parts of Giambo's soul that no sitter could possibly wish to reveal. She will never permit any likeness of her to do that.

'In all honesty, Algardi,' she says, staring out at the parched garden, 'I am surprised that *you* could spare time for *me*. I have heard that your shop has as much work as it can manage – and that a good deal of it comes from this Spaniard, the portrait painter.'

The sculptor does not pause in his sketching, but the line between his eyebrows deepens with discomfort. 'I am a humble man, Excellency,' he replies guardedly. 'I cannot refuse the envoy of a king. The work itself is uninteresting, in truth. I have given most of it to my boys.'

'What is your opinion of the man himself – of Don Diego Velázquez?'

Algardi sees that he has no choice but to answer. 'I have met the gentleman only once,' he says, his voice now a little flat. 'He seemed distracted, as if a certain portion of his thoughts were elsewhere. But his eye was keen. He knew what his royal master required. And I am told that his own portraits are without equal. There is a tale going around that Ambassador Sagredo, when brought before his likeness of the Holy Father, bowed down before it, honestly believing it to be the real man.'

'Remarkable,' says Donna Olimpia.

'Sagredo is said to have spoken to the portrait for almost a minute before realising his error,' adds Ludovisi with a smirk.

'What this tells us about the Holy Father's conversational skills we should perhaps refrain from pointing out.'

It is plain that no more information will be extracted from Maestro Algardi. Donna Olimpia bats away a large, buzzing insect with her hand. It is getting even hotter, she is sure of it; her entire body prickles with fresh sweat and irritability. She longs for the parlour in the small, secret villa she owns among the vineyards of Esquilino, over by the western wall. The heavy shutters. The cool, tiled floor. The darkness.

'How much longer will it take you?' she asks. 'To finish the bust, I mean?'

The sculptor exhales, lifting his graphite from the paper. 'Three weeks at most,' he says. 'It will be ready for viewing in my studio by the feast of San Giacomo.' He hesitates. 'You do wish for me to proceed then, Excellency? Forgive me, but if I am to arrange for its delivery, I must . . .'

Donna Olimpia pulls back her shoulders. 'And why in heaven would I not?' she says tersely. 'Do you think I might have been driven from the city, or something of that nature? Ejected forever from my home? Do you believe that I am without resources, unable to plan or adapt? A beaten woman, with no other course but retreat?'

Algardi is mortified. He lowers his paper and begins an earnest denial.

Donna Olimpia won't hear it. She raises a forefinger. 'I will tell you this, Maestro Algardi. You have no idea of my situation — you or any other man in Rome.' She shifts herself around so that her glare takes in Ludovisi, the dirty river, and the whole stinking city beyond. 'None of you have the slightest sense of what I might do.'

*

The grey carriage waits on a street behind the Rotonda. Inside, Donna Olimpia fans cards out across a cushion, playing a hand of Scopa against herself to stop the usual dark thoughts from piling up in her mind. Only the top slats of the shutters are open, in case of prying eyes, but the sun is so bright that this is enough to illuminate the cabin. She keeps as still as she can, ignoring the gathering heat, trying to savour the soft slip of the cards as she draws them from the pack; the delicate expertise of their illustrations; the strategy of the game itself, with its calculations and captures. She is so absorbed, in fact, that the knock causes her to jump, inhaling sharply through her nostrils.

'Excellency,' says Baron Mattei, from the other side of the window. 'We have her.'

Donna Olimpia starts to gather in the three hands she has in play. 'Very well,' she replies. 'I am ready.'

The left side door opens a few moments later, flooding the stuffy little cabin with light and noise, and the smells of Rome: woodsmoke, sizzling meat, cut flowers and ordure. A woman's voice is raised nearby, making a futile complaint. Donna Olimpia's view is blocked by one of Mattei's larger men, who appears briefly in the doorway, frowning with exertion – and then the person she seeks is deposited on the carriage floor, laid out at her feet. Mattei peers in to check that all is well, his head held at an angle to account for his sightless eye. Baron Luigi Mattei is Donna Olimpia's favourite kind of servant, being unquestioning, highly capable, and indebted to her for almost everything he is; she nods and he withdraws, closing the door behind him. The new arrival picks herself up, sitting warily on the seat opposite as the grey carriage starts to move.

'Flaminia Triunfi,' says Donna Olimpia, tapping her deck

straight. 'How long has it been since we spoke last? Six years? Seven?'

It has to be admitted that she wears the time well. She is poor, that much is obvious – the simple costume, the lack of paint or jewellery, the scent of lye only – but her skin is still smooth enough, her features even, and her eyes clear and clever. An excellent match could once have been made, enough to salvage the Triunfi name and restore a portion of their fortunes, despite everything that had happened to them. It is far too late now, of course. For all her barely diminished beauty, Flaminia has plainly grown strange and unbiddable. Furthermore, she is thoroughly spoiled; Ludovisi's spies say that she has given herself away for nothing, to numerous men, and continues to do so. *A waste,* thinks Donna Olimpia. *A most lamentable waste.*

Flaminia is staring over at her. She is trying to appear confident, defiant, even a touch amused by the turn her morning has taken. 'Everyone thinks you've left,' she says. 'All of Rome. Yet here you are, riding around in this secret carriage, like . . . like some kind of spymaster.'

Donna Olimpia studies her passenger more closely. Something is there in her complexion, in her jawline perhaps, and the faint shadow beneath those eyes. Something else that can be made use of.

'I have been thinking,' she says, 'of your sister.'

And across the carriage, lovely Flaminia goes pale as marble, all the fight emptied out of her with a single firm shake.

'Claudia, I believe her name was,' Donna Olimpia continues. 'I found myself recalling what a dreadful trial she proved for your poor father – this impossible creature who would not leave the comfort of her holy books, or eat a decent meal, or even comb her hair, without much violent resistance. And she had been that way since her earliest girlhood. It was widely assumed that she was unmarriageable, but he found her a suitor nonetheless, didn't he? I was impressed by that.'

This is not true. Donna Olimpia was deeply annoyed. At that time, she was the foremost matchmaker of Rome. She had certainly thought that Claudia would be a challenge, especially considering the meagre proportions of a Triunfi dowry and the fact that she was a few years older than was normal. There were still options, though: an array of second or third sons whose family name compensated for club feet, or withered limbs, or some unappealing speech impediment. Donna Olimpia approached the father, a haughty widower, only to be informed that the task was already complete. A willing groom had been found and terms reached. Her assistance was not required. She left the Palazzo Triunfi in high dudgeon, resolving to discover everything she could about this groom and make sure that his family knew precisely what they were committing themselves to.

But that same week Pope Urban died. Rome was gripped by a frightful convulsion. There were lootings, many hundreds of murders and all manner of public outrages. The Holy Conclave was called to appoint Urban's successor – and amid the negotiations, the switching allegiances, the bribes and empty pledges, came the wild excitement of victory. A Pamphili pope! Her Giambo, her own brother-in-law, on San Pietro's throne! Consumed by triumph, and then buried beneath the mighty labours that followed, Donna Olimpia had forgotten the Triunfis entirely. It was only months later that she learned what had become of Claudia's betrothal. Her information was incomplete, but shortly before the couple's first meeting, it seemed that some manner of disaster occurred at the Palazzo Triunfi. There was an accident, a dire injury that wrecked the nascent union and left the girl's father with just one course open to him.

'It is a terrible shame what happened,' says Donna Olimpia. 'Although I must say I thought the Blessed Visitation at Castro a peculiar choice.' She shrugs, looking down at the intricate red and black pattern printed on the reverse of her playing cards. 'But then, your late father was not known for the wisdom of his decisions.'

What self-control Flaminia has managed to retain deserts her now. 'You *destroyed* it!' she spits, her eyes bright with loathing. 'You had your army destroy that town without a thought for the souls inside – for Claudia or anyone else!'

Donna Olimpia meets Flaminia's gaze; no fault or uncertainty can be admitted here, even if she had a mind to. 'It was a place of heresy. Surely you are aware of this. The house of Farnese rejected the Holy Father's authority and had Bishop Giarda cut down in cold blood. A price had to be paid for that.' She starts to shuffle her cards. 'But we must always trust in the Lord, Flaminia. For I can tell you that He has spared your sister. Claudia is back in Rome, among the pilgrims of the Jubilee. By God's grace, she has been walking these very streets.'

Donna Olimpia was looking forward to making this revelation, and the astonishment it would provoke; however, as she speaks she sees that Flaminia knows already. Looking over at the shadows that are playing across the right-hand shutter, her passenger nods and begins to talk about rumours she has heard, the fruitless searches she has conducted, and the people she is paying to keep an eye out.

Donna Olimpia soon grows weary of it. 'I have her,' she interrupts. 'I have your sister. Her mind is as disordered as it ever was,

I am told, and her defacement on full display.' She snorts. 'The years have only made Claudia Triunfi more distinctive.'

This gets Donna Olimpia her reaction. At first, Flaminia is speechless, quite stunned; then slowly, understanding begins to dawn inside her, tinted with a yet darker shade of abhorrence. 'You *have* her? You mean Claudia is your prisoner?' She is thinking furiously, bless her – and fast becoming mired in mystification. 'But why would you do such a thing?'

Donna Olimpia continues to shuffle. 'You know what has befallen me.'

Flaminia glowers at her for a few seconds. 'They say that the pope has expelled you,' she replies. 'That he shut you out of the Quirinale and evicted you from his family's palazzo. That he has seen through your wiles at last.'

Donna Olimpia narrows her eyes; there is some backbone here. 'That palazzo is mine,' she corrects. 'It has always been mine. And within a single beat of Gabriello's wings, it will be mine again.'

Flaminia is looking a touch worried now, as she senses where their conversation is heading. 'What do you want from me?'

'The Spanish,' Donna Olimpia begins, 'are the close allies of my enemies. All of them are against Rome – against the pope, although the old fool does not see it yet. Their concern lies not with him, but who they mean to place upon the throne when he is gone.'

Flaminia is shaking her head. 'I don't see how I—'

'My men have been following you for some weeks now. You are often in that embassy on the Piazza Trinita. It seems that you come and go as you please, heeded by no one.' Donna Olimpia stops shuffling the deck and addresses her passenger with cold frankness. 'You no doubt consider yourself very quick, Flaminia. Very *astute.* But events are moving in a dangerous direction indeed. You will be caught up in them, you will be trapped, and by God, you will surely be destroyed.'

Flaminia has nothing to say to this. She looks at the floor, removing her shapeless straw hat and mopping at her brow with a corner of her shawl. Donna Olimpia notices that her hands are trembling.

'This need not happen. If you help me, there will be a life for you afterwards. A life with your sister.' Donna Olimpia tucks the deck of cards inside her sleeve. 'I have a town, some distance from here. San Martino is its name. There is a fine old church, an abbey, and a network of new streets, sketched out to my own design. Much is still to be done, but soon there will be houses, a great many freshly built houses, looking for people to live in them. For *women* to live in them. I have decreed that an unmarried woman can own a house in San Martino. She can open a shop and ply a trade, should she wish it.'

Flaminia is staring across the cabin again, but there is no defiance or hatred in her now. Donna Olimpia recognises her expression: an entirely new possibility has been revealed to her, and she cannot help but imagine the way things could be. She is almost there. Just one final weight, provided so fortuitously, remains to be set upon the scales.

'Prove yourself my friend and a place will be kept for you within its walls,' Donna Olimpia says. 'The Triunfi family can live in San Martino at complete liberty, free from judgement or stricture.' She pauses, folding her hands in her lap, and directs a meaningful glance at Flaminia's midriff. 'All three of you together.'

This meets with a startled blink; a wordless opening of the mouth. She is not far gone, and Donna Olimpia wonders if she has even admitted the truth of it to herself. It occurs to her that the child could well belong to the Spanish painter, which would lend a certain poetry to the situation.

'This chance will not be offered a second time,' Donna Olimpia adds. 'I would say that you do not have a choice.'

Flaminia swallows, gripping the brim of her hat with her long fingers. 'So tell me what you want from me.'

Donna Olimpia leans back. 'Come now, Flaminia,' she says. 'I believe you already know.'

Sorores

Sister Serafina stays where she is dropped. Orsola tries unsuccessfully to rouse her; and then, with much hesitation, she peels the bloody veil back from the choir nun's brow. This uncovers a large, livid bruise with an ugly split down one side. She attempts to clean it with her own grubby cuff, but this only seems to make things worse.

They are in a chapel, but it is unlike any Orsola has ever seen before. The room feels like it was hewn directly from the damp, chalky stone, its vaults and floor so crude they could almost be the work of nature rather than man. There is a single semicircular window, barely three hands high and fitted with iron bars. A large Madonna has been painted on the altar wall, with a host of tiny, doll-sized people clustered beneath Her blue cloak like so many ducklings. She is faded and crumbling, with weeds trailing over Her elongated, greenish face; but Orsola kneels before Her nonetheless, appealing helplessly for aid, for intercession, for some small indication of what action she might take.

Surely it cannot end like this. Not after everything they have endured, the great distances they have travelled, and the many trials they have somehow managed to survive. Orsola thinks it is more than her soul can bear. The memories begin to press in on her, to suffocate and blind her, their sounds deafening and horrible. It is very difficult, for a while, not to become lost in wailing.

Eventually she calms, or at least runs out of strength to panic any further. She lies down beside Serafina, and after a period of exhausted blankness her mind starts to search for an explanation. The *barone*'s words seem to be key: *she wants this done quickly*. Orsola knows of just one woman with the power to order such things. Donna Olimpia must have learned that some of Castro's survivors were in Rome, planning her death. Tullio and the others had not been discreet; the details of their scheme could have leaked from a dozen different places. Through spying and subterfuge, the widow had set another trap around their own, allowing them to come out into the open so that they could be extinguished completely.

And yet there was more to it than this. Those men were looking for Serafina. They had information that she would be there, and instructions to capture her – to bundle her into that carriage, drive her across the city, and then drag her down into this ancient, mouldering prison. Orsola becomes convinced that the reason for this must involve Serafina's former life, before she took her holy vows. The choir nun has demonstrated time and again that she is familiar with Rome – and that she is most definitely *fearful* of Rome, as if it is a place where she has known great suffering.

A while later, Orsola rises. Her toe aches dreadfully, and her throbbing scalp is sticky with drying blood. She goes over to the wall with the window at its top. Along its base is a simple stone bench; she discovers that if she stands atop it, craning her neck, she is rewarded with a limited view of the yard outside. Through the spokes of a cartwheel, she can see an open-fronted, empty stable and a double gate, firmly closed. This dull scene is shrouded in the flat blue shadows of early evening. There are no people at all.

Orsola climbs back down and sits on the bench. Growing

fearful once more, she devises a tale intended to save her life for a second time. She is Sister Serafina's devoted companion, appointed by the Mother Abbess many years ago, and the only person on God's earth who can calm her. Tullio Botta captured them immediately upon their arrival in Rome, forcing them to beg along the procession route and then take part in his bloody plot. They are victims, in short, wholly without blame. Orsola realises that if it works, such a story could well result in her being returned to the Benedictine Order along with Serafina. She tries her best to make peace with this. It is better than death, just about; and there might well be some way to slip off before the final lock is turned.

The light in the chapel ebbs away, until the painted Madonna's face is merely a pale oval hanging in the gloom. A Vesper bell chimes nearby; Orsola is trying to identify the church it belongs to, so that she can work out where in Rome they are, when Serafina begins to stir. Going over at once, Orsola kneels beside the choir nun and attempts to lift her head from the floor. She is shrugged off with some vehemence.

Serafina must be in quite formidable pain but she shows none of it. She struggles up, fighting against the filthy folds of her habit, fumbling for her rosary – which is still in her sleeve, no effort having been made to rob either of them. The silver beads glint as she draws them out; muttering rapidly, she begins to work them between her fingers, as if finding her place again after a minor interruption. In moments, she has returned to Santa Catarina, to the dungeons of Alexandria, to conversions and tortures and righteous speechifying.

Orsola sits back, asking God for patience. Serafina is launching into an account of her beloved saint's final days, before Emperor Maxentius ordered her end and ensured her place in Paradise. The choir nun's voice is cracked and hoarse; her feverish energy frequently fails, leaving her groping dizzily for her next word.

'Why is this happening, Sister?' Orsola interrupts, after a couple of minutes. 'Did you know that man – the *barone*? What do they want?'

Serafina stops speaking. She is quiet for a while, her lips moving soundlessly; then she swallows hard. 'They are hers,' she says.

Orsola stares at her. 'Do you . . . do you mean Donna Olimpia's? Do you know her, Sister? Did you know her before you came to Castro?'

There is a longer silence. Serafina lifts a hand to her head, laying it heedlessly against her wound and then recoiling with a yelp. 'The saint . . . the saint asked Maxentius which one she should choose,' she mumbles, glancing at her bloody fingers. 'One who is powerful, eternal, honoured by every righteous soul . . . or one who is mortal, ignorant and repulsive?'

Orsola wants badly to scream; to squeeze Serafina's hands in hers, and kiss them, and implore her for help. 'Sister,' she says. 'Sister, listen to me, I beg you. Those men might soon return. They might come to kill me. I . . . I was only just spared in the alley. There was a blade at my throat, and it . . . it . . .'

Suddenly, she can feel the fist gripping her hair, twisting around two, three times, impossibly tight. She can see the coachman's squinting eyes as he takes aim. The recollection is so terrifyingly vivid, it sends her listing breathlessly towards the floor; just as she is going over, though, she sets her hand against the stone, closes her eyes for a few seconds, and firmly pushes it all aside.

'Didn't you see what happened to Tullio and the others? Didn't you see how they died?' Orsola lowers her voice to a deliberate, emphatic whisper. 'I need to know why they want you, why they spared you, so I might get them to spare me too. *Please*, Sister.'

Another lengthy pause follows. Serafina continues to fuss with her silver rosary; her brow furrows and she rocks a little, back and forth. A couple of times she seems ready to start speaking, but stops herself. Orsola clenches her jaw, digging her fingernails into her palms.

'Torments were threatened,' Serafina murmurs at last. 'The most dire torments. But Catarina welcomed them. My one desire, she declared, is to offer my flesh and blood to Christ as He offered Himself to me. He is my God. My shepherd. My one and only spouse.' She hesitates, looking up towards the window. 'And so the wheels were brought forth.'

Serafina commences her description of this hideous machine – four interlocking devices, designed to rotate in different directions and tear Catarina asunder between their cruel hooks and serrated blades. Orsola slumps forward, tears blurring her sight. She sees that if her survival is to depend in any way upon Sister Serafina, she is very probably lost. She will not be returning the choir nun to the Benedictine Order. She will not be able to atone for her carnality, in coupling so readily with Jacopo Bruni; for her deception, in concealing the pregnancy from all who might have helped her; for her shameful neglect, in letting the child die. Her daughter's soul will remain stranded on the grey hill, while her own will surely be delivered to hell, to receive its just punishment. There had been a chance: a narrow and most difficult path that she has followed as best she could. But it has come to nothing. The path has led her here.

The light in their chapel cell is almost gone. Serafina is only a dark shape now. She stops her account and begins to move, shifting around until she is kneeling directly opposite Orsola. They are close together, their knees almost touching. Orsola can smell her; she can hear the shallow rasp of her breaths. The story of the saint's end resumes, but Serafina has lost her sermonising manner. She is speaking quietly, intently, as if she is addressing Orsola alone.

'The day arrived, and Catarina was led out to die between the wheels. These wicked devices towered before her, waiting like a set of open jaws. All around was a great pagan carnival, filling the main square of Alexandria, celebrating her demise.' Serafina unclasps her hands and reaches over to pinch a fold of Orsola's sleeve between her thumb and forefinger. 'But Catarina walked with the blessed Virgin Mary at her side. And she was not afraid.'

*

The widow comes to them on the third day.

From early morning, it is plain that something is about to happen. After endless hours of emptiness, the little yard is brought to life. Male voices echo around its walls, swearing, complaining and issuing orders. The gates scrape open repeatedly; Orsola is up on the stone bench each time, peering past the carts and horsemen, hoping for clues of their location. She sees only a shabby stretch of street: tenements, dusty flagstones, a ropemaker working beneath an awning. Nothing of any help at all.

Not long after the Angelus, a carriage arrives. It is modest by Roman standards, with two mismatched horses and grey, weathered panels. As it draws up in front of the chapel's window, a couple of riders follow it in through the gates and dismount. Orsola curses softly; one of them – tall, straight-backed, severe – is unquestionably the half-blind *barone* from the alley. She watches him pass his reins to a stable boy and approach the carriage, soon disappearing behind it. The cabin rocks slightly, and she hears the voice of an older woman – an aristocratic voice, hard-edged and testy. A second or two later, the bottom of a black silk gown appears below the carriage, beside the *barone*'s riding boots. This visitor walks off, making no effort to save her hem from the dirt.

'Sister,' Orsola says. 'I think that Donna Olimpia is here.'

Serafina is curled at the base of the wall painting, where she has been for most of their time in this chapel cell. From where Orsola stands, it looks almost as if she is attempting to insert herself amongst the Madonna's miniature disciples. She seems to be sickening; her head wound has left her immensely tired, drained of all vigour. The sound of Orsola's voice makes her shift about, but she does not reply or show any sign of comprehension.

Orsola can feel herself beginning to fade as well. They have been fed just once, to keep them weak she supposes: milk and stale bread, brought in by the same coachman who aimed his sword at her throat. She recoiled at the sight of him, preparing to resist, but he simply set down their meagre meal and dropped a misshapen leather pail by the door.

'Shout for help,' he said, jabbing his finger at the barred window, 'and you'll lose an eye.'

A door closes somewhere above. Several pairs of feet descend a flight of stone steps, and then advance along the passage to their door. Orsola gets down from the bench, and after a second's indecision she sits upon it. She is keenly aware of how dirty she is, and how badly she smells; she is so scared and nervous she cannot keep still. As the chapel door is unlocked, she prays for a clear head, sound speech, and a virtuous countenance. This could well be her one opportunity to convince these people not to kill her.

Two men enter: the coachman, holding a short staff this time, and a learned-looking fellow with a barbered beard, a smart black cape, and an officious manner. He goes at once to the leather pail and inspects the contents without so much as a flicker of disgust.

When this is done, he advances purposefully towards the insensible Serafina.

'Wait,' says Orsola, 'what are you—'

The coachman steps between the nuns, ready to beat her back. She can only watch as this second man pulls on a pair of sleeved gloves, tilts Serafina's head to study her eyes, her nose, and her neck, and then pulls aside a fold of her habit to peer into her right armpit. She makes a feeble, mewling protest, trying to shove him off, but he's plainly well practised at this. Adding a sudden firmness to his grip, he rolls up her sleeve so that he can examine her forearm and the crook of her elbow.

'All is well, Excellency,' he says, rising and turning to the doorway. 'She requires food and drink, and perhaps a poultice for that injury above her brow, but there is no contagion here.'

'What about the other one?'

The gloved man, obviously a doctor of some sort, shakes his head. 'How long have they been in here – two days, three? There is no way that one would be infected but not the other. It is a medical impossibility.'

Apparently satisfied, Donna Olimpia Maidalchini comes into the chapel. She is a stout, rather plain old woman, clad in widow's weeds and shorter even than Orsola herself. Orsola is seized by the urge to laugh aloud. *This* is the Queen of Rome? The woman who held the Holy Father in thrall? Who has claimed untold riches, marshalled vast armies, and brought down entire towns? It seems like a mistake. Like some kind of trick has been played. Then the widow glances over at her – and the expression in her eyes is so forbidding, so empty of pity or patience, that Orsola's heart constricts and she lowers her gaze abruptly to the floor.

'Who is she?' Donna Olimpia asks someone behind her. 'What is she doing here?'

His work complete, the doctor bows and withdraws, eager to be gone. Once he has left the *barone* enters, looking vaguely bored, and stops just inside the door.

'They were together, Excellency,' he replies. 'There appears to be a connection between them. A bond of intimacy, or the like.'

'I am a nun also,' Orsola says, starting to get up. 'A servant nun from the same house as Sister Serafina. Our abbess tasked me with—'

The coachman steps forward and swings his staff in a neat, expert arc, cracking it against her shin. The pain is excruciating; she lets out a choked, disbelieving cry, dropping back immediately onto the bench.

'Blessed saints!' shouts Donna Olimpia. 'Where in God's name do you think you are, man? Do you imagine that this is a dungeon of the Tor di Nona – that this is a murderess, perhaps, being made to confess her crimes?'

The coachman is taken aback. 'I was quietening her, Excellency, to halt any threat before it—'

'*Threat?* Holy Madonna, what conceivable threat could this miserable scrap here pose to me?' Donna Olimpia turns to the *barone*. 'You must train your beasts better, Mattei. This one here is practically wild.'

The *barone* jerks his head, dismissing the coachman, who gives a flustered bow and retreats to the corridor. Orsola flops onto her side, gulping down the sour lump of nausea that is rising in her throat. Her shin feels like it has been cleaved open. Puffing in a few quick breaths, she pulls up her grimy gown, expecting to see an unnatural bend or a splinter jutting out gruesomely through the skin. To her surprise, there is almost nothing, just an angry red stripe with a little blood bubbling through. Orsola gasps thanks, blinking with relief. She is attempting to sit up again when a darkness gathers before her. Donna Olimpia has crossed the chapel, she realises, and is standing barely two yards away.

'I will have an explanation,' she says. 'What were you planning, you and those brutes in that alley? It was to be an assassination, yes?'

'I never meant you harm,' Orsola answers, speaking more loudly than she intended, a horrible, frantic sensation tightening around her. 'I swear it, mistress. By the Virgin and the holy saints. I only wanted a chance, that's all. A chance for me and my sister.'

'A chance? You mean money?'

Orsola nods, wiping away her tears. 'A . . . a few coins. Maybe a jewel. Enough to get us out of Rome.'

Donna Olimpia sniffs, considering this; and then, to Orsola's great consternation, she moves to the bench and sits down beside her with a small groan. 'The brutes did not want money,' she says. 'They wanted my head on a pikestaff. Were you intending to rob my corpse, I wonder? I am afraid there is not much to be had at present.'

Orsola looks at Serafina, who hasn't stirred since the doctor's examination. She has no sense whatsoever of how this might go. The widow's manner is entirely perplexing. There is power, and more than a little menace; a stern, honest attempt at understanding, not unlike that of the Mother Abbess; and also, Orsola is increasingly sure, something that edges close to kinship.

'We were their prisoners,' she says. 'We were on the penitential procession, seeking to gain the Holy Father's indulgence as we sought out a new convent. They found us there and beat us most harshly. They told us we would be killed if we did not help with their scheme.' She leans forward, her breathing short, trying to ignore the vicious pulsing of her shin. 'With their vow of vengeance for Castro.'

'You did not take this vow yourself, then? You do not blame me for all the ills that have befallen you, as they did?'

Orsola recalls everything Tullio and the others told her. The murder of the bishop, the devious provocation of the war, and the death and devastation that followed. The theft of relics, of gold, even of the bells of Castro's duomo. If true, these are terrible crimes; but there is nothing that she, Sister Orsola, can do now to see them punished. What purpose would any accusations or denunciations serve, apart from to ensure her own end? She decides that it is best left to the hereafter and the eternal wisdom of God.

'I do not, mistress,' she replies. 'Duke Ranuccio sinned against the Church. It was his doing.' She bows her head in supplication. 'All Rome speaks of you as a . . . as a defender of women. They say that you are our guardian, and have extended your personal protection to many. I beg you now to show us the mercy you have—'

'The nun of Castro,' Donna Olimpia pronounces. 'That is what they called her, is it not? My people tell me she was quite the sight, with her visions and heady tales – and that awful scar, of course. She seems to have walked the penitential circuit on a veritable carpet of coins. Coins, sister, that *you* gathered up.'

Orsola freezes. Donna Olimpia does not believe her – not for an instant. She can see the truth as clearly as if it was written across Orsola's forehead.

'This girl here,' the widow continues, 'is from a line that goes back to the first Pope Clement. And you have put her to work begging in the streets. I wonder what that proud father would make of such an outcome – one daughter a beggar, the other a whore.' She looks over at the *barone*. 'See how we can fall, Mattei. How quickly and absolutely.'

Orsola forces herself to think. 'This old family . . . do they want her back? Is that why you had her captured?'

'There is no place in Rome for Claudia Triunfi,' says Donna Olimpia. 'That was settled for good, many years ago. Different things lie in store for her.'

Claudia Triunfi.

Orsola looks again at Sister Serafina, bony and ailing, huddled before the Virgin on the wall. This was who the choir nun had been, before the Convent of the Blessed Visitation had rubbed it away: a daughter of Rome, a young woman of wealth and breeding, with carriages and banquets and grand, gilded palazzos. It is a life Orsola can scarcely imagine.

Donna Olimpia fixes her with an appraising stare. 'You are her keeper, I see. This was your role at Castro, and the one you have performed ever since – even as you made poor Claudia your dancing bear.'

Orsola tenses at this description, but she knows better than to object. Donna Olimpia begins to pray, murmuring an Ave Maria as she kneads her kneecaps gently through her gown. The sight brings Orsola a sudden memory of her own aged relatives in Castro, back when she was a small girl; of their decline, suffering, and death. She feels an incongruous twinge of pity.

After a few seconds, Donna Olimpia turns towards Serafina. 'They tried to make me a nun,' she says, almost to herself. 'But I would not let them.'

Then she draws in a breath, rises from the bench, and hobbles towards the cell door without a backward glance. Orsola listens to them turn the lock and walk off along the corridor.

'Keep them both here for now,' Donna Olimpia says. 'Feed them, for God's sake – and bring that doctor back with his poultice. I need her well, do you hear?' Her voice grows strained as she begins to labour up the stairs. 'The moment is close, Mattei. It is close indeed.'

Orsola stands gingerly, flinching a little as pain spears down into her foot. Using her good leg, she climbs onto the bench, gripping the bars and hoisting her face to the window. Donna Olimpia emerges into the yard and crosses to her carriage at the same halting pace. She gets inside with a grunt of discomfort, the black folds of her gown disappearing into the cabin.

The *barone* orders the gates opened and the carriage starts out into the street, slowing as it navigates an awkward right turn. A half dozen beggars promptly move towards the carriage doors, rattling wooden cups and raising their hands in prayerful appeal. They are ignored, and most soon drift off again – but one does not. Rather shorter than the rest, this beggar is clad in a grubby turban and dark blue cloak, from which spills a thick, reddish beard. He lingers around the gates as the carriage completes its turn and clatters away, then takes a couple of stealthy steps towards the threshold. Orsola sees that his cloak has a simple yellow cross upon its back; and she frowns, for a garment very like this circulated among the residents of the grain loft, adorning a variety of soldiers and warrior saints. She slides her hand between the bars and opens it up, hoping that her pale palm will stand out against the surrounding brick and dirt.

A stable boy trudges over to the gates, grumbling a threat at Redbeard as he begins to close them up again. The beggar duly retreats, but he notices Orsola's hand. Their eyes lock across the dreary yard – and Orsola starts so sharply she nearly knocks her head against the bars. Just before the gates swing shut, the beggar tugs his bushy beard downwards, pulling it clean off his chin to reveal the grinning face behind.

Lontra.

Servus

De Pareja sits cross-legged in a dark corridor on the lowest level of the Palazzo Panciroli, waiting for the banquet upstairs to conclude so that he can accompany Don Diego back to the embassy. Satchel laid across his lap, he is attempting to write to Señora Inés on the Plazula de Santiago, by the light of a hissing tallow candle which he begged from the kitchens along with his supper. It is proving difficult, as his desire to reveal what is happening is so powerful and urgent, it seems to be hindering its own expression. I am almost there, he wants to say; I am so very close. When we meet again, señora, if it is the will of Almighty God, the world could be changed.

Since the presentation of Innocent's Jubilee portrait, all the collections of the Vatican have been opened up to them. The old palace of the popes is Cardinal Panciroli's domain, de Pareja senses, now that the Holy Father has chosen to house himself in the Palazzo del Quirinale. Panciroli often escorts Don Diego as he surveys the courtyard of the Belvedere. The little cardinal is both amiable and amenable, permitting his Spanish guest to make whatever new casts he desires; Don Diego's royal mission, their reason for coming to this strange, turbulent land, will be gloriously complete. Just that morning, de Pareja watched as a team of

Maestro Algardi's assistants set boards around the famed statue of Apollo standing with his bow raised, as they prepared to capture it in plaster before casting it in bronze.

And Panciroli's favour has extended even beyond this. The cardinal has penned a formal letter to the Papal Nuncio in Madrid, expressing his support of Don Diego's admission to the Order of Santiago, on account of his miraculous skill in art. This caused Don Diego some private exasperation, for it is exactly that – his reputation as an artist, rather than as a gentleman of the Spanish court – which he likes to blame for impeding his rise thus far. But even he cannot deny that the recommendation of the Secretary of State to the Holy Curia, the second man in the entire Catholic Church, will carry serious weight. At last, it seems probable that the cross of Santiago will soon be placed on Don Diego's chest; and then his slave will be granted manumission, and life can begin.

De Pareja stares at the chipped floor tiles before him, rolling a short quill slowly between his fingertips. After a year of absence, he finds that he can still bring Inés to his mind with perfect clarity. The beautiful, owlish roundness of her eyes. The lines at the sides of her mouth, impressed there by her ready laughter. The way her voice would change when they made their projections – their cherished, heartfelt jests about the future they would have together, if ever he was free.

But much else is uncertain. De Pareja has not tried to write to Inés before – not knowing, in truth, if she can read. This letter would have to go via his cousin Miguel, a carpenter in one of the workshops of the Alcazar, who would be able to get permission to take it out to her stall. If Miguel has to read it to her – or if she is gone for some reason and he opens it for himself, which de Pareja can easily imagine him doing – word of his hopes would surely be spread around the royal palace. Manumission is rare, God knows, and must be handled most carefully. Such an untimely disclosure could place Don Diego in a difficult position at court. It could make de Pareja appear presumptuous, as if he were boasting about something that has yet to come to pass, and end up undoing the very news he seeks to share.

It is too much. The mere thought of manumission, of the liberty that will follow, is oddly frightening. It feels so fragile and unlikely that de Pareja is convinced that the slightest obstacle or interference will cause it to melt away. He rests his head against the wall behind him and lets out a long breath.

The Compline bell rings at the nearby hospital of San Spirito. The party upstairs has been assembled now for just over two hours. De Pareja has learned that these dinners can go on well into the night, even in the houses of clerics. Deciding that Señora Inés' letter should best be left for now, he flexes his arms and looks along the gloomy passage. A scrawny, dappled cat is watching him from the corridor's end. It has stopped in a shaft of light cast from a room somewhere beyond, one of its front paws slightly raised. They consider each other for a few seconds. De Pareja holds out a hand, inviting it to approach. The cat, accustomed to the casual brutality of kitchen servants and street children, does not move. De Pareja persists, murmuring softly under his breath. Eventually, the cat lowers its head, as if relenting – then it twists around towards the light, dropping low and flattening its ears, and darts away so abruptly it seems almost to disappear.

The next moment, shouts are echoing down through the palazzo's stone stairways. 'Raise the alarm, raise the alarm! Seal the building at once – all the gates, all the doors! *Now*, damn you!'

'Fetch Doctor Mormando! Go, as fast as you can!'

De Pareja pinches out his candle, stuffs his writing materials back into his satchel and rises as quickly as his stiff limbs will allow. He realises that the entire household is being brought to a state of high alert; before he has even reached the stairs a pair of footmen hurry past him, heading for the kitchens, shouting for the scullery door to be locked. Guards are taking up positions at every door and staircase, whilst servants are bolting the shutters in place over the windows. His first thought is that they are under attack – that enemy raiders, Frenchmen most probably, are trying to force their way inside. Upon arriving in the main courtyard, however, he realises that the opposite is true. Panciroli's people are trying to prevent somebody from getting out.

De Pareja walks through a shallow colonnade, intending to ask one of the servants what is happening – but before he can speak a passing guard doubles back, takes him by the shoulder, and slams him against a column. A flushed, slab-like face looms into his own, the eyes bulging with fury.

'Who is this?' the man shouts. 'What's his business here?'

Straight away, a number of others are pressing around him also, seizing his arms. Half a dozen questions are yelled simultaneously; then someone strikes him hard in the belly, doubling him over.

'Heathen dog!' they spit. 'Godless worm! Keep hold of him there – don't let the devil escape!'

De Pareja struggles to breathe, his sight dimming as he stares down at the boots that are deliberately treading upon his own. He lifts his head, trying to stay calm, hoping to spot a person of authority to whom he can make his usual appeal. There is nobody: only guards and footmen, every one of them blazing with hostility and excitement.

'I am a Catholic,' he croaks, bile burning in his throat; then he swallows and repeats as loudly as he can, 'I am a *Catholic*, and a member of the Spanish party. I was admitted with my master, the painter Don Diego Rodríguez Silva y Velázquez.'

'Is a Spanish painter dining with his Eminence tonight?' a guard asks. 'Did you see their ambassador arrive?'

'The fiend is lying,' another declares. 'He is a spy, brothers! Rome is packed with them – with heathens and heretics of every stripe!'

'I've heard they're coming from African lands,' a third agrees, 'or the pagan kingdoms of the East. Their rulers have sent them to despoil the city of the pope. They see the Jubilee as a great chance for havoc and blasphemy.'

The men all nod and mutter, apparently convinced; their grip grows rougher, their fingertips digging deep into de Pareja's flesh. A sword is drawn and lifted up, the scratched blade flashing in the torchlight.

'Signori, please,' de Pareja says, his voice quickening, 'look at my clothes – at my satchel. I am a God-fearing Christian, just as you all are. We walk . . . we walk the same earth. We live beneath the same skies.'

As he says this, as he sees the implacably suspicious way they are regarding him, he wonders if it can ever be true. If his freedom would be enough, should he gain it. If there is something here that will never be overcome. He is attempting to speak again, to keep them talking, to ask what in heaven's name has just occurred, when a cry goes up by the main gates: someone has been seen in the lane outside, running from the palazzo in the direction of the river.

The currents in the courtyard promptly shift. De Pareja's captors move off to join the chase; he is released, shoved a couple of times and punched again, at the top of his chest. Once the pain has subsided, he wipes his eyes on his sleeve and looks around. Servants are flowing up and down the grand staircase, exchanging instructions, panicked remarks and snatches of prayer; and as de Pareja weaves across the courtyard towards them, he catches the same word over and over.

Poison.

Numb with dread, he starts up the broad, white steps, heading for the balcony of the palazzo's first floor. He might typically expect to be stopped and made to explain himself again, but the furore at the gates is causing enough of a distraction that night for him to be able to slip past. A single terrible image crowds all others from his mind: Don Diego dead at Cardinal Panciroli's table, slumped in his chair with his head on his plate, his earthly advancement halted permanently. Everything ruined. Everything lost.

De Pareja reaches the balcony. Along to his right, a set of tall doors stands open. The dining room beyond seems strikingly still after the furious activity of the courtyard. It is furnished in the lavish style of a senior churchman; he sees the gleam of pewter and polished glass, the cool smoothness of marble, the rich colours of the tapestries. He goes through the doorway. A long table is set for a banquet, with silver candelabra and extravagant centrepieces of fruit and flowers arranged down its middle. Not a single person is sitting at it. Lined up along one side of the room are the servants, both the waiters and kitchen staff by the look of them. Several are in tears. On the other side, standing back almost at the windows, are the masters – and praise God in His eternal glory, there at the margins is Don Diego, pale and profoundly discomforted but very much alive. De Pareja mutters a breathless prayer of thanks; and then, suddenly conscious of the great impropriety of his presence, he slides into the shadows behind a large antique urn, its glossy black surface circled by lithe, long-limbed dancers.

From here, he makes a more careful survey of the company. If any ladies were present, they have been dismissed. Cardinal Astalli is there, of course, and a few other clerics and gentlemen, both Roman and Spanish. De Pareja notices a bad smell: the curdled, vinegary reek of vomit. Searching for the source, he spies a yellowish splatter on the pristine white tablecloth, beside one of the central places — and then, with a start, he sees Cardinal Panciroli laid out in the corner of the room. The churchman is dead, for certain. His face is a horrible grey, with darker blotches around the neck, while his lips are drawn back unnaturally, exposing blackened gums and a set of uneven, discoloured teeth.

Looking to his master again, de Pareja finds that Don Diego is staring straight back at him. He does not seem surprised to see de Pareja in the dining room. His eyes are wide and alert, and his thoughts quite plain: he wishes to flee this place at the very first opportunity.

A voice is raised nearby, taut with impatience. De Pareja realises that the Duke of Infantado is among the servants, questioning them one by one in a blunt, aggressive manner. From his queries, it seems that he is seeking to establish that Panciroli alone was the assassin's mark.

'So you prepared particular dishes that were just for the cardinal's consumption?' the duke is asking, in response to a cook's stammered reply. 'Simple, frugal fare — things that would have been easy to identify?'

It goes on for a while longer. Infantado knows his business, and a dishearteningly clear picture is formed of what has occurred that night: a poisoner crept in through the kitchens, added a deadly draught to Panciroli's supper of steamed turbot, and then stole away again unseen. Word arrives from the captain of the household guard that despite an extensive search, no one was caught in the streets outside the palazzo. Whoever laced the cardinal's fish is gone.

Infantado stands rigid with anger. Addressing the assembled servants, he leaves them in no doubt that they have failed their master most grievously and can expect no charity from the Church in the wake of his death. They are ordered from the room, and file out swiftly; it is all some of them can do not to run. De Pareja remains where he is, reasoning that he is not one of their number, but sticking close to the shadowy urn nonetheless.

Once the doors have been secured, Infantado crosses over to a window, stopping only a couple of yards from Panciroli's body. 'She has done this before?'

Cardinal Astalli clears his throat; his hands, which rest upon the back of one of the upholstered dining chairs, are shaking badly. 'Nothing has ever been proved, your grace,' he says, his usual smoothness considerably diminished. 'But many in Roman society believe that Donna Olimpia has had several opponents silenced in this way. There are instances, also, where she is suspected of . . . removing certain Vatican officials, so that she might profit from the sale of their positions, via her creatures in the Church hierarchy.'

'Lord Almighty,' Infantado murmurs, gazing down into the street. 'The *dishonour* of it. That a noblewoman would order the death of the second man in Rome. That she should arrange it so that he died in front of his allies in his own house.'

Astalli is staring at Panciroli's body. 'We . . . we should have taken more care,' he says, his voice thick with remorse. 'Donna Olimpia herself might be gone, but her people remain. They are everywhere, your grace, infesting all of Rome. And they will commit grave wickedness on her behalf.'

De Pareja watches the other men of rank shift about, crossing themselves and eyeing the doors. This evening, intended as a celebration of their victory, has been plunged into disaster. Talk of peace is surely now to be replaced with talk of war, and they are reluctant to be carried along with it.

Infantado is not about to excuse anyone. 'That much is plain, Eminence,' he says. 'And this . . . *obscenity* before us surely demonstrates that papal favour alone is not sufficient. Cardinal Panciroli, God rest his soul, thought that replacing the Cardinal Nephew would rid the Holy Church of that woman and her noxious influence.' He gestures towards the corpse. 'And this is the result. Our enemy is without mercy. She will not rest until we are all banished from this city or laid out beside poor Panciroli. Our strategy must change, signori. We must strike back.'

Cardinal Astalli concurs. He straightens his crimson robes, attempting to assert something of his own authority. 'Don Diego, I take it that you are still receiving the papers from Naples?'

There is a pause.

Don Diego's eyebrows rise, his nostrils flaring as he inhales; de Pareja can tell that he hasn't been listening to the discussion, being concerned wholly with his desire to depart. 'Naturally, Eminence,' he says now, with a slight bow – although he has no idea, having left this particular duty entirely to de Pareja. 'They are safe and can be delivered whenever they are needed.'

'Delivered to Pope Innocent, you mean,' says Infantado, as if identifying a further flaw in a plan of which he has never approved. 'So much depends upon him, does it not? Cardinal Panciroli succeeded in placing himself between the pope and his wretched sister-in-law, and he kept the Holy Father's wrath towards her burning as brightly as he could. But now, Astalli, you know as well as I that it will start to cool. In fact, with his dear friend gone, he may begin to pine for her at once, as a source of consolation and comfort. These papers of yours may well lay out a detailed and irrefutable case against Olimpia Maidalchini – but if Innocent is set upon her return, and is prepared to deny even the evidence of his senses to bring this about, then what real use can they possibly be?' The duke points again to Panciroli. 'This shows her strength. An immediate blow must be landed in return. Something that will weaken her, here in Rome. Something that will truly *hurt*.'

A clear sense of horror is building throughout the dining room. Don Diego has bowed his head and is shifting his weight from foot to foot; he almost looks ready to disavow Spain, to disavow his king and his church, and make a break for the doors.

'That may be so, your grace,' Astalli says faintly, 'but I am afraid I—'

'You spoke of her people,' Infantado interrupts. 'Her *creatures*. You know who they are, I take it?'

'I do – the more prominent ones, at any rate. However, I—'

Infantado's composure vanishes. 'By the saints, Astalli!' he shouts. 'This woman has murdered your protector, the man who made you what you are! She thinks that by removing him she will weaken us. That we will falter and fail, and she can return. Is that what you desire?'

Once more, Astalli tries to gather himself. 'It is not, your grace,' he says. 'Of course it is not.'

Infantado turns to the company. 'Look at him,' he commands. 'All of you – look upon Giacomo Panciroli. Look at what she has wrought. And find your damned courage.'

The group stirs, attempting to express its abhorrence of Donna Olimpia and her near-Satanic turpitude, as well as its own determination to defeat her. It is not persuasive.

A thought, however, has occurred to Cardinal Astalli. 'There are rumours connected to certain of Donna Olimpia's subordinates,' he says. 'Rumours of truly vile deeds, committed with impunity during the widow's reign. Cardinal Panciroli and I had only just begun to investigate them.' He hesitates. 'This process, with regard to a couple of individuals, could possibly be expedited.'

Infantado appears not completely unsatisfied with this suggestion; he indicates to Astalli that he will hear more, when they are alone. De Pareja senses that the small company is about to be dismissed. The duke has one more matter to clarify, though. He turns to an older gentleman, slightly vague in manner, clad in dark green, who is standing close to the fireplace.

'Doctor Mormando,' he says, 'how did our friend Panciroli die?'

The gentleman appears confused. 'My diagnosis has not changed, your grace, since my initial examination. A tincture was added to the cardinal's food, that of a botanical perhaps, which caused him to—'

'It was a seizure,' Infantado tells him, in a tone that forbids dissent. 'Or a sudden inflammation of the brain. Say what you like. But let it be known that an aged and most blessed man was gathered to God, surrounded by his friends, as calmly and peacefully as any of us can hope for.' He faces the room. 'We will not give her this. Do you hear me? She will *not* have it.'

Mormando assents, as he must. The clerics and gentlemen also signal their agreement with varying degrees of robustness. Don Diego nods a touch too emphatically, his hair falling forward over his eyes. De Pareja glances towards the doors; if he moves as soon as the party dissolves, if he is quick and discreet, he should make it onto the balcony without being seen.

The Duke of Infantado draws back his shoulders, laying his hand on the jewelled pommel of his sword. 'Stay the course, signori,' he instructs. 'We will honour Cardinal Panciroli and serve the cause of Catholic virtue. We will bring about God's plan.'

*

'We must leave,' says Don Diego, the instant the door latch clicks in place behind them. 'As soon as can be arranged. This is not our place, Juan. I feel this . . . *most* powerfully. These are not our struggles.'

A deep, unfathomable weariness has settled upon de Pareja during the carriage ride back to the embassy; he tries to shrug it off, so that he might address his master's fears and steer him away from any imprudent decisions. 'Don Diego, the king desires that—'

'King Felipe desires me to return to Madrid,' Don Diego cuts in, as he lifts the pope's golden medallion from around his neck and drops it noisily upon the dresser. 'He has written many letters to that effect – several of them in his own hand. He believes that I delay my return unnecessarily, that I do not wish to see my wife, that there are things keeping me here, certain distractions, that I am loath to . . . to . . .' He stops talking, frowning at the patterned rug, thrown by the truth in his own words and how it undermines the argument he is attempting to make.

'I was referring to the king's business,' de Pareja says. 'Much of it is incomplete. Maestro Algardi's men are hard at work in the Belvedere, making their casts. Pieces are still arriving from Naples. A wondrous collection is being assembled, Don Diego, truly beyond all expectation, but it requires more time.'

His meaning is plain enough: if they leave now, they risk the success of their mission. The cross of Santiago. The freedom of Juan de Pareja.

Don Diego can see the sense here, despite his unwillingness to accept it. 'Agents can surely be employed to oversee Algardi and dispatch his works as they are finished,' he says. 'And the Neapolitan pieces need not come here at all. They could be sent directly to Spain and would very probably arrive at the Alcazar before we do ourselves.'

'It could be done that way,' de Pareja admits. 'There are dangers, of course. We would be trusting these agents with much and presenting works to the king we had not inspected ourselves.' He lowers his voice a touch. 'And Cardinal Astalli's conduit would be lost. There would be no new papers from the Count of Onate in Naples.'

Don Diego snorts. 'What of it? Our noble ambassador does not seem to place any great value in them, despite the risks I am taking. You heard him just then, in poor Panciroli's dining room. He has no interest in building a case against this widow, to demonstrate her perfidy to the pope. I truly believe that he would rather have her knifed in the street.'

'She has fled though, hasn't she?' de Pareja asks. 'To a stronghold in the north?'

'They do not believe it,' Don Diego replies. 'There was lengthy discussion of this before Cardinal Panciroli . . . before he was . . .'

His voice peters out. De Pareja fetches wine and he drinks deep, then drops into the nearest chair and covers his face with his hand. Standing there beside him, de Pareja feels the slightest itch of impatience. It is no small thing to see a man die; to see him poisoned at his own table. But much is at stake.

'Do they think Donna Olimpia is still in Rome?'

Don Diego struggles back up, propping himself on an elbow to drain his wine cup. 'Indeed they do. She lurks about, they say, like a fat black rat that has been chased beneath a sideboard – where she now sits sharpening her fangs, plotting her return.'

He begins to talk again of the absolute necessity of their departure, in less than a week if possible, and perhaps without informing Infantado, Astalli or anyone else beforehand. De Pareja's impatience grows. His master has not thought this through: like any gentleman of the court, he has no real conception of what leaving like this will involve.

'What of the paintings?' he asks, coming within a whisker of interrupting. 'Would you simply abandon them?'

This succeeds in giving Don Diego pause. He falls into a longer silence, pulling at the ends of his moustache; then he rises abruptly, takes a lit candle from a sideboard, and strides off through the dark apartment to the studio. De Pareja follows a few steps behind.

The four clerics are arranged in a line atop the dresser. There is the pope's chamberlain, Monsignor Massimi, in blue velvet; Monsignor Brandano, the chief officer of the Vatican Secretariat; a third de Pareja does not recognise; and Cardinal Camillo Astalli, clad in his red robes and biretta. Each is a slightly different size, but all are shown at bust length, head and shoulders only, against a bare background. For all his private assertions of reluctance, the experience of painting the pope and the great clamour of praise that followed has awakened something at Don Diego's core. A man does not possess a God-given talent such as his, and have honed his art as assiduously as he has done, without developing a deep and abiding love for it, whatever its effect upon his standing in King Felipe's court. Don Diego knows what he has wrought – how could he not? His abilities are at a point they have not approached for the better part of a decade, if ever. He could hardly refuse to exercise them further.

Don Diego goes straight over to the canvases, setting his candle incautiously close to Cardinal Astalli. Only this portrait and that of Brandano are complete, but the genius of all four is perfectly clear. These men, so proud and pompous, are there in the studio with them. The feather-light, almost liquid brilliance of his master's technique – impossible to describe satisfactorily, let alone emulate – fills de Pareja with the familiar combination of elation and despair. Normally this feeling is a spark only, fading as soon as it is struck. That night, however, it catches and flares up with sudden, startling brightness. It seems highly unjust that one who desires rank and wealth more than art, who seeks a knighthood rather than a painter's laurels, should be granted such miraculous ability. *How can I possibly equal this?* de Pareja thinks. *How can I learn from it? What will I ever be, with these works always before me?*

Since the Chinea, also, his labours have been unceasing. There have been canvases and paints to prepare, and expeditions across Rome to the houses of sitters, as well as the same endless tasks pertaining to King Felipe's statues. De Pareja has not opened his sketching folder for many days. The scarred nun has been forced to languish. He has an agonising sense of the heat and life ebbing from the idea, as the definition of memory begins to dwindle. *How can I be a painter,* he wonders, with an intense jolt of anger, *when I am allowed no damned time to paint?*

De Pareja takes a breath; he smells his own sweat and a trace of lavender, mixed with the thick odour of linseed oil. Whispering a prayer, he makes a determined attempt to damp these thoughts down. Disaffection is futile; he has long known this. He has watched it ruin others. He must weather his trials, these unending assaults upon his person, his mind, his dignity. He must keep to the plan.

Don Diego is leaning in, squinting as he studies the portrait of Astalli, perhaps noting something that he wishes to alter. De Pareja steps forward, taking the candle and holding it up, to distribute the light more evenly across the canvas and save it from immolation. The portrait itself is a most mysterious thing. Once more, he marvels at the enthusiasm with which these gentlemen sit before Don Diego, for the nature of Camillo Astalli is opened up before the world. Well-barbered curls glisten at the collar of his scarlet vestments, while the attempted serenity of his expression is spoiled by the very faintest beginnings of a smirk; and atop it all, his scarlet biretta has been knocked off centre, setting it at an oddly jaunty angle. The image suggests unseriousness and complacency: a facile man lifted far beyond his rightful place.

'These works are favours only, for members of Panciroli's faction,' pronounces Don Diego, straightening up again; he points to Astalli and Brandano. 'Those two I will deliver. The others can be left.'

De Pareja bows in obedience, posing no more questions: his master has convinced himself that they must leave, so he must bring it about. He looks around the gloomy studio, trying to assess the labours that lie ahead. The room is scrupulously clean as always, but it is also very full. Several tables are laden with artistic equipment. There are bowls, bottles and rags; jars filled with brushes, and stacked palettes of various sizes; canvas knives, grinding boards and mullers. A number of other canvases are propped against the walls, with two more fastened upon the easels. One of these, close at hand, is a copy of the papal portrait, begun while the original was still with them – a smaller work, just the head and shoulders, intended as a placatory gift for King Felipe. A good deal remains to be done; at present, Innocent's gnarly head floats against an expanse of grey ground, his mozetta a russet triangle.

The other canvas, larger and horizontal, is as different from the others as can readily be imagined. Don Diego retrieved this painting from de Pareja's chamber soon after he finished the papal portrait and has done much to it since. The woman is complete, in fact, absolute in her nakedness. De Pareja takes in the fall of daylight on her skin; the careless grace of her pose, with her back to the viewer and her face turned away; the loose knot of chestnut hair, tied up on her head. It is Flaminia Triunfi, of course. Every last brush mark seems to speak of his master's enthralment. The staggering fineness of it, and the sheer folly of its existence, makes him want to shout out in frustration.

'A classical subject,' says Don Diego, his tone slightly defensive. 'Venus at her mirror. See the space to the left – that is where I shall place Cupid, who will be holding up the mirror for his mistress. I suppose it is inspired by the statues we have collected, and the many masterful representations of the goddess I saw in Venice.'

'A classical subject,' de Pareja repeats.

'I have painted the figures of pagan myth before, Juan, if you recall,' says Don Diego. 'Several times. They are among the king's favourites of all my works.'

This point is made without much conviction, as Don Diego is well aware of its inadequacy. He has painted Mars, and Vulcan at his forge. Never has he painted the goddess of love. Never has he painted a female nude. Madrid is not Rome – not by a very significant distance. Upon their return, the Inquisitors of Santo Tomas will certainly comb through the collection they have assembled, questioning the moral worth of each and every item, and the necessity of placing it in the royal palaces. Discovery of this painting might not lead to immediate calamity; Don Diego is protected, always, by the favour of the king. It will most definitely affect his reputation, however, and the way he is perceived throughout the court – which is something that cannot be risked if he is to be considered for the Order of Santiago.

De Pareja says a few words of praise, trying hard to keep the exasperation from his voice. 'Forgive me, Don Diego,' he asks, 'but what do you mean to do with it?'

His master glances at him in surprise. 'Why, bring it with us to Spain – what else? Such a thing cannot be left behind.' He looks back tenderly at the Venus. 'Never before, in all my art, have I felt such . . . have my senses become so . . .'

'What of the Inquisition, though? What of your name?'

Don Diego blinks, then dips his head in acknowledgement. 'Discretion will be important, certainly,' he admits. 'But there will be a way around those troublesome friars. We will think of a solution, Juan, I am sure of it.'

De Pareja adjusts his grip on the candle holder, whose iron ring is growing hot against his skin. He has been contending with the more whimsical, unpredictable aspects of Don Diego's character for almost two decades now — and with particular frequency during this past year, as they travelled alone through Italy, with all the danger and wonderment that has involved. Once again, the only course open to him is to swallow his doubts and his vexation, and voice his agreement.

Don Diego is pleased by this, and relieved also. 'You are a man of true loyalty,' he declares, 'who will soon receive his just reward. We simply need to get back to our home, to our rightful place, and everything will begin to improve.'

De Pareja nods, and thanks his master — all the while looking over at the Venus, at the elegant, sinuous line of her body, and wondering what in God's holy name they are going to do.

*

A new consignment of statues arrives from Naples the next morning, shortly after the Angelus. Don Diego has already gone, summoned by the Duke of Infantado to a special Mass in the Cappella Paolina al Quirinale for the soul of Cardinal Panciroli. De Pareja himself has hardly slept, his mind seething with worries. He is light-headed and sore-eyed; but after so many shocks and setbacks, he is determined to put everything in order.

This time the papers are in with a small bronze Mercury,

merely tucked beneath one of the statuette's arms. De Pareja soon sees that they are different, obviously composed with a good deal more haste and containing rather less actual information. As he flicks through them, he discovers that the final sheet is not even ciphered, but a page of notes written in Latin on buff paper. De Pareja's knowledge of the language is limited, learned through necessity in the course of his master's business; he has only been permitted formal instruction in art, so that he can serve as Don Diego's assistant. He can tell, however, that this is a report of a conversation overheard in a taverna frequented by French agents, where repeated mention was made of the pope himself. A letter was being discussed, sent to their masters some months before: a pledge of support, bearing the papal seal and signature, stating that the Holy See would legitimise any actions taken against Spanish rule in Naples.

De Pareja lowers the page. If this report is accurate, Cardinal Astalli has made a serious miscalculation. The scheme to assist the French invasion of Naples does not just involve Donna Olimpia Maidalchini. Pope Innocent seems not only to be aware of it, but to endorse it — to be implicated in it, even. Back in Cardinal Panciroli's dining room, the Duke of Infantado claimed that Innocent could not be relied upon to use the evidence they are gathering against Donna Olimpia, due to the unaccountable hold she still has over him. But this report suggests that the pope will not act because he is a willing participant in this scheme — meaning that all these hard-won, carefully concealed intelligences are utterly worthless.

Heavy with misgiving, de Pareja adds the latest papers to the torso of the Mars, secures the cellar, and starts up through the embassy's system of back staircases. Disaster feels ever more imminent. He decides that Don Diego is quite correct: this is not their fight. They can do nothing more in Rome but be used for others' ends, and risk lasting damage for no good purpose. He begins to run through his duties, compiling a schedule for their departure and identifying tasks of particular difficulty.

Between the second and third floors, de Pareja realises that someone is standing on the staircase ahead, just around a shallow bend. Three more steps and he can see something of them – and he almost trips over, for their profile is exactly that of the large painting upstairs, which is among the most pressing and awkward of his problems.

Flaminia Triunfi is tired and none too clean, but the warmth of her smile still causes de Pareja's breath to catch a little in his throat. They have not spoken since the day she had him show her the oil study of the scarred nun, and then fled so inexplicably. He has seen her through the cracks in half-closed doors, or climbing into hired carriages in the lanes around the piazza. At times, their eyes have met, and she has given him nothing, a blank barrier only – no hint of apology or an explanation to come. Accordingly, he merely nods in response, intending to cut by her and carry on his way.

As he passes, however, Flaminia extends a hand, her fingers shining white as they touch a narrow sunbeam that falls across the staircase from somewhere above. 'Good morning to you, señor,' she says. 'How very hushed it is in here today. Almost like church.'

De Pareja stops. She will surely know the reason for this, as word of Cardinal Panciroli's death has spread throughout the city. He looks at her for a second, noticing the slight chapping on her upper lip; the single silver hair in her left eyebrow.

'Don Diego is not here,' he says. 'He will be gone until noon at least.'

Flaminia gives a small shrug, as if this is not important. 'How goes the sculpture collection? Will your king be pleased?'

'We hope so, signorina,' de Pareja replies; a spiteful impulse comes over him. 'Our labours in Italy are nearly complete. My master and I will soon be ready to return to Spain.'

Flaminia smiles again, rather more tightly. 'So I have heard. I shall pray that you both receive the advancements you deserve.' She looks off to the side, towards the floor below. 'You are a talented man, señor. It is only right that you be given the chance to express it freely – to bring forth that which God has—'

De Pareja has heard enough. 'Why did you leave like that?' he interrupts. 'Did you know the person in the sketch – the scarred nun?'

Flaminia hesitates, then nods; she has been expecting this question and believes she is ready for it. 'I came across her, out in the city,' she says. 'It was a week or so before I saw your work, close to the Piazza Navona. She was speaking of the life of Santa Catarina with great passion.' Her voice grows quieter; more halting. 'Catarina was . . . she was beloved by my younger sister, who died some years ago. We would read the saint's legend together and recite its lines. It was . . . very strange to listen to it again after so much time.'

De Pareja is not convinced. He has thought of that moment often, poring over exactly what Flaminia said and the expressions upon her face, and has decided that there is only one plausible explanation. 'You seemed to know her, signorina,' he insists. 'To recognise her.'

Flaminia shakes her head. 'You are mistaken. I was upset to be reminded of my sister, that's all. Most upset. She left me suddenly, señor. She left me quite alone.'

Despite his doubts, a part of de Pareja's mind is now busily picturing this encounter near the Piazza Navona – a fresh view of the scarred nun, engaged in a new and dramatic composition. His ill temper recedes; he regards Flaminia with sympathy and a certain puzzlement.

'Then surely there is solace to be found in this,' he says. 'God was awakening these memories within you, signorina. Perhaps He was showing you that your sister dwells with this holy saint in Paradise. That she is saved.'

Flaminia will not hear this either. She looks back briefly at de Pareja, a line etched in the middle of her brow; all her amiability and confidence have gone, like a changing of the light. It is clear that whatever she wanted from him when she reached out a minute earlier, he has failed to supply. Gathering in her shawl, she carries on towards the top floor, not seeming to care if he follows.

'My sister is not saved, señor,' she says over her shoulder. 'She is among the lost.'

PART THREE

The Mirror of Venus

Domina

The grey carriage is tucked in a shadowy alley off the Via della Mercede. Inside, Donna Olimpia fumes and sweats, her playing cards lying forgotten upon the cushion beside her. So aware is she of the time that is passing, of Rome flowing ever onwards while she remains mired at the margins, that she cannot rest or think; she cannot *live*. Everything she sees is an annoyance. A provocation. An *insult*. The Holy Jubilee, for example, still grinding on so many weeks after everyone of any taste or judgement has tired of it. The performers, prancing and warbling like musicians nobody any longer cares to hear. The wretched, malodorous pilgrims, whose welcome has become so threadbare that if it was held up to the light, you could see straight through it.

And then, perhaps worst of all, there are the Spanish. A detachment of their soldiers is marching past the carriage at that very moment. Through a crack in the shutters, she glimpses the morions, the flags and the hooked halberds, as they head out from their piazza like men at war – like they are about to *do something*, to strike some blow on their king's behalf. It fills her with an unutterable scorn. It worries her.

Ludovisi sits opposite, in a state of some disarray. He climbed aboard only a few minutes previously, as the carriage passed the church of Sant'Andrea delle Fratte. They have important matters to discuss, but the fat prince appears to have dozed off, oblivious to the heat and noise, his head tilting back until it crushes his hat's brim against the side of the cabin. When he starts to snore, Donna Olimpia wants very much to lean over and give his nose a hard tweak. Instead, she taps the tops of her knees with her knuckles, and Madonna it makes them hurt; but she finds herself tapping them again, and harder, because *damn* them, and *damn* the God that has cursed her with them, and—

The voice comes first, rich and studied, filling the alley and echoing in through the carriage window; that Cavaliere Bernini struts about his chambers rehearsing his remarks seems beyond all doubt. He is annoyed, as Donna Olimpia was warned he would be, complaining to Baron Mattei about the interruption. A master disturbed is an offence to God, so they say; the Cavaliere has been sheltering behind this notion his entire damned life. She finds that she does not care in the least. That she is glad of it, even, and is spoiling for a fight.

Donna Olimpia flings open the door, almost knocking it against the western wall of the Cavaliere's palazzo. The lauded sculptor is standing there before her, with Baron Mattei at his back. Briefly, she considers him: the eagle brow, the bony nose, the oiled moustaches; the thinning black hair atop his bare head; the affronted masculine pride that blazes in his eyes. She feels herself begin to sneer.

'I am most busy, Donna Olimpia,' he begins stiffly, refraining from a bow. 'You are aware, I think, that your brother-in-law's latest fountain will not fashion itself. If the boards are to come down, if the waters are to gush and spurt, if the work is to rise above absolute *wretchedness*, then these hands' – here he holds them up, with no small degree of self-reverence – 'must be applied to their labours throughout every hour of the day.'

'Have you heard from her?'

The Cavaliere knows who she means, but he brushes at his smock – which she notices is tailored rather better than many noblemen's doublets – and continues as if she has not spoken. 'I do wonder what business we could have, you and I, as all Rome is talking of Alessandro Algardi, and the surpassing likeness of a portrait bust he has recently completed. A marble Donna Olimpia remains in Rome, they are saying, even as the living woman takes herself away to San Martino! I am told it is a masterpiece – so what use, dear lady, could you possibly have for another sculptor?'

Donna Olimpia does not bother to hold back her laugh. 'Just this moment past,' she says, 'you were complaining about the grand commission my family has bestowed upon you – a commission, I might add, that was intended to salve your own bruised fortunes. Tell me, am I to offer *everything* to Cavaliere Bernini? Am I to wait until I am gathered to Almighty God for him to complete what I ask of him, and view his productions from my seat in heaven?'

Bernini pouts and tuts, his moustaches twitching. 'Algardi is an ape,' he says shortly. 'He isn't fit to chisel the sign for a Pigna shithouse. I tell you, Donna Olimpia, I would not let him clean my tools. Why, the last thing of his I saw had—'

'Cavaliere,' Donna Olimpia says, more loudly. 'Have you heard from Flaminia Triunfi?'

The Cavaliere releases a monumental sigh; then he leans to the side, planting one of those precious hands against the wall of his house. He is tired, Donna Olimpia sees, although whether this is due to overwork or something else she can only guess.

'She was angry with me,' he says at last. 'By the saints, she was *very* angry with me. I was sworn to secrecy, you understand. It is a most delicate thing, her connection with this Spaniard. She reveres him, Donna Olimpia. She values his example, and what she believes he is able to teach her, so very highly. By telling you of their affair, I was betraying—'

'Where has she gone? Is she still in Rome, even?'

'Don Diego is a difficult man, she says,' the Cavaliere goes on. 'He thinks everything of his art, and nothing of it at all. The Spanish are barbarians, of course; everyone knows that. She says that he does not seem to understand his own talent — that at times he seems almost to resent it. It is a confounding circumstance, to be sure. If such ability had been imbued in the soul of an *Italian*, well . . .'

'Cavaliere Bernini,' says Donna Olimpia, 'I swear by the Blessed Virgin that if you do not answer my questions, I will have Baron Mattei break your thumbs.'

The Cavaliere pauses, apparently unmoved by this threat. 'Flaminia is a dear girl,' he says. 'She is very dear to me, Donna Olimpia, do you hear? Her poor mother did me a great service in our youth, and I will not see her compromised. Honour will not permit it. Her circumstances are so very fragile. I would have thought that you, in particular, would understand.'

Donna Olimpia scowls, shifting on her cushion, her patience all but gone. She is about to give her unvarnished opinion on the Triunfi family and their dissolute daughter, and the arrogant, ageing sculptor who is wasting her time with such swaggering profligacy, when it occurs to her that Bernini simply doesn't know. Flaminia Triunfi no longer trusts him.

Narrowing his eyes slyly, the Cavaliere attempts to move their conversation on to a rather different subject. 'I must say, Donna

Olimpia, that I am surprised to see you so agitated. Cardinal Panciroli, your most steadfast opponent, has been claimed by the Lord and will injure you no more. I might add that the circumstance has been managed to perfection. There has been no capture, and no suspect named. The good cardinal was struck down in his home, as if by divine will.'

'I do not understand you,' says Donna Olimpia.

The Cavaliere claps his hands together. 'It is *courage*,' he says firmly. 'Holy scripture urges us to show courage for ourselves, and also for our people. You have acted for everyone in Rome who would see balance restored, and the influence of Spain reduced to its rightful extent. You have *resisted*, when so many would not dare to. You are Daniello, dear lady, in the lions' den. You are David.'

Donna Olimpia is not about to discuss any of this with Cavaliere Bernini. Seeing that nothing more can be gained from their discourse, she glances at Baron Mattei; the soldier promptly steps aside, clearing the Cavaliere's path back to his studio.

'If you happen to see Flaminia,' she says, leaning forward to take hold of the door, 'send her to me.'

The carriage leaves the alley and turns along the Via della Mercede. Donna Olimpia watches the Cavaliere through the gap in the shutters, walking to his gate. He spots her, and consents now to make a quick, neat bow, shot through with mockery.

'That coxcomb thinks that I ordered Panciroli's death,' she says. 'He honestly thinks that I would have a cardinal poisoned. My brother-in-law's secretary of state.'

Ludovisi sniffs and begins to pull himself up, lifting a haunch to release a surreptitious squeak of wind. It is unclear how long he has been awake or how much he has heard, but he was plainly content to stay out of sight; he has a wish to avoid Bernini at present that Donna Olimpia suspects is to do with money lost at the gaming table.

'That was certainly his implication,' he murmurs, mopping away some drool on his fine lace cuff.

'It is astonishing, Ludo, truly it is. Quite apart from fear of hellfire, how would such an act possibly serve me? Whatever advantage I might derive from Panciroli's death pales beside the effect it must be having upon the pope. He will . . . He will be . . .'

Donna Olimpia stops, recalling how Giambo and Panciroli were together: the scholarly bond between them, in all its strength and oddness, so inexplicable to more practical minds; the infuriating ease with which the cardinal could turn the pope's thinking around with a carefully chosen passage of scripture.

'Well, he will be heartbroken. If he really thinks that I killed his friend, it will set him against me most powerfully. It must be made clear to him that I was not involved. Giacomo Panciroli was an old man, after all, who could be expected to pass on at any time. He was not well; *none* of them are well. Is it so ridiculous that he died just as his doctor has proclaimed?'

Ludovisi rubs his eyes, making a visible effort to rouse his intellect and apply it to their conversation. 'Some are saying that the Barberini were responsible,' he volunteers. 'Perhaps encouraged by their friends in France. Panciroli had definitely set himself up as the primary obstacle to their ambitions.'

Donna Olimpia has already pondered this possibility; she has spent far longer speculating about who might have caused Panciroli's demise, in fact, than she has dwelling upon the departed cardinal's memory, or praying for his soul.

'They do have a reputation for such things,' she says. 'And one that is justified, I might add, unlike my own. But it is disappointing that they would take such a step without consulting me, or even issuing a warning. It was a move devoid of strategy, Ludo. Of any deeper understanding of Rome. Panciroli we knew; the man who will replace him, we do not.'

Ludovisi leans back, yawning hugely. 'Many favour Fabio Chigi,' he says, as it ends. 'Some considerable sums have been wagered on him already.' He chuckles, picking at his teeth. 'Our slippery comrade Mascambruno also tried to put himself forward for consideration, but the word is that Cardinal Astalli forbade it in the most absolute terms.'

Donna Olimpia lets out a dark laugh, for she can hardly think of anyone less suited to the role of secretary of state than her conniving datary. Ludovisi has been keeping her apprised of the grave animosity that is building between Mascambruno and the traitor Astalli. This has led to Mascambruno deliberately impeding Astalli's efforts to enrich his family members from the papal treasury, as is customary for the Cardinal Nephew. The sheer stupidity of this chills Donna Olimpia's blood. Once again, she can only wonder as to Masco's intentions. The datary imagines that he is a master tactician, an operator of the highest order, yet he is in danger of exposing them utterly.

Of Bishop Fabio Chigi she has no real opinion. Nuncio to Germany, he has been away at Munster for the whole of Giambo's reign; he is known among the Curia as the calm, measured voice that relayed the Treaty of Westphalia, which ended the northern wars on such ignoble terms, to the increasingly despairing pope. She can remember some cardinal or other describing him as incorruptible, without ambition, and entirely above the games of the Vatican. But this is said of many clerics.

The grey carriage begins to circle around towards Esquilino, using a familiar network of backstreets and alleyways. Donna Olimpia's thoughts return to the question Cavaliere Bernini could not answer for her. She glowers across the stuffy cabin at Ludovisi, who has embarked upon the laborious patting of his person that she knows is the search for a pipe. It could be argued that the fat prince has failed her, failed her badly, but there is not a speck of contrition or discomfort in him, beyond that inflicted by his excesses.

'How could this have happened, Ludo?' she says, the desire to attack him creeping back. 'How could you and all of your people across Rome have possibly lost sight of Flaminia Triunfi? Is this due to inattention, I wonder – to drunkenness, laxity and sloth?'

Ludovisi suspends his pipe search. 'It often goes like this, Mama,' he says, with a dash of condescension. 'The strumpet knows that we are watching her, so she has made a particular effort to hide herself away.' He clears his throat noisily, popping open the top two buttons of his doublet. 'There are various . . . resources I could still call upon to draw her out, but I believe that they are best saved for a moment of true need. Flaminia will do what was asked and then she will return to you – for what choice does she have, if she wishes to fulfil your bargain?'

Donna Olimpia scoops up the playing cards from the seat beside her. She thinks of Claudia Triunfi collapsed on the floor of that chapel, stinking, starving, hopelessly mad – and has a sudden, startling sense of the narrowness of this course she has selected. Of how perilous it could prove, and how great the costs even should it succeed. She quashes this feeling at once. She is merely adapting her plans to the shifting of the city, as she has always done – throughout her marriage to Pamphilo Pamphili, when she slowly made herself so essential to his overcautious fool of a brother; and then for the eleven years of her widowhood, as she engineered Giambo's rise to the papal throne. It is how she survives.

'What of my granddaughter?' she asks, shuffling her cards briskly.

Ludovisi blows out his pasty, unshaven cheeks, and then summarises a series of confidential conversations with people inside the Palazzo Giustiani, from the lowest servants to the senior Latin tutor. The girl is reported to find the company of her parents distinctly trying; to miss Donna Olimpia most sorely, and ask after her several times a day; to be keen to leave Rome, and join her grandmother in San Martino at the earliest opportunity.

Donna Olimpia nods. 'Guard her closely, Ludo,' she says as she shuffles on. 'Olimpiuccia may still be required.'

*

The church was chosen for its widows. Hidden away in the north-eastern corner of Esquilino, it is dedicated to Santa Barbara; the saint has been daubed in a side chapel by some third-rate master, draped sadly around her tower. The building itself has a small, plain dome, still mildewed somehow after this desperately arid summer, a dull, peeling altar, and a collection of rickety chairs, all of which seem equally likely to collapse during Mass and deposit you unceremoniously upon the flagstones. It is a miserable place.

The immediate neighbourhood, however, is home to a great many soldiers, Barbara being the patron saint of armourers and artillerymen. During the recent conflicts in the north, Almighty God saw fit to carry a good number of them off to Glory, and the bereaved wives now flock to this church on every day of the week. Ragged infants in tow, they badger the deacons for alms; exchange tips about good places for piece work, or decent charitable kitchens, or grand houses looking to send out their laundry;

and they pray, endlessly and with much emotion, for the souls of their fallen warriors and the fortunes of those left so dismally behind.

As one more widow, carefully clad in her plainest weeds, Donna Olimpia draws little notice here. The priest, also, is so short-sighted that he does not recognise her as she limps to the communion step; and so simple-minded and incurious that he hears her confession without a murmur, and makes a penitential prescription of the very mildest variety. There in that fusty little box, she owns up to envy, to greed, to vengeful and wrathful thoughts, and he assigns her prayers that she has said before she has even stepped back out into the sunshine.

It is convenient, certainly, but also profoundly unsatisfying. Hiding does not suit her, and neither does forgiveness. Amid the bustling, chattering widows, she longs for confrontation – for the stark definition of enmity. She needs to feel her foes' dismissal, and their contempt; and then to savour that exquisite moment when they see that she has outplayed them once again, and their cause is quite lost. Within that sorry heap of a church, spiritual succour is thus in short supply. Typically, Donna Olimpia leaves it in the blackest of tempers, aching with frustration and knees afire, ready to swipe at anyone who comes close.

It is in this condition that Baron Mattei discovers her, although he does not acknowledge it. He nods towards the grey carriage, which is waiting on the next corner, and tells her the news the moment they are inside. It hardly improves her mood.

'Raided,' she repeats.

Mattei nods. 'Papal investigators are emptying Monsignor Mascambruno's offices at this very moment, Excellency. Every last scrap of paper is being carried along the Via della Dataria to the Palazzo del Quirinale.'

Donna Olimpia arranges her skirts. She is frightened, she realises, her body jangling with an unbearable imminence. It is a strange feeling, remarkably intense, and most unwelcome. 'What of the Monsignor himself?'

Mattei regards her coolly through his good eye. 'Word of the raid got out at dawn,' he tells her. 'A number of the clerks took to their heels immediately, fleeing the Dataria with whatever they could carry. But Monsignor Mascambruno stayed to face them. He was led from the building in chains, then transported to the Tor di Nona. I hear that his house has been placed under heavy guard, ahead of a formal search.'

Donna Olimpia attempts to recover her composure. So here is the Spanish faction's revenge for Panciroli — their act of misplaced retribution. The possible consequences make her head swim. Mascambruno is a weakness; she has long been aware of that. Holy saints, he has been a party to so much. So many years of petitions and dispensations. So many gifts and indulgences. So much blessed *gold*.

And that house. Donna Olimpia has never been there; it would not do to visit the residence of a man such as Mascambruno. On occasion, however, he could not help alluding to the existence of a personal archive that was stored in its attic, a library of material of quite extraordinary delicacy. What it might contain, and what this might mean for her, is a thought so unnerving that Donna Olimpia does not dare even to approach it.

'Astalli,' she says. 'Astalli did this.'

Amid everything else, she feels the stirrings of a peculiar, unexpected satisfaction. She had thought Camillo Astalli to be gutless — capable of treachery but little else. Raiding the datary's offices suggests otherwise. The death of his patron has plainly brought about a change in Astalli. This is the move of an adversary.

'It is being done with the full authority of the Curia,' says Mattei. 'Concerns were raised by a Jesuit from Portugal, a Father Brandano. They suspect forgery.'

Donna Olimpia orders their return to her villa. 'Astalli is behind it, Mattei,' she says. 'He aims to scare Mascambruno witless and wring confessions from him that will end me as well. To rid himself of two annoyances with a single strike.'

As the carriage turns, she tries to plot a path through what now surely lies ahead. From time to time, usually after liquor, she and Mascambruno talked of the possibility of this outcome. He assured her that if their enemies ever came for him, he would hold. He would reveal nothing whatsoever of their business. She had given him everything that he had, and in return she had his loyalty. He would hold.

But this is Masco, a man as lacking in honesty and integrity as he is in Christian virtue. It was a large part of what made him so useful. Donna Olimpia thinks of the medallion he slipped into that coin coffer and the mysterious intent behind it. The datary is a schemer of the lowest kind, and one who fancies himself supremely clever; and now he has been pulled from his hole, dangled by his tail, and dropped into a bucket with no chance of escape. Above all else, of course, he is a coward. And cowards are capable of doing unholy damage indeed.

They are underway now, heading down a gentle slope. The more Donna Olimpia mulls it over, the more impressed she is by Astalli's nerve. Whatever happens next, this move of his will have serious repercussions. Mascambruno might be her creature in particular, but he is far from exclusive. With her blessing, the datary has made sure to weave himself into the fabric of Giambo's papacy and the offices that support it. Many important clergymen and nobles know him; they have had him dine at their tables and do them various services. Will they defend him now and perform that awkward dance that allows for both his exoneration and his condemnation? She almost smiles at the thought. One thing is certain, though: Astalli is forcing her hand. The plan must be advanced, and quickly.

Donna Olimpia looks over at Baron Mattei. 'Go to Prince Ludovisi,' she says. 'Tell him that our moment of need has arrived.'

Servus

Maestro Algardi is there to greet them with a dozen assistants and apprentices assembled around him. De Pareja recognises Finelli, the principal, along with a few of the others; they have kept him waiting for many hours over the course of the summer and shown him their progress with offhanded rudeness. The mood today is rather different, however. Each one is attentive, respectful, as if awaiting an honoured guest. They have brushed the marble dust from their clothes and beards, or at least made an attempt to do so. A degree of order has also been imposed upon the materials piled about the yard: the bronze ingots are now stacked neatly, the pieces of cut stone set in even lines, and the planks and poles leaned up against the walls.

The masters bow, embarking upon the customary praise of each other's work. Don Diego delivers a fairly convincing account of his recent tour of Buen Respiro, the papal villa beyond the city walls, which contains many of Algardi's productions. Predictably, the sculptor talks of Pope Innocent's portrait and the wonder it has caused — and the deep misery, he adds with a laugh, among any who seek to make their living painting likenesses. Don Diego thanks him with an uneasy smile. Algardi then proposes that they go across to his studio for refreshment and to survey the original works he has been preparing for His Catholic Majesty King Felipe. Don Diego bows again in acceptance, and they leave with Finelli in tow.

The assistants begin to drift apart, muttering and spitting on the flagstones. Bonarelli, the next in seniority, issues a series of instructions, reminding everyone of their duties – and is met with some instructions in return, involving lengths of wood and the orifices of his body. De Pareja finds himself ignored. He lets them run on for a minute or so, then reminds Bonarelli loudly of their particular business that morning: he is to be shown the cast that is being prepared ahead of the main commission, so that it can be shipped to Spain and presented to King Felipe as Don Diego rejoins the royal court.

Mention of the king proves effective. Bonarelli promptly breaks off from his hectoring and leads de Pareja out of the yard into one of the casting workshops. It has a high ceiling and a row of windows on the southern side; all of them have been thrown wide open, but this does little to relieve the stifling heat given off by the several stoves that are placed around the room. De Pareja follows Bonarelli's broad back among tables strewn with sculptors' tools. Lumps of clay glisten in bowls of cloudy water; sticks of wax the colour of wine are bundled like firewood; blocks of plaster have been split open to reveal exquisitely detailed impressions of bearded heads or muscular limbs. Between these tables stand buckets and barrels, the occasional complete statue, and the disembodied parts of many others. De Pareja recognises some of these works as belonging to their commission, but many more of them he does not. Algardi's is one of the largest shops in Rome, a place of constant industry, fulfilling many different contracts at once – a worthy example, he tells himself, of what can be done.

The Apollo is in the south-west corner. It has been cast in red wax and divided into four separate sections, which are laid out in a row upon a battered workbench. There is the head; the torso and right arm; the outstretched left arm, and the magnificent fold of the cloak; and the legs with the tree trunk beside them, a python edging its way across the bark. This is the initial model, made from the casts taken in the Belvedere, which will serve as the basis for the bronze copy Don Diego has ordered for their king.

De Pareja thanks Bonarelli and asks that he be allowed to make a proper inspection. The assistant shrugs and leans against the wall, folding his thick arms. A couple of others are back in the shop now, returning to their work; and before long, like everyone else in the city, they are talking of the trial underway in the courts of the Vatican.

This event is preoccupying all of Rome, from its gilded state-rooms and marble-clad apartments to the kitchens, cellars and tavernas, eclipsing the Holy Jubilee entirely. As de Pareja understands it, the situation is this: Monsignor Mascambruno, Pope Innocent's datary and one of his most trusted officials, has been found to be a forger of quite astounding greed and ambition, supplying a corrupted network that extends throughout the Catholic world. One particularly salacious case has brought about his downfall. A Portuguese count, discovered to have married a boy of seventeen, was due to stand trial before the Inquisition – who would surely have sentenced him, his unholy bride, and the priest that married them to burn at the stake. After a payment of some forty thousand scudi, however, a papal bull miraculously appeared. This document ordered that the count's case be placed under the jurisdiction of a local bishop, who also happened to be a relative of the disgraced nobleman. Sure enough, this bishop turned out to be far less disposed to burning, or indeed any punishment beyond a small fine.

'Fellow feeling, it was,' Bonarelli proclaims. 'This Mascambruno is known to have a boy here in Trevi, and one in Pigna and Trastevere too. He saw himself in this sodomite nobleman – a vision of his own future. That's why he took such a risk. Well, that and a cartload of gold.'

Among the laughter, de Pareja makes a show of studying the head of the Apollo: the line of the profile, the shape of the brow, the tight curl of the hairs. Algardi's shop know their business, he has to admit; this will be among the finest bronzes in Madrid. King Felipe will surely be pleased.

The assistants are talking now of how the datary's crimes were committed – how he exploited the pope's weakness of mind, and the trust in which he was held, to trick the old man into signing these fraudulent documents.

'It's the nerve of it,' says one of the others. 'Did he think no one would question such a thing? Did he honestly imagine that nobody would investigate?'

'There it is, brother,' says Bonarelli. 'There it is exactly. Monsignor Mascambruno thinks himself protected. Even now, he does not believe any ill can befall him.'

'Does he think that the pope will intervene on his behalf? They say that the matter has left Innocent awash with sorrow. Beyond all consolation.'

'So he should be,' replies Bonarelli tersely. 'He's been made to look like the lowest breed of donkey. Like an absolute shit-eating fool.'

De Pareja examines the folds of Apollo's cloak, admiring the soapy smoothness of the wax and the crisp precision of its edges. Then, as he reaches the legs and tree trunk, he opens his satchel and takes out the length of twine he measured and cut before they left the embassy. This section has been stood upright on the bench;

the trunk is set at a slight angle to the ground but it is straight enough overall. There is a join at the top, also, where two parts of the cast will be fitted together. His heart lifts. This might actually be possible.

'But Mascambruno does not look to the *pope*,' Bonarelli continues. 'His attachment is to a far greater power. He has named no one else, you notice. Who knows what they did to him in the Tor di Nona, and still he has said nothing. Mark my words, the Monsignor sees his angel up above. He has only to remain loyally close-lipped, and she will swoop down to save him.'

De Pareja unravels his twine. There seems to be rather more of it than he remembers; he knows before he holds it to the trunk that it is not quite tall enough for the purpose he has in mind. He curses softly.

Bonarelli hears this. 'Is everything well?' he asks, a slight defensiveness entering his voice.

De Pareja turns from the cast. Four of Algardi's men are watching him from their different places around the room, waiting for his answer. All are well made and strong, and the oldest of them is ten years his junior. Abruptly, he is transported back to Cardinal Panciroli's courtyard. The close, yelling faces, filled with loathing and suspicion; the boots and punching fists; the drawn sword. He takes a breath, blinking the memory away.

'Signor Bonarelli, I must request, in my master's name, that you make a small adjustment. The figure itself is beyond criticism. It is this base.' De Pareja taps the oval disc, also wax, to which both legs and trunk are attached; it is presently no thicker than his drawing folder. 'It will need to be somewhat taller, so that the bronze cast is properly suited to its intended place in the gardens of the Alcazar.' He indicates the disc's side. 'I believe that two hand-widths of additional elevation would suffice.'

De Pareja has no idea whatsoever where the bronze Apollo might eventually be situated, but he speaks convincingly enough. The four assistants look at each other for a long moment, as if deciding how to react. They settle upon amusement.

'Tell us, friend,' chuckles Bonarelli, 'what are they saying about the trial on the Piazza Trinita — no, I humbly beg your pardon, on the *Piazza di Spagna*? Was Mascambruno's arrest a surprise to your ambassador, the noble Infantado? I hear he is a staunch ally of Cardinal Astalli. How much did he know about what was to be done?'

De Pareja demurs, pushing his twine back into his satchel. 'It is not for me to consider such things, signor,' he says. 'I perform the tasks I am set, that is all.'

Bonarelli smirks at the others. 'Come,' he says, walking off between the workbenches. 'We have something else here that might be of interest to you.'

De Pareja does not know what to make of this. He repeats some of what he just said about the base, raising his voice a little. Is it possible? Can he tell his master that it will be completed in time? Bonarelli merely beckons in reply, without looking back. He reaches a narrow door and walks through. The others are returning to their work, shaking their heads and grinning, refusing to meet de Pareja's eye. He sees that he has no choice but to follow.

The door leads into a storeroom, a single skylight set into its angled ceiling. Finished pieces stand along the walls, four or five of the life-sized portrait busts for which Maestro Algardi is deservedly famed. De Pareja sees a bishop wearing a neat biretta; a gentleman in a large ruff, the folded lace carved with extraordinary skill. A couple of the others are covered with white sheets, to keep them free from dust. Bonarelli has stopped by one of these, which has been placed centrally in the full glare of daylight; and as de Pareja approaches it, he snaps off its cover with a sardonic flourish.

De Pareja is adept at concealing his reactions, but still he feels himself flinch. Donna Olimpia Maidalchini has been captured, held forever in marble, her plain black garb reversed to gleaming white. It has the odd lifelessness of these busts, of course – the head and shoulders cut from the body and set on a plinth; the eyes blank, inscrutably empty. The effect of it, however, the sheer *presence* of it, cannot be denied. The widow's hood billows out like the wings of a bat, or the petals of some veinous tropical plant. The face has neither beauty nor majesty; the truth of life, of time, has not been evaded or reduced. Algardi has shown an old woman, her jawline lost to jowls. Her expression is not wrathful nor openly defiant, but there is an unnerving directness to it. An assertiveness. A clear, unrepentant sense of purpose.

'Dear God,' says de Pareja.

'We have just finished polishing it,' Bonarelli informs him. 'I am told that it is to stay here for a while, though, on account of its owner being . . . inconvenienced at present.'

De Pareja murmurs some words of praise, but alarming thoughts are crowding his mind. Why exactly is Bonarelli showing him this? Is it an attempt at intimidation? Could this man be an agent of Donna Olimpia – or of the Barberini, of the French king? Or is he simply making mischief – having his fun at the expense of the Spaniard's Morisco slave? Either way, he finds that it angers him. His patience with this situation, with these assistants and their games, is at an end.

'So your master has been taking her gold at the same time as King Felipe's.'

Bonarelli shrugs again. 'This is Rome,' he says; then his smile grows conspiratorial. 'Now it's just the two of us here, friend, I wonder if you might aid my understanding of this trial we are all talking about so much. Was Monsignor Mascambruno unmasked as revenge for the death of that old cardinal? Many think that the widow had him killed – that this trial is retaliation by his allies. By Cardinal Astalli. By you Spanish.'

De Pareja finds that he wishes only to be gone – away from this workshop and the marble widow, who gazes out beside him with such unsettling, unchanging determination. 'Please, Signor Bonarelli,' he says firmly. 'I have told you already. I know nothing of this. Forgive me, but I must take my leave. I have much to see to.'

Bonarelli sucks his teeth in disappointment, but he makes no attempt to ask any more, seeming to think that de Pareja's refusal to discuss these matters offers its own kind of confirmation. He listens with reasonable attentiveness as de Pareja repeats his request regarding the thickening of the Apollo's base, and asks that the completed bronze be delivered at the start of the following week, so that it might be shipped to Madrid ahead of Don Diego himself.

'It will be done,' Bonarelli says. 'You may assure your master of that.' Then he shakes out the dust sheet and throws it back over the widow, covering her entirely.

*

Don Diego has plainly taken wine with Maestro Algardi. Disregarding protocol, he orders de Pareja to ride with him in the cabin of their carriage, rather than up on the roof with the guards Infantado has assigned to all Spanish gentlemen in the wake of Cardinal Panciroli's death. De Pareja sits in a corner, while Don Diego sprawls across the seat opposite, removing his hat and running a hand through his well-oiled, greying hair.

'Donna Olimpia is in Rome,' he announces, his manner alarmed but also strangely pleased, as if his fears have now been supplied with an unimpeachable justification. 'Algardi just told me. She has *always* been here, Juan – watching everything and issuing her directions. She has houses all over the city, apparently. Her exile to that town of hers near Viterbo never occurred.'

De Pareja thinks of the bust, so recently completed – its finishing touches no doubt taken from life. 'It would explain a great deal,' he says.

'The trial of this datary that Astalli has brought about, that he imagines will reveal Donna Olimpia somehow and cause her final downfall – she is observing it, as she does everything else. And it leaves her . . . *wholly* unperturbed.' Don Diego sighs. 'She has a plan. That much is definite.'

'Does she mean to reconcile with the pope?' de Pareja asks. 'To see the datary pardoned, and the charges against him dismissed?'

'I do not know, Juan. *Nobody* knows. But it is not our fight. Our work here is done, and I must return to my king. To my wife and my daughters. To my grandchildren.' Don Diego sits up a little, twisting one of the points of his moustache. 'Algardi is a solid sort. He assured me that everything will be delivered as requested, so that we have something to show Felipe on our return. What was your impression, down in the shop?'

De Pareja decides that the bust is best left unmentioned. 'All is in hand, Don Diego, like you say. The work looks to be most excellent, in fact.' He clears his throat, signalling a shift to a more sensitive matter. 'I made my measurements and suggested an alteration, and they agreed to it at once. The cast of the Apollo will be tall enough for our purpose. The scheme I proposed to you for the Venus will work.'

Don Diego appears satisfied by this, although he does not ask for any more details. He stretches out his legs as far as the confines of the cabin will allow, the rich smell of Algardi's wine wafting over from him. 'And what of your own portrait? How have you fared there?'

In a manner typical of him, having barely mentioned de Pareja's likeness since its exhibition in the Rotonda, Don Diego suddenly decided that he wished to take it back to Madrid, for the amusement of the royal court. De Pareja duly headed out into the city and began to hunt his own portrait through the palazzos of Rome. It was a stern test, he discovered, to present yourself at a steward's doorway and attempt to explain that you were searching for a painting that was *you*, mirrored in pigment, on behalf of the King of Spain.

So far there has been no trace of it. Someone told him that the portrait was in the possession of Cardinal Panciroli at the time of his death; his servants recalled it being there, saying that it was loaned to him by Cardinal Astalli, who had borrowed it in turn from the Duke of Infantado. The painting was not in Panciroli's house now, though, the cardinal having passed it on himself to another unnamed churchman. The essential problem was that nobody had ever laid proper claim to it – not even Don Diego, before now at least. The irony of this has not escaped de Pareja: the portrait of an owned man had itself no owner.

'I will find it soon, Don Diego,' he says. 'Do not worry.'

His master is regarding him fondly. 'I knew I could rely on you, Juan,' he says. 'On you and you alone, in this entire damned city. This is a trying circumstance indeed, far beyond anything I feared we might encounter in these lands. But we are nearly free, you and I. The cords are being severed. One by one, they are surely being severed.'

Just as Don Diego makes this assertion, the same thought

arrives in the minds of both men: one of these cords is rather different from the others and might not be cut through quite so easily. Don Diego falls quiet, looking out at the line of pilgrims that snakes along the wall of the Palazzo del Quirinale. De Pareja knows that his master has been delaying this matter; it causes him pain and a measure of confusion, dimming his desire to be gone. But he knows what he must do.

Don Diego picks up his hat and brushes some marble dust from the brim. 'She will be in the apartment when we return,' he says. 'I will speak with her then.'

*

De Pareja discovers Flaminia Triunfi in the studio. She is standing by the Venus, which is now the last painting that remains at the Piazza di Spagna, wearing a cloak the colour of old Douro wine. It is disconcerting to see her directly beside her own naked likeness. Cupid has been added to the left of the composition, kneeling upon the disordered bedclothes, as Don Diego described. The winged boy seems to have been drawn from his master's recollections of his own children and grandchildren. He is propping up a mirror taken from the apartment's reception room, so that his divine mother – and whoever stops before the painting – might see a reflection of her features. This is the one part of the work still incomplete; the unrivalled painter of faces has yet to give one to his reclining goddess. The mirror holds only a grey rectangle.

Flaminia herself looks markedly different. De Pareja has not seen her for well over a week and has begun to suspect that she is avoiding him. He detects a deep fatigue about her now, and a slight fullness in her face and figure – and all at once he perceives that she is with child, perhaps three months' gone, just passing the point where such a thing will usually become noticeable. What bearing this might have upon their plans he does not dare to contemplate.

'Signorina, forgive me,' he says, glancing back towards the bedchamber into which Don Diego has just withdrawn. 'I have been thinking of my words about your sister and regretting them greatly. It was not for me to say what I did, and I am sorry for it.'

All of this is true. Flaminia's response both to his oil sketch and his suggestion of salvation surely indicates that her sister's death was not a good one – a murder perhaps, or worse. De Pareja cannot escape the notion that she might have died by her own hand. He has known of several such cases in Spain, servants and slaves driven beyond reason by cruelty, bereavement, or despair. The pain of it is unmatched, as the act is among the very gravest of sins: a person is lost, and their soul consigned to the raging fires of hell.

Flaminia simply nods. 'Please,' she says, without meeting his eye. 'Fetch your master.'

De Pareja hesitates, somewhat wrong-footed, frowning down at the paint-spattered floorboards. Then he bows and obeys, lingering in the corridor outside the studio to overhear what transpires. It is soon evident that the conversation will be entirely opposite to the one Don Diego imagined in the carriage – for Flaminia is cutting him loose, rather than the other way around.

'It is too dangerous,' she tells him; she is sad, weary, and utterly certain. 'I must think of when you are gone, Diego. I cannot be seen as an enemy of Donna Olimpia and her allies – that would surely mean my ruin. God knows, it is difficult enough already to be a woman and a painter. Having the widow as a foe would make it impossible.'

A woman and a painter. De Pareja swears under his breath,

cursing his stupidity. He has heard of such things several times in Italy, elsewhere in Rome, in Venice, and in Naples also — another sign, he thought, of the country's great liberality. These female painters are normally the daughters of established artists, who work in their fathers' studios; and even, in some rare cases, open modest shops of their own. And of course Flaminia Triunfi numbers among them. It was *there*, directly in front of him. It was there throughout.

Don Diego attempts to argue. Now that he is standing before her — and surely realising that she is carrying his child — he forgets everything he has said about departing Rome and its trials, about their futures in Spain, about freedom.

'This is love,' he says. 'Flaminia, this is *love*.'

'How can that be true?' she asks him, her voice sharpening with exasperation. 'Where can it go? What can it ever hope to be?'

'Why in heaven does it need to *go* anywhere? Why can it not just—'

'You are leaving. Deny it.'

Don Diego pauses. 'Flaminia, I—'

'You are *leaving*,' she repeats, bitterly triumphant. 'You are going back to Spain. To your king. To your wife and daughters. Were you even going to tell me?'

'You could come also,' Don Diego says. 'There are places in Madrid where you . . . where you could live. Where we could be together. I have friends. There are possibilities.'

Almighty Christ, thinks de Pareja, lifting a hand to his brow. *Holy saints.*

Flaminia will not consider this, thank God; her refusal has an odd, awkward note to it, beyond the aversion many Italians seem to feel towards the idea of Spain. 'I must stay here,' she says. 'Rome is my home. And I must not make an enemy of Donna Olimpia.

You must understand this, Diego. She is still here, in this city. She always will be.'

De Pareja furrows his brow, trying to untangle Flaminia's meaning. She seems to be alluding to the tumults of the summer, as if she has been caught up in them somehow; as if Donna Olimpia has some power over her, some pressure she can exert. The widow is a prominent patron of artists, as Flaminia has said, and can influence a great many others. But de Pareja can tell that there is more to it than this.

Don Diego is growing agitated. 'I cannot just let you go, Flaminia. You are with child. It is clear to see. You are . . . you are with my child.'

A silence follows. Tentatively, de Pareja steps towards the studio doorway. He can hear their shoes scraping on the floorboards; the faint rustle of a hand passing over fabric.

When Flaminia speaks again her voice is colder, faster, and more determined than ever. 'I want nothing from you,' she says. 'I want only to be away.'

'This is not right. This is—'

'It is not your concern, do you hear me? It is *not your concern*. I do not regret this, not any of it, but I must leave. May God be with you.'

Don Diego pleads some more; he sounds defeated now, though, as if he sees that Flaminia's departure is inevitable. There are footsteps, rapid and purposeful, and before de Pareja can step back she is out in the corridor. He opens his mouth to speak, to repeat his apology perhaps, but she will not even look at him. Passing at a diagonal, she strides across the reception room and through the main door, shutting it loudly behind her.

De Pareja nearly gives chase, thinking to stop her on the stairs and have her spell out what it is that binds her to Donna Olimpia.

Just then, however, Don Diego calls his name. After a second's hesitation, he hurries to the parlour, fetches a cup and a pitcher of wine, and returns to the studio. His master is at the window, staring over the terracotta rooftops towards the twin belltowers of Trinita dei Monti. De Pareja stands and waits, his heartbeat subsiding. He looks at the line of the Venus's backbone, and the gentle impression it leaves in the flesh.

'You were by the door, weren't you?' says Don Diego. 'You heard what was said?'

De Pareja sees no point in lying. 'I did, Don Diego.'

'That is good. You are concerned for me. And I am glad you know, Juan. I am glad you know that . . . that there is a child.'

De Pareja senses trouble. This development cannot be permitted to weaken Don Diego's resolve and put their departure from Rome in jeopardy. He tries to work out what to say.

'It is a strange thing to consider,' Don Diego continues. 'A child of mine, to be born in this city. To be raised an Italian, with their language and customs.' He falls quiet again, raising a forefinger to his lips; then he waves de Pareja over and takes the empty wine cup. 'But it is in the Lord's hands now, I suppose. We have our duties to attend to.'

De Pareja almost grins with relief. 'This is how it must be, Don Diego,' he says. 'The cords must be severed, like you said, however painful this might prove.'

Don Diego rests a hand upon his shoulder. As de Pareja pours, filling the cup in a single, well-practised movement, he feels very strongly the unique and peculiar bond that has formed between them during these months in Italy: a reliance that runs in both directions, albeit for the provision of quite different things. And now, with Almighty God's assent, their great trial will soon be complete. Lifting the pitcher upright, de Pareja's thoughts drift towards the future, and the life that might await. It occurs to him that he has not looked at his sketch of the scarred nun for many weeks; suddenly he longs to take the sheet from his folder and make a fresh assessment of its virtues, to see if anything is there.

But it is not yet time for this. Despite his talk of duty, Don Diego is fast sinking into dejection. The cup of wine is thrown back and refilled; the hand on de Pareja's shoulder grips him a little more tightly. His master's mind is plainly fixed upon Flaminia Triunfi and their unborn child – on this situation he has created and now must leave behind forever. As always, de Pareja sees that it will be up to him to keep them on course.

'Just one matter remains, Don Diego,' he says. 'One final cord that must be cut.'

Don Diego lowers the cup, his face quite blank.

De Pareja supresses a twinge of irritation. 'The documents from Naples. The ones entrusted to your care, that expose the widow's treachery and her plotting with France. They should be given to his grace the Duke of Infantado as soon as possible, to make use of as he chooses. I believe this will serve as an appropriate announcement of your intention to depart.'

Don Diego is nodding, as if he knew all along what was being referred to; he releases de Pareja's shoulder and takes the pitcher from his grasp. 'Go now,' he says, made more emphatic by wine. 'Go and fetch them. I will present the damned things to Infantado before this day is out.' Squinting those hooded eyes, he fills his cup to the brim. 'And then, Juan, we are done with this place. We are done with Rome.'

A minute later de Pareja is descending through the embassy. Each of the stone steps seems to bring him closer to freedom; closer to his workshop, to Señora Inés and the household they might build, to a life that is truly his own. After so much complication and confusion, everything appears blessedly simple. He offers up a quick prayer of thanks and finds himself suffused with a bright, irrepressible energy. With hope.

It is unusually dark in the cellar, a stationary cart up in the street having blocked out much of the daylight. De Pareja walks in, his eyes adjusting to the gloom; and as he heads towards the crates, his boot strikes against a piece of hollow metal. He looks down and his hopefulness vanishes, swept away by an abrupt, absolute disbelief – as what he sees there is so unlikely, so unlucky, that it cannot possibly be real.

'No,' he says aloud. 'Dear Lord.'

He crouches, lifting the Mars with Helmet and Sword from the ground, already knowing what he will discover. Sure enough, the antique cast, survivor of so many centuries, has been split almost in two. Someone has thrown the god of war against the flagstones, pried him open like a clam, and scooped out all that was inside.

Sorores

It takes so very long for anything to happen. Days become a week, and then another; summer's glare begins to fade, the shadows softening, the nights before the crumbling Madonna gaining the slightest chill. Orsola soon learns that the yard is generally quiet. The gates are opened once in the early morning, and riders leave; and then again when they return, often in the depths of the dusk. Each time she is at the window, her face against the bars, searching in vain for that cape with the yellow cross. Was Lontra seen, she wonders – did they chase her, and kill her perhaps, remembering her part in Tullio's attack? Or did she escape them, yet was left so scared she did not dare return? Or was she simply unable to think of how she might help the nuns without personal risk? This is Lontra, after all; her greatest talent is self-preservation, and her one consistent trick has been running away.

Eventually she reappears, however, watching the gate from the ropemaker's shop across the street. Her costume is the same, even down to the beard. She tries to sneak in but is seen almost at once and repelled with a hard kick. Two further tries are made after that, a couple of days apart, with a little more caution – but she barely takes more than three or four steps past the threshold before fear of discovery prompts her to retreat.

It begins to look impossible. If Lontra is to free them, she will have to make it across the yard to the doorway that lies somewhere to the right. She will have to creep through the rooms upstairs, down the steps to the cellars, and along the corridor. She will have to open the door somehow, by stealing the key or picking the lock. And then they will have to gather up Sister Serafina, retrace Lontra's route back outside, and flee into the city, all without being seen by Donna Olimpia's men. Orsola tries to believe that it can be done; she prays to the Virgin and to the saints, imploring them for guidance. But she cannot do it. Her faith, it seems, is exhausted. There is no plan here. They are doomed to whatever fate the widow determines for them.

Their food, meanwhile, has improved: soup and bread, sometimes with salami or pecorino, brought in each morning. The doctor has visited again, to see to Serafina's head and apply his poultice. She doesn't seem to be recovering, though; her utterances remain confused and rambling, and her strength is drained almost to nothing. Donna Olimpia talked of needing Serafina well – of the approach of some significant moment. Orsola starts to think that unless it comes soon, the choir nun's soul will no longer be lodged within her body.

Much of Orsola's time is spent laid out on the stone bench, or slumped on the floor beside it. Her toe heals, and her shin, and her torn scalp as well, but the inaction is difficult to bear. That damp chapel becomes a stage upon which her darkest memories re-enact themselves over and over again. The bright, grisly redness of Tullio's broken skull, and the eyes of the coachman as he angled his blade towards her throat. The screams of the horses trapped in Castro's burning stables, and the bank of bobbing dead that dammed the river in the valley below. The still, newborn body of her daughter, blue and bloody on the washhouse floor, and her brother's unpitying face as he prised the child from her arms, so she might be buried in an unmarked corner of the churchyard. Orsola often finds herself staring over at the Madonna and her little flock, asking only for emptiness.

Then one morning, the pebble comes. There are roughly twenty yards between the chapel's window and the alley beyond the gates, but Lontra was raised on the streets of Rome and her aim is good. The stone is very small, the size of the nail on a little finger, but the sound of it pinging off the bars and skittering across the chapel brings Orsola immediately to her feet. Another follows, and another; and then a flint the size of a silver scudo, which flies a good distance into the nuns' prison, nearly striking against the Madonna's robes.

Orsola realises that Lontra is testing out the throw, gauging its angles and distances, and the exact degree of force required. The gates close again before anything more can occur; but that same evening, just after the horsemen have entered the yard and are preparing to dismount, a large red apple is lobbed through the gates. Aimed low to avoid notice, it falls a few yards short, bouncing against the dried mud and rolling in an odd curve that suggests it is rather heavier and more unevenly weighted than an ordinary apple. It stops an arm's length from the window, settling in a shallow rut.

Terrified that it will be spotted, Orsola reaches out at once, pressing her shoulders and neck against the bars. She strains her muscles, her teeth clenched, the coarse iron digging into her flesh as she opens her fingers as wide as they will go. The tip of the middle one brushes against the apple's dusty skin. Pushing herself yet further, she gains a tiny degree of purchase, finding the dip on its top where the stalk attaches, and managing to roll it very slightly towards her.

The horsemen are all off their mounts now, and have started to lead them to the stables. Orsola redoubles her efforts, opening her mouth in a silent cry – and suddenly the apple is out of the rut, fitted firmly in her palm, coming back through the bars and down with her onto the stone bench. She sits for a moment. There is no shout of alarm; no thud of approaching boots. She was not seen.

Orsola studies the apple in the dim light. It is indeed heavier than it should be, and seems partially distended. Turning it about, she discovers a metal hook poking from its bottom. She pulls on it – and out slides a narrow strip of metal with fine serrations down one side. It is well made, like it might have been stolen from a metalworker's shop. The intention here is plain enough. Orsola looks back up at the bars; she hefts the little rasp in her hand and takes a big bite of the apple. The flavour of it, that crisp, acidic sweetness, seems so miraculous that she lets out a bark of involuntary laughter, spraying fragments of fruit across the dirt floor.

Serafina stirs at the sound, peering at her in mystification.

'We are blessed, Sister,' Orsola tells her, taking another ravenous bite and talking around it with some difficulty. 'We are truly blessed.'

She begins work shortly after nightfall. The yard outside is quite dark, illuminated only by a weak patch of moonlight that falls into a far corner. There are three bars in the chapel's window; Orsola starts with the one on the left, sawing at the base. She has never done this kind of labour before and is surprised by the speed with which one piece of metal can cut its way through another. In ten minutes she is finished and moving to the top; another ten and the bar is out, there in her hand. She lays it quietly upon the bench below.

Orsola has almost removed the second as well when the candle appears, set in a window beside the stable, with the shadows of men moving behind. She curses, sawing faster, her fingers and wrists aching with exertion. Any hesitation is time in which her efforts could be discovered and a dreadful punishment come crashing down, burying all hope beneath it.

The second bar is detached in a small cascade of powdered plaster. Standing back, panting a little, Orsola decides that the third can stay put; lean as they are, the nuns can slip through this gap. She sets the severed bar beside its brother and goes to Serafina, who is curled at the bench's end. The choir nun is in her usual condition, neither fully asleep nor awake, wandering through dreams and visions, murmuring in a barely audible croak. It is distressing to see how frail she has become. You are saving her, Orsola tells herself. You are freeing her from the widow's grasp and bringing her back to God. And the soul of your daughter, released from the grey hill, will surely follow after.

'Sister,' she says. 'Sister, we are leaving. You must ask the Holy Virgin for strength. You need to move as quickly as you can.'

Serafina's head lolls; she mumbles a few half-formed words and draws up her bony knees. Orsola looks at the window again. She realises that Serafina must go first, otherwise there is a good chance she will not go at all — that she must push the choir nun out into the courtyard and pray with her entire soul that she does not give them away.

'Think of Santa Catarina,' Orsola says, a note of desperation entering her voice. 'Think of how she was imprisoned by the emperor, and how dark and frightening it was. Think of how she was brought out once more, up into the sunshine. Into the Lord's light.'

This succeeds in rousing Serafina from her torpor, although she is distinctly unimpressed by Orsola's evocation of her favourite saint. 'An altar,' she mutters, rising onto an elbow. 'I will pray at an altar.'

'We will go to Mass, Sister, as soon as we can,' Orsola tells her. 'We will take communion and have a priest hear our confession. But we must leave here first.'

Serafina sits up. 'The procession,' she says. 'We must rejoin it, Sister. We must repent.'

At this point, Orsola would commit herself to a pilgrimage to the Holy Land if it would get the choir nun moving. 'Tomorrow. We will walk it tomorrow, I promise you.'

Somehow, it is done. Serving as a ladder, and then pushing from behind, Orsola manages to work Serafina through the window and onto the mud-caked cobblestones. She follows as rapidly as she can, her every muscle protesting and her hip scraping against one of the raw ends of the bars. But she makes it. The night air is like a draught of cool water, and as she stands the world seems to open out around her. The dull, rutted yard; the stables, and the horses standing peacefully within; the boundless reach of heaven, its stars glittering so far above.

Nearby, a voice rises in anger and a chair bangs violently onto the floor. Orsola twists around, her heart lurching, but they have not been seen – an argument has begun in the room with the candle in the window, over cards from the sound of it, and it is fast growing vicious. Hurriedly, she pulls Serafina up and leads her to the gates. There is no lock, just a bar and bolt, and in seconds they are out in the street. Orsola eases the gates back in place as best she can, to delay discovery of their escape. Then she whispers thanks for their deliverance, and they are gone.

*

Orsola wakes with a gasp, her head jerking up from her arm. Lontra is crouching in front of her, and has just given her foot a firm shake. She is huddled with Serafina beside the fountain in the Piazza San Paulo; immediately to her left, a pair of old donkeys are drinking from the basin. The piazza, so quiet when they arrived a couple of hours earlier, is now completely full. As she tries to get her bearings, a strong breeze cuts in from one of the surrounding streets, rippling across the canvas of the market stalls, knocking over jugs and piles of fruit, and setting chickens scrabbling and squawking inside their cages.

It has been an exhausting, terrifying night.

Once out of the yard, Orsola had quickly ascertained that their prison was close to the Piazza del Popolo, on Rome's north-western edge. She stole a ragged sheet from a washing line to disguise Serafina's habit, then took them south, back towards the procession route. Thinking to stay out of sight as much as possible, she tried to avoid the main avenues and use the alleyways instead. Lontra had always told her never to do this, and especially not at night. Many of the crooked, stinking streets were almost totally dark, and clogged with vagrants, drunks and thieves. As they passed, obscenities rose up in a muttered clamour, while hand after hand reached out to grab and grip, attempting to drag them into the shadows.

Before long, Orsola abandoned her plan and started out onto a broad, straight stretch of the Via della Scrofa, striding swiftly between flickering pools of torchlight. They were being followed now by a leering, snickering mob; with each block these men and boys grew more menacing, throwing insults and threats, and then a barrage of stones. It was only when one of these struck a bystander, and his companions promptly attacked the nuns' pursuers, that they managed to slip away. Panting with fright, Orsola rushed Serafina down a flight of steps, along a lane, and into a small, musty church dedicated to San Antonio. Here they hid in a side chapel for a few hours, praying at the altar, until they were found by an ill-tempered deacon and moved on.

Dawn was still a way off, but Orsola decided that it was time to seek out Lontra. Approaching the players' grain loft was too dangerous; Donna Olimpia's spies would surely be watching it. Instead, imagining what she would do in Lontra's place, Orsola selected a spot along the route of the Jubilee Procession, where Serafina used to speak. The fountain in the Piazza San Paulo was an obvious choice. It was close to the loft, but not too close; the Corsican Guard were usually posted there also, to supervise the Jews who sold their wares around the ghetto gate, during the few hours of the day they were permitted to step through it. Should the *barone* and his men appear, and Orsola shout for help, there was at least a slim chance that it might be provided.

Lontra still has the blue cloak, but is now wearing a stained gown beneath it. The beard and turban are gone, and she looks thinner; her lip is bruised and she has lost another of her front teeth.

'How about that,' she says. 'I'd only just started looking for you.'

Orsola blinks and coughs, rubbing her eyes. She hadn't meant to sleep; she feels disorientated and slightly ashamed. 'The apple,' she says. 'That was a good throw.'

Lontra gives her a strange grin, both confused and confusing — somehow suggesting amazement, gratification, and a profound, inexplicable anger. 'God is with you,' she says. 'Truly. To make it out as you did . . . Long odds, Sister Orsola. Long odds indeed.'

Orsola looks to Serafina. The choir nun hasn't slept; her eyes are red and her hands clasped in prayer, the silver beads of her rosary winding around her knuckles. Orsola's clumsy mention of Santa Catarina back in the chapel cell has returned the saint to the forefront of Serafina's mind. She has been running through Catarina's legend all night, with varying degrees of intensity and expressiveness; right then, she is back at the four hideous wheels, mounted in the marketplace at Alexandria.

'The soldiers brought Catarina before this infernal machine,' she says. 'It bristled with blades and hooks and . . . and cruel serrations. It was a sight so horrific, many swooned to behold it. But not holy Catarina. She stood without fear. She looked upon the wheels as old friends, who would bring about her greatest wish: to sacrifice herself to Almighty God.'

'There she is,' says Lontra, not without affection. 'The nun of Castro. Get her up, will you? We shouldn't stay out here any longer than we need to.'

Orsola rises, wincing at her numerous aches and stinging cuts. She glances over the drinking donkeys at the mass of Jubilee pilgrims that are tramping steadily across the piazza, on their way between San Pietro and San Paulo Outside-the-Walls. Then she leans down, as she has so many times before, slides her hands beneath Serafina's armpits, and eases the emaciated nun to her feet.

The three of them start through the crowds, Lontra leading them around the blackened walls of the ghetto and towards the hill of Campidoglio. The street is lined with the shops of tailors and corset-makers. Business is good, customers thronging around the shopfronts, talking loudly as they survey wares arranged in windows, mounted on frames, or piled on tables out in the street. One subject dominates: a trial in the courts of the Vatican, of a priestly official caught in acts of the most ungodly forgery. He was found guilty the afternoon before, Orsola gathers, and has been sentenced to die. The people appear largely satisfied by this verdict, and a good number are amused. For them, it is another entertainment of the Jubilee – and the more embarrassment it brings to the Church, to the Holy Father, the better.

'Could this help us?' Orsola asks hopefully. 'Doesn't the widow rely on the pope for her power? Might this weaken her?'

Lontra snorts. '*Nothing* can weaken her, Sister. She can stop it at any time and have this miserable priest returned to his vestry within the hour. Just you watch. It is theatre, as fake as anything I ever did.'

She takes them to a tenement not half a mile from the Tor de'Specchi, where all of this began. It is no well-appointed convent, however, but a giant, dilapidated block, like a thousand others that stand around the city. The doors are warped, the shutters split, and the stairwells heaped with filth. Ragged children run and shriek; women and men sit wherever they can, slumped and desolate. The nuns, even after their weeks in Donna Olimpia's chapel, do not stand out at all.

Lontra has a room somewhere in the middle, so narrow you could extend your arms and touch each wall. It contains a basket of clothes, a dented pail, and a grubby mattress packed with straw. The smell in there is close, animal, thick with grime. Noise pours in through the uncovered window: shouts and screams, the slamming of doors, the constant clatter of copper water pots, going up and down the sides of the buildings on lengths of wire.

Orsola cannot hide her dismay. 'What happened to the grain loft?' she asks. 'What happened to the players?'

'That's done,' Lontra replies curtly. 'They would not have me any more, Sister. Not after what we did. They said I was *marked*. That the widow would be after me for sure.'

Orsola remembers those first weeks in Rome, up there among

the roof beams; the sense of friendship and shared purpose, which she has treasured ever since. 'So they just threw you out? They threw you out with nothing?'

Lontra shrugs and gestures at the clothes basket – a small sample, Orsola now realises, from the chests of costumes in the loft. 'They let me take that. To sell, and to disguise myself. To give me a chance.'

Serafina has retreated to a corner and is arranging herself against it, with her head propped between the two walls, much as she would back in the chapel. It suddenly seems to Orsola that they have merely traded one dire situation for another.

'And yet you sought us out,' she says. 'You . . . you came for us.'

'I asked some questions. You can't kidnap a nun in full daylight using one of Donna Olimpia Maidalchini's carriages without anyone noticing where it went.' Lontra's manner hardens. 'The way I see it, Sister Orsola, *you* did this to me – you and your holy seer over there. You cracked my Venetian eye on the Via Monterone. You had me join with your Tullio and his stupid scheme. And now I am finished in Rome. I've got to leave before the widow's brutes catch up with me.'

Orsola crosses her arms and leans against the pockmarked wall. She resents this account of their association – Lontra has only ever been her own mistress, treating them as an opportunity to be taken up when convenient, and then dropped again in the face of trouble. At the same time, though, she can see that there is truth in what Lontra says. She was certainly heedless, in following Tullio; she made foolish choices. In part, at least, she is to blame. She slides down the wall to the floor.

'They wanted Serafina,' she says. 'That's what it was about. They knew she was with me – with Tullio and the others. They used Tullio's desire for revenge to draw us out, so they could capture her.'

Lontra looks over doubtfully at the choir nun, who seems to have fallen into a deep, obliterating sleep. 'But why?'

Orsola tells what little she knows about Claudia Triunfi. The name means nothing to Lontra; if the Triunfi family was ever spoken of in the streets and piazzas, it was plainly a good while ago now. Unable to make any sense of it all, they fall into a disconsolate silence. Lontra sits down herself. Outside, the bells begin to chime, spreading through the city like the barking of dogs.

'Why did you help us, anyway?' Orsola asks. 'It was a grave risk.'

'Everything else is gone,' Lontra says simply. 'You are all I have.'

Orsola does not know how to respond to this. She swallows, trying to blink away her tiredness, and looks up bleakly at the mildewed ceiling. 'Lontra,' she says. 'What in the Virgin's name are we going to do?'

And now, rather to her astonishment, Orsola learns that Lontra has a plan. In that tiny, filthy room, she speaks of a place below, accessible through an entrance out in the ruins of Celio. It is a whole underground world, she says, carved from the stone and mud, with churches and grand halls and mile upon mile of passageways. And there are rivers too, a great system of them, extending beneath the city like the roots of a tree, running under each of the seven hills and back to the Tiber. Lontra has made use of this place numerous times, when she has needed to keep out of sight for a while. There are dangers, certainly; it is easy indeed to get lost, or to fall. Those corridors are also home to many restless spirits, who delight in tormenting anybody who ventures down there. But they really have no other option.

'Donna Olimpia has people everywhere,' Lontra says. 'In every piazza and avenue, and at every gate. These underground rivers are the one path they might not be watching.'

Orsola is sceptical. 'Do you have a boat, then?'

'There are many down there already. Left by smugglers, I think.' Lontra's voice is quickening with excitement. 'I've seen them, heaped up on the banks. They're old, but there'll be one that'll serve us. All we need to do is plug the leaks and ride the current out of Rome.'

'Where will that take us? Do you even know?'

Lontra sighs in exasperation. 'Holy Madonna, what does it matter? It won't be *here*, will it? Donna Olimpia will be left far behind, and we will be able to begin again. This will *save us*, Sister. Believe me, it will save us.'

Orsola thinks for a minute, and in truth she can see it. A shallow-bottomed skiff could carry them out onto the river and beyond the city walls without drawing any undue attention. Afterwards, away in a small town somewhere, they might well be able to find a convent where Serafina can safely be lodged. She will have atoned for her greatest sin, and rescued her daughter from the grey hill of Limbo. And then she and Lontra would be free, starting off together into a new and blessed world.

Orsola folds her legs beneath her, listening to rodents scratching inside the walls. She takes a steadying breath.

'Very well,' she says.

*

They leave late that afternoon, clad in hooded cloaks taken from Lontra's basket, and head east into Celio. A light rain has begun to fall, the first in months, lowering a grey veil over Rome. Soon the three woman are crossing the region where Tullio and his comrades made their camp, with its rows of columns and stretches of wild scrubland. On the horizon is the gigantic, ruined arena, standing starkly against the dull sky, the alcoves of its massive walls lit from within by many dozens of pilgrims' campfires.

Serafina begins to mutter, pulling upon Orsola's cloak with increasing determination. Orsola has done what she can to tend to her: to clean her person, or her face and hands at least, and brush the crusted filth from her habit. She has also tried to explain what lies ahead, persevering with the old untruth that their ultimate goal is for them both to rejoin the Benedictine order, and enter a holy house – that they just need to trust in the Lord's wisdom a short while longer. Serafina seemed content, joining in Orsola's amens and returning to her rosary peaceably enough. Now they are out in the open, though, she is starting to object, and for the very reason Orsola was dreading – the thing she has avoided making any mention of, in the hope that it might have slipped from Serafina's mind. She curses her folly, for the choir nun never forgets anything. Some thoughts are merely obscured by others, for a time; and then they reappear without warning, at the most inconvenient moments, having lost none of their urgency.

'This is not the procession,' Serafina says, bringing her mouth to Orsola's ear. 'We have to return to it. You said we would walk it, Sister. You *promised* we would walk it.'

They are approaching one of the grand pagan arches that stands in this part of the city. It is huge, almost as tall as the church that is being built on the sloped ground beside it. The ancient stonework is cracked and pitted, and streaked with silt. A number of Jubilee pilgrims have made shelters within its three passageways and put up awnings around its base, further blackening the marble with smoke from their fires.

Seeing what is happening, Lontra comes over to reassure Serafina, telling her that the Laterano is not far – they are making a brief detour, that's all. This is not helpful. Lontra has never quite understood that Serafina is not a simpleton and cannot be lied to in this way – and indeed she reacts with anger, glaring at Lontra and pushing her back.

'You are false,' she declares. 'You are not taking us to the Laterano. You are empty-hearted and ... and Godless and *false*.'

Heads are turning now. Some of the pilgrims seem to recognise Serafina, or at least know her by reputation, the fame of the nun of Castro plainly having endured throughout her imprisonment. As Orsola tries to calm Serafina herself, she notices something odd: past the choir nun's shoulder, just behind a group of sun-burned women wearing strange, squared-off hats, is a lean, watchful man in a black cape who is obviously no kind of pilgrim. Seeing that she has spotted him, he murmurs an instruction to a boy of eleven or twelve, who scampers off towards the centre of the city.

Orsola stops for a second; and then she feels an alarm so terrible and all-consuming, she wants to throw Serafina over her shoulder and break into a run. There can be no mistaking what that was, and what has surely been set in motion. They pass through the central passage of the arch, Serafina's shouts echoing off the patterned stonework high above. Onlookers flank them on either side, their faces mystified, concerned or mirthful, calling things out in several foreign tongues.

Beyond the arch is a long rectangular square, fringed with ruins and a ramshackle market. The rain is growing heavier, tapping insistently on the hood of Orsola's cloak, and the baked mud underfoot is beginning to soften. Serafina stumbles, partly on purpose, falling against Orsola and dragging her down as well. They are on their knees, struggling for balance, their faces close together; the choir nun's sunken eyes are filled with a deep, gnawing worry.

'I *told you*, Sister,' she insists. 'We need to *repent*. We need the

Holy Father's indulgence, if we are ever to be brought back into the Lord's grace. We must walk the circuit. We *must*.'

Suddenly, Orsola realises what she has to say. 'There is no need, Sister. Almighty God is pleased with what we have done in Rome. Can you not see it? He has prepared a new path for us.'

Serafina begins to protest, but Orsola presses on.

'He knows that you have suffered here, within this foul city. When you were Claudia Triunfi, before you pledged yourself to His son. He knows that you have suffered upon your return also, suffered most badly. He wishes you to leave this evil place well behind you. To leave it once and for all.'

And holy saints, it works. These words seem to resonate through Serafina; to leave her a little stunned, in fact, gazing up imploringly towards the dark rainclouds. Orsola sees again how spent she is, how close to some kind of final collapse, and feels a sharp ache of guilt. She reaches out for the jutting end of Serafina's shoulder-bone, just as the choir nun releases a great stream of Latin, so fast that the words jumble together and lose all form.

The man in the black cape is still there, lingering beneath the arch as if sheltering from the downpour. Orsola gathers up Serafina, and with Lontra's assistance they start across the muddy square. Serafina's Latin begins to falter, and then to emerge as anguished yelps – and abruptly, as she casts around for solace, she is speaking once more of Santa Catarina's wheels; of the crowd's devilish delight in the spectacle to come; of the saint's serenity in the face of her gruesome end.

'There,' pants Lontra. 'To the south. That big ruin.'

It looks like a church whose roof has long since fallen in, the whole thing overgrown with bushes and small trees. To reach it, they must pass through the market that borders the square. This appears to be devoted to meat and livestock, with goats, pigs and sheep roped up inside the open-fronted tents, their plaintive cries drifting on the air.

'Catarina was ready to die,' Serafina says. 'To be bound between the wheels and brought to glory. But the Holy Virgin . . . the Holy Virgin had another plan.'

A whistle sounds across the square, clearly audible over the hiss of the rainfall and the sounds of the market. Orsola looks back to see two black-clad figures rounding the grand arch – and another coming from the north, starting through the sparse crowds. Donna Olimpia's men.

'Madonna,' she gasps. 'Blessed Christ.'

'Don't worry, Sister,' says Lontra. 'We'll lose them. You'll see.'

They hurry among the stalls and find themselves in an open-air slaughterhouse. Three large pigs, recently killed, are being butchered on a trestle table. Innards lie in steaming piles, while freshly cleaved flanks drip on their hooks, the split flesh livid in the gloom. Orsola trips on a guy rope and flops down into the bloody mud, raising a cackle from the butchers' boys. For a few moments she cannot move. The mud is soft as lard and revoltingly warm, its sweet coppery smell coating the inside of her nose and throat. When she pulls her hand free it is streaked with red, thick rivulets running along her forearm; then Lontra grabs hold of it, hauling her up with a sucking squelch, and they stagger on towards the ruin.

'The skies of Alexandria were torn asunder,' Serafina says, staring at the gory work underway on trestle table, 'and a . . . a bolt of holy wrath fell directly from heaven. In an instant, the monstrous wheels were blasted to pieces and two thousand pagans lay dead, their bodies pierced through with . . . with shards of wood and metal . . . and . . .'

Clearing the market, they dive through a screen of scrubby

trees, twigs scratching at their arms and faces. They are close to the derelict church now. One of the outer walls has partly collapsed, allowing them to clamber into the southern aisle. The roofless nave is empty save for weeds and heaps of rubble. Lontra takes them across the shattered, mossy flagstones, through a tall archway, and into the remains of a cloister. Here they are confronted with a new degree of ruination – for the very ground has been overturned, and channels carved deep into the mud. This has exposed the beginnings of a system of passages, their entrances yawning open like the mouths of caves.

'This is it,' says Lontra. 'This is the way inside.'

She hops down into one of the broader channels. Orsola sees that there is a gate a short distance along it. Lontra heaves it open, the rusted metal grinding against stone, and starts into the darkness beyond. Orsola looks back towards the ruined nave. There is no sign yet of any pursuers. At her side, Serafina is still talking of destruction and death in the main square of Alexandria, and the miraculous preservation of Catarina herself, standing alone in her white martyr's surplice. Orsola snatches a few desperate breaths, trying to shore up her will and keep her fears contained; then she takes hold of the choir nun's hand and they go after Lontra together.

Beyond the gate, the muddy trench becomes a corridor hewn from rough, grey stone, unlike anything Orsola has seen in the city above. The rain is reduced to glistening drips, and then disappears altogether. They follow Lontra around a bend, heading down beneath the earth. A tiny amount of light filters in through unseen fissures and holes; it has a muted, colourless quality, and reveals very little.

'Hell,' says Serafina, her voice reverberating flatly in the uncertain space ahead. 'Hell claimed all who died in Alexandria that day. For those pagan souls, the dreadful tumult of the square was replaced in an instant with the eternal torments of the pit – with hellfire and lamentation and . . . and the most crushing and overwhelming agony.'

Her recitation has quickened, as it always does when she is scared. She draws in close, repeating certain phrases several times, her fingernails sinking into Orsola's arm.

They continue for perhaps a hundred yards. It is becoming plain that this is no neat network of tunnels but an endless warren, dug for unknown reasons, filled with dead ends, sudden drops and strange, murky chambers. Creatures shift in the deeper blackness – beetles, rats, and larger things as well, possibly cats and dogs that have become trapped down here and have adapted to the smothering dark. The air is dry as old paper and difficult to inhale, with a desiccated, crypt-like smell. Orsola's head is growing light, and her heart thudding thickly.

'How much further? I can't see any rivers. Are you sure—'

A loud clang comes from behind them, echoing through the maze.

'That was the gate,' Orsola says. 'They're at the gate. Holy Christ, they're coming for us!'

Lontra is just a silhouette ahead. 'We're almost there,' she says. 'Only a few yards more.'

They arrive at an intersection – three or maybe four passageways, it is difficult to tell. Lontra leads them right, down some crude steps, and along a corridor so low Orsola's hood almost brushes against the ceiling; Serafina, deep in her meditations on hell, is obliged to hunch over most awkwardly. This brings them into what feels like a far larger, more open area. Orsola can make out a series of carved blocks, almost like altars, that are set across the floor at even intervals. Stone shelves, four or five high, seem to have been built into the walls. There is still no sign of any water. Her unease grows.

'What is this?' she asks. 'Where are we?'

Lontra has gone off into a corner. She is fumbling with something, then makes an abrupt motion with her hand. Orsola hears the chipping sound of a tinderbox; Lontra strikes a spark and catches it, lighting a candle. The glow spreads, reaching through the room and away down the corridors.

'Are you mad? They will *see it*, Lontra! It will lead them straight to—'

As she speaks, Orsola realises what is happening. Lontra did not have a candle and tinderbox with her when they left the tenement block. They must have already been here, brought down by her in preparation at some earlier time — and she is using them now with the precise intention of guiding the widow's men. This is the candle's purpose. This is Lontra's entire aim.

'Go,' she says, her voice hard with resolve; then she draws out a small coin pouch and sets it on the stone slab in front of her. 'Take that and *go*.'

Orsola stares at the pouch in horrified bewilderment. 'You broke us out,' she says slowly, 'just so you could give us back. You did it for the widow's pardon. You . . . you did it for coin.'

Lontra doesn't bother to deny it. 'We each look out for ourselves. I told you this, Sister. I had nothing else left.' She glances impatiently towards the corridor they came in through. 'But I did it for you as well — can you not see it? They don't want *you*, Orsola. Like you said, it's all about Sister Serafina, or Claudia Triunfi, or whoever she is. I'll just tell them that you ran off — that I had to choose between the two of you.'

Orsola hears several pairs of heavy boots, walking rapidly. The shadows outside are diminishing, becoming tinted with velvet browns; another light, brighter than the candle, is approaching through the passageways. At her side, Serafina continues to talk.

'The destruction of the wheels won over many to the way of Christ. Seeing the true . . . the true and holy power of Almighty God, the pagan multitude fell down on their knees and renounced their false idols – they renounced them with the passion and the fervour of—'

Orsola's spirit starts to return. She takes a closer look around her. In the new light, she can see that the shelves in the walls are stacked with human bones, piled up like kindling. The blocks set down the middle of the room are not altars but tombs, covered in inscriptions and sealed with slab-like lids; several have been cracked open, spilling yet more bones across the floor. To her right, in amongst the shelves, is another doorway, a broken gate hanging half open before it.

'You have *betrayed us*,' she says, her fury rising. 'You have doomed us both!'

Lontra steps forward, picking up the pouch again, and tries to push it into Orsola's hand. 'I have *saved* you,' she insists, at once angry, guilty and oddly tender. 'If I'd left you in that prison, you'd have ended up floating in the Tiber for sure. This way you can escape. You can *live*.'

Very briefly, Orsola feels the old temptation of a life without Serafina. But she is well practised at resisting it. The duty is like a hook, buried in the deepest part of her soul, impossible to disregard. She has taken on a sacred charge, an act of atonement, and she must see it through – for the sake of Serafina and herself, and for that of her daughter. She pulls back and the pouch falls to the ground between them, the coins shifting within as it strikes against the stone.

'I made a promise, Lontra,' she says. 'You know this. I must make myself right with God.'

The footsteps are getting closer, and the light brighter; the candle's flame wobbles in a breeze, making the shadows around them dip and sway. Serafina has dropped to her knees beside the nearest tomb. Her voice a hoarse murmur, she is talking still of Catarina, and the emperor's terrible reckoning as he begins to execute his newly converted subjects.

'His wife the empress was first among this number. At the . . . at the moment her head was struck from her shoulders, her Christian soul winged to heaven like a silver dove. And her guards, when it was done, found themselves converted also, and said they were ready to die as well. Which they did. Which they . . . they did.'

Orsola grabs hold of Serafina and begins to work her upright again. Lontra forces herself between them, seizing Orsola by the shoulder. She has entered into a bargain with the widow's men, and must deliver: there is as much at stake here for her as for anyone else.

'I can't let you, Sister,' she says, as they struggle. 'I *can't.*'

Orsola has kept the rasp that Lontra threw to her in the apple, tucking it inside the strap of her gown. She fumbles for it now, gripping the serrated strip and scoring a line into Lontra's forearm. There is blood immediately, a lot of it, dark in the candlelight. Lontra recoils, spitting a curse – and Orsola bundles Serafina towards the rusted gate, wrenching it from its hinges and letting it crash to the floor, before plunging into the black corridor beyond.

Male voices echo behind them, raised in urgent censure; and then there is Lontra's also, attempting vainly to reject all fault. Orsola tries to think, but this is a wild and most dismal circumstance, with no hope of escape. They have been betrayed and deserted. They are surely finished.

No – she cannot allow this. She has the Madonna and the Saints. She has the breath in her lungs, and the heart that thumps so violently in her chest. She has to save Serafina; to save the soul of her daughter and perform her atonement. She presses onwards, taking them around a corner and down some steps – and from somewhere up ahead, as clear and bright as birdsong, comes the sound of flowing water. Orsola nearly laughs. So there is truth to Lontra's tale after all. There are rivers here. Perhaps there are those boats she spoke of as well. Perhaps her plan will still work.

The passage turns again and opens out, becoming a stairway that runs into what might be a hall or nave. There is a wall on their left, while on their right is a vast darkness – a space whose dimensions can only be guessed at. A distance below them, however, somewhere past the stairway's base, dim, blueish light is reflecting off water, rippling a little as it moves.

'There, Sister,' Orsola pants. 'Look there.'

Serafina is uncertain; she adjusts her hold on Orsola's sleeve, pinching at the fabric. 'Santa Catarina was led to the place of . . . of execution,' she mumbles. 'It was barren, and marked with . . . much marked with . . .'

The going is treacherous; the steps are coming apart, crumbling to mud, threatening to send the nuns tumbling into the black chasm beside them. They have descended perhaps two storeys when the light changes, the darkness growing softer. Orsola has a momentary sense of figures and faces, arranged in rows, watching her from afar – and then an arc of flame is drawn before them, curving downwards, its whites and yellows blazing over clusters of columns, walls crowded with ancient paintings, and the looming outlines of tall, rounded arches. Serafina ducks down with a wordless shriek, her grip constricting sharply, while Orsola throws out her other arm to stop them toppling off the stairs.

The flame strikes the ground about thirty yards away. Orsola realises that it is a torch, thrown from above — from up behind them, at the top of the stairway. She turns to see three or four men, just like those from the alley where Tullio and the others were killed. One of them is raising what looks like a long rod of wood and metal, and pointing it in their direction.

The sound claps against Orsola with an almost physical force, sending her stumbling down the steps. This thunderous blast is followed instantly by a loud ping and an odd, zipping whistle, the noises coming so quickly that they merge into one — and then seem to roll around the ceiling, as if trapped in the vaults high above. Shocked into silence, Serafina presses herself close against the wall, her black habit blending with the shadows. Orsola feels a keen desire to join her there — to draw close to her as they have done so many times before, their bodies fitting together with such familiarity and relief. Instead, she leans back to lift Serafina up, and hurries her on down the twenty or so steps that remain.

The floor of this enormous chamber is covered with sandy silt that runs at a gentle slope to the channel of water in its middle. The thrown torch is guttering a little now, but it still casts enough light for Orsola to see the brick archway ahead, through which the channel flows. Beyond is darkness — yet it surely leads to a stream, or an underground tributary, and then on to the river.

The men are coming down the stairway behind them, talking to each other in low voices. 'Take care with that thing,' says one. 'By God, you'll answer for it if she dies.'

Orsola starts them towards the water. It looks shallow; they will splash through the arch, she thinks, and then—

And then she is on her knees, despite having no recollection of falling. The second report echoes overhead, deep and immense, like the sound of a building suddenly collapsing. She begins to rise; her body seems heavier than usual, though, slower to react. It is as if her garments have become snagged on something, and are twisting more tightly around her with every movement. A bitter, mineral smell reaches her nostrils, drifting across from the stairway – gunpowder smoke, she thinks, like that from the coachman's pistol.

She looks for Serafina. The choir nun is a few yards away, praying the rosary, or one of her own variations of it. Orsola tries to run over, but the ground slips and sinks beneath her feet. There is a jarring collision, and a quite unbelievable jolt of pain. The torchlight dims yet further; the shadows stretch and join; and she is at the channel's edge, lying on her back with her legs in the water. It must be cold indeed, but she feels nothing.

Serafina is next to her now, kneeling in the silt, her forehead laid against Orsola's shoulder. 'The axeman stood by,' she is saying, 'sharpening his dreadful blade. But Catarina was not afraid. She turned her face to heaven and she said, "Oh Jesus, oh good king – may any in need who invoke my name receive the benefit of your holy kindness."' The choir nun sniffs and glances up nervously, her eyes reflecting the flame of an approaching torch. 'And her prayer was answered. Heaven's gates did open wide. Christ Himself did honour her and pledge the help she had requested.'

A tingling sensation is creeping around Orsola's spine, seeping into the bone, and a heavy numbness settling upon her chest. Her voice, when she gathers the energy to speak, sounds so broken and distant, she barely recognises it as her own.

'We must rise, Sister,' she whispers. 'We must keep going.'

Up above her, a vision of the journey ahead begins to form amid the shadows, becoming vivid and real. The two of them reach the Tiber and float out past the walls, departing this rotten heap of a city forever. After gliding for a while through green meadows and woodland they arrive at a holy house, welcoming and secure, with a kind Abbess. Sister Serafina is taken in and is safe. Orsola's task is done. All blame lifts away, like the shedding of a dark mantle. Her daughter is found, and led from the grey hill into this brighter world; she is a child now, and so pretty. Orsola gives thanks, wipes her tears, and walks off into the woods to meet her.

'The saint knelt down to die,' Serafina says. 'And when the act was done, angels came to claim her blessed body and bear her to her rest.' She pauses, releasing a shivering breath. 'Santa Catarina was dead. And she was free at last.'

Domina

The river has risen. Throughout the summer it has been a meagre, sluggish thing, humming with ordure, its exposed banks crawling with street people and treasure-seekers, rooting around in the mud for any precious objects that might have been brought back into the daylight. Now though, after only half a week, it is beginning to overflow, creeping up onto the lower lawns of Donna Olimpia's garden and flooding the parched grass. From the loggia, she watches a pair of mallards being carried along quickly by the current, ruffling their feathers in the steady rainfall.

Donna Olimpia takes a mixed view of this shift in the weather. The new coolness is welcome, naturally, and all life requires water. She can sense it stirring around her now: beetles clambering up dewy stems, spiders scurrying across webs laden with droplets, worms rising through the loosened earth. There was something in the heat that she savoured, though – a stilling, at certain hours, when any movement became onerous, and the din of Rome diminished almost to nothing. That is quite gone now; for even in the rain, the city seethes. The damp, also, can already be felt in her accursed knees. They are worsening, despite her prayers. It is starting to seem that they must be rubbed ceaselessly if she is to know any peace at all.

A tray has been set on the stone bench beside her. It holds a fine glass beaker of apple brandy, a saucer, and a plate of almond biscotti, bought the day before from a renowned sweetmeats shop on the Viale Trastevere. Donna Olimpia glances at them with dissatisfaction; she still resents the loss of Signor Gallo the *pasticcere* more than nearly anything else. With a sigh, she pours a little brandy into the saucer, soaks a corner of the largest biscotto, and chews on it reflectively. *The end is in sight*, she thinks. *We must make do until then.*

'Excellency,' says Baron Mattei. 'You have a visitor.'

Donna Olimpia dips her biscotti back into the brandy. 'Does she have them?'

'She says so. But she will show them only to you.'

Sighing again, Donna Olimpia turns slightly upon her cushion. Mattei has brought Flaminia Triunfi beneath the loggia. She stands perhaps four yards from Donna Olimpia's bench, wearing the same damson cloak as before, the hood and shoulders darkened by rainwater. Her arms are crossed in front of her, holding something tightly, and she is gazing out across the gardens with open astonishment.

'Are those the documents, Flaminia?' Donna Olimpia asks, taking another bite of biscotto; it dissolves on her tongue in a rush of sweetness, the brandy's glow spreading through her chest. 'Did you succeed?'

Flaminia seems not to hear. 'This is yours, I take it? This and that villa in Esquilino? And the Palazzo Pamphili, and the estates around Viterbo – with the entire town of San Martino? *All* of it is yours?'

Donna Olimpia shrugs, and wipes away a crumb; there is also a rather splendid apartment in the Borgo district, a manor out in Valmontone, and a prime tract of coastal land on the edges of Ostia. But she does not care to mention these now.

'You would not be here, I think,' she says, 'if you had not met the terms of our agreement.'

Still Flaminia does not appear to be listening. 'It is incredible,' she says, 'that a woman can own all of this, and not be subject to any man. It is the fruit of sin, of course – of base theft and wickedness. But it is quite incredible nonetheless.'

Donna Olimpia purses her lips; so this is how it will be. 'I suggested we meet here in Ripagrande as I know it is convenient for you,' she says. 'You are still living on the Vicolo della Renella, are you not, in that miserable pile your parents had us all call the Palazzo Triunfi – even though it was scarcely large enough to host a game of cards?'

This wins Flaminia's attention, at least. She leans against a column, glowering at Donna Olimpia with great ferocity; her left hand, meanwhile, slips down unthinkingly to her midriff, rubbing the faded green silk of her gown. She is beginning to show. The Spanish face-painter's bastard is growing inside her, and she will surely be a mother by next Lent. The discomfort will be starting; the aches, the flushes. She would probably very much like to sit.

'Where is my sister?' she demands.

'Documents first,' Donna Olimpia tells her, as she finishes the biscotto. 'You disappeared, Flaminia. It took much effort to locate you again. Wherever did you go?'

Flaminia's eyes dip; she does not reply. Donna Olimpia suspects that it has to do with the child – that perhaps, when its existence could no longer be denied, she sought out some form of remedy. If so, it evidently came to nothing.

'Where is Claudia? Is she nearby? Answer me!'

Donna Olimpia regards her visitor coolly. 'She is safe enough. You can be sure of that.'

Flaminia glares back at her. 'You said we would be together. You said a place would be kept for us in San Martino – a house, where we—'

'All of which will still occur. But I stand at an important point, Flaminia. I believe you know this. When I am secure once more, when my fortunes have been resolved, then I will see you and your sister reunited. You have my word.'

Flaminia flattens herself against the column, as if to relieve her shoulder muscles, conflicting feelings flitting across her tired, lovely face. There is deep anger, at having been so comprehensively outplayed; self-reprimand, for not seeing this in advance, as she really should have done; and the dragging dejection that comes with defeat. Reluctantly, she reaches beneath her damson cloak and draws out a thick packet, wrapped in oilskin to protect the papers inside.

Donna Olimpia waits for a few seconds, her hands crossed in her lap, tapping a forefinger against her wrist. Then she realises that Flaminia is not quite done.

'You are trying to defeat the Spanish,' she says. 'That's what this is about, isn't it? You wish to regain the favour of the pope. So that you can get your palazzo back, and save your man in the Tor di Nona.'

'I'm sure I don't know what you mean.'

Flaminia persists. 'Innocent's datary has been sentenced to death. But it is said that despite the horror of his circumstances, he has revealed nothing of any accomplices in his crimes. He has held his peace, as if expecting such a show of loyalty to be rewarded.'

Donna Olimpia's patience leaves her. 'Enough of this,' she says, extending her arm and gesturing with her fingers. 'The documents.'

With a slight, bitter smile, Flaminia steps forward and presses the packet a touch too firmly into Donna Olimpia's palm.

'Now go back to your little palazzo,' Donna Olimpia instructs. 'And stay away from the Spaniards. I cannot have them guessing our connection, or you choosing to tell them of it. This is part of our agreement, do you understand? Break it and I will release your sister into a place where she will not be found.'

Flaminia seems to consider a response, but thinks better of it. She looks out at the waterlogged flowerbeds for a moment; then she turns and walks back towards the gates. Donna Olimpia holds up the packet and Prince Ludovisi appears from a doorway behind to take it from her. Before Flaminia has left the estate, he has peeled off the oilskin and begun leafing through the contents.

'So tell me what happened,' says Donna Olimpia, as she watches a large bluebottle inch along the patterned rim of the biscotti plate. 'Tell me why my little gaol now has but one resident.'

Baron Mattei has been waiting at the loggia's end. 'There was an escape, Excellency,' he admits, shifting uncomfortably. 'A failure in the pattern of the guard. It has been addressed.' He nods towards Ludovisi. 'With his excellency the prince's help, the nuns were quickly trapped again, in the catacombs beneath Campo Vaccino. But they tried to flee. Warning shots were fired – and by some dire misfortune, a ricochet brought one of them down.'

Donna Olimpia makes a short, disgusted sound. 'Warning shots!' she repeats derisively. 'Was that warranted, Mattei? Your men were chasing a pair of runaway nuns.'

The lid twitches above Mattei's blind eye. 'They believed the women had knives, Excellency, as one of them had just attacked a—'

'She is well, though? Claudia Triunfi is well?'

'She is. It was the servant nun who died. Signorina Triunfi is . . . unsettled, for sure. Like one possessed, my men say. But she is unharmed.'

Swatting away the bluebottle, Donna Olimpia slides a second biscotto from the plate and rests it in the brandy saucer. She recalls her visit to the captives – how the peasant girl who had attached herself to poor, mad Claudia begged for her life, as she tried to understand the larger events in which they had so unwittingly become ensnared. It is a shame, certainly, to think of her dead; but at times, the loss of such people seems all but inevitable.

'So be it,' Donna Olimpia says, as the reddish liquor seeps up into the biscuit. 'The servant nun is with God. We will include her in our prayers.'

The soldier and the fat prince murmur their agreement. Donna Olimpia then dismisses Mattei, ordering him to maintain a close watch over Flaminia Triunfi. 'The Spanish might still seek her out,' she says. 'The prospect of a child may trouble the face-painter's conscience. These things are not completely unheard of.'

As Mattei departs, Ludovisi perches his sizeable frame on the far end of the bench, his nose held close to the thin pages of the packet.

'Is it all we hoped for?' Donna Olimpia asks.

'Oh, a good deal more, Mama,' he replies with a chuckle, as he turns a sheet over. 'The Spanish have been monitoring our friends in Naples . . . *very* closely. This is exactly the tool that we require.'

'And you can gain access to Astalli's residences?'

Ludovisi tilts his head. 'The cardinal is presently based at your own palazzo, of course. They've changed the locks, but I have people inside – one of them a priest, in fact, a most ambitious and effective man, who has full access to Astalli's papers.'

Donna Olimpia nods; she feels the first real stirring of satisfaction. 'It is here, Ludo,' she says. 'The hour is finally here.'

Ludovisi begins to wrap the packet back up in its oilskin. 'I should point out, Mama, that what Signorina Triunfi just said was true. Masco doesn't have long. If you are to intervene, it must be soon indeed.'

Donna Olimpia detects a note of malicious pleasure in his voice at Mascambruno's plight. She lifts the biscotto from the brandy, shaking a few drops back into the saucer. 'Should he die, the pope will be most upset,' she observes. 'Not knowing Mascambruno very well, he holds him in high regard.'

Ludovisi concurs. 'The disgrace of it also – one of his officials, whom he appointed personally, put to death. Why, the old fellow would be distraught.' He pauses meaningfully. 'Much reduced.'

Donna Olimpia glances over at him. 'Well then, Ludo,' she says, bringing the biscotto to her lips, 'we must do whatever we can.'

*

The grey carriage clatters across the cobbles of the Ponte Sant'-Angelo. Opening the shutter beside her, Donna Olimpia sees the statue of San Luca, pocked and weathered, missing fingers and an ear; and then a stretch of the water below, brown beneath the leaden sky. The carriage bumps down the ramp, passes through the toll gate, and circles left, the coachman slowing the horses to a walk as the platform comes into view beside the bridgehead.

Mascambruno is bound to the post, a cord around his shoulders and waist, clad in a stained prison smock. Early word was that his body would be hung upside down, with his head set on a spike out somewhere on the bridge itself. He has plainly been spared this; for a second, in fact, the datary seems oddly unscathed, like he might start to struggle against his bonds or try to rise. Then, as the carriage draws closer, a street dog springs up beside him. It begins to lick at the dried blood that coats his throat and streaks his chest and shoulders. Mascambruno makes no reaction. His skin is a grubby white, bruised blue in places; his neck is criss-crossed with crude stitches; his delicate features are slack, his eyes like those of a fish laid out on a stall.

Donna Olimpia pulls back a little, crossing herself. 'Holy Madonna,' she mutters, 'they've sewn his damned head back on.'

Executing an ordained man is a contentious business. Prince Ludovisi's spies reported widespread disquiet throughout both the Curia and the Governor's offices – but Cardinal Astalli was said to be set upon the datary's death, asserting that it was necessary for the redemption of the papacy. And so the previous day, Mascambruno was taken from his prison to the church of San Salvatore in Lauro and publicly defrocked before the altar, in front of a crowd of cardinals, ambassadors and noblemen.

Ludovisi was among them. 'A ghastly spectacle, Mama,' he said, when he came to Esquilino later that evening. 'Once poor Masco realised that it was really going to happen, that they meant to see him die, he began to wail – and Christ, did he wail! On and on it went, about how he pardoned his persecutors, how they would see their error and beg forgiveness, how he was innocent as a lamb . . . in the end, the prison guards had to gag him.'

Back at the Tor di Nona, the unlucky datary had found the Brothers of Compassion waiting in his cell, ready to perform their duty of consoling the condemned. As fortune would have it, Ludovisi has a man with the Brothers, who told of the fresh terror that consumed Mascambruno – and who brought Donna Olimpia a note from him, while she was still dining with her son-in-law. This was a sign of his desperation, for he would be well aware that she would not welcome such a thing in the least. It said – in his typically insinuating manner – that he had thought of her often since his arrest, and throughout his trial, stressing that he had always been devoted to her above all other people.

Donna Olimpia sighed as she read this note; only Masco could make an appeal for his life a matter of blackmail. After throwing it on the fire, she called for paper and penned an equally elliptical response, advising him to attend to his prayers, and to remember that Almighty God spares those who repent in earnest. This prompted a full confession, the likes of which even the Tor di Nona rarely heard. Ludovisi's man reported that it took more than seven hours, and included many outrageous crimes that the datary's prosecutors had been unaware of, such as several large thefts from Donna Olimpia's own family. Nothing was revealed that would cast the slightest suspicion upon the lady herself, however; her missive worked precisely as intended, delaying Mascambruno's threat until it was removed for good. The wretch thought that her call for repentance was in fact a test of his loyalty – that word of his salvation would come at dawn, while he waited in his cell with the Brothers; or in the prison yard, perhaps, as he said his final prayer; or as he mounted the steps, and was pushed down onto the headsman's block.

Donna Olimpia looks at him again, mutilated so peculiarly, presumably in ham-fisted deference to the vestments he wore until the previous afternoon. Guards chase off the licking dog, only for it to be replaced by another, and then two more. The body slumps, a couple of stitches give out, and it looks briefly like the head might come loose and bounce away down the street.

As she watches the guards boot off the strays and prop the corpse back up, straightening the blankly staring head atop the blood-blackened neck, Donna Olimpia feels an unexpected pang of sadness. She remembers the secret conversations in darkened chambers and carriages, and at the ends of secluded balconies; the coded notes that would pass between them, sometimes four or five in a day, along with stacks of bulls or petitions; the boxes of gold scudi that would appear, as if by sorcery, in the vaults of her bank. In Mascambruno she had found a commendably quick mind, sworn to the service of the Church, yet almost entirely devoid of morality or restraint. He was outclassed by her, of course, in every conceivable way, while imagining that things were the opposite. She thinks once more of that medallion with its vicious caricatures, surely intended to inspire her retreat – but which has quite demonstrably brought them all to this moment.

The coachman whips the horses, speeding up the carriage. Donna Olimpia closes the shutter and sits back, moving her hands to her throbbing knees. She has taken the correct path. This cannot be doubted. Mascambruno was a double-dyed rogue with a clacking tongue, wholly selfish and privy to far too many secrets; any pain she experiences is merely that of an effective medicine, purging her of corruption. It will soon pass.

And now the ground has been prepared for a far more significant action.

*

The room in which Donna Olimpia and Olimpiuccia are left is reassuringly fine: expert stonework and furniture, immaculate parquet, walls hung with gold-framed paintings of the first rank. It sits within a tall townhouse close to the Piazza della Minerva, where the Holy Inquisition has its headquarters, and where Cardinal Francesco Barberini thus spends much of his day. The Barberini do own grander residences – notably their vast palazzo just behind the Quirinale, with a wing set aside for each brother – but these remain under papal confiscation for now, obliging the cardinal to dwell here. And as a back-up, as your third or fourth best Roman property, this place is truly remarkable, fashioned by that hallowed combination of refined taste and immense wealth. Awaiting its master, Donna Olimpia feels that she has chosen her allies wisely.

Olimpiuccia is growing apprehensive, however. Regrettably, the girl is dressed in everyday clothes: a simple gown and shawl, with her hair tied up beneath a length of blue satin. This couldn't be helped, for their time is in precious short supply. Donna Olimpia tells herself that Cardinal Barberini will know what he is being shown. An able enough display will be made.

At first, Olimpiuccia was very pleased by their reunion, and filled with a child-like excitement at the prospect of this mysterious little adventure they were to have together. As they were shown through the house to this room, she'd become concerned by Donna Olimpia's gait and occasional groans, both elicited by the damned knees. Taking her grandmother's arm, she led her to the two chairs that had been set in the middle of the floor, and then attempted to divert her with a tale from the Palazzo Giustiniani, concerning a macaw owned by one of her brothers that had run amok in the kitchens. Now though, this kind, rather self-possessed girl is peering at one of the gold-framed paintings in a state of mild alarm — for it is a classical subject, the rape of someone or other Donna Olimpia thinks, featuring a copious number of unclothed bodies roiling around in a lush, expansive landscape.

'What . . . what is that, Nonna?' she asks at last.

'French, I believe,' Donna Olimpia replies shortly. She is in no mood to be indulgent; the conversation ahead promises to be both sharp and consequential, and she needs to keep her wits applied to her purpose.

Olimpiuccia changes tack. 'Who is this person we are to meet?

My uncle Niccolò would tell me only that he is very important, and that I am not to speak a word.'

'Quite right,' says Donna Olimpia. 'You would do well to heed him.'

Olimpiuccia will not let it rest there. She has been raised in palazzos and villas but still knows Rome well enough to be able to tell roughly where they are. She is speculating as to how this location might identify their host when, without preamble or announcement, he enters the room. To her annoyance, Donna Olimpia hears the girl catch her breath at the sight of his crimson robes. Olimpiuccia has been around clerics all her young life – her great uncle is pope, for heaven's sake – yet in the past year she has started to affect a deep, unquestioning reverence for the Church and its ministers. Donna Olimpia suspects that she will now imagine a religious purpose for their visit – that her piety is to be examined, her knowledge of the catechism tested, or something of that nature.

Cardinal Francesco Barberini is not pleased to see them. He eyes Olimpiuccia with particular distaste, being well aware of Donna Olimpia's reason for bringing her: so that he might behold the girl, and acknowledge that she is ready to be betrothed to his nephew Maffeo. Donna Olimpia should get up from her chair, but she decides to stay where she is. In contrast, Olimpiuccia drops forward onto her knees, her head bowed in veneration.

A single chair, heavier and more ornate than the rest, stands at the front of the room, obviously intended for the cardinal. Ignoring it, he walks directly up to them, up to Olimpiuccia, stopping when he is barely a hands-width away from her. A strange, pointed silence ensues. Cardinal Barberini's rich red robes are virtually brushing against Olimpiuccia's shoulder; she glances back at her grandmother from the reception room floor, uncertainty and mortification in her eyes. After a moment, Donna Olimpia sighs loudly and instructs the girl to take herself to one of the chairs that are lined up against a far wall. Olimpiuccia obeys straight away; as she rises she turns her head very slightly towards the motionless cardinal, but does not quite dare to look at him.

Cardinal Barberini waits until Olimpiuccia has reached her new chair, then sits beside Donna Olimpia and begins to hiss out questions with quick, hostile intensity. 'What is this, Donna Olimpia? What in the Lord's name are you doing? I have duties to attend to – and you are not even supposed to be in this city. I cannot be seen to be providing assistance to a—'

'There is news, Eminence,' Donna Olimpia interrupts, her voice a firm murmur. 'Of the most urgent and sensitive variety. I am afraid it could not be delayed. I have rushed over here, as you can see, with my poor Olimpiuccia in tow, so imperative did I think it that we speak.'

The cardinal's anger ebbs somewhat, his black-brown eyes blinking as he considers the possibilities. 'Your brother-in-law's datary has just been put to death,' he says. 'It is a bad day for Pope Innocent, I would imagine. A bad day indeed.'

Donna Olimpia shrugs. 'A guilty man has paid for his crimes. The Spanish faction was thirsting for blood after the loss of Cardinal Panciroli, and Monsignor Mascambruno was dragged forth to provide it.' She pauses. 'Not that the unlucky wretch had anything at all to do with Panciroli's demise. That was the work of another, was it not?'

Cardinal Barberini refuses the bait, his expression indicating nothing. He leans back, arranges his robe with an odd, fastidious elegance, and waits for her to continue.

'No, Eminence, I am afraid that a rather more important reversal has occurred. Our Neapolitan stratagem must be abandoned. My people have uncovered evidence that Spain is forewarned. She is readying defences that would make an invasion extremely costly and very possibly unsuccessful. It would be gross slaughter, I am told. Pope Innocent cannot supply his sanction to such a doomed endeavour.'

Donna Olimpia says this with authority, and Cardinal Barberini does not contest it; the news can hardly be a surprise to him, as the French have many spies of their own in the Kingdom of Naples. He retains his composure, but his eyes darken with a new, noxious loathing.

'My brother will be most aggrieved to hear that,' he says. 'Antonio was set upon that territory – on seeing our nephew crowned its duke. He will be asking me, Donna Olimpia, why we should continue in our alliance with you. If there is to be no invasion, we will no longer need the sanction of this foolish, declining pope – even if you, in your present state of disgrace, were really able to secure it. Antonio will be wondering what conceivable use you can be to us now.' The cardinal's gaze flicks over to Olimpiuccia. 'You or any of your family.'

Donna Olimpia nearly smiles at how neatly this conceited churchman's response matches her anticipation of it. 'I have prepared for this, Eminence,' she replies, keeping her tone low. 'Our stratagem for Naples has faltered, yes, but it has yielded something else – a valuable and unexpected weapon that can be used against our enemies, and return me to my rightful place at Pope Innocent's side. That will see the Barberini family restored to all its former greatness.'

Cardinal Barberini is sceptical. 'Is that so? Will this . . . *weapon* allow you to meet the more recent threats that have appeared? Such as this Fabio Chigi, back from the north, who has already been raised to the Sacred College and set in Panciroli's place as secretary of state?'

Donna Olimpia waves this away. 'I ask only for your patience,' she says, 'and for the smallest amount of trust. Soon I will be back beside the pope, with all other voices silenced. The adversity of this fevered summer will be but a memory.' She casts a glance of her own at Olimpiuccia – who sits earnestly with one hand clasped in the other, trying vainly to listen in. 'Our families will be united, in the happy manner I have long proposed. We will be ready for the next stage, where we will make plans for the lasting benefit of us all.'

The cardinal's thin eyebrows contract, his doubt edging into exasperation. 'And how exactly will this be achieved, Donna Olimpia? Pope Innocent will not receive you. It is said that he still believes you to be the source of the misfortune that has hobbled his papacy.'

Donna Olimpia nods slowly; she sees that for all his acrimony and resentment, Cardinal Francesco Barberini will do precisely as she requires. She looks towards the door, preparing to depart.

'Do not trouble yourself with that, Eminence,' she says. 'Just watch.'

*

Olimpiuccia does not speak until they are back in the grey carriage, on their way to Donna Olimpia's next destination. 'So what did you want from him, Nonna?' she asks. 'What were you talking about?'

Once again, Donna Olimpia is both impressed and vaguely disturbed by her granddaughter's confidence, and apparent disregard for the boundaries of discipline within which the young are supposed to live. She wraps her black shawl around her shoulders. 'That is not your concern,' she says.

As ever, Olimpiuccia persists. 'If that is so, why am I here? Did you honestly have me taken from my lessons in the middle of the day just to ride around Rome in this little carriage, and then sit upon a chair while you quarrelled with his Eminence the cardinal?'

'We did not quarrel,' Donna Olimpia corrects her. 'Cardinal Barberini is a close friend of our family. A close friend indeed.'

Olimpiuccia plainly thinks this unlikely. She starts to pose another query, but Donna Olimpia has had enough.

'Quiet, by God,' she says. 'No more from you, do you hear? These are not matters for a young mind.'

The remainder of the journey passes in a rather tense silence. When it is over, Donna Olimpia considers Olimpiuccia for a few seconds, staring sullenly out of the window, before reaching across to cup the girl's cheek in her hand. Olimpiuccia flinches and nearly moves away, but then bears the caress like a disgruntled cat.

'This carriage will return you to your parents' house,' Donna Olimpia says. 'I will see you again very soon, and we will go back to the Palazzo Pamphili together.' She strokes her granddaughter's warm, smooth skin. 'Always remember that I am toiling for you, Olimpiuccia. For everyone you hold dear.'

The sedan chair has been set down close to the carriage, so that Donna Olimpia can climb into it directly, planting just a single footstep on the streets of Rome. It is carried around a corner and up a long flight of steps; the bearers begin to pant but their pace remains steady. They pass through a low stone gateway – one she suspects is used by lesser people, clerks, messengers and the like. She refuses to let this vex her. It will happen only once.

As expected, nobody dares to issue a challenge. This ban, this foul prohibition, is merely a matter of will: all she needs to do is act and it is dispelled. Moving at speed, they reach the papal chambers in a couple of minutes. Donna Olimpia has left one of the chair's curtains open, so that she might survey the grandeur of the Palazzo del Quirinale. She shifts upon her cushion, straightening her spine, and finds that she is most glad to be back. It feels righteous.

A pair of cardinals are standing outside the main reception room, deep in conversation. Donna Olimpia's bearers have instructions not to stop or slow for anybody; the leader mutters a respectful warning and the clerics step aside. One of them she cannot place at first. He has a large, aquiline nose, a neat, greyish beard and a slight stoop; there is a strong impression of dampness about him, created by his moist lip and lined, watery eyes. She realises that this is the recent arrival just mentioned by Cardinal Barberini: Fabio Chigi, called back from Germany, elevated in some rushed consistory and then installed at the very heart of the Curia. The new secretary of state has yet to develop the vigilant obstructiveness of Giacomo Panciroli, however, and simply watches her pass.

The other cardinal Donna Olimpia knows immediately. It is the sleek betrayer, the traitor to his blood, the lapdog of Spain — and most recently, the agent of Mascambruno's demise. Camillo Astalli is as well groomed as always and a little plumper than she recalls, a change for which she suspects Signor Gallo's creations may be responsible. She makes sure that he sees her as the chair charges by, savouring his dismay — for he is very aware of what she can do.

Prepare yourself, fool, she thinks. *Prepare for the end.*

In the reception room itself Donna Olimpia notices a rectangular object on the wall, where previously there had been nothing. It is the Spanish portrait — the magnificent masterpiece lauded from one end of Rome to the other, and taken as absolute evidence of

God's favour for the bond between the papacy and the Spanish crown – and it has been covered over completely with a sheet of deep blue velvet.

An order to halt comes now, from just ahead; it seems that a Swiss guardsman is blocking their path to the library. Donna Olimpia sits forward very slightly, allowing a fold of her black gown to fall from the chair. The guardsman apologises at once and opens the library door.

'Admit no one else,' she says to him. 'The Holy Father and I will speak alone.'

She finds Giambo weeping at his desk in the papal study. His camauro is clutched in his hand, which is trembling more severely than ever. A small team of valets hovers nearby, waiting to dress the old man for Mass, eyeing him with a mixture of concern and caution. Ludovisi has said that the pope became increasingly irascible during Mascambruno's trial, threatening even the most devoted and longstanding of his servants with dismissal – even, at times, with excommunication.

Sight of the chair startles the valets from the study. Donna Olimpia climbs out at the threshold, sending her bearers away, thinking it better that she come before Giambo on foot. She says his name as she approaches the desk. The weeping tails off; he does not turn towards her, but neither does he demand to know what she is doing there, or who let her in, or order her to go. She can tell that their last conversation has been forgotten – whether by accident or design, or some eliding of the two. He raises his camauro to dab the velvet against his streaming eyes, and she knows that he wants her back; that he will reinstate her in every way; that this victory, as she suspected, is hers for the taking. Events have battered Giambattista Pamphili most soundly. His defences have fallen. She need only march in through the breach.

'It is ashes.' His voice is a croaking husk; a wisp of nothingness. 'All of it. My triumph, the triumph of the Church . . . it is lost, Olimpia. It is gone. Ashes.'

Self pity: of course. This is how he reacts. This is *always* his reaction. As Ludovisi predicted back in the loggia at Ripagrande, it is the undoing of Mascambruno that has induced this particular convulsion. Giambo has much indeed to say on the matter; Donna Olimpia wonders, after a while, if it will ever end.

'The Blessed Jubilee was intended to save my papacy, to restore its honour – yet now it is stained, stained indelibly with the very blackest scandal! The holder of one of the most senior posts in the Vatican has been *executed*, Olimpia – beheaded in the prison yard and exposed on the street like the lowest of thieves, like a brigand or pirate!' The pope gasps and gurgles, wringing the camauro like a dishcloth, struggling to hold back a new wave of sobs. 'Mascambruno erred. This is . . . this is above dispute. But in his heart, he was a faithful servant – a good Christian and a good man. He did not deserve such an awful fate.'

Donna Olimpia raises an eyebrow at this, for Masco's loyalty to anything at all save Masco was an issue of serious doubt, and almost nothing about the datary's conduct upon this earth would qualify as goodness.

'The Epistle to the Hebrews instructs us to think of the prisoner,' Giambo goes on. 'To remember them as if we were there with them, sharing their ordeal. But I can scarcely bear to do it. The thought of his final night, Olimpia . . . it will haunt me to my death. The cells of the Tor di Nona are surely the most miserable places in Rome. To have been confined there, to take your last meal there, to . . . to . . .'

Donna Olimpia puts a hand on the back of his chair. 'The Lord gives especial succour, does He not,' she says, 'to those who are imprisoned?'

Holy Madonna, she knows him, this broken old beast; in seconds, his spirits have begun to lift and he is talking of Samson, of Joseph, visited in their dungeons by angels, doves or ghostly lambs.

'It is plain,' she interrupts, after another minute or so, 'that a gesture is called for. Have the prison razed, Giambattista. Have its bars and chains melted down, its timbers burned, and each and every brick ground to powder. Give the order now.'

As these words pass her lips, evoking this vision of destruction, Donna Olimpia finds herself thinking again of the servant nun, shot down in the darkness of the catacombs; of the desperate band who came for her blood, and failed so signally to spill any of it; of the town wiped away by a papal command she did much to support, so that an example could be made of the doltish Duke of Farnese. Suddenly, a connection forms.

'Also,' she says, 'I believe the time has come to find a home for the bells of Castro. They have been standing quiet in a warehouse in Regola for more than a year. You know that it has long been my wish that they should be hung in the church of Sant'Agnese beside the Palazzo Pamphili, as part of a renovation performed in our family's name.'

The truth is that Donna Olimpia has hatched this scheme just then, in that moment, but she knows that she simply has to assert it with sufficient confidence and Giambo will pretend that he remembers. Better that than to admit ignorance, and reveal the diminishing of his once-renowned mind.

'Yes, Olimpia,' he says, even managing some enthusiasm. 'Yes, I recall.'

Donna Olimpia moves around him, sliding her hand from the chair to his shoulder, and feels him start slightly at her touch. She looks into that familiar, ill-favoured face, raw with weeping and pale with fatigue; she is standing close enough now to smell his curdled, oniony breath.

'Well, it is time for this to come about. Two works, Giambo, to put this behind us. Think of it: a black stain washed away, and a holy beacon restored to glory. It will serve as a statement of our intentions. Of how we mean to proceed.'

This — the *our*, the *we* — slips by without a murmur of complaint or qualification. He is pleased, in fact, his lips twitching into the beginnings of a sad smile.

'We cannot link dear Mascambruno's name to our actions, of course,' Donna Olimpia adds, kneading the bony joint at the top of his arm. 'But I believe his presence will be felt. Almighty God will see to it.'

There is a pause.

'You are right,' Giambo says. 'Holy Christ, Olimpia, you are right. Praise the saints. A . . . a weight is beginning to reduce. And by God's divine grace it will soon be gone.'

He lays the camauro on the desk before him, pushes the chair back across the marble floor and starts to lower himself down to pray. This is a lengthy, painful process. Donna Olimpia takes a half-step back, watching dispassionately as gnarled hands are clasped together and pressed to the papal brow, and an expression of earnest thankfulness and obeisance is begun.

'I heard that it was Camillo Astalli who oversaw Mascambruno's arrest,' she says. 'And who demanded the harshest penalties for his crimes.'

Giambo stops his prayer mid-phrase and lowers his hands. 'This is true,' he says regretfully. 'Cardinal Astalli would have no other outcome. A terrible hatred had developed between them. There were offices and preferments due to Astalli that he believed Monsignor Mascambruno, in his role as datary, was deliberately denying him.'

He hesitates, as if debating whether to go on. 'Also . . . the Cardinal Nephew felt very strongly that Mascambruno was not telling everything he knew about the death of poor . . . of poor Giacomo.'

And here it is: the weasel Panciroli. Another swamp of sorrow seems to open up before them, threatening to slow the old sheep to a dismal, boggy halt. Giambo will have heard the stories, even the most lurid and slanderous ones, no doubt presented to him as unquestionable fact; and he will have begged the Lord for guidance, asking if his sister-in-law could possibly have ordered the murder of his dearest friend. Donna Olimpia pulls in her shawl, her brow darkening. She will put an end to this right now.

'Cardinal Panciroli died of a seizure,' she says curtly. 'Astalli is wrong, Giambo. His suspicions are utterly misguided. He has caused all this monstrous damage for nothing. For *nothing*, do you hear?' She takes a breath, looking out through the tall windows. 'And he means to do more. To do *worse*. For it is not just Mascambruno that he hates.'

Perversely, given the trouble they suggest, these words bring Giambo visible relief. He wants to believe her more than anything in Creation. She looks down at him, into those rheumy eyes, and she feels herself relax a little as well. The pope might have accepted Astalli's appointment as Cardinal Nephew, but the traitor will always be Panciroli's man, brought in from outside – whereas Giambo is *hers*, now and forever, to lead exactly where she chooses. If that summer has taught them both anything, it is this.

'Whoever do you mean?' he asks. 'Who does Camillo Astalli hate?'

Donna Olimpia pouts slightly, as if this is obvious. 'Why, *us*, Giambo. You and I. Astalli saw that Monsignor Mascambruno was loyal to the Pamphili and Maidalchini families, and that he would never betray our interests. That he was, in effect, an obstacle.'

This merely deepens Giambo's incomprehension.

'Like his master, like poor Panciroli, Astalli is bound to the Spanish,' Donna Olimpia enlarges. 'You must surely be aware of this. It is the reason for the terrible fuss you have endured of late. All those parades and presentations.' She glances back towards the reception room. 'And that Spanish portrait, so very *admired* – which I notice you have covered up, Giambo, as if you cannot bear even to look upon it.'

The kneeling pope demurs, and begins a mealy-mouthed explanation that shows quite plainly that Donna Olimpia is correct. Standing there is bringing her the usual discomfort. She considers sitting, in his vacated chair perhaps; but something about their current position feels appropriate, with her drawn up before him like a holy visitation, so she makes do with propping herself against the desk.

'But I fear Astalli's aims are greater than Panciroli's ever were,' she says, 'and a good deal more perfidious. He is a young man still, and a formidably ambitious one. With the backing of King Felipe and his faction here in Rome, he sees the Fisherman's Ring on his own finger. He imagines the long and glorious reign of an Astalli pope, forming the foundations of a dynasty that will rule over the Catholic world for decades to come.'

Giambo leans back from his prayerful posture with a small groan, his long face growing yet craggier as he thinks this through. 'How do you know this?'

Donna Olimpia regards him with a passing imitation of patience. 'Do you remember our plan for the Kingdom of Naples?'

This is the moment of greatest risk – for as the invasion was conceived, and the initial agreements made with the Barberini and the French Crown, Donna Olimpia left Giambo out of the negotiations entirely. When it reached a point where he had to be told something

– to ensure that he was implicated, and their fates entwined – she rattled through complicated preparations with a deliberate, obscuring haste, omitting details she knew he would find unsettling or distasteful. And then later on, she had him sign certain letters that she hadn't actually permitted him to read, or at least not in full.

'We thought of it together, Giambo,' she tells him. 'A stratagem to guide us into the future – into a time beyond.' *Specifically a time beyond YOU,* she thinks, *surely no more than a year or two away now.* 'It was our attempt to consider the generations that will follow. To guarantee that our families remain in Rome's first rank, with friends who will protect them. Who will *empower* them.'

Giambo is nodding in apparent understanding, but then he asks: 'And how does this involve Naples, precisely?'

'Dear Giambo,' Donna Olimpia replies, after a short, faintly mystified hesitation, 'it was your idea.'

Keeping her tone brisk yet admiring, as if marvelling still at its simple genius, she explains the whole enterprise. How France was to seize Naples from Spain and award it to the Barberini, to give them a proper foothold in Italy. How this family would then make their full return to Rome, bringing their exile to an end. And how all of this would be fully sanctioned and legitimised by the papacy of Innocent X.

'Thereafter, we would have been bound both to the Barberini and to Catholic France by ties of gratitude and lasting friendship. These are superior allies in every respect to the rotting throne of Spain.' Donna Olimpia looks down, briefly studying the back of her hand. 'I am embarrassed, quite frankly, to be describing your own scheme to you in this manner.'

Giambo is frowning. 'I think . . . I think I can recall our conversations on this matter,' he says. 'But Olimpia, the Barberini . . .'

Donna Olimpia will not hear it. 'That is the past,' she declares.

'They did wrong, Giambo – this is not disputed. But they have been punished for it. Francesco, as you know, is back already, and serving the Church with great distinction. And Antonio longs to return as well, and will pledge himself to you without reserve or restraint.' She sighs, allowing her expression to soften by the slightest degree. 'You know all this, Brother. It was to be a chance for forgiveness – for their redemption. And one of Italy's great kingdoms would once more be under the control of an ancient Italian family, not a viceroy of Spain. We would have had a powerful new ally, and the future would have been secure.'

Giambo squints up at her, considering her words. 'It has . . . failed, then?'

'It will do very soon.' Donna Olimpia pauses for emphasis, her nostrils flaring. 'For we have been betrayed. The Spanish know of our stratagem for Naples. Their spies have been busy indeed, and they are ready to resist – to defend their stronghold. France will quickly lose heart. King Louis envisaged a coup, a rapid seizure; he has no appetite for another war.'

The pope has fallen silent. His breathing is growing heavy, as if kneeling on the parquet requires a degree of effort he can only just uphold.

'And Camillo Astalli is an important part of this. He hates us, like I said. For almost a year now, he has been setting up hidden conduits, to collect together information from the Spanish spies of Naples. His purpose is exposure, of course – to frustrate our plan while it is still under formulation. To humiliate us both, and erode your support among the Sacred College. And it looks very much like he will be successful.'

Giambo has turned his face away; now he extends a trembling hand towards his chair, so that he might rise again. 'There is proof of this, I assume?'

'Search his residences,' Donna Olimpia says. 'Do it today – this very hour. Send your own guard. And may Almighty God strike me down if I have spoken a word of untruth.'

Giambo grips the chair arm, his knobbly fingers sinking into the green velvet. Gathering his strength, he starts to climb back to his feet, calling for the guard sergeant as he does so. Halfway through, however, his right leg gives out and he stumbles to the side. Donna Olimpia grabs at him, largely through instinct; this slows his fall, preventing injury, but pulls them both down into an awkward embrace on the study floor. Immediately, he is clinging to her in the old familiar way, his head pressed to her breast, emitting little gasps of gladness. The knees are screaming – they are screaming like scorched, maniacal monkeys released from the blackened gates of hell – but Donna Olimpia swallows her agony, glares up at the lavishly patterned ceiling and calls out for the sergeant herself.

It has begun. Her vengeance is approaching, and it will not stop with Camillo Astalli. Any man who has opposed her, or slighted her, or thwarted her aims to even the smallest extent will be swept aside.

Including you, old sheep, she thinks, as she pats Giambo's wizened shoulder. *Including you.*

Servus

De Pareja rises early and makes for the studio. The sky above Trinita dei Monti is untouched by the dawn; Matins are still being said in a chapel a few streets over, the choir's chants drifting between the rooftops. He lights a candle and turns towards the Venus. Flaminia Triunfi's features are in the mirror now but her reflection is indistinct, as if seen through a pane of misted glass. The face appears distant, its lines and details dissolving, like something already being lost to memory – and quite separate from the reclining goddess before it, who is so filled with presence and life that she seems about to shift her position atop the coverlet.

De Pareja straightens his doublet and takes a breath. The time has arrived. If this is to be done, it must be done now. He must trust himself, and act without hesitation, or everything will be lost.

Rather to his amazement, the theft of the documents caused Don Diego only the slightest concern. They agreed that Flaminia had to be the culprit. She had watched de Pareja go about his business, and deduced where the documents were hidden; and then, after waiting patiently for an opportunity, she had gone down to the cellar and stolen them. It also seemed likely that Olimpia Maidalchini was involved, and that Flaminia had acted on her behalf. They couldn't be sure of the precise nature of the connection, but Don Diego said that the two women had several mutual acquaintances, the widow having been a great patron of artists and architects before her expulsion.

'Rome is a small place, really,' he said. 'They all seem to know one another.'

'What shall we do, then?' de Pareja asked. 'Will you go to confront her? Will you alert the ambassador – bring out the guard?'

Don Diego fell quiet at this suggestion, pulling absently at a loose thread on his cuff. They were both well aware that the Duke of Infantado would be gravely unimpressed by their failure to safeguard the Neapolitan documents and would take it as confirmation of his worst fears.

'I . . . think not,' he said at last. 'I cannot blame Flaminia for this, Juan. Her life is a most precarious one. The choices she must make, and the alliances she must form merely to survive – it is hard to imagine. To be a female painter in a city such as this, where artists fight and steal from each other as a matter of course . . . She will not have done this lightly. There will be a good reason.'

De Pareja barely managed to hide his exasperation. 'What about the widow? If she really is behind it, what use might she make of those papers?'

Don Diego shrugged. 'Astalli intended them to serve as a weapon against her. I would think she has put them straight on the fire.'

'So we do nothing. Signorina Triunfi comes in here and betrays your trust in the lowest manner, and we do nothing.'

This comment earned de Pareja a reproving glance. 'No, Juan. We will return to our rightful station. I am the king's painter, and the keeper of his pictures. My place is at his side, in his royal court. We will absent ourselves from Rome as soon as we possibly can and pray that nobody learns of this before we go.'

De Pareja was unsatisfied by this course; it seemed evasive to him, like some important task was not being addressed. But he could most definitely understand the appeal of leaving all this subterfuge and struggle behind. Instructing himself to think of their advancement – of Señora Inés, his workshop, and everything else he intended to achieve in Madrid – he set about hastening their departure.

And this, the Venus, is the first and most pressing of his duties. After double-checking the painting's dimensions, he sweeps the studio floor and lays out a large piece of clean linen. Then he takes the canvas from its easel and removes the supports, stacking them away in a corner. For all the freedom of his technique, Don Diego insists always on a very thin pigment, almost liquid, which he will apply with a minimum of impasto. This means that the Venus, now turned into a painted sheet, can be rolled inside the linen to form a fairly tight tube; de Pareja is well practised at this, having prepared many pictures for transportation between the royal palaces of Spain. He tucks the linen in at both ends and wraps a piece of heavy, untreated canvas around the whole, for the purposes of protection, before binding the result with twine.

When this is done he collects together his things, leaves the apartment, and starts down through the embassy, the rolled Venus carried over his shoulder. He looks constantly this way and that, for the building is never still. Even in the darkest hours of the night, there are people at work in the kitchens and on guard in the courtyard; but he knows their posts and patrols, and makes it to the cellars without being seen.

The Apollo stands at the end of a row of casts and statues. It was delivered without fanfare a few hours earlier, precisely as agreed. Maestro Algardi's men have built a frame around it, with a solid top and bottom, but have left the cast open at the sides so it could be inspected before the packers arrive the following day. De Pareja has brought his candle with him, carried in a shuttered lantern. Now, as he slides back the front hatch, he cannot help smiling a little – for down there in the murky cellar this Apollo appears close to perfect. The shop of Algardi, for all their gossiping and strange games, have fully justified their reputation, recreating the beautiful, nonchalant god in the glossy blackness of bronze. The graceful contours of the original have been replicated exactly, and the locations of the various joins and sprues can barely be seen.

Crucially, they have also carried out de Pareja's request, inserting an oval plinth beneath the statue that will supply the additional height required. He sets the rolled Venus against a wall, and the lantern upon a nearby crate. Then he approaches the Apollo, crouches beside it, and runs a finger over the tree trunk at the figure's rear, quickly locating a join amongst the bark and bulging knots. In his satchel is a set of unfamiliar tools, acquired specifically for the task ahead: a fine saw, a mallet, and a selection of chisels. De Pareja glances up apologetically at the bronze god. It is true that he made similar use of the Mars with helmet and sword; there, however, existing damage was adapted to a new purpose. This has an inescapable feel of vandalism. But if he is to serve his master, he has no choice. He selects the mallet and the sharpest, narrowest chisel. Placing its head in the trunk's near-invisible join, he murmurs a brief prayer for forgiveness and brings the mallet down.

After an hour or so of chiselling and sawing, de Pareja manages to detach a segment about three hands wide and four long. The bronze is barely thicker than the rind of an orange; he lays it gingerly on the ground, dry-lipped and trembling, dazed by his own audacity. Rising to his feet, he brushes off the metallic dust that glitters on the front of his doublet, and goes to fetch the Venus.

His measurements were correct. Indeed, the rolled canvas disappears inside the Apollo as neatly as if the cast had been fashioned solely for that purpose. It actually seems to *fit*: to be held securely within. De Pareja gives thanks to the Holy Madonna, earnestly and repeatedly; then he takes out some strips of sackcloth and packs them in around the roll, to provide further protection.

When this is done, he takes a small leather pouch from his satchel. It contains a gobbet of soft putty, made with linseed oil and whiting – similar to that used on the Mars, but matched to the tone of freshly cast bronze by mixing in black ink. He hooks out some of this concoction with his forefinger and spreads it evenly along the raw edges of the hole, before replacing the sawn-out segment. It settles back into place almost undetectably, like a piece of cleanly broken china.

To finish, de Pareja smooths a tiny amount of putty along the crack. By noon it will be dry, leaving only the very faintest unpolished line in the bronze, on a part of the cast that no one will inspect with any care. The Venus is hidden, sealed inside the Apollo for its trip to Madrid. There it will elude the attentions of the Inquisition, he is sure of it; the friars will check that the crates contain what is on the manifest, but nothing else. And once the cast has arrived at the Alcazar, he will have ample opportunity to remove the Venus in secret. Then he will make new supports, apply a coat of varnish, and return the canvas to Don Diego for whatever future he envisions for it.

The absurdity of it all, of these elaborate and extensive pains he is taking, strikes against de Pareja with sudden force. For what exactly does Don Diego propose to do with this Venus of his – this large painting, replete with sin, that cannot ever be shown to anyone? Will he hang it in his rooms, to be seen by his wife, his daughters, his grandchildren? Will he tell them how it came to be made, and who it was who modelled for him in that luxurious pose? Or of the child he left behind, its fortunes entrusted to Almighty God?

De Pareja dismisses these thoughts, for they will do him no good. This is his duty. He is serving his master and working towards his reward – which is surely now all the closer. He puts away his tools and starts back up towards the apartment.

To his surprise, he finds Don Diego out of bed, passably washed and coiffured, and sitting in the reception room in one of his finer doublets. He considers relating his success in the cellar: the cleanness of the cut, the neatness of the fit, the absolute invisible smoothness of the join. It is still early, though, less than an hour since the Angelus; for his master to be up and dressed when there are no paintings underway suggests that something urgent is afoot.

'The duke has sent word,' Don Diego informs him nervously. 'He is coming here to speak with me.'

'How soon?'

'At any moment.'

De Pareja has stopped by the kitchens and is carrying a jug of fresh milk, along with bread still warm from the ovens. He starts for the parlour, saying that he will prepare some breakfast; but before he has taken a half dozen steps the Duke of Infantado is upon them, flinging open the apartment door and striding through it with ferocious energy.

'Astalli has fallen,' he says, by way of greeting.

Don Diego jumps up from his chair, attempting to combine his bow with an exclamation of dismay. 'Not dead?'

Infantado halts in the middle of the room; he shakes his head. 'Disgraced. Stripped of all honours, incomes, benefices and titles, save that of cardinal itself. They say he will be exiled from Rome within the month.' The duke's voice is level, his arms folded before the knight's cross on his chest, but the tension in him is so formidable that de Pareja thinks he will very soon draw a blade or kick over a table. 'We are speaking of the *Cardinal Nephew*. One of the foremost men in Rome. This is not merely a fall — it is a damned *plummet*, from the absolute pinnacle of the city to its lowest gutter. Camillo Astalli has been destroyed in the span of a single night.'

'By the saints, your grace, I have—'

Infantado holds up a black-gloved hand; he is not interested in Don Diego's thoughts. 'The widow is back. Many have seen her, at the Quirinale and elsewhere. She has crept beneath Astalli's defences and burrowed her way inside.' He swivels sharply on his heel, glaring towards the window. 'She should have died at the outset. I told Panciroli this — I told him *repeatedly*. Whilst she breathes, there is no safety. Not for any of us.'

Don Diego tries again. 'But how is this possible? Her man, her own creature, was tried and executed as a forger. I heard that the proof of corruption and theft was overwhelming, and that much of it suggested a—'

'The datary did not name her. Of course he did not! The poor dog believed that if he remained quiet, she would stay the axe — right up to the instant it was brought down upon his neck.' Infantado lets out a low, mirthless laugh. 'And now she has managed to work it all in her favour. Perhaps she made it seem as if the datary was the sole source of evil, and that she was deceived along with everyone else. But whatever her manipulations, this accursed fool of a pope has restored her to the position of trust she occupied so undeservedly — and straight away she has done for Astalli, almost as thoroughly as she did for his master.'

Don Diego's expression has grown a touch queasy, for like de Pareja, he is beginning to sense where this is going. 'How did it happen?'

'His offices were searched,' says Infantado, 'much as Monsignor Mascambruno's were. A cache of ciphered documents was uncovered. Word is going around that they contain evidence of espionage and collusion, and show quite indisputably that Cardinal Astalli was plotting against the interests of the papacy.'

De Pareja tightens his hold on the milk jug as his palm begins to sweat. They have not been fast enough. *Another day,* he thinks. *Another day and we would have been gone.*

Infantado does not look around but his anger undergoes a subtle change, as its focus shifts from a scheming widow somewhere across the city to the man standing not five yards away from him. 'I strongly suspect, Don Diego, that if you were to go to wherever you have so ingeniously concealed those Neapolitan documents, they would no longer be there.' The duke's hands form into fists; he rolls his shoulders like a man preparing to fight. 'This was another area where the cardinals chose to ignore my counsel. Involving you in their machinations was a sure and obvious path to disaster. You are a *painter*, by God. You are not to be trusted with such things.'

Don Diego's face is flushed with alarm and embarrassment. 'Forgive me, your grace,' he murmurs, 'but I do not understand. The documents from Naples were proof of Donna Olimpia's own treachery – of her conspiracy with France. Why would she want such a thing brought into the open? How could it possibly help her?'

As he hears this, de Pareja recalls that one report he saw while standing among the statues in the cellar – the notes of a taverna conversation indicating the pope's support for the invasion of Naples. He gets a sudden, chilling intimation of what has occurred here.

Infantado stalks over to the window, moving into a shaft of early morning sunlight. He has plainly seen little rest that night. Running through his anger and incredulity is a seam of unease – for it could certainly be said that his diplomatic mission, upon which so many hopes rested, is now marked by an undeniable failure.

'Pope Innocent was a party to these plans for Naples from the start,' he says. 'Neither Astalli nor Panciroli knew anything of this. Almighty Christ, *nobody* knew. The seizing of the territory from King Felipe, the gifting of it to the Barberini, the bolstering of France – it was all the papal will. Or at any rate, that damned widow has managed to convince him that it was.' De Pareja detects a dark amusement in the duke now, as if he is grudgingly impressed by what he describes. 'It would appear that whatever sorcery she has worked upon Giambattista Pamphili allows her to assert that night is day, that vile sin is purest virtue, and be believed without pause or question. And now Camillo Astalli, whose only wish was to strengthen and purify the papacy, finds himself treated as if *he* was the traitor. The wretched woman has flipped everything on its head.'

Don Diego adopts a pensive air, as if he is trying to set out the sequence of events. 'So having ordered that the documents be concealed within Cardinal Astalli's offices, Donna Olimpia reported him to the pope . . . and this was sufficient to win her the Holy Father's forgiveness?'

Infantado snorts. 'The old reptile was desperate for her return – all Rome knows that. I do believe that almost any justification would have served, once Cardinal Panciroli was no longer there to argue against it. The widow will be back in her palazzo before the next sabbath, and will already be deciding which of her many scores she will settle first, now that Astalli has been dispatched. Perhaps I am on that unlucky list. I suppose we will find out.'

Don Diego glances over worriedly at de Pareja. 'What will you do, your grace?'

'I am beaten,' Infantado replies flatly. '*Spain* is beaten. Honour demands that this be recognised. The Kingdom of Naples seems to be safe, for now at least; but this woman, our determined foe, is more powerful than ever before. I will salvage what I can, of course – but King Felipe must understand that when he binds his servants to amateurs, to weaklings and neglectful fools, there is a distinct chance that they will disappoint him.'

It is clear enough to whom he is referring.

Don Diego swallows; he lays a remorseful hand against his chest. 'Your grace,' he says, 'I fear that I may have incurred your—'

The duke twists back into the room, blazing with an abrupt, savage rancour. 'Who the devil *are* you, Don Diego Velázquez?' he spits. 'A Sevillian interloper of dubious breeding, impudent enough to aspire to a knights' order – yet skilled only in *illusion*, in the plebian trade of painting? Your carelessness has cost Spain dearly, most dearly indeed. If it were my decision, you would be whipped through the streets, and then sent in chains to the galleys of Cadiz!'

Infantado steps forward purposefully, as if set upon more immediate punishment; but he checks himself, turning away again, cursing under his breath. Don Diego and de Pareja both stand very still, hearts pounding and eyes staring wide. De Pareja realises that his thumb has dug into the loaf he is holding, tearing through the crust. What would he do, he wonders, if Don Diego was actually attacked by the king's ambassador to Rome? Would he have to stand there and watch his master be battered bloody, perhaps even killed, by this rabid duke?

Infantado paces back and forth across the room, three, four, five times – rapidly at first but gradually slowing, like a clockwork mechanism winding itself down. Eventually he stops, and breathes for a while, seeming to recover a portion of his temper; then he rips open his crisp white golilla, sending a silver pin skittering across the floor.

'You are the king's special creature, however,' he says, his tone now bitterly cold. 'He writes to me about you more than any other damned thing, inquiring about your mission and your productions, and urging your return to Spain. So you will go to him, with all speed – and by the Holy Madonna I will be heartily glad to see the back of you.'

Slowly, de Pareja begins to release the breath that is pent up inside his lungs. Don Diego continues to stand in a stunned approximation of a courtier's pose. He does not dare to speak.

Infantado is grimacing at one of the sideboards, his hands on his hips. 'But before that, a final task remains. It is now my duty to make whatever peace I can with this putrid papacy, and the grasping witch that squats so determinedly at its head. And herein lies our single scrap of good fortune.' The duke looks around, fixing Don Diego with an icy stare. 'It is a game of some sort, no doubt. But it appears that there is one thing she wants from us.'

*

Don Diego's attendance is requested on the feast day of San Luca, Evangelist, doctor, and the patron saint of painters; de Pareja suspects that this might be mockery. By the time they set out, the saint's feast is being celebrated with all the fanfares and revels that have come to distinguish the Jubilee year. From his place atop an embassy carriage, de Pareja once more looks out over streets and piazzas made bright by new banners; parades and performances of every imaginable kind; crowds joined in song, or gathered around a roasting pig, or playing at loud, rowdy games. They arrive in the Piazza Navona to find it filled with lowing oxen. These beasts, San Luca's symbol, are being led around the perimeter in pairs, their horns garlanded with flowers, accompanied by trumpets and drums.

The carriage works its way across the square to the Palazzo Pamphili, only to discover that the main entrance is blocked by a wall of furniture. Beds and chairs, trunks and armoires, all of the very finest quality, have been heaped high on the flagstones. De Pareja's first thought is that the beleaguered Cardinal Astalli must be barricaded within, defying the pope's command that he vacate the building, and then Rome itself shortly afterwards. But no: he soon sees that this furniture is for sale, right there and then, to anyone with coin and the means to carry it away. He realises that it must be Astalli's, only moved in that summer, now being sold in the street by the palazzo's returning mistress.

The gate itself is sealed tight, despite the hour of the visit having been arranged well in advance; their coachman is obliged to drive round to a small piazza at the rear, so that Don Diego and de Pareja can be admitted through a side door. A steward greets Don Diego courteously enough, before leading them through a series of passageways to a wide marble staircase. De Pareja hears conversation, a ripple of laughter, and the warm trill of music. Peering over the folded easel he carries on his shoulder, he sees a large number of nobles and churchmen up on the first floor, spilling from grand rooms onto a balcony. Some at the fringes glance over the balustrade at Don Diego, recognising him perhaps from the ceremonies and banquets of the summer, but none offer any acknowledgement. De Pareja spots Cavaliere Bernini, who so praised his own portrait at the Rotonda; upon noticing the two Spaniards, he makes a great show of sighting a dear friend further along the balcony, and pushes his way towards this person with exclamations of delight.

They reach the top of the stairs. Instead of Don Diego being announced to the company, as befits his rank, they are taken promptly into a corridor, at the end of which is a large, chilly chamber that seems to be awaiting refurbishment. Blinds cover three of its four windows, and a black sheet has been pinned across the western wall. Before it sits Donna Olimpia Maidalchini, her face pale and unpainted, positioned in the single beam of daylight that has been permitted to enter.

The widow is imperious without possessing majesty or magnificence, and formidably alert whilst being entirely at her ease. She is rather smaller than Algardi's bust led de Pareja to expect, but this does not diminish her authority in the least. On the floor beside her is a silver tray bearing a pitcher of wine, a crystal glass, and a plate of fine pastries, whose broken arrangement suggests that at least two have been consumed.

'You have an hour,' she says.

Her manner forbids all conversation. For a couple of minutes Don Diego walks about the chamber, considering various angles and the fall of the light, then points out his chosen spot. De Pareja steps forward smartly to put up the easel and set the primed canvas upon the stocks. The widow watches them all the while with keen distrust, as if confronted with a pair of charlatans who she is on the brink of having thrown from the building.

De Pareja retreats a few paces with the paint box and crouches on the bare floorboards to load the palette, which he does more hastily than he ever has before. When the spread of pigments is complete, he hurries it over to Don Diego, along with a mahlstick and three of the smaller brushes, which he judges to be suitable for laying in the initial oil sketch. Don Diego takes all of this without meeting his eye. Then he breathes in deeply, selects a brush and a warm shade of ochre, and sets to work.

Standing off to the side, de Pareja waits to be dismissed as he usually is, to linger somewhere downstairs until the sitting is complete. But Don Diego does not do this. De Pareja senses that his master wants to keep an ally present, however modest – to serve as a witness, perhaps, as he contemplates this woman in the intent and prolonged way that he must, and is confronted with the unrelenting fact of her enmity. This feat is made yet more difficult by the noise that issues from the palazzo's other regions. Don Diego is not precious. He is used to painting in the king's rooms at the Alcazar, through which people are moving constantly, and in all sorts of trying combinations. This, though, is different: it is an assembly of their opponents and false former friends, celebrating a victory against the Spanish faction in Rome. Against them.

The steward can be heard out on the staircase, announcing new arrivals. From the sound of it, several of Donna Olimpia's relatives are among their number, but the grand names and titles elicit only muttered exclamations of disdain from their sitter. These guests are a nuisance to her, it seems, and she shows no inclination to welcome them.

An image begins to appear upon the canvas, in accordance with Don Diego's method. Inwardly, de Pareja urges his master on, praying that he obtains what he requires as quickly as possible so that they can take their leave of this place. He could swear that Don Diego heeds him – for he is bringing the brush to the palette, then to the canvas, and then to the palette again, with a swiftness that borders on urgency. The widow is a good model in one sense: she hardly moves, save the occasional rubbing of her kneecaps, her unnerving stare barely straying from the man before her.

As he watches Don Diego work, de Pareja realises that the

portraits his master has completed over the summer have left him better practised than he has been for some years. He captures the contours of the face with careful efficiency, tracing its jowls and wide, rounded chin, leaving dabs of colour here and there to be used for reference when he paints the features in properly. As always, he gives an extra measure of attention to the eyes, finding life in the shaping of the lids and irises, before dotting the pupils with spots of unmixed black.

The Nones bell sounds somewhere outside; by de Pareja's calculation, only a handful of minutes remain before their allotted hour expires. He shifts about, discreetly flexing a muscle in his lower back. *Heaven be praised,* he thinks.

An odd shiver runs through the widow, like someone waking from sleep; when she speaks her voice seems unnaturally loud, and is as blunt as a watchman's cudgel. 'I understand that you will be departing soon,' she says. 'Returning to your king.'

Feigning regret, Don Diego tells her that this is true and begins to describe the route they will take to Genoa – with a stop at the court of Modena, and perhaps—

Donna Olimpia is not interested. 'You must be sad indeed to be leaving so much behind you,' she interrupts. 'So very much of yourself.'

De Pareja tenses; the widow's meaning is plain, and the knowledge it reveals unmistakable. Here is confirmation of her connection with Flaminia Triunfi, if any were needed.

Caught utterly off guard, Don Diego carries on working. 'I beg your pardon, Excellency,' he murmurs, making three quick marks around the nose, 'but I am quite certain that I do not—'

'Flaminia will be well enough,' Donna Olimpia continues. 'They tell me that she has already survived several similar situations. A means of provision will be located before too long, I am sure, and the fruit of your wayward loins reared into . . . some form of adulthood.'

At this, Don Diego stops. He lifts his brush from the canvas and gazes at the floor with a pained smile, in order to show as little of his feelings as he can. He does not offer any reply. De Pareja finds himself frowning in sympathy; he wants badly to go to his master's side, gather up their things, and head back out into Rome.

Donna Olimpia has more to say, having whetted her obvious appetite for humiliation and cruelty, but before she can begin there is a shout from the stairway. A young woman is calling for her — screaming her name, in fact, with both despair and indignation. The widow hesitates; then she sighs, and rises with some trouble from her chair. Don Diego and de Pareja watch as she hobbles across the room to the door, wincing with each step.

There is nothing infirm, however, about the way she addresses the woman on the staircase. '*Enough*, Catarina Maidalchini,' she shouts, causing a hush to fall over her assembled guests. 'What is the meaning of this?'

'Please, Aunt Olimpia, you must help — you must help my poor family! Camillo is a fool, a prideful fool! He did not think of what might result from his actions — of who he might injure, of what damage he might do, of what—'

'And now,' the widow cuts in, 'thanks be to God, your Camillo is finished. He will damage no one else.'

De Pareja looks over at Don Diego. His master is wiping his brush with a rag, turning it over in his hand; his lips are moving, his brow raised slightly, as if he is addressing someone who is not present.

The woman on the staircase — the widow's niece, presumably — attempts to moderate her tone. 'Dear Aunt — I beg you, in the Blessed Virgin's name. Find it in your heart to be merciful. Think of my husband. Poor Tiberio is blameless, utterly *blameless*. He knew nothing of his brother's crimes against you. He reviles the very thought that—'

'I think it would be best,' Donna Olimpia continues, 'if you Astallis simply followed your wretched cardinal into exile. Lord knows, there is nothing for you in Rome any longer. I hear that the family owns an old castle away in Sambuci that is not too broken down. I am sure that you will all fit within it quite adequately.'

This meets with laughter from her guests, and a round of applause so loud that she can only just be heard ordering that Catarina — who is wailing now, like one bereaved — be ejected from the palazzo without delay.

Donna Olimpia reappears in the doorway a moment later. She is stony-faced, showing no satisfaction at her niece's removal. Her desire to torment Don Diego by dangling his unborn child before him has disappeared also, along with any patience she had for the business of portraiture.

'Begone,' she says, heading for the silver tray beside her chair.

'Forgive me, Excellency,' says Don Diego, 'but my work is so nearly complete. Only a few minutes more and I will have enough to—'

'Begone,' the widow repeats, without looking around. 'You are done here.'

*

Finding the Palazzo Triunfi is not easy. It is deep in Trastevere, a region of Rome de Pareja has only ever skirted before. He finds it to be a place of smoky workshops, small, sooty churches and meandering bends, lacking much of the grandeur found so commonly in the districts across the river. Its stallholders, also, prove themselves more suspicious than most; he has named the site of his baptism and affirmed his love of the Holy Virgin more than a half dozen times before anyone agrees to give him directions.

The palazzo itself is a strange thing: not much larger than the more ordinary houses around it, but darker and more dilapidated, with peculiar crenulations on its topmost storey and heavy iron bars rusting over the lower windows. De Pareja watches it for a while before approaching. The evening clouds are low, making Rome cool and gloomy, but he can detect no trace of life within — not a wisp of smoke, nor a single chink of light between the warping shutters. As he walks along the façade, however, he hears a harsh, trembling cry, coming from somewhere inside the building.

De Pareja hurries to the gate. It is very old, a single panel sitting poorly in its frame. He brings his eye up to a narrow gap in the wood, just as a form flashes past on the other side. A figure clad entirely in black is rushing about the dingy yard in the centre of the palazzo. After a few seconds it seems to trip on its robes, staggering a short distance before folding almost gracefully to the ground.

De Pareja starts — for it is the scarred sister, the Benedictine nun from the procession route who he has pictured so very often, summoned with such effort, drawn and painted over and over again. And now she is right there, her habit heaped around her and her clasped hands raised aloft, running through a *De Profundis* at frantic speed.

Too late, de Pareja realises that he is pushing against the gate. Something gives way, old wood cracking apart and nails falling to the flagstones with a dull jingle — and the gate swings inward, causing him to stumble a couple of steps into the shadowy arcade beyond. He recovers his balance and begins to return to the street, thinking he will close the broken gate behind him as best he can and make a more formal announcement of his arrival. But then his eye snags upon the nun, who is still praying with such intensity, her remarkable scar on full display – and an unreasoning part of him considers reaching for his satchel, taking out his drawing folder and some graphite, and setting down the beginnings of a—

'What is this? What does he want?'

Flaminia Triunfi has appeared in a doorway nearby. She is wearing a familiar dark green gown, adjusted for her condition, and seems more tired than ever. A lock of greasy hair is tucked behind her ear; a fierce red pimple hums on her chin. De Pareja perceives another change in her as well, alongside the pregnancy. In place of her curiosity and good humour is a determined hardness – that of someone set upon a path they have not chosen, but which they will follow to its end.

De Pareja looks from Flaminia to the nun, who has halted her prayer to gag and cough – and he sees something else, very clearly. He furrows his brow, opening his mouth to speak.

'She is my sister,' Flaminia says. 'You were right, señor: I was lying to you. Her name is Claudia.'

And there it is. Her reaction to his oil sketch is explained at last. Someone lost, perhaps long lost, has been returned. But it is also evident that this is not the whole of the tale. The nun's distress is too acute; and Flaminia is too wearied, appearing resentful both of this situation and the world that has brought it about. De Pareja wonders how the nun – Claudia Triunfi – made her way from that spot on the Corso, where he was so struck by her, to this decaying palazzo in Trastevere.

He bows to Flaminia. 'I apologise for the lock, signorina,' he says. 'There was no indication that it might—'

'You should not be here,' she interrupts. 'Donna Olimpia is back. Her men are all about. They are watching me – watching my house.'

De Pareja inclines his head; he is well aware of this, but the duty he has to fulfil is a delicate one. It must be done in person, and he has assured Don Diego that he will see it through. 'We will be leaving the city soon,' he says. 'I believe she knows that we pose no threat to her.'

'She certainly poses a threat to *me*, señor,' Flaminia retorts. 'A deal was made. If she feels I am betraying it in any form, and consorting with her enemies, I will be finished.'

A deal, de Pareja thinks. He tries to imagine what the terms might have been. Flaminia agreed to steal those documents from Don Diego – but in exchange for what?

The answer, of course, is there in front of him. Flaminia is advancing towards the nun at that very moment, speaking soothingly as one might to a startled animal. The nun has stopped coughing; she wipes her face on her black sleeve and looks around her, fumbling with a string of silver rosary beads. De Pareja can see now that she has a form of lunacy; that this is the source of her inexhaustible fervour. He has encountered such people in the past, when they were brought into the Alcazar for the diversion of the court. It is as if an outer layer has been peeled back from their souls, opening them up to God, bestowing both confusion and profound clarity. Flaminia does not touch her, or even address her directly. This seems to demonstrate a far greater knowledge and tenderness than if she had attempted to wrap her sister in her arms.

De Pareja watches this with growing embarrassment. He was intending to confront Flamina about the theft of the documents; to tell her of the disgrace in which he and his master languished, with both their futures in jeopardy. Now, though, a new light has broken over it all. Through her many spies, Donna Olimpia plainly learned that Don Diego was receiving and storing compromising intelligences from Naples. This same network of agents then told her of his connection with Flaminia, and that Claudia was holding forth on the streets of the Jubilee. So the widow had the sister seized, and brought about a forced exchange: the scarred nun for the Neapolitan documents. Flaminia Triunfi has been extorted. She has been used.

'Still you have not answered me,' she says. 'What are you doing here? Why has your master sent you?'

De Pareja clears his throat; he draws himself up. This, at least, he knows how to meet. He takes a slim sheaf of papers from his satchel and presents them with another bow.

Donna Olimpia's crude provocations at her sitting left a lasting mark upon Don Diego. Once they were back inside the Spanish embassy, he brooded for a while, then had de Pareja fetch a lawyer from the offices below. These papers are the result: a formal pledge, fully admissible in Roman law, that Don Diego Rodríguez Silva y Velázquez will provide for the child of Signorina Flaminia Triunfi up to the date of its First Communion. Also included is a banker's draft for a sizeable initial payment.

Flaminia understands immediately what is being proposed. She does not even look at the sheaf in de Pareja's hand. She seems affronted; even faintly disgusted.

'My master urges you to accept,' de Pareja says. 'For the sake of his child. An innocent soul beloved by God, wholly free from the sins of—'

'After all of this,' she says, 'he offers me gold.'

De Pareja is unsure how to proceed. He has become aware of the crates and boxes that are stacked at the edges of this little courtyard. Now, in his awkwardness, he takes an unthinking glance to the side, through the doorway by which Flaminia first entered, and he sees further signs of a house that will soon be packed up and vacated. By a staircase rests what is clearly equipment from a painter's studio – while off against a wall stand several large canvases, out of their frames, waiting to be prepared for transportation. Even at a distance, and in imperfect light, de Pareja can tell that they are pieces of considerable proficiency, painted in the Roman style, busy with figures and colours. There is a Baptism of Christ; one that he thinks shows Susannah and the Elders; a Santa Catarina, praying beside a studded fragment of wheel. Briefly, he is confounded – for they are by no hand he recognises, and he has become versed in the work of almost every master in this city. And then with an odd jolt he realises that these are Flaminia's, that she has painted them all – and that she is leaving Rome as well, taking her pictures and her sister along with her.

De Pareja turns to face her again, thinking to say something – to offer his compliments, perhaps. To ask to see her work as she once asked to see his. To listen to her plans for the years ahead, and share his in return. This seems absurd, however, so he stays quiet.

With some difficulty, Flaminia has lowered herself to a crouch. She sits cross-legged at her sister's side, gazing at her – at the hollow cheeks, the black habit, the dreadful scar – as if she is searching for something.

A few seconds pass. The nun resumes her prayer. De Pareja looks over at the paintings for a final time. Then he lays Don Diego's papers on the corner of a crate and withdraws.

*

Next comes the business of departure. Clothes must be laundered and brushed, boots and buckles polished, and hats boxed; and then it all must be stowed away in trunks, along with books and art materials, and the various soaps, oils and powders with which Don Diego tends to his person. It is not a massive undertaking, in all honesty, for Don Diego means to exit Rome with a good deal less than he entered. Many of his possessions – the easels, several unused canvases, numerous gifts and trinkets – will simply be left in this apartment for whoever wishes to claim them.

The statues down in the cellar are to be sent back directly to Spain. De Pareja looks on as a team of carpenters packs them up, so they can be hauled to the nearby port of Civitavecchia. The timings are arranged so that the pieces will not reach the Alcazar before Don Diego himself; it is vital that he is present when they arrive, so he can show the king personally what he has achieved.

Travel with Don Diego is an inexact process, however. Their loose plan is to head north to the court of Modena; then go to Venice again, to purchase some paintings by the maestro Paulo Veronese; and once winter has passed, proceed to Genoa, where they will sail at last for Spain. De Pareja does his best, but a certain amount of guesswork is required. He knows from experience that even the soundest co-ordinations can easily be spoiled by the weather, or the tides, or his master's whim. There is always a degree to which everything must be entrusted to prayer.

Don Diego is not involved in any of this. He hardly speaks at all, in fact, remaining almost entirely in the studio, applying himself to the task Infantado has set with an unstinting, joyless dedication. It is here that de Pareja discovers him, after the last arrangements have been made. He is over at the window, his elbows resting on the frame, and once more seems to be murmuring to a person who is not there.

The portrait itself is complete. Straight away, de Pareja notices that it is unlike any of Don Diego's other works – for of all his master's sitters, from noble knights to dwarfs, from court fools to the king of Spain, this widow has defeated him. Donna Olimpia Maidalchini's every feature has been portrayed with Don Diego's merciless accuracy: the sag of the jaw, the mottling of the skin, the grim line of the mouth. But she is opaque. Her black, sunken eyes are a barrier; a blank wall, lacking even a crack in the plaster; a door locked and barred. There is no intimate perceptiveness here, no inner contradiction laid bare, no insight into the condition of this woman's immortal soul. Her expression is forbidding, confrontational – and yet also oddly bland. It gives away nothing that it does not intend.

'My congratulations, Don Diego,' de Pareja says; then he swallows and blinks, for he can find nothing more to say.

'It will serve,' Don Diego replies curtly. 'I will not give Olimpia Maidalchini another minute of my time.'

'Should I arrange for its delivery to the Palazzo Pamphili?' de Pareja asks – thinking of paint drying, of varnish, of a delay of a day at least.

'Leave it there. Infantado can see to it. God knows, he will need all the help he can get if he really is to woo that monstrous woman.' Don Diego turns from the window, wiping his hands on his grubby painting smock; his manner grows a little lighter. 'What of your own portrait, though? Has there been any sign?'

'I am afraid not. I have made urgent queries in your name at many of the city's grandest houses. It was among the cardinals for a while, but appears to have moved into other regions. Word is going around, certainly; it may be that it will be found before . . .'

Don Diego is shaking his head. 'Leave that also. The work is lost to Rome.' He seems to spot de Pareja's dismay, for he adds: 'It is but one painting. Such is the price of escape. And Juan, the time has most definitely come for us to escape.'

De Pareja bows, in part to conceal his mixed feelings. Abandoning a task upon which he has expended so much energy seems deeply wrong. It is strange, also, to leave this uncanny likeness of himself to gaze out forever from unknown walls. But Don Diego is right: an old order has returned, strengthened and invigorated by victory, and it regards them as its enemies. As he goes about his duties, he has a sense that the entire city has turned on them. Adversaries are emboldened in their censure, and allies suddenly scarce; even the beauty of Rome has begun to repel him. This is not their place. They are not wanted and do not belong.

And there is something else. It has been several months since he last looked upon the portrait – but he remembers very clearly the doubt in it, which his master perceived and set out with such unsparing plainness. That this will remain here, many hundreds of miles from his home, does not cause him undue sorrow.

Don Diego now begins to inquire about de Pareja's progress elsewhere: first the statues and the arrangements for their shipping, and then the Venus. Quite deliberately, he has not enquired in any great detail about the scheme for smuggling the painting back to Spain – and de Pareja's assurance that it is stowed away safely and secretly, and will appear in Madrid at the same time as the statues, is all he wishes to hear about it.

After this, growing slightly coy, Don Diego asks how de Pareja fared that morning in Trastevere. 'She took them, though,' he says, once the account has been made. 'She took the papers.'

De Pareja considers this for a second. It is true that Flaminia reacted to Don Diego's gesture with injured scorn; but from what he has learned, her ultimate concern will be her own survival, along with that of her child – and now, perhaps, her sister as well.

'I left them with her, Don Diego,' he replies. 'She will make use of them.'

Don Diego nods, twisting his moustaches; then he looks to the apartment's door and exhales heavily, like a man who feels a burden beginning to lift. 'We can go, then,' he says. 'Back to the Alcazar at last. Back to our king.'

A silence falls. De Pareja glances over at the widow – at her dull glower, so assessing and unimpressed – and he knows with absolute certainty what is coming next.

'Will it be enough, though?' Don Diego asks. 'The pains we two have endured, Juan, here in this . . . this most perplexing place. The trials we have undergone since that day, so long past, that we left our home. Will it see me granted the cross of Santiago?'

De Pareja takes a breath. He thought himself ready to meet this, as he meets all of Don Diego's worries, but now he feels a pang of hopelessness. 'We have statues, Don Diego,' he says. 'We have a great many statues, all of them surpassingly fine. You have done what was asked of you. How can King Felipe not be pleased?'

Don Diego is unconvinced. 'The Duke of Infantado has taken against me,' he says. 'He will always blame me for Astalli, and will communicate his doubts to various people at court.'

De Pareja cannot reasonably deny this, so instead he talks about Cardinal Panciroli. 'His Eminence wrote to the nuncio in Madrid, did he not, in full support of your elevation? Surely this will count for much?'

'Panciroli is dead, God save him. And his successor in the Curia, this Cardinal Chigi, is no friend to Spain. He sees the shift that is coming with the widow's return – the shift to France, to the Barberini.' Don Diego sighs. 'No, Juan, we must not deceive ourselves. It could well be that the only result of this great labour of ours is the enrichment of King Felipe's palaces.'

De Pareja nearly remarks that this should be enough for loyal subjects such as themselves, but his master's careworn expression makes him think better of it.

'It is not fair,' Don Diego states. 'I feel this most strongly. It is not fair in the least.'

He goes to the dresser and starts to sift through a heap of papers. De Pareja is wondering what he is searching for — what line in the king's correspondence he wishes to read out that will further stoke his grievances — when he notices that there is a small piece of board amid the sheets. Pinned upon it is his oil sketch of the scarred nun, Claudia Triunfi, which so provoked her sister. Painted with such urgency and inspiration, and the focus, briefly, of so much hope, he has since lost track of it in every sense. Indeed, before this moment he had almost forgotten it existed.

'Forgive me, Juan,' Don Diego murmurs, showing the sketch to de Pareja before studying it himself. 'I came across this among the materials that we are leaving behind. While you were out in the city.'

De Pareja longs to speak; to explain how the image came about, and what it was working towards; to apologise for its failings, and promise to do better; to ask Don Diego's honest opinion of it. Instead, he remains completely quiet, nailed in place, his cheeks, brow and neck all burning — not daring even to blink, lest he miss some passing nuance in his master's features as he contemplates the sketch.

Eventually, Don Diego taps the corner of the board with his knuckle. 'I mean, you have something,' he says. 'The style is old fashioned, perhaps; the expression a touch maudlin, a touch forced; the technique overplayed, shall we say, especially around the knees and elbows.'

De Pareja flinches at each step of this appraisal. He can see at once that all of it is true. Doing what he can to hide his smarting soul, he nods stoically and waits, for his master is not finished yet.

'But you . . . you really do have something, Juan.' Don Diego squints, holding the sketch out a few inches further from his face. 'There is aptitude, yes, but invention also – a sense of the life within, that art alone can realise. I knew you were able, of course. I have known that for years. But this shows you are ready. That you can stand on your own.'

De Pareja goes cold. A strange charge seems to be gathering in the air; a sense of change fast approaching. He bows and thanks his master, and asks what he means.

In reply, Don Diego sets the sketch aside, unfastens the top three buttons of his smock and slides what appears to be a formal letter from within, stamped with his own seal. Then he hesitates, looking down at this letter, shoring up his resolve; there in the near-empty studio, he seems older, deeply weary, weathered by Rome. De Pareja knows that he hates to make any kind of performance, just as he hates praise and almost all types of attention, but he is clearly determined that this be a moment of significance. When he speaks, his tone is earnest and tinted with shame.

'I may be judged worthy of the cross, Juan, or I may not, but this must be done nonetheless. In Madrid, back among King Felipe's court, matters might prove . . . more complicated. So I have decided that it must happen here, before we leave. You have not wavered once, throughout every turn of this damned summer. Such constancy deserves to be rewarded.' He glances at the oil sketch. 'And you have the seed of mastery. It is there, plain as the sun. Keeping you bound to me is beyond all justification – a crime against Almighty God. Your fortunes must be untethered from my own.' Don Diego holds out the letter. 'Rome is the last place you will be a slave.'

De Pareja feels a great and tumultuous rushing, like a sudden gale; and then half a second later, he is enveloped in an absolute stillness. He becomes acutely aware of his surroundings. The black rectangle of the widow's portrait, its paint glistening damply. The scuffed varnish upon the floorboards beneath his feet. The citrus tang of Don Diego's hair oil, and the colour spreading over his master's cheeks.

His blood surging, he accepts the letter, breaks the seal and unfolds the fine, heavy paper. Before him is an official document, written in Latin in a precise, orderly hand, very different from Don Diego's own. His eyes skim down it, trying to absorb the words and their meaning as rapidly as they can. And yes, it really is so: he is holding a full declaration of the manumission of Juan de Pareja, in the eyes of Almighty God and the Holy Authority of Rome, drawn up no doubt by the same lawyer who authored the pledge to Flaminia, signed by his master and witnessed by a licensed notary. Following a four-year probationary period, providing he commits no criminal act nor attempts to escape, he will be free.

Don Diego is watching him with pride and a trace of guilty discomfort. 'My apologies,' he says, indicating this last passage. 'It is a standard clause, and can safely be disregarded. A copy has been lodged here, with the office of the governor. That one can come back to Madrid with us. It is binding, I believe, and within my rights as a gentleman of the court. It will stand.'

De Pareja realises that he has not taken a breath for almost a minute. He gulps one in, his throat raw, the document shaking in his grasp. How does it feel, this moment – so longed for, so keenly imagined? It feels right. It feels *just*. It feels like the will of God.

A hot tear runs across de Pareja's cheek. He wants to cast off his hat and stamp on it; to run out into the piazza and bellow his name. For everything is changed: the curtain has dropped, cut from the pole, revealing the open window behind. He considers this new prospect before him and is nearly overwhelmed by a fearful, light-headed elation. No longer will he fetch meals, wash plates, polish boots, or visit laundries. He will be a painter. This will be his profession, his sole occupation – his God-given purpose. He will take on commissions of all kinds: portraits of Madrid's notable citizens; scenes from the bible and pagan mythology, rendered with all the life and ingenuity he can muster; landscapes and still lives too, if such things are wanted. Perhaps there will even be a chance for a single figure in the Sevillian style, lit powerfully from above, showing a scarred nun at prayer.

And he will go out to the Plazuela de Santiago. He will find Señora Inés standing behind her stall, framed by bunches of dried herbs and flowers, and he will tell her what has happened. He will tell her that he is free. Slowly, their plan will be made real. He will leave the Alcazar for good. There will be a well-appointed house, and a family perhaps; assistants, apprentices and servants. A painter's studio. The workshop of Maestro Juan de Pareja.

He stays quite motionless for a while, recovering his breath, a steady tremor humming through his bones. Then he folds the document up again and holds it tightly to his chest.

'Praise God,' he mutters. 'Praise God.'

Domina

Donna Olimpia enters the bedchamber without announcement, goes over to an upholstered stool and drops down upon it like someone about to fall, her black gown billowing out around her. She breathes in sharply through her nose, and for an instant everything is unmoored. Her head swims; the fire seems to flutter from the grate like a blazing flag. She wipes her face and clutches one hand with the other, waiting for the pain to fade, as it sometimes does. As it surely used to do.

Olimpiuccia's maids have risen; they bow their heads and smooth their clothes, stealing quick, anxious glances at each other. Donna Olimpia dismisses them with a curt gesture. She yanks up the hem of her gown and glares at her right foot – at the black slipper that contains a toe so swollen, it bulges visibly beneath the fine, shiny silk. It is said that if God wishes to curb you, He sends the podagra. She straightens her back, flattening her palms upon her thighs. *We'll see about that,* she thinks.

The girl herself is away in a corner, a candle by her side. She has taken that panel off the wall – a Madonna and Child with Angels, given to her upon her Confirmation, claimed by the dealer to be from the shop of Giulio Romano – and is kneeling before it, rosary in hand, murmuring her prayers. This has become a common practice of hers during the Jubilee year, according to reports from the Palazzo Giustiniani. It does not bode well.

'Olimpiuccia,' Donna Olimpia says. 'I have wonderful news.'

The girl does not reply, or even pause in her prayer; her devotions have become noticeably more ardent since her grandmother's entrance. They have the quality of a performance, the words and expressions slightly exaggerated, knowing that they are observed. She is saying the *Tota Pulchra Es*, as today is the feast of the Immaculate Conception of the Virgin. The timing is unfortunate; the palazzo around them is full of guests, who are expecting to pay homage to its mistress. But this matter must be attended to straight away.

Donna Olimpia shifts, reaching for her knees – for their assaults continue, as if in unholy competition with the accursed toe. She looks at Olimpiuccia again, suppressing her irritation at this display of earnest, youthful piety, and resolves to be direct.

'You are to marry,' she says. 'I have found you the best young man in Rome – a prince, no less. It will be done by the spring. By summer at the latest.'

Still the prayer continues.

Donna Olimpia narrows her eyes. 'His name is Maffeo Barberini,' she goes on, a little more loudly. 'Since you ask. The second son of the departed Taddeo. You came with me to visit his uncle, Cardinal Francesco, at the end of the summer – and were very impressed by him, as I recall. He has just written to me, after some final communication with his brother Antonio in Versailles, to confirm the arrangements. You will have a palazzo, Olimpiuccia. *Several* palazzos. You will sit at the heart of one of the foremost families of Rome – a family which is on the cusp of a great and glorious return.'

The prayer ceases now, at least. The girl leans back from the panel and covers her face with her hands. She does not speak.

Donna Olimpia takes in the large, luxurious chamber, with its costly fabrics and finely carved furniture. 'Maffeo is a fine man,' she says. 'The more handsome of Taddeo's sons, all agree. A skilled horseman, also, and a hunter, whose aim is—'

'Nonna.' Olimpiuccia is gazing over at her with a calmness that is faintly disquieting. 'I am twelve years old.'

'I would have you older,' Donna Olimpia admits. 'I make no secret of that. But I am afraid we must act. Maffeo is twenty, and will not be available for long. And you are of age, Olimpiuccia. This is what the Church has decreed. Your courses have begun. Twelve is old enough.'

The girl turns back to the panel, casting a long look at the Holy Mother; at Her smooth, creamy skin, and those eyes like clear blue jewels, brimming with love. 'Well,' she says, 'I do not wish it.'

Donna Olimpia blinks; her lip twitches. 'You do not wish it.'

'I have decided to take Holy Orders. I will join my Aunt Agata in the Tor de'Specchi, or go elsewhere in Italy. It does not matter. But I will not marry Maffeo Barberini or anyone else. I will give myself to God.'

Donna Olimpia allows a pause, so this may settle. It does not surprise her, exactly, although she certainly hoped for better. A laugh rises from the celebrations downstairs.

'You are an intelligent girl,' she says, aiming for kindness, 'in whom I have long taken a special interest, so I will tell you plainly how things lie. You will have noticed that your great-uncle the pope is ailing. When he has been gathered to God there will be a contest, and if we are on the losing side, the Pamphilis, Maidalchinis and Giustinianis will face a harsh reckoning indeed. The security in which you have lived your young life will disappear in days, and a far less comfortable time will begin.' She inclines her head. 'If you are a Barberini, however – if that connection is firmly made, and their faction is protecting us – we will be safe. All will be well, don't you see? For you and your children, and their children also, leading off far into the future.'

Olimpiuccia nods again, with slight impatience; she knows all this. She has surely deduced her Nonna's design some time ago, and is determined to resist. She stands now, facing Donna Olimpia in her plain silk gown, her chestnut hair coiled in two tight plaits, and in truth she does seem very much like a child – albeit one with a long Maidalchini nose, and a hard Maidalchini look in her eye.

'I will not do it,' she says simply. 'You have always told me to know my own heart. To fight if I must. And so I will not marry. I do not choose to. I will give myself to God.'

Donna Olimpia marvels briefly at the clarity and self-assurance of this declaration; at the almost successful concealment of fear. She sees that this is a problem of her own making. It is the direct result of the lessons she was so determined to teach this girl – the precise reason she removed her from her parents and had her raised here, in the Palazzo Pamphili. She thinks of her own girlhood: how her father, facing three dowries, tried to force his inconvenient daughters into the convent; how she battled him, and defied him, and went on to marry Paulo Nini instead, then one of the richest men in Viterbo. It did not last, sadly, a fever claiming him at only twenty-three – but she was left with his gold and a plan to go to Rome, already sensing what might be possible there.

This situation is different, of course – the same adamant will applied to the very opposite end. It occurs to her that she has a Claudia Triunfi on her hands, which is enough to dampen any amusement or pride immediately.

'You know what would await you in a convent,' she says, kneading her kneecaps. 'How your life would be.'

'I know what awaits me in marriage,' Olimpiuccia retorts. 'I know what a man would expect. And I will not do it.' Her voice is rising, her composure beginning to slip; the hands at her sides have balled into fists. 'I will *not*, Nonna!'

Donna Olimpia remains quite calm. 'It is a life of privation, Olimpiuccia. Of hunger and hardship and the deepest boredom imaginable.' She waves a hand at the chamber around them. 'With all this, with the way you have been raised, I fear you have little notion of what true tedium can be.'

The girl's eyes grow yet brighter: she has anticipated this argument and believes she can meet it. 'You do not know either. You do not have a *single* idea. I have spoken with Aunt Agata. She told me of her life of study – of contemplation and . . . and serenity, and—'

'Your Aunt Agata,' Donna Olimpia states, 'is a strange and shrivelled creature, whose views are not to be relied upon for one instant. The convent is her world entire. She has no comparison – no knowledge of anything else.' She leans forward on the stool. 'Listen to me. It is *imprisonment*.'

This prompts a predictable flood of counter-charges, made with mounting vehemence: so is marriage, so is a husband's will, so is the tyranny and peril of childbearing, so is—

Donna Olimpia does not attempt a riposte. The discussion has run its course and can serve no further purpose. She adjusts the position of her throbbing toe, fixing her eye on the richly patterned rug beneath it.

'You will meet him,' she interrupts, 'in one week's time. At the Barberinis' Palestrina estate, a short distance outside the city wall. Believe me when I say that it is a dream made real. A prince, a most handsome prince, in the full splendour of his palazzo.'

Olimpiuccia falters, realising the futility of her circumstances; that her consent is not required, or even desired; that the deal has been done, in fact, and she has already been traded away. Her shoulders fall. She takes a half-step forward.

'Nonna,' she says, her voice now small and faint with horror. 'Please don't, Nonna.'

Donna Olimpia does not reply. Wincing, she hoists herself to her feet using the edge of a nearby table, trying to disregard the new agonies that riddle her knees. At the door, she glances behind her. Olimpiuccia is weeping, something she does not do easily; she has returned to the panel of the Virgin and Child and is praying before it with tearful fervour, begging for an intervention that cannot come.

'You will see that this is right, Olimpiuccia,' Donna Olimpia tells her. 'I know it.'

*

The corridor outside is filled with servants. Thinking still of Claudia Triunfi – of that gaunt body, that horribly scarred face, that desperately disordered mind – Donna Olimpia beckons to the steward and instructs that the closest watch be kept on her granddaughter at all times, throughout the day and night. Noises begin to issue from behind the door of Olimpiuccia's room. There is a moan of distress; the crash of something falling; a choking sob.

Donna Olimpia does her best to ignore it. She takes a heavy cloak from a maid and orders a footman to have her carriage brought into the courtyard, so she might go out into the city. Then she makes for a rear staircase that will take her down past the state rooms without attracting any attention. It is a slow descent, with several stops to permit her pains to subside. At one point, she remembers the half-empty bottle of the physician's opium draught, stored in a sideboard upstairs. The temptation to call for it is strong, but she pushes it away: this is no time for dullness. She hears more laughter, the clink of glass, and a few familiar voices raised in mirthful disputation. The occasion for which these guests are gathered could hardly be more holy, but they are plainly finding their way to their usual earthly pleasures.

The courtyard is quiet and dark; a few footmen stand about, shivering and stamping their feet, while a boy sweeps the stones with a long-handled broom. As Donna Olimpia leaves the staircase and steps into the arcade, she catches the sour whiff of tobacco — and there he is, propped against a corner column with a clay pipe jutting from his mouth, pretending not to have seen her.

'Ludo,' she says, rather frostily. 'Shouldn't you be upstairs?'

Prince Ludovisi exclaims as if startled, despite obviously having been waiting for her to appear. 'My dear Mama, shouldn't *you*?' he replies. 'This is your palazzo, after all. I believe this awful year has settled that, at least.'

'What do you want?'

'I confess that I was searching for your likeness,' Ludovisi says, knocking out his pipe and tucking it inside his long, fur-lined coat. 'Everyone is wondering where it is — and its model as well, of course, for surely—'

'It is at the base of the grand staircase,' Donna Olimpia tells him. 'I would have thought it difficult to miss.'

The fat prince hesitates. 'Ah, no,' he says, smiling apologetically. 'Not the bust by Maestro Algardi, glorious though it is. No Mama, I meant the Spaniard's portrait — the one he painted just before his departure. It is most unusual, I must say, that you do not have it on more prominent display . . .'

Donna Olimpia barely looked at this work before ordering it to be wrapped in a sheet and stowed away in an unused part of the east wing. She offers no explanation now. 'That man's talent,' she says, 'was grievously exaggerated.'

Ludovisi stares at her for a moment. 'Quite,' he says, with mild disbelief. 'Anyway, Mama, since I have stumbled across you so very fortuitously, I must insist that you come back upstairs with me. *Your guests are* asking after you.' He lifts his fleshy hands aloft. 'The victor of the Holy Jubilee! The great unifier, who has achieved the impossible in gathering together the entirety of our family beneath one roof!'

Donna Olimpia purses her lips, suspecting one of Ludovisi's snide jokes, for it could reasonably be claimed that it was she who forced the family apart in the first place. And the truce – with her son and his wife, and various relations of Giambo's – has been made somewhat reluctantly on both sides, for the sake of the broader campaign. All of them know what is at stake, though, despite not having a single blessed clue what to do about it.

'Dear Maria has been enquiring about her daughter, also,' Ludovisi continues, 'in the hope that young Olimpiuccia might be brought down as well – to sing for the company, maybe, as she used to do on holy days?'

Donna Olimpia sighs at his unsubtlety. There are rumours, naturally, about her plans for her granddaughter; she has not manoeuvred in secret, and word could have leaked out from a number of different sources. Wearily, she meets her son-in-law's eye and provides him with a quick summary – and he murmurs an oath, grinning in admiration.

'Maffeo Barberini,' he says. 'As we all had hoped and prayed. Christ's blood, Mama, that is a triumph. A damned *triumph*.'

'The pope has yet to be told,' Donna Olimpia adds, 'and many arrangements remain to be made.' She shrugs. 'But yes, it is done.'

In truth, it has been a mighty labour indeed. With the Kingdom of Naples no longer in play, Donna Olimpia has had to promise the Barberini much in the way of compensation to obtain their assent to Maffeo and Olimpiuccia's betrothal. First and foremost, a truly titanic dowry will be paid. Then all Barberini properties and titles will be restored to them, and their many outstanding debts cancelled. And finally, the notorious Cardinal Antonio will be welcomed back from his exile in France, and paraded through Rome with great ceremony. Explaining the terms of this deal to Giambo will involve a little tact.

Ludovisi looks upwards, as if he might spy Olimpiuccia somehow through the palazzo's stonework. 'And the girl is . . . willing?'

Donna Olimpia remembers the fall of those slender shoulders; the imploring look in her eyes. *Please don't, Nonna.* 'She will come to accept it.'

Ludovisi thinks about this for a few seconds, thinks of his own daughters perhaps, and his countenance darkens. 'Olimpiuccia is just twelve,' he says. 'That she does not understand is to be expected.'

Donna Olimpia is shaking her head. 'Her understanding is of no consequence. This marriage is now our only course. Maria will perceive this, and her husband also. They know what we stand to lose, all of us, if we do not lose Olimpiuccia.'

The fat prince begins to smile again, his conscience apparently salved; he pinches the end of his nose and lets out a wily chuckle. 'This really is astonishing, I must say. You have secured the favour of the Barberini. You have fashioned a true and lasting connection.' He applauds her softly, bowing in deference. 'Bravo, Mama. Bravo.'

There is a hideous twinge in Donna Olimpia's left knee, like the parts of the joint are being very slowly prised apart. She grinds her teeth until she feels them shift in her jaw; then she sucks a breath in through her nostrils and glances towards the courtyard's rear gates, wondering where in God's holy name her carriage might be.

'Sometimes, Ludo,' she says, 'Almighty God provides more than one path to victory.'

'And if victories are defined by the condition of your foes,' Ludovisi declares, 'this one is *magnificently* complete. I've heard that when Astalli realised the great trick that you had worked on him – that it was *he* who was being accused of treachery, rather than yourself – he broke down and wept in this very courtyard!'

Donna Olimpia nods; several others have already told her this. Since Camillo Astalli's exile, she has seen to it that every last part of his wealth has been confiscated and will now be put towards Olimpiuccia's Barberini dowry. A trial was staged in absentia, at the pope's express command, during which proof of the young cardinal's duplicity and gross carnality was aired for the condemnation and entertainment of Rome. It is as if he has been tipped into the ocean with weights strapped to his ankles, sinking all the way to the bottom. He is gone.

'Astalli was a traitor,' she says. 'He was lucky not to die.'

At last, the rear gates open and her carriage comes forth, pulled by four ebony mares. Donna Olimpia's soul lifts at the sight; very briefly, she forgets the toe, the knees, and everything else. Here is her full glory, restored to her after an ignominious summer in that little grey carriage – which she ordered to be broken up for firewood in the first hour of her return. It pulls past them into the centre of the courtyard. The blue panels are glossy and deep; the polished gold sparkles even in the low winter light; and on the doors, crisp and perfect, a white dove flies above the crossed keys and tiara of the Holy See, an olive branch clutched in its beak.

'Are you going to call on the Holy Father, Mama?' asks Ludovisi. 'To, ah, finalise the marriage contract?'

Donna Olimpia readies herself for the short walk to the carriage door and the suffering it will bring. 'His blessing is required, along with his signature. Much preparation lies ahead.'

'And will you be going alone?'

Donna Olimpia considers Prince Niccolò Ludovisi, standing there in her arcade with a hopeful expression upon his plump, devious face. Since her restoration, she has made a point of loading her son-in-law with prizes, with treasure and sinecures and property, to recognise his loyal service over the summer. Yet word has reached her that he has been complaining to carefully chosen members of their circle – complaining about *her*, criticizing her stratagems and circulating injurious rumours. He is working some scheme, no doubt; perhaps laying the grounds for a faction of his own.

She turns to the carriage. A footman is at the door, opening it smartly. 'Yes,' she says. 'I believe I will.'

*

Darkness is creeping up on Rome, although it is only the middle of the afternoon; the sky is clear and divinely smooth, its blues melting into shades of pink and gold. The city below seems almost empty, despite the sacred occasion. What crowds there are collect in tavernas or lantern-lit tents, to watch the performances being staged within. Huddled in her carriage, half-buried beneath furs, Donna Olimpia glimpses the courtship of Santa Anna and San Gioaccino, and the chaste kiss that led to their holy daughter's conception, while players in angels' wings prance around them with peacock feathers. Elsewhere, she sees plaster-cast Virgins propped on corners and in the centre of the piazzas, each one surrounded by a host of flickering candles; a few modest parades, away in the smaller streets, with torches, chanting, and statues borne aloft; and even the trailing remnants of the penitential procession, a last cohort of pilgrims shuffling onwards through the cold. But it all feels like yesterday's spectacle. The Blessed Jubilee has nearly a month left to run, with numerous rituals, feasts and solemnities still scheduled. Looking out at Rome now, however, Donna Olimpia feels that it has already reached its end.

Giambo is at the Vatican, as is typically the case on feast days. A runner has been sent ahead, to warn the staff of Donna Olimpia's arrival. Monsignor Scotti, the pope's unappealing new majordomo, is waiting just inside the gates. He approaches the carriage door but makes no move to open it for her.

Donna Olimpia shakes off a fur and pulls down the window. 'What is it?'

'Excellency,' Scotti begins, in a tone of clipped apology, 'I am afraid there has been an error. I tried to have your carriage intercepted, but evidently word did not reach you in time for—'

'Where is my chair?' Donna Olimpia interrupts, squinting out into the gloomy yard. 'Why has it not been brought?'

'His Holiness is preparing for a special Mass in the Sistine Chapel,' the major-domo tells her, 'to mark this holy day. It is to begin imminently, I am told – within an hour of the Nones bell.'

'You are surely mistaken. I know nothing of this *special Mass*. What in God's name are you talking about, Monsignor?'

Scotti attempts to hold his ground. 'It has been convened at the particular request of the secretary of state, Excellency. For members of the Sacred College and the Roman Curia only.'

Donna Olimpia stiffens in her seat, sensing trouble. As Panciroli's successor as secretary of state, Fabio Chigi has thus far been a curious proposition. She has encountered him several times since Astalli's fall, as they attended to their business about the Quirinale – and she has been testing him in the usual fashion, sending lavish gifts and offering various pensions and preferments for his relatives, all of which he has refused or returned within the day. For his part, Cardinal Chigi has treated her with a scrupulous, faintly pointed politeness, as one might a notable but not entirely welcome visitor. Although not ideal, there has been reason to hope that they might be able to accommodate one another and share this space that they both wish to inhabit.

But not any longer. Chigi's purpose seems clear enough. After a fractious year, he has gathered together the senior clergy of Rome for this special Mass, to demonstrate the unity he will now help Giambo achieve – a unity that is to exclude Donna Olimpia Maidalchini completely. A memory returns, startlingly clear, of the clashes she would have with Panciroli; of Camillo Astalli in the Palazzo del Quirinale, slamming a set of doors in her face.

Heaving away the remaining furs, Donna Olimpia snatches up a leather document folder fat with Barberini correspondence and throws the carriage door open with such abruptness that Scotti is obliged to take a backward step.

'This is nonsense,' she says, as she begins to disembark. 'I have urgent business here, Monsignor. My brother-in-law will make time for me, and what I have to tell him – and I guarantee that if you bar my path, or cause me any delay whatsoever, you will quickly come to regret it.'

The threat works. A chair is brought, and Donna Olimpia orders its bearers to proceed to the Sala Regia with all haste, so that she might talk with the pope before this special Mass begins.

Monsignor Scotti starts to protest, but he has been defeated and is ignored.

Donna Olimpia's mind has now been whetted to razor sharpness, her blood thrumming through her veins. She sits up keenly, savouring the thought of the revelation she is about to make, which will surely break over poor Giambo's head like a thunderclap. Being wholly oblivious to gossip, the old sheep has no notion of her labours in this quarter. He will assent to whatever she proposes, though; this is beyond question. He will praise her with his customary earnestness, affirm his absolute reliance upon her, and lament for the hundredth time the dreadful folly of the summer. And then he will sign the documents she has prepared, granting the Barberini what they require – and thereby damning himself to complete and eternal insignificance. Her safety and influence, her place in Rome, will depend upon that inconstant fool no longer. He can be cast aside, as he did to her. All that will be left for him is to die.

They arrive in the frescoed vault of the Sala Regia. The chair is set down and Donna Olimpia clambers out. The hall is quite empty save for the Swiss Guard, and its patterned marble floor is so cold she can feel it through her velvet slippers. The gouty toe bulges demonically, seeming ready to burst, while the parts of her knees grate together like skewed millstones. But she knows what she must do. She pulls in her black cloak and turns towards the chapel's open doors.

The holy congregation is assembled inside. Monsignor Scotti was not exaggerating: the service will be beginning very shortly. Donna Olimpia resolves not to hurry, however; to walk at an even pace, and betray not even the slightest trace of her pain; to act as if she was a part of the ritual, with a natural right to be present. She knows that Giambo will be in the vestry at the chapel's far end, dressed in his golden robes, bracing that wizened turkey neck for the weight of the papal tiara. And so that is where she will go.

She walks to the doorway and the chapel opens up before her, its every surface crowded with colours and forms. It is filled with churchmen, the marble screen halfway down dividing the bishops and monsignors from the cardinals. She is noticed at once, disquiet rippling out through the assembly. She lifts her chin and begins her march, keeping her eyes fixed upon the mighty spread of nakedness painted on the altar wall. Inwardly, she dares them – she *dares* them – to step into her path; to lay their hands on her, and turn her back; to shove her out into the hall.

None do. A few find the nerve to address her, raising their voices above the general murmur, quoting familiar lines of scripture about woman's rightful submission to man; about the Lord's decree that she stay modest, pure, and reverent. Donna Olimpia does not react. She passes beneath the screen and starts among the cardinals, a single black gown moving between two large blocks of red; and now she looks around her, taking them all in with a swift, sweeping glance. There are her enemies, scattered about or gathered in groups, mostly allies or acolytes of the departed Panciroli. Balancing them, however – and outnumbering them, she believes, by a slender margin – are her friends, fronted by the august, rather severe figure of Francesco Barberini, whose letters she carries beneath her arm. She directs her gaze straight ahead again – for she will not meet his eye, lest this be taken as a sign of reliance. Of weakness.

Her goal approaches. The chapel seems to grow darker, its candle-flames each acquiring a golden corona; she feels sweat spring out across her back and brow. The knees and the toe are beyond pain now, consumed by a tingling, white-hot numbness. She can only keep walking; it is a sensation almost like floating, the specific movements of her legs and feet quite lost to her. Four shallow steps lead to the altar level. Donna Olimpia girds herself, pinches up her gown, and climbs them slowly, taking care to lift the toes of her slippers so she does not trip. Then she advances towards the altar and the huge, muscular Christ who looms above it, cleaving humanity apart with a powerful flourish, forever separating the righteous from the damned.

A trio of cardinal-bishops are waiting there to assist Giambo with the Mass. They brace themselves, moving together, as if preparing to repel her. She nearly smiles; and just for them, corrects her course only at the very last moment — swerving to the right, gliding from the chapel through a door beside the altar, as the muttering gathers behind her like an inrushing wave.

Donna Olimpia stops in the gloom beyond, leaning against a wall. She breathes, whispering a prayer, and gradually the feeling in her knees becomes familiar again; excruciating, yes, but something she can manage. And she has reached Giambo. He is just a few yards away, in the papal vestry. She will make her revelation and secure his consent for Olimpiuccia's betrothal; and then she will retreat to her apartments in the Palazzo Pamphili with a plate of Signor Gallo's *cannoli*, and perhaps some of his *struffoli* as well, and take a healthy dose of the physician's draught. She will be able, briefly, to rest. The thought spurs her onwards, through an antechamber and a heavy velvet curtain, into this most private of papal sanctums.

'Giambo,' she begins, 'you will not believe it. I swear by the Blessed Virgin, you simply will not believe what I have—'

Someone is in there with him — not a valet or a butler, but a cardinal clad in his most splendid vestments. He is standing before Giambo and seems to be listing points of advice. Donna Olimpia tenses, drawing herself up; it is Fabio Chigi. Everything is exactly as she suspected. He is making himself a barrier between Giambo and any outside interference. Between Giambo and *her*.

Chigi turns with an expression of icy surprise – and sure enough, Donna Olimpia can see something different in him now. This cardinal is offended by her presence, by her unannounced arrival, by the unchecked excitement in her voice; by every last aspect of her existence. He hates her, of course, as they all do in their hearts – but by coming in here she has forced him to reveal it.

Chigi shifts, deliberately blocking Donna Olimpia's path; he is a tall man despite his stoop, his angular, monkish frame made rather wider by his vestments. All she can see of Giambo are those bony hands, the left twisting the Fisherman's Ring upon a finger of the right, and the top of the papal tiara that trembles very slightly upon his head. The old sheep has not yet acknowledged her in any way. She wonders if he has even realised she is present.

'Donna Olimpia,' Chigi says, his tone quiet but unyielding. 'The Holy Father is preparing to lead a special Mass. You should not be in here, or anywhere nearby.'

So there it is. The next enemy has declared himself; the next battle has begun. Donna Olimpia takes the cardinal in, from his robe's embroidered hem to the freshly pressed peak of his white silk mitre. She doesn't see anything much. If this man truly thinks that she can be ousted once more from her rightful place, Almighty God is about to teach him a terrible lesson indeed.

Donna Olimpia steps forward, nearly treading on Chigi's foot. Then she casts a hard look up into his eyes and opens her mouth to speak.

Sorores

Claudia is already aboard the carriage, folded onto a small patch of seat that has been kept empty among the trunks, musical instruments and boxes of artistic equipment. She crept up there as soon as she could, perceiving that Flaminia's promises of departure were to be acted upon at last. This has plainly caused her despair to lift a little, for she has fallen fast asleep.

Flamina climbs in with a grunt, heaves aside a book of drawings and sits down heavily. The child begins to wriggle, its heels pressing against the inside of her hip; she strokes the contour of its tiny back, smothering a yawn, and is nearly overcome by exhaustion herself. The overloaded carriage rocks as the coachman clambers up to his bench; across the cabin, Claudia twitches and begins to murmur something. Flaminia tries to listen, but it is unintelligible.

The coachman whistles to his horses and they start off, heading through the narrow gate of the Palazzo Triunfi. Flaminia watches her sister with careful attention. It has become very clear that for Claudia, their childhood home is a place of unfathomable darkness. Since the hour Donna Olimpia's men delivered her, she has been in a state of near-constant distress. On occasion, she would run around, shrieking as if she was on fire; but mostly she has huddled away in shadowy corners, often for days, immersed in her endless prayers.

Flamina could provide no solace. Claudia has not yet spoken to her, in fact, and will barely even glance in her direction. At moments of particular agitation, she has appealed dismally to a missing sister — words that made Flamina's soul leap, the first few times she heard them. But she quickly came to realise that it was not her Claudia was addressing. She could only guess that it was another nun from Castro, lost at some point during Claudia's ordeals.

They inch out of the palazzo, the coachman easing the carriage into the morning crowds that jostle along the Vicolo della Renella. The weather is fine for early winter, a strong sun rising in clear skies, but it is still cold enough. Flaminia takes up a woollen blanket and leans forward to lay it over Claudia, tucking it around the sharp edges of her body. She looks at her sister's wasted face, at the scoured tracks of the scar, and curses herself for not foreseeing this further tribulation — for not warding it off somehow. She was there, after all, through the very worst times. She saw it happen.

At the root of this great pain lies their father. Widowed shortly after Flaminia's birth, Andrea Triunfi had been unyielding in his refusal to make any form of allowance for his elder daughter. When Claudia would not speak or eat, he tried to compel her; when she found some commonplace sensation unbearable, he would force her to bear it, often to the point of crazed anguish. Flaminia's earliest memories are of Claudia being pursued, Claudia being confined, Claudia being beaten. It was a brutal regimen to which she did not respond — to which she was incapable of responding. Her nature was immutable, fixed since her first days. This was something Andrea could not be made to understand.

At some point, however, he seemed to give up: on the impossible

Claudia, on Flaminia too, and on any pretence of a respectable life, devoting himself instead to the gaming houses and brothels of the city. Largely forgotten, the sisters became constant companions. Flaminia discovered that although oblivious to the patterns and obligations of ordinary life, Claudia had access to the deeper truths of religion and could lay open its mysteries with a fluency that defied explanation. Their father often claimed that his elder daughter was half-witted, mired in childhood, her intellect forever unformed. This was evidently untrue. Claudia could read, in Italian, Latin and Greek, without ever having received instruction, and seemed to have committed every sacred volume in the Palazzo Triunfi's library to memory. These holy stories would emerge from her quite transformed, enriched and enlivened, her usual halting sentences replaced with a rare, astonishing eloquence. As she listened to Claudia's words, Flaminia found that vivid images were taking shape within her mind. Before long, she had reached for quill and paper and was attempting to bring them forth.

For a while, all was well. Both sisters became more practised, fuelling one another with their words and drawings. Flaminia's artistic impulse grew into an earnest ambition. She also developed a profound affection for Claudia, which was not reciprocated in any obvious way – but a tolerance was there, a kind of trust, beyond anything her sister had ever shown towards anyone else.

It could not last. A few months after Claudia's seventeenth birthday, Andrea Triunfi suddenly became fixated upon the notion of his daughters' marriages; of finding good matches for them both, and thus restoring the family name. Unexpectedly, Claudia was to go first. Andrea had already secured her a suitor, it transpired: a former commander of cavalry, crippled but rich, who was inclined to view her intractable character as a challenge. Flaminia readied herself to deal with Claudia's desolation, but it did not appear. Indeed, there was no real sign that she understood what was to occur – until one day at dawn, just before she was due to be introduced to her betrothed, she went to the kitchen, heated a small copper pan of walnut oil, and poured it over her face.

Flaminia was woken by the screams. Scrambling downstairs, she was confronted by a cook and a maid, both wailing for all they were worth – while her sister knelt before the range in an attitude of prayer, her skin livid and bubbling, tilting sideways as she fainted from the pain.

After that, everything changed. Claudia was gone, borne away hurriedly to Castro. Now the subject of calumny and gossip, his marriage plan horribly spoiled, Andrea was consumed by misery – and then he was dead, broken by his troubles, joining their mother in an early grave. The Triunfi fortune was found to be almost completely spent, squandered by their father on gambling and dissipation. As one, the servants departed, with whatever valuables they could find. At sixteen years of age, Flaminia was left alone in an empty, crumbling palazzo, without guardian or income, to glean what she could from the artistic world of Rome. The life that ensued has made her resilient and practical before all things; and now, as the Palazzo Triunfi passes by the carriage window, and she looks out at that tarnished façade for what must surely be the last time, she feels only relief.

The carriage rattles away down the street. Flaminia puts a hand to her throbbing forehead and makes a more critical survey of the packed cabin. It was loaded in haste by Donna Olimpia's men and is distinctly unstable, her possessions swaying and shifting as they cross the uneven stones of Trastevere. The vehicle turns a corner, the light changing; and an eye catches hers amid the clutter, startlingly real, from a canvas propped against the opposite panel. It is that of Juan de Pareja, peering out at her between a long blue feather and a rolled rug. This man, so doggedly alert, had threatened to become an obstacle; but looking at him now, amid his apprehension and his pride, she swears that she can see a flicker of collusion.

The portrait was a parting gift of sorts, presented to Flaminia by Cavaliere Bernini; he came to call the previous day with it under his arm, to bid her farewell. Typically enough, the painting was not really his to give away. He explained that it had been circulating through some of the finest and most learned households in the city – but with Donna Olimpia's restoration, it had come to seem rather too *Spanish* for any loyal Roman citizen. It had no owner, and its creator was long gone; the Cavaliere's fear was that it could easily end up in a mildewed cellar, or a cupboard, or even on a fire. It was an extraordinary piece of work, almost without compare, and it needed to be with a painter. It needed to be with her.

'It can serve as a memento of your affair, perhaps,' he observed; then he cast a sly glance at the belly that rose tightly beneath her gown. 'One of the mementos.'

Theirs was an association of some years, the Cavaliere having extended Flaminia intermittent, rather slapdash assistance in memory of her parents, and there was a measure of genuine concern behind his flippancy. Plainly thinking that she was finished, and was being sent away into dire exile, he was at pains to exonerate himself; to stress once again that he had not told Donna Olimpia about her dalliance with the Spanish painter; that he had played no part in her ruination. Despite all the contacts he supposedly had around Rome, Flaminia saw that Cavaliere Bernini knew almost nothing of her actual situation. As she lifted the portrait from his hands, she decided not to enlighten him.

What Flaminia said to Diego as she took her leave holds true:

she has no regrets about what happened between them. When they first met at the Cavaliere's table, she swiftly realised that this was someone from whom much could be learned. It is her belief that an artist is forever incomplete – forever being schooled and improved by their experiences. In this spirit, Flaminia dedicated herself to the study of Don Diego Velázquez, painter to the king of Spain. During their time together, she discovered that the gifts of genius can coexist with gnawing frustration and disappointment – and that an eye of miraculous astuteness could also be pitiless, laying bare what should rightly remain hidden. Knowing this, when he proposed to paint her in the guise of a living goddess, she made just one condition: that her face be turned away, seen only at a remove, as a reflection in the mirror of Venus.

And this mirror had still been empty when she left. At the time, Flaminia regretted her betrayal, and resented how she was being forced to spy and steal. But God's will can be opaque. Against all prediction, Donna Olimpia – so dreadful, so scornful, so indifferent to the dangers of her commands – has kept her word. She has been liberal beyond imagining. There has been a delay, it is true, to allow the construction of her town to advance; as the year's end approaches, however, and Rome moves on to new intrigues, the Triunfi sisters have been given leave to depart. Flaminia supposes that she is privy to secrets; that she could tell of the widow's methods, and of her trickery; that she is being bribed, in a way, after having been exploited so ruthlessly. So be it. She will take what has been offered. She will hold her peace for now.

The carriage has reached the river, which is dark and fast-flowing. As they bump up onto the ramp of the Ponte Cestio, Flaminia glances at the three letters tucked inside the book that rests at her elbow. All were delivered in the past month, having been sent to the Palazzo Triunfi from the town of San Martino.

The first is from a local contessa, who claimed to know Maestra Triunfi by reputation. She wrote that she had long desired a fresco in the hall of her villa – an allegory of the seasons, maybe, rendered in the forms of pagan mythology – and asked that the Maestra call upon her, to see the room in question and discuss her terms. The second is from the abbess of the town's Cistercian cloister, inquiring about Flaminia's sister, who had been recommended to her as a woman of extraordinary piety and devotion; was it true, the woman asked, that she had taken holy vows and was in need of a place in a closed order? The third, a more formal document, was from San Martino's principal magistrate. It provided the address of a newly built house on the Via del Monte, and stated her legal ownership of it – identifying her as Signora Flaminia Triunfi, recently widowed, with one child.

Flaminia runs a thumb over the ends of these letters, a slight smile on her lips. She knows that there is only one way these people could have learned all of this about her, both that which is true and that which is not. But none of them so much as alludes to Donna Olimpia's existence.

They are on the Tiber's northern bank now, climbing uphill towards Campidoglio. The vastness of Rome opens out before her, hazed by a thousand strands of drifting, sunlit smoke. Flamina takes a trembling breath. They are leaving. Already, Trastevere is becoming lost in the distance. She lays both hands upon her belly, and the little body still stirring within. One thing is certain: the childhood that awaits her daughter or son in San Martino will be very different from her own. This brings her an inexpressible gladness. Flaminia had greeted the pregnancy with dismay, yet to her surprise this feeling did not last. God has granted her acceptance. It is experience, after all. It is life.

She settles back upon the cushions, looking through the shutter slats at a row of grimy tenements, their bold Jubilee banners now tattered and dull. A group of riders pass close by, calling to each other; a knife sharpener works his wheel, spraying orange sparks into the street; there is soft music somewhere, the trill of a flute, and several voices joining in song.

And then the carriage halts, rocking everything forward and back, shaking Flaminia awake. She sits up, rubbing her eyes and nose, and sees that they have reached the wide road that leads to the Porta Pia. She has slept through her last ride across Rome. Pilgrims fill the street outside, walking with their belongings in bundles on their backs, or riding in carriages and carts. They begin to move again, and Flaminia has a sense of joining a tide; of crawling along on a slow current, towards the mouth of a drain. This, she knows, is the daily situation: Rome's Jubilee guests are streaming out through the gates in their hundreds, and are not replaced.

The carriage stops once more, for longer this time. Those nearby start to complain, in three or four different languages. Flaminia feels a passing unease; she shivers within her cloak, drawing it more tightly around her. At this final stage, she cannot help worrying that something is amiss. That they are to be questioned or detained.

It does not happen. The carriage rolls forward, soon passing into the deep shadow of the gatehouse. The walls press in; hooves echo upon stonework, and salutations are exchanged between their coachman and the guards; and then the shadow disappears. They are pulling clear of the Porta Pia, away from the knots of pilgrims. They have left Rome. The carriage is going faster, faster than Flaminia has ever gone in her life, the horses approaching a canter as they start onto the northern road. The buildings outside the city wall are already becoming small and scattered, seeming almost to disperse. Between them are not walled gardens or ancient ruins, but fields, gentle hills, stretches of winter woodland. The world beyond.

With some effort, Flaminia reaches over a large trunk to open the window shutter fully. A cold breeze blows in, catching her hair and the folds of her cloak. She raises her chin, angling her face this way and that, as if washing herself clean.

Claudia begins to stir. Flaminia closes the shutter and turns back inside. Her sister is shifting awkwardly, pushing off the woollen blanket and pressing her silver rosary briefly to her brow. Then she hesitates, her lower lip quivering, as if she is on the verge of speech.

A few seconds pass. The carriage follows a bend, its panels creaking; a shaft of sunlight moves through the cabin, becoming dappled as they start into a wood.

'I must speak,' Claudia whispers, 'of a holy saint.'

More than anything, Flaminia wants to take hold of her sister's hands. She wants to say her name over and over, and promise her that all will be well – that they are safe at last. But she knows she must not. She stays on her seat, rubs her belly, and waits.

'Santa Orsola,' Claudia says, staring at the floor. 'Santa Orsola, virtuous and brave, made a perilous journey in the name of God. A journey beset with perils. I have seen it. I have seen her acts and her holy countenance. I have… I…'

Flaminia leans a little closer, into the space between them. Claudia senses this and lifts her grey eyes. The sisters look at each other, their gaze unbroken by the sway of the carriage.

'Tell me,' Flaminia says.

Author's Note

These Wicked Devices is a work of fiction that manipulates the historical record in many ways. I will confess to some of these here, as well as relating the fates of the various real people who have been conscripted into this story.

Events that were spread over a roughly three-year period have here been condensed into a single year. Olimpia Maidalchini's exile from Rome lasted rather longer than I have portrayed it, and did actually involve a period of residence in San Martino. Cardinal Girolamo Panciroli died on 3rd September 1651, almost certainly from natural causes, and was succeeded by Fabio Chigi shortly afterwards; Chigi would go on to become Pope Alexander VII. The trial and execution of the priest known as Mascambruno occurred a little later, in the early months of 1652, but the circumstances and details are the same.

Pope Innocent died on 7th January 1655, with Donna Olimpia at his side – although she insisted upon this more to upset Cardinal Chigi than to console her brother-in-law. Once he was dead she would do no more for him, refusing to pay for his coffin, attend his funeral or even remove his body from St Peter's. It was eventually buried in an unmarked grave in the basement of the basilica, in a cheap coffin paid for by his major-domo.

Concerted efforts were made at the outset of Pope Alexander's reign to bring Donna Olimpia to justice for her years of outrageous theft from the Vatican Treasury. She mounted a spirited defence of herself, mostly by blaming Pope Innocent. Her enemies were determined, however, and in July 1655 she was exiled to San Martino while a formal case was assembled against her. These proceedings were comprehensively derailed the following year by a major outbreak of Plague, which killed more than twenty thousand Romans. The disease lingered, spreading through the surrounding regions, and eventually found its way to San Martino. Donna Olimpia fell ill and died in September 1657 at the age of 66. Camillo Pamphili is said to have arrived at her palazzo to discover his dead mother lying naked on a stripped bed, her home having been looted by her departing servants.

Olimpiuccia could not prevent her marriage to Maffeo Barberini, which occurred in the Sistine Chapel on June 15th 1653, after the payment of a colossal dowry of one hundred thousand scudi – seventy thousand of which allegedly came from Donna Olimpia. But this victory was short lived. Directly after the wedding feast, in a final act of protest, Olimpiuccia locked herself in her room at the Palazzo Pamphili and refused to come out, shouting from her window of her desire to enter a holy order and die a virgin. This went on for five months, much to Donna Olimpia's embarrassment, the girl proving resistant to all arguments. Eventually her grandmother lost patience, took her to the Palazzo Barberini 'almost violently', according to the ambassador of Mantua, and pushed her into the arms of her husband. The marriage was consummated not long afterwards – and on January 6th, 1654, Pope Innocent instructed the Vatican Treasury to nullify all remaining Barberini debts.

Very little information survives about the city of Castro, which was erased from the earth by the mercenary armies of the Pope. Accordingly, all details included here about its Duomo, Benedictine convent and the layout of its streets are invented.

I could also find out nothing about Flaminia Triunfi beyond her profession, her relationship with Diego Velázquez and the son, Antonio, that resulted – who is known about only due to documentary evidence that Velázquez made financial provision for the child before he left Rome. None of her paintings have been identified, if any survive.

The model for Velázquez's *Venus at her Mirror* (or *Rokeby Venus*, now in the National Gallery in London) is unknown, as is its exact date and place of execution. More than one art historian has argued that it was painted in Madrid at the end of the 1640s. For a historical novelist, however, the idea that the only surviving female nude in Velázquez's oeuvre might coincide with his second trip to Italy, and an affair with a much younger woman in a liberal environment very different to that of his homeland, was impossible to resist.

Velázquez was not made a Knight of Santiago as a result of his trip to Italy. In fact, the requisite royal nomination was not granted until 6 June 1658. A formal investigation of Velázquez's credentials – both social and genealogical – was begun that November by the Council of Military Orders, and continued until February 1659. 148 witnesses gave evidence that he was of noble blood, which appears to have been true, and that he had never accepted payment for his paintings, which most definitely was not.

Nonetheless, the nomination was rejected, meaning that King Philip IV had to obtain a papal dispensation to excuse the disproven nobility. This was presented to the council – who then found another flaw in Velázquez's genealogy, requiring a *second* dispensation. He was finally ennobled by the king and admitted to the knights' order on 18 November 1659, but then died after a short illness on 6 August 1660. His final masterpiece, *Las Meninas*, finished around 1656 and now in the Prado Museum in Madrid, includes a self portrait of the artist at work, with the elaborate red cross of Santiago emblazoned on the front of his doublet. Velázquez's first biographer Antonio Palomino claimed that this cross was added by another hand after the painter's death, on the orders of the king.

Several of the details of Juan de Pareja's life given here are my invention. It is known that he was born into slavery in Antequera, southern Spain, around 1606. He had joined Velázquez's studio and household in Madrid by 1642, and was granted his freedom in Rome in November 1650, where a copy of the manumission document was discovered in the state archives. Upon their return to Spain, he stayed for a while in Velázquez's workshop, then began to work as an independent painter, taking on commissions of his own. His surviving masterwork is *The Calling of St Matthew* of 1661, now in the Prado. There is no evidence of a wife or offspring, or of a painting of a Benedictine nun. He died in Madrid in 1670.

Many books were consulted in the writing of this one; any errors and distortions are my own. I am indebted to the scholarship of Eleanor Herman, Jonathan Brown, Jose Lopez-Rey, Gregory Hanlon, Thomas Dandelet, Sylvia Evangelisti, Franco Mormando and numerous others. All details on the lives of the saints are taken from *The Golden Legend* by Jacobus de Voraigne.

More personal thanks are due to my agent, Euan Thorneycroft, for his counsel and friendship; Suzie Dooré, for her patience as the years piled up; Jo Thompson, for a brilliant edit; the teams at A. M. Heath and the Borough Press; Logan Macx and everyone who enabled him; my family and friends, who have listened to me go on (and on); and Sarah and Kester, who have kept me together throughout it all.

I would also like to express my deep gratitude to Susan Watt, who passed away recently. Susan published my first novel, *The Street Philosopher*, and was a very wise and inspiring editor. Her guidance made me a better writer and gave me the courage to try again.